The DUKE'S LAST HUNT

OTHER BOOKS BY ROSANNE E. LORTZ

MEDIEVAL FICTION
I Serve: A Novel of the Black Prince
Road from the West: Book I of the Chronicles of Tancred
The Splintered Oak: A Short Story of the First Crusade

REGENCY FICTION
To Wed an Heiress

HISTORICAL ESSAYS IN ANTHOLOGY
Castles, Customs, and Kings: True Tales by English
Historical Fiction Authors (Volumes 1-2)

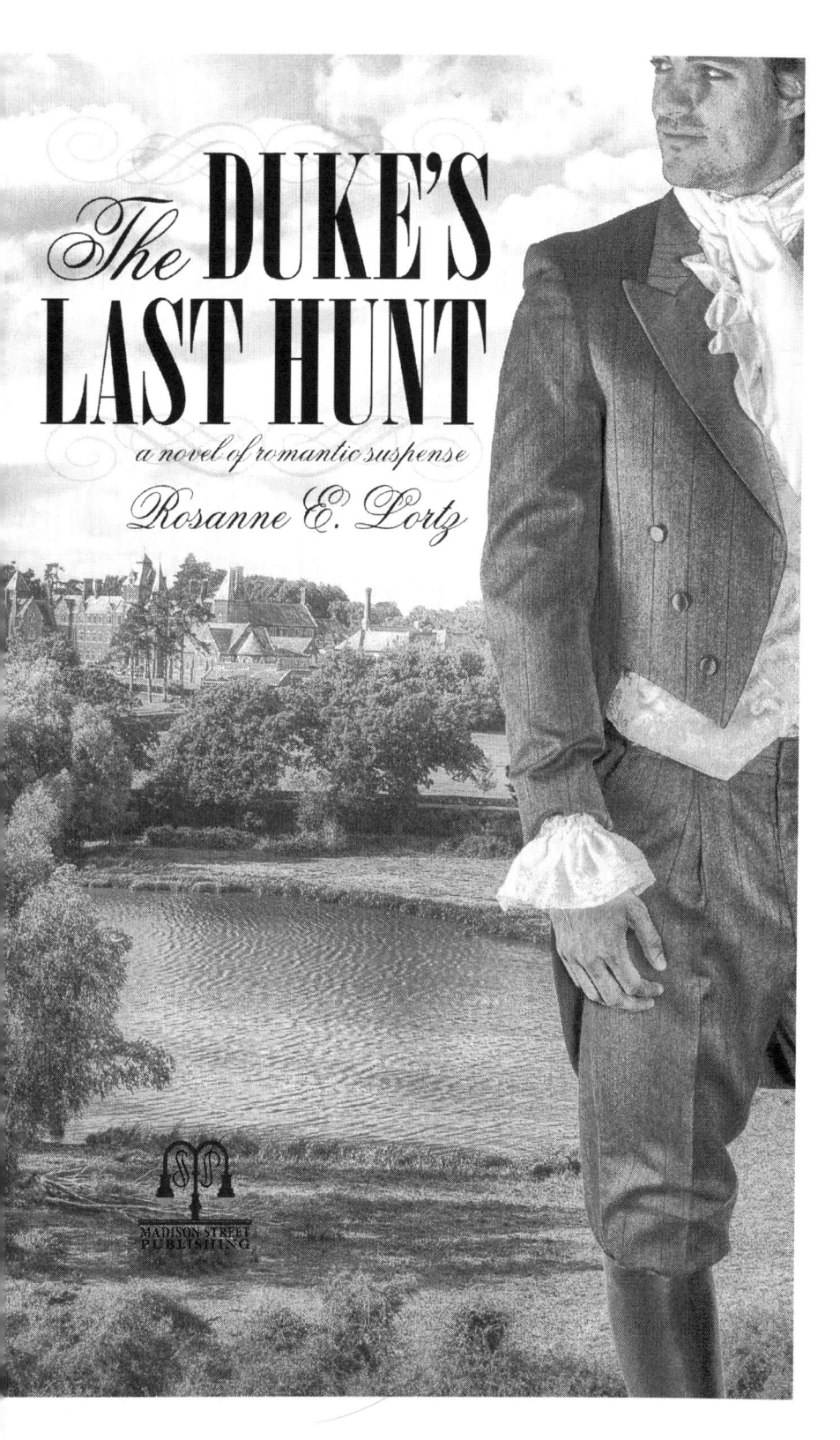

The DUKE'S LAST HUNT

a novel of romantic suspense

Rosanne E. Lortz

MADISON STREET PUBLISHING

Copyright © 2016 by Rosanne E. Spears

Cover and interior design by Masha Shubin
DreamsTime.com: English Countryside in Suffolk © stanzi11;
Autumn Sky © Serg64. Regency Man © PeriodImages.com

All rights reserved. No part of this book may be reproduced or transmitted in any form or by any means whatsoever, including photocopying, recording or by any information storage and retrieval system, without written permission from the publisher and/or author.

ISBN-13 978-0-9962648-3-9
Publisher: Madison Street Publishing

Printed in the U.S.A.

3 5 7 9 10 8 6 4 2

PART ONE

1

*E*LIZA STARED INTENTLY OUT THE WINDOW, IGNORING THE argument taking place across from her in the carriage.

"But my dear," said Lady Malcolm. "How can you possibly desire our daughter to ally herself with an irreligious man? How could she ever trust his prudence, his honesty, or his morals?"

"Upon my word, Margaret!" said Sir Arthur with a glare of annoyance. "It's not as if the man is a confirmed libertine. So what if he does miss a Sunday service or two? And I'm not asking her to accept his offer right away. I'm simply asking her—and you—to keep an open mind on the matter."

Lady Malcolm sniffed. Eliza recognized it as the sniff of longsuffering, somewhere in between the sniff of bearing one another's burdens and the sniff of embracing one's calling to living martyrdom.

"Come now, Eliza," said Sir Arthur. "What have you to say on the matter?" He drummed his fingers on his knee.

Eliza opened her mouth and then shut it again. She had landed in the middle of her parents' quarrels before and knew better than to do so again—although, in this case, she could hardly help but be in the middle of it. It was *her* future they were considering, *her* marriage to Rufus Rowland, the Duke of Brockenhurst.

"Well?" It had been a long carriage ride. It was a warm August day, but the dust from the road did not permit them to open the carriage windows. Sir Arthur's patience was wearing as thin as the auburn hair receding from his high forehead.

"I feel...." Eliza hesitated. "I feel that I hardly know the man, Papa." She glanced over to her mother and gained some courage. "I've stood up with him at a few balls over the course of the season, and I spent one half hour of awkward conversation with him at Almack's. But it was a complete surprise to me when you said he'd called and asked permission to pay me his addresses."

"And a complete surprise to me that you would say yes so readily!" interjected Lady Malcolm, fixing her husband with a steely glare. Her own hair was far darker than Eliza's reddish brown curls, but they shared the same deep green eyes.

"And why shouldn't I say yes?" Sir Arthur blustered. He had never been one to hesitate when a bird was in the hand, or in the bush, or in the tree, or over the hill. "He's a duke, Margaret! And it's not as if it's Eliza's first s—"

He caught himself abruptly, and an uncomfortable silence settled over the closed compartment. No, thought Eliza bitterly, it was *not* her first season. It was the end of her third—and still no matrimonial prospects on the horizon other than this sudden and perplexing interest shown by the Duke of Brockenhurst.

"In any case," said Sir Arthur, "he's called upon us in Grosvenor Square—"

"Twice," said Lady Malcolm, acidly.

"—and you'll have time to better your acquaintance during our stay at Harrowhaven, time to be certain before you make your decision."

Eliza felt a new wave of warm air turn her cheeks pink. "Are you so sure, Papa, that he will even…ask?" How mortifying it would be to go to all this trouble to visit his country estate and then discover that the duke's intentions were not serious. She pulled out her fan and tried to drive away the heat.

"Of course he will! The man's smitten!" Sir Arthur's voice was much too loud for the smallness of the carriage. "And who wouldn't be?" He gave his daughter an encouraging smile.

Plenty of men, Eliza thought, unable to manage a smile in return. Every man who had danced with her during her first and second seasons—danced with her once and never approached again after a taste of her shy conversation. She moved her fan faster and began to breathe more quickly.

Lady Malcolm emitted another principled sniff.

Eliza laid down the fan. She *would* stay calm. She *must* stay calm. She touched the glass of the windowpane, once more feigning preoccupation with the scenery. They had entered a colonnade of tall oak trees lining the roadway, their full branches creating a screen that filtered the rays of the summer sun.

"Almost there now," said Sir Arthur.

Eliza was not sure whether to be glad or begin to cry.

The carriage drive leading up to the house was interminable. The avenue of oaks, planted a hundred or more years ago by one of the Rowland ancestors, stretched out in a straight line far into the distance, paralleling the road on either side. The house, at first just a pinprick of stone amidst a sea of green, grew steadily larger until Eliza could make out the square towers and tall windows. Behind the house, the measured planting of oak trees gave way to the more natural growth of forest, wild and unrestrained.

"Prime place for hunting," Sir Arthur noted approvingly.

"I believe the duke mentioned he is fond of hunting," said Eliza, swallowing hard. The house was larger than she had expected. Would she know anyone else in the house party? Probably not. It was not as if the duke and she traveled in the same circles.

"More than fond of it!" said Sir Arthur. "He's devoted to it!"

It was an unfortunate choice of words. Lady Malcolm uttered a tight-lipped comment about idolatry, and Eliza felt her ribs constrict even further.

On the edge of the forest they saw a small country church, its whitewashed stone a pleasant contrast with the green. "At least there will be *somewhere* for us to worship our Lord tomorrow," said Lady Malcolm grimly.

"Of course there will be!" retorted Sir Arthur. "They're not all heathens in Sussex, Margaret!"

The post chaise rounded one half of the circular drive to pull up at the door of the house. The wheels came to a stop. In the rear, Sir Arthur's valet hopped down from the seat on the back of the carriage, covered with a yellow cloud of dust from the journey. In the front, the coachman handed down Frances Ollerton, Lady Malcolm's lady's maid, who had been mounted precariously in the box beside him. It would have been pleasanter for all concerned to have taken two coaches down to Harrowhaven, but then, reflected Eliza, they could not have gone to the expense of renting a second one. This journey was costing her father enough money as it was.

The carriage door opened, but instead of the driver waiting to hand her down, Eliza discovered two perfectly matched men in immaculate livery ready to perform the task.

"Thank you," Eliza said, giving the nearest footman a faint smile. She was rewarded by a look of surprise.

"You're welcome, miss," the footman said tentatively and then faded away into the background behind the wheel of the post chaise.

They walked up the steps and in through the marble columns flanking the front door. Eliza's lower lip dropped a little as they came into an entrance hall that seemed half the size of their entire London townhouse.

A welcoming committee had formed; however, a cursory glance showed that the greeters were composed entirely of domestics. Eliza, who had been dreading a conversation with the Duke of Brockenhurst, found herself disappointed that he was not at hand to welcome them. And neither was his mother, the dowager duchess.

The butler came forward with a bow and introduced himself as, "Hayward, at your service." He beckoned for two more footmen to assist with unloading the carriage. Then he introduced the housekeeper, a Mrs. Forsythe, and assured them that she would attend to their every need.

Mrs. Forsythe briskly escorted the Malcolms out of the entrance hall, through the saloon, and over to the great oak stairway that led up to the next floor of the house. All the while, she kept them apprised of the history of the rooms they were passing through and asked questions about their own needs and comfort. "I see your valet and one lady's maid have arrived. Will Miss Malcolm's lady's maid be coming in another carriage?"

Eliza flushed pink. Her mother saved her the embarrassment of responding.

"My maid attends to Miss Malcolm's hair and gowns as well as my own."

"I see," said Mrs. Forsythe, in a tone that was both polite and unreadable.

Eliza supposed it would be unheard of for the dowager duchess to share a lady's maid with her daughter, Lady Adele. She sighed. Here was one small incentive to entertaining the duke's suit—as mistress of this house she would be able to have her own lady's maid at last.

"When will the family be expecting us to join them?" Lady Malcolm asked.

Mrs. Forsythe hesitated, the first pause that Eliza had noticed in the housekeeper's effortless industry. "I will let her grace, the duchess, know that you are here. Tea will be served in the drawing room in one hour."

"Thank you," said Lady Malcolm.

Eliza echoed the thanks, but her thoughts were more filled with apprehension than gratitude. What did the housekeeper's hesitation mean? Was the dowager duchess even planning to receive them?

She wished she had been introduced to the duchess prior to this visit. How strange to be staying in someone's house that one had never even met! But it was not the duchess' house anymore, she reminded herself—it was the Duke of Brockenhurst's. And with him she was acquainted—or as acquainted as a few dances and morning calls could make them.

The curving stairs paused on a magnificent landing, the walls decorated by a plethora of portraits in gilt frames. The portrait of the current Duke of Brockenhurst was situated most prominently. Eliza lingered in front of it. She had always found portraits to be a fascinating study. Those done by the best painters—such as the ones the Rowland family could afford—revealed a glimpse of something far deeper than the flat physiognomy of the subject.

Rufus' eyes—could she call him *Rufus* in her mind? It was so strange to think of being that intimate with him!—were the first thing she noticed about the picture: bright, glittering, alive. She had never seen them that animated in person—certainly not on the dance floor or over the glass of punch they had shared at Almack's. No, there was one time she had witnessed that excitement—when he had waxed eloquent about the merits of the hunt and the delights of the forest adjoining Harrowhaven.

She smiled wryly to see that the artist had toned down the brightness of the duke's red hair. In the picture, it was more of an auburn color, the same shade as her own, not the shocking, brilliant red it was in real life. Perhaps the duke was not fond of his coloring—or perhaps his mother was not, since it was probably she who had commissioned the portrait.

Mrs. Forsythe had paused in her ascent of the stairs, noticing Eliza's interest in the portrait. Eliza's eyes flicked over the wall hurriedly—she did not want to keep the others waiting, but her curiosity had gotten the better of her.

There was another painting, placed higher and more out of the way than the duke's, which looked like it had been done by the same artist at much the same time. The subject was darker, with brown hair and a more even complexion. He had the same broad shoulders as the duke, but his brows were more heavy set, his smile more serious. There was a steadiness about this one, especially in the eyes.

The housekeeper walked back over to where Eliza was standing and, following her eye, gazed up at the same picture. Eliza sensed a hint of approval in her eye and gained the courage to ask a question. "Please, Mrs. Forsythe, who is this one?"

"That would be His grace's brother, Lord Henry."

⁂

HENRY ROWLAND TIPTOED INTO THE cavernous library with care. It was as he suspected—the only person wasting a hot summer's day in the library at White's was his friend Stephen Blount. Light-footed as a cat, he glided over to the wingback chair where his friend sat, and without warning, threw down a silver case on the ebony table nearby. "What do you think of this?"

Stephen Blount jumped in his chair as if he had sat on a pin. "Might give a fellow warning! I thought you'd gone to the races."

"No, I went to the stationer's." Henry sent a meaningful glance at the case he had dropped. He needed to show this to someone—it might as well be Stephen.

Setting down his newspaper, Stephen dutifully extracted a

small white card from the silver case. He adjusted his spectacles to read aloud.

HENRY ROWLAND, DUKE OF BROCKENHURST
HARROWHAVEN, SUSSEX

Stephen started again. The card slipped from his fingers, clipping the edge of the ebony table before fluttering to the floor. "I say, Henry! What's this supposed to mean?" He rubbed a knuckle against a left sideburn that was so thin as to be scarcely there. "Duke? You? I didn't know your brother was so eager to abdicate the position...."

Henry smiled devilishly, flexing his broad shoulders with enjoyment. "I'm riding out to the old house to visit Mother tomorrow. I thought I'd leave one on the tray for him to remind him that I'm still alive. He's having a house party, I hear. Strange—he didn't think to invite *me*!"

Stephen took off his spectacles and shifted uncomfortably.

"Oh, you know about that, do you?" Henry's dark eyebrows fell into a frown.

"Well, I...I...yes, dash it all, Henry! He invited me to come down for the week."

"And you said yes, I take it?"

Stephen's tentative smile was confirmation enough.

"Not on account of Rufus' merit, I hope?" Henry already knew the answer to that question. "Don't tell me you're still dangling after that headstrong sister of mine!"

Stephen rose from his chair, a wounded look on his face. "I'm sorry if that offends you, but yes, I *am* still dangling after her, as you call it. And she has given me some reason to hope that my suit will not be in vain. I understand that you may see our situations as somewhat unequal—"

"Good Lord, man," said Henry, clapping him on the shoulder.

Why was it always the gentry who were so old-fashioned about these things? "I've no worries on that score. I was thinking more of your own domestic happiness." He cleared his throat. "Adele's a willful woman, Stephen...."

Willful? He was putting the matter far more politely than it deserved.

Stephen colored. "I'm not such a milksop as all that!"

Henry raised both eyebrows. It took all of his willpower to refrain from argument. "Well, good then! You'll be there when I leave my card at the door. I shan't stay long enough for him to throw me out. You can tell me how Rufus takes it."

"If I know your family's butler, he'll throw the thing in the rubbish heap and not even give it to him."

"Hmm...." said Henry. It seemed that Stephen *did* know their butler. He wouldn't put it past Hayward to hide the card knowing the tempest it would create. "Who else is going to be at this house party?"

"Walter Turold, of course."

Henry growled in annoyance. There was no point in hiding how he felt about Walter in front of Stephen. There was a time that Henry and Walter had been as close as a stand of silver birch trees, but that time was long since gone.

"And...Rufus didn't say who else, although I gathered that there were to be ladies in the party, for he told Adel—I mean, *Lady* Adele that he was bringing some pleasant company for her."

"Perhaps he meant that *you* were the pleasant company."

Stephen blushed. "I hardly think—"

"No, quite right. I hardly think so either." Henry gave another devilish smile as he snatched up the loose card from the floor and the silver case from the table. "Well, who these ladies are, I shall be eager to discover. My brother's not usually one for inviting *respectable* females to his house parties."

"Perhaps he's turned over a new leaf."

Henry's mouth fell open, and all his willpower disappeared like water through a broken dam. "Stephen, you're a babe in the woods. An utter milksop! It's good I'm coming after all, I think. And perhaps I'd better stay at the house instead of simply stopping by to see Mother. Between Rufus and Adele, you wouldn't stand a chance...."

※

HENRY STRODE INTO THE BLUE Boar and called for Ned Hornsby to give him a pint of his finest. He had left early to reach the village by noontime and was thirsty enough to drink a whole hogshead himself.

"Back in the country, eh, Lord Henry?" said Ned with a grin that was nearly lost in the big brown beard which hid his neck and came down over his shirt collar. He pulled down a tankard from the shelf and shined the outside with his apron.

"For the time being," said Henry, returning the grin. Ned was much of an age with him and, before he had taken over proprietorship of the Blue Boar, had always been ready to come along for a hunt, a wager, or a bout of boxing.

"You staying at the big house?" Ned gathered up a tray of dirty dishes from the counter. "Or will you be needing a room here?"

Henry might have stiffened if any of the other villagers had asked that question, but Ned was too old a friend to take offense at—and besides, the whole village knew the Rowland brothers were on bad terms. "That's yet to be determined. Do you have a room for me if I should need it?"

Ned gave a laugh that shook his great brown beard. "That depends. You's not the only one waiting on the duke's pleasure." He jerked his head toward the table by the window.

Henry's eyes followed Ned's until he saw a dark-haired gentleman sitting alone—a slender man with a light-colored coat in the pink of fashion, eating his luncheon and squinting at the counter. "Hello, Hal!" he said abruptly once his presence had been discovered.

"Robert!" said Henry in a tone of surprise that was not precisely good-natured. How many times had he told his half-brother to leave off calling him *Hal*? "What the devil are you doing here?"

"Here to visit Mother, of course." The dark-haired man lifted his monocle and adjusted it to get a better look at Henry.

"And to apply to Rufus for some money while you're at it?"

"Well, yes, there is that too." The man let the monocle drop. "There's this fellow in London with a locomotive machine...."

Henry turned away. He did not care to hear about another of Robert's foolish speculations. As the son of the duchess' first marriage to an untitled landowner, Robert Curtis had always ranked below his brothers in consequence and—now that Rufus has come into his own—in fortune. Ten years Henry's senior, Robert never ceased importuning Rufus for money, both to support his highbrow style of living and to finance a perpetual string of unwise investments.

"Perhaps we can ride up to the house together," Robert said brightly. He stood up, his willowy frame contrasting sharply with his brother's sturdy physique. Then he put on his beaver and headed for the door of the tavern.

"Aren't you forgetting something?" said Henry, looking pointedly at his half-brother's empty plate.

"Oh...." Robert's fingers fished around in his waistcoat pocket but came up empty. "Ned, might I trouble you to...?"

"Put it on your account? Of course, Mr. Curtis." Ned's brown beard split into a half smile. One did not have to know him well to see that it was forced.

"Thank you," said Robert. He gave Henry a shrug and stepped out onto the porch. The door swung shut behind him.

Henry's dark eyebrows beetled into a frown. He picked up the empty dish from the table and carried it over to the counter. The innkeeper reached for it with a look of confusion on his face, probably able to count on one hand the times an aristocrat had cleared a table in the inn.

"Ned," said Henry firmly. "You've been tavern-keeping long enough to know that what I'm about to say is true. Always insist the customer pays before leaving. You'll never get on in life if you keep letting fellows like that shoot the crow." He pulled a guinea out of his own pocket and slapped it on the counter. "Hopefully this will settle whatever he has owing."

Ned took the coin and put it in the moneybox under the counter. "Funny thing, your lordship, but seems like someone might offer you the same advice. How are *you* supposed to get on in life? I shouldn't think you'd be having guineas to spare for paying others' reckonings, what with—"

"Never mind that," said Henry curtly. "I don't want it talked of."

"What you want said and what the village wants to bandy words about ain't exactly the same thing now, is it, Lord Henry?" Ned waggled his eyebrows as he spoke, and Henry could hardly keep from laughing in spite of himself.

"'Tain't right, Master Henry. 'Tain't right." Ned slid an arm over the counter to wipe off the crumbs. "And there ain't a single one of my regular customers but would rather that *you* were still in charge up at the big house."

Henry snorted. "An unlikely eventuality. No, I'm simply here to visit Mother and then back to London. I'll stop back in tonight for a room if I find I'm less than welcome. And now for that pint, if you please. You'll find that I'm good for it." He placed another coin on the rough wooden counter.

2

ELIZA TOOK SOME WATER FROM THE WASH BASIN AND splashed it over her face. It had been warm in the carriage, and this room at Harrowhaven, with the sun beating down on the tall windows, was not much cooler. She could not unlace her traveling dress herself, so she waited patiently, fanning herself when the air grew too close, until Ollerton would be done with her mother and come attend her.

The minutes ticked by. Eliza walked over to one of the three windows that overlooked the circular drive. Riding up the paved driveway was a thin man in a light-colored coat. Her breath caught a moment. Was it the duke? No, she chided herself, he was much too slender. Rufus Rowland's shoulders would nearly double this fellow's. The man rode up to the stables near the right side of the house and disappeared inside.

She looked over to the door to her chamber. Ollerton still had not come. She wondered if she should try to dress her hair herself. It was not the first time Ollerton had forgotten her, and she did not want to be late for tea.

She was about to move away from the window when she spotted another rider coming up the drive. This one rode straight up to the door, dismounting by the front steps and casting the reins of his horse to a footman with an imperious fling. Eliza began to breathe a little faster. The shoulders were right, the air was right—this must be him, the master of the house. She could not see his hair or his face—from this vantage point, his beaver concealed them both—but she knew it was Rufus.

She looked at the door again. Her hand ran over her gray traveling dress; she could feel the dust, but the color concealed it. There was a small looking glass on the bureau. Her auburn curls were pinned more loosely than she liked, but they were not in complete disarray.

A daring thought came to her. What if she were to go downstairs—by herself—and greet the duke as he came into the house? A tremor of trepidation almost extinguished the idea as soon as it had formed, but the spark refused to die.

She would be brave. She would go downstairs. And perhaps the look in the duke's eyes, when he saw her so unexpectedly, would tell her whether he truly had an interest in her…or whether this whole trip was a waste of time and expense.

Eliza opened the bedroom door and peered down the hallway. The appearance of a footman carrying candlesticks or an encounter with a maid bearing linens would have halted her in her tracks. But no one was in the corridor, not a soul. She tiptoed down the floral rug until she came to the stairs. Her hand glided over the polished banister as she descended. She glanced up at the portrait wall over the landing to shore up her courage.

As the staircase led into the saloon, she heard voices. She leaned breathlessly against a column close to a bright floral arrangement and listened to the conversation in the entrance hall.

"Good afternoon, Hayward. If I might trouble you to place my card on the silver salver for my brother."

"Your…card, Lord Henry?" The butler sounded perplexed.

"If you would be so kind."

There was a pause. Eliza's heart fell. It was not the duke after all, but his brother. She could not see him from where she stood in the adjoining room, but she could imagine that dark, serious face from the portrait gallery conversing with the immaculate butler.

"Lord Henry, I regret that I cannot—"

"Oh, do be a good fellow, Hayward."

"*No*, Master Henry."

There was another pause. Eliza thought it very strange that a servant would speak so to a son of a house. But then, it was no stranger than a man wanting to leave his calling card for his own brother.

"Very well then. I'll hand it to him myself. Is my mother at home?"

"In the drawing room, sir, waiting for tea to be served."

Before Eliza had time to wonder where exactly the drawing room was located, the duke's brother strode into the saloon. She froze like a deer trapped behind a thicket, staring at him intently with her green eyes.

"And who might you be?" he demanded, looking Eliza up and down as if she were some sort of trespasser.

Eliza's face flushed as pink as a summer sunset. "Miss Elizabeth Malcolm," she said. "I'm afraid I've not had the pleasure of making your acquaintance either, Mr.…?"

He ignored her and continued on with his own line of questioning. "And what are you doing here?"

Eliza lifted her chin and folded her hands in front of her to stop them from shaking. "My parents and I are guests of the duke."

"The duke!" His dark eyes narrowed. "Whatever for?"

His rudeness was unlike anything she had ever experienced. Part of her wanted to slap him. Part of her wanted to run away and cry. She was certain that the latter outcome would occur if she were not rescued soon.

"I could not say, sir. As the duke's guest, though, I suppose I have as much right to be here as you—"

"More right, I should think," said another voice coming in from the opposite door of the saloon.

Eliza and the dark-haired man turned sharply to see Rufus Rowland, the Duke of Brockenhurst saunter into the room. He was in his shirtsleeves and vest, having divested himself of his jacket on this warm August day. His wavy red hair was wet from exertion, and his buckskins were caked with dust.

"Enchanted to see you again, Miss Malcolm." Rufus walked across the room, took Eliza's hand in his, and lightly kissed it.

He turned to his brother. "And you, dear Henry—not quite so enchanted."

"Likewise, my dear Rufus." Lord Henry glanced from Eliza to Rufus and then back again.

Eliza was struck by the contrast in manners between the two gentlemen. Her hand still tingled from the brush of Rufus' lips. Her spirit still smarted from the incivility of Lord Henry's words.

"You're not staying?" said Rufus. It was more of an assertion than a question.

"Would you rather I didn't?"

Eliza felt the younger Rowland's eyes dart toward her again.

"Whatever you like, brother," Rufus said dismissively. He turned his attention back to Eliza. "As you can see I've been shooting. I'm mortified to say that I had exceedingly poor luck. Only two braces of pheasants. But now that you're here, perhaps my luck will improve."

He pressed another kiss on her hand. Eliza's eyes grew big. He had never been this familiar when calling on them in Grosvenor Square. Perhaps he really did mean to court her.

"I must change into something more presentable," said the duke, mopping his hair away from his face with a large hand.

Eliza looked down at her own dusty traveling dress, wondering, with a tinge of panic, how soon tea was.

"But I imagine my mother is eager to see you, so let's not keep her waiting. Henry,"—the duke's eyes glittered—"you can make yourself useful and take Miss Malcolm to the drawing room."

Lord Henry made no answer, watching as his brother disappeared toward the staircase.

Eliza took a deep breath and stared at the floor.

"Well then, shall we?"

She looked up. Lord Henry was offering her his arm. She took it and they walked back through the entrance hall toward the double doors that led into the drawing room, Lord Henry maintaining an aloof silence and Eliza summoning up the whole of her courage to face a room full of people she did not know on the arm of a man she did not much like.

∞

HENRY HAD ESCORTED ENOUGH NERVOUS debutantes to sense when one was about to dissolve into a puddle. He cast a curious glance at Miss Malcolm's profile as they approached the drawing room. She was biting her lower lip and her face was still a half-shade of pink, but despite that, or perhaps because of it, she was rather pretty. He would almost think her beautiful, if it were not for the red in her hair which reminded him of his brother.

Where had Rufus come across this girl? And why had he invited her here? Henry knew all too well that she was not the usual sort of woman that the Duke of Brockenhurst preferred. Her dress was plain and genteel, and she did not seem the least bit forward. She had said that her parents were here as well, which lent an unexpected air of propriety to the situation.

He was already regretting his incivility to her in the saloon. It was not his habit to insult young women on first acquaintance—but then, previous encounters with ladies of *Rufus'* acquaintance had left him ill-prepared to encounter someone modest and demure.

Henry could feel Miss Malcolm's grip tighten on the crook of his arm as his opposite hand pushed open the doors of the drawing room. She was terrified. But just as quickly, her hand relaxed—she was determined not to show it.

The group of four seated around the tea table looked up as Henry and Miss Malcolm entered, and the two gentlemen rose to their feet in courtesy to Henry's companion.

"Henry! What on earth are you doing here?" demanded Adele with a shriek. She tapped the gentleman next to her with her fan. "Mr. Blount! Did you know my brother was coming down to the country?"

Stephen smiled. "He told me he might, but I did not think it my place to tell you."

Henry and Stephen exchanged a nod of greeting.

"Well, that was very wrong of you," said Adele, shaking her brown curls with a toss of her head. "I forbid you to keep secrets from me, Mr. Blount."

Henry groaned inwardly. It was ghastly watching one's sister flirt with one's friend.

"So delightful to see you," said his mother, with a little more decorum than her daughter. "The day is full of surprises—first your brother Robert arrives, then you."

"Hello, Hal!" said the slender man standing behind the duchess. He gave a smirk, as if their chance meeting at the village tavern was some sort of clandestine act that bound them together.

"And who is this on your arm?" asked the duchess, gesturing graciously to Miss Malcolm.

Henry started. He had assumed that Miss Malcolm would have met his mother before now, but apparently Rufus had sent this wilting flower into a room full of strangers. "I beg your pardon, Mother. May I present Miss Elizabeth Malcolm?"

"How do you do?" said the girl a little faintly. She let go of his arm to bob a brief curtsey.

The duchess murmured something polite while Adele displayed another of her irrepressible outbursts. "Miss Malcolm? But I thought you were visiting Rufus? How is it that you come in with Henry?"

Miss Malcolm colored from the edges of her ears to the tip of her nose. Adele certainly knew how to infuse a situation with awkwardness. Henry felt sorry for the young lady. But not sorry enough to dismiss the mischievous thought that came to him. Hayward had thwarted his plans to vex Rufus with his new calling card—but circumstances had provided another opportunity with which to vex him. He would still be able to put some pebbles in Rufus' boots today.

"Miss Malcolm is a great friend of mine from London," said Henry, spilling forth this fabrication with enthusiasm. "I heard that Rufus had invited her to Harrowhaven, so naturally, I decided to pay a visit to you, Mother, at the same time."

Miss Malcolm stared at him, her lips slightly parted. She was tall for a woman, and he was only of average height for a man, making their eyes nearly on a level. He wondered if she would have the courage to contradict him. But no—she kept silent and her opportunity was lost.

"I see," said his mother, her eyebrows crinkling together in foreboding. It was not the first time Rufus and Henry had been rivals.

"How interesting!" trilled Adele, spreading her fan in front of her face to hide a grin. Henry gave her a wink—he might have known that Adele would appreciate the situation as much as he did. He could see his sister cast an appraising glance at Miss Malcolm's plain gown and pretty features. "Please, sit down, my dear," she said to their guest, gesturing to the empty sofa. Henry deposited his charge and stepped back, giving her an encouraging smile.

"Aren't you going to introduce the rest of us?" asked Robert, perching himself primly on the edge of his chair so as not to wrinkle his coattails. He lifted his monocle to examine the fair intruder.

"It would be my pleasure," said Henry. "Miss Malcolm, allow me to present my half-brother, Robert Curtis. My sister Adele needs no introduction, I suppose. And this is Mr. Stephen Blount, a longtime friend of mine—although something tells me that he is not here to visit *me*."

Adele giggled at this last part, and Stephen cleared his throat in annoyance.

"Do you paint, Miss Malcolm?" Adele asked, leaning in confidentially. Henry sat down on the other side of the sofa, a little closer than he normally might to a lady not his relative. He watched as Miss Malcolm's right hand, which was trailing absently over the upholstery, moved suddenly into her lap.

"Yes," said Miss Malcolm, fixing her attention completely on Adele.

"And play the pianoforte?"

"A little."

"And sing?"

"Not at all."

"That is no matter. I don't think Rufus much cares for music. Although Henry might." Adele smiled archly.

"Miss Malcolm," said the duchess, no doubt determined to intervene before her daughter humiliated their guest entirely, "I suppose we have the honor of your parents visiting as well?"

Henry frowned. Had Rufus not informed his mother which guests they would be receiving? He knew all too well the autocratic control that Rufus exercised over the estate since their father's death, but he had assumed that his mother was still mistress of the family home.

"Oh, yes," said Miss Malcolm. The dark lashes around her green eyes fluttered in surprise. "I do apologize that they are late for tea. They were removing the dust from travel."

She blushed again as she said this, and her fingers rubbed a fold of her skirt. She was still in her own traveling dress, Henry noticed, the plain gray a great contrast to the frilly white chiffon that Adele was sporting.

"No matter, for here they are now!" said the duchess, and pulling his eyes away from Miss Malcolm's face, Henry saw Hayward opening the drawing room doors to announce Sir Arthur and Lady Malcolm.

ELIZA BREATHED A SIGH OF thanksgiving as her father and mother entered the room. The last fifteen minutes had been almost unbearable, first Henry Rowland's insolence in the saloon and then his outrageous claim to friendship with her. Rufus' mother seemed kind enough, although how peculiar that she should not know ahead of time that they were coming! Rufus' sister she was not so sure about—she seemed mischievous, though one could hope it was only high spirits and not maliciousness.

Eliza felt the sofa shift as Lord Henry stood up and offered his seat to her mother. She took her mother's hand as she sat down and squeezed it, but Lady Malcolm, with a pointed look at Eliza's gray dress, released her hand just as quickly in a gesture of disapproval.

Eliza touched her fingers to her hair and felt a few tendrils coming loose. Why had she not waited in her room for Ollerton to come?

The Duchess of Brockenhurst was making the necessary introductions to Eliza's parents—"...and my son Henry you must already know."

Eliza shot a look of desperation over to her father. What would they all think if Lord Henry was acquainted with *her* and not with her *father*? She cast a sideways glance at Lord Henry and saw the hint of a smile on his face. How unkind of him to get so much amusement at another's expense!

"Erm, yes, of course," said Sir Arthur, always ready to sacrifice a little truth for the sake of social niceties. Eliza released the breath she had been holding.

Lady Malcolm, however, was not so easily swayed by convention. "I do not believe *I* have had the honor. You are...?"

"Henry Rowland, my dear," said Sir Arthur. "Surely you remember."

"Always a pleasure, madam," said Lord Henry, reaching for her mother's hand and kissing it gallantly.

Eliza's mouth nearly fell open. So he *did* have some manners after all, just none that he had cared to display for her.

The Duchess of Brockenhurst ordered more tea things to be sent for and, when the requisite cakes and cups had arrived, distributed them to the late arrivals. Mr. Curtis, Rufus' older brother, engaged Sir Arthur and the other gentlemen in conversation about a new machine that ran on steam. The duchess began commenting on the hot summer weather to Lady Malcolm.

Eliza saw Rufus' sister leaning in for another round of questioning and braced herself for the onslaught.

"How do you enjoy the country compared to London, Miss Malcolm?"

"It is a pleasant change," rejoined Eliza, relieved that her accomplishments were no longer being put on display. "I have not been much in Sussex."

"Ah, what county is your family seat in then?"

"We reside in London for the whole of the year." She did not think it necessary to mention that her father had sold their country estate three years ago to add some wind to their sails.

"Oh!" said Lady Adele. She seemed genuinely dismayed by the admission, her tone hinting at the universal understanding that the best sorts of people always quitted London by the beginning of August.

It was not *so* bad, thought Eliza ruefully. She loved the hustle and bustle of the streets, the anonymity of the crowd, the life and the colors. And in the summer, one could easily become accustomed to the heat and the smell and the absence of friends while others were enjoying rural life.

"How pleasant," said a voice behind her, "to have an excuse to forgo the call of the horn and the hounds!"

Eliza tilted her chin upwards and saw that Lord Henry had vacated his place in the men's conversation to stand directly behind the sofa. "You are not fond of hunting, Lord Henry?"

"No. That is my brother's province." His tone indicated that anything in favor with the duke would be out of favor with him.

"Well, if you mean to stay the week, you'll have to ride out with Rufus," said Lady Adele, "for he's organized a large hunting party this Wednesday."

"If I mean to stay," echoed Lord Henry. His dark eyes looked down at Eliza thoughtfully. "What think you, Miss Malcolm? Is it worth my time?"

Eliza felt heat burning in her cheeks. Other women could bear embarrassment gracefully—why must *her* complexion betray her at every turn? "I could not say, sir."

"Of course it is, you gudgeon," said Adele, striking at her brother with her fan. "What can you possibly have to do back in town? Mother will be delighted to have a long visit with you, and did you not say it yourself, that Miss Malcolm is a great friend of yours? How can you possibly come all this way and then desert her because you dislike the hunt?"

A̲FTER SIR ARTHUR HAD INGESTED THE LAST TEA CAKE, the Duchess of Brockenhurst invited the Malcolms to take a tour of the house and gardens. "It may have been a while since I've been a proper hostess," she said, "but I still remember where everything is."

Rufus entered the drawing room just after the Malcolms had left it, dressed in a gray coat with a freshly starched cravat. Henry thought it a strange omen—Rufus never wore a cravat in the country, not while he could live all day in his riding boots.

"Robert!" said the duke, eyeing his elder brother. "You're here too?"

"Just a filial visit to Mother," said Robert reassuringly. Henry suspected he would try to tap the duke's financial casks when a more opportune moment arose.

"Hmm, very well," said Rufus. "*You* can stay. But as for Henry,"—he looked at his younger brother—"I'm sure your horse is rested well enough by now—"

"Oh, you can't boot Henry out," said Adele matter-of-factly.

"Can't I?" Rufus' eyes glittered dangerously.

"No," replied Adele. She set her teacup down and rose from her chair. Stephen Blount, who had been ignored by the rest of them, jumped to his feet as well. "He's great friends with Miss Malcolm, and you do want to make a good impression, don't you?"

Rufus turned on Henry. "How do you know Miss Malcolm?"

Henry smirked. "Hard to say, really. A dance here, a ride in the park there. No need to be so proprietary, dear chap. She's certainly given *me* no reason to hope."

"What!" barked Rufus. "Did you offer for her?"

Henry nearly fell to pieces laughing but managed, with effort, to keep a smile off his face. "Not in so many words...."

Rufus snorted. "You're lying. We both know that you're in no position to set up a household."

"And whose fault is that?"

"Now, now," said Robert stepping between the two men. He was the tallest of the three, but also the slightest and least imposing. "We're all together again...let's not spoil it by quarreling."

"And besides," said Adele with a winning smile. She thrust her fan at Stephen to hold and hung persuasively on Rufus' arm. "You were never afraid of a little competition, were you, brother? It should be amusing for all of us to see Henry try to best you."

"Try and fail," growled Rufus.

"Oh, I could never be as tempting a matrimonial prospect as a duke," said Henry, imbuing his voice with a false sincerity that was certain to irk Rufus.

"It's decided then," said Adele. "Henry stays." She let go of Rufus' arm and retrieved her fan from Stephen. "Shall we take a turn in the garden, Mr. Blount?"

"Of course, Lady Adele," said Henry's friend, no doubt relieved to escape the familial quarrel. Adele rang for a footman and sent him to fetch her parasol.

Rufus stalked towards the drawing room door, then looking over his shoulder, delivered one last parting shot. "Since you're staying, Henry, you'll be happy to know that I've another guest arriving tonight."

"I can only imagine who that might be," said Henry dryly.

He was glad that Stephen had already forewarned him of Walter Turold's impending arrival. Still, he would be even less happy to see Walter than he was to see Rufus. It was always easier to face someone who had wronged you than someone who knew the wrong that you yourself had done. His lips set in a firm line, and he walked over to the drawing room windows to stare at the perfectly trimmed hedges outlining the garden.

As soon as Rufus' shoulders had disappeared, Robert left the drawing room as well. The footman returned with Adele's parasol, and she walked over to a small mirror by the mantel to ensure that her brown curls were still properly arranged. "I would invite you to walk with us, Henry, but I daresay you remember how to amuse yourself at Harrowhaven."

"Of course," said Henry. He walked over to Stephen and put a none-too-gentle hand on his friend's shoulder. "And in my experience, getting lost in the garden maze is not quite so easy when the lady's brother joins the expedition."

"Insightful as ever," said Stephen with a faint smile. He extricated himself from Henry's grip and offered Adele his arm. "We really shouldn't mind though, if you want to join us...."

Adele sent a petulant glare in Stephen's direction. If she had not already put away her fan, she would most certainly have rapped his knuckles with it.

"No, no, enjoy yourselves, children," said Henry. "I know my way around, and there's someone here at Harrowhaven I very much want to visit."

༺❦༻

THE EXTENSIVE TOUR THAT THE Duchess of Brockenhurst had planned was perhaps better conducted in winter than in summer. Eliza's face began to glow with the heat before they had finished viewing the main floor. She stifled expressions of surprise more than once—the country house that her father had sold was a hovel compared to this palace! Her mother remained silent, casting measured looks at the high ceilings of the library and the intricate wainscoting of the blue room. Sir Arthur filled the void, engaging the duchess with questions and compliments since his wife and daughter would not.

They had just begun ascending the grand staircase when a figure hailed them from below. Eliza smiled tentatively to see Rufus coming toward them, hand on the banister, taking the steps two at a time.

"Ah, there you are, Rufus," said the duchess evenly. "You see I am showing your guests the house." A look passed between them, but Eliza could not decipher what it meant.

"Thank you, Mother," said Rufus. "I can relieve you of the duty now if you wish." He smiled at Eliza and, stepping up alongside her, offered her his arm.

The duchess inclined her head in a slight bow, a very formal gesture to make to one's own son, thought Eliza. Without looking back, she climbed the rest of the stairs and disappeared down the corridor, presumably to her own chambers.

"Please take no offense," said Rufus hurriedly. "My mother is feeling indisposed today."

"Oh, of course not," said Sir Arthur, beaming profusely. "The heat, no doubt. A little rest will do her some good."

Eliza looked up. They were standing on the same large landing where they had stopped earlier that day, the gilt-framed portraits staring from the corner wall.

"How long ago was this done?" she asked, releasing the duke's arm and walking over to his image.

Rufus followed her. "Four years ago. It is a good likeness, I think."

"Yes," said Eliza, looking back and forth between the two.

A good likeness and, indeed, a flattering one, she thought, now that she had the opportunity to see the duke again in person.

"And was this one done at the same time?" She gestured at the picture of Lord Henry.

Rufus frowned. "Yes, and that one of Adele as well."

Her parents walked to the other side of the landing to examine the picture of the buoyant Lady Adele. Rufus leaned in, his face close to Eliza's as she examined his own portrait. "I did not realize you were acquainted with my brother Henry."

Eliza started. "Only a very little."

"I see."

She kept her eyes on the painting, but she could feel Rufus studying her face.

"He means to stay for the hunt on Wednesday," he said abruptly. "I hope you don't mind."

"Mind?" Eliza wished she were a more accomplished actress. "Why should I?" What had Rufus' brother told him? It almost seemed that the duke suspected some romantic connection between the two of them. Merciful heavens! She said a silent prayer. Why had she not contradicted Henry Rowland the moment he claimed they were acquainted?

"Oh, no reason." Rufus snapped his attention back to the tour of the building. "Shall we?" He offered her his arm again.

Eliza cast one backward glance as they ascended the staircase, seeking a glimpse of the painting she had refrained from studying too closely. While the duke's portrait from four years ago was a touch too complimentary, she discovered that his brother's portrait had the opposite flaw. The Lord Henry of four years ago was a serious-looking adolescent, but the Lord Henry of today was a handsome, albeit ill-mannered, gentleman.

Henry watched as Adele and Stephen stepped out the French doors into the garden, his sister's white parasol twirling gaily between her fingertips. He wondered if his mother had given Adele any instructions on how to behave in the company of admiring suitors. Even if she had, he doubted that Adele would pay heed. Propriety was never Adele's strong point if it got in the way of her whims. About Stephen's morals he had no qualms. If those two were planning on stealing a kiss in the garden maze, it would be *Adele* doing the stealing.

Miss Malcolm, on the other hand, looked far more mild-mannered and biddable. He imagined Rufus leading *her* behind a hedgerow, then found himself unwilling to imagine anything further. What on earth did his brother want with a blushing rose like that when the brash peonies of Covent Garden were more his style?

Henry shook his head and went down a narrow corridor to the back of the house. His mother would hardly be conducting her tour of the house here, but it was the very place to find the person he was looking for.

Sweat began to drip down his neck as he entered the kitchen. Shadrach, Meshach, and Abednego would have been right at home in here. He loosened his collar. There were some pheasants on the counter, plucked and dressed for roasting on the spit—Rufus must have desired the fruit of his labor to be displayed at tonight's table. Cook had stepped outside, however, in search of a cooling breeze.

"Master Henry!" said a shocked voice from the storeroom next to the linen closet. Henry turned around and bumped into a string of ladles, sending them clattering onto the floor.

"Mrs. Forsythe! I was looking for you."

The housekeeper set down the jar of spices she was measuring and wiped her hands on a cloth. "I suppose I should be angry with you, after what happened with Jenny the last time you were here, but it seems I cannot be. It does a body good to see you, Master Henry."

Henry grinned and enveloped the old housekeeper in a bear hug. Mrs. Forsythe had been the housekeeper at Harrowhaven when his parents married, the housekeeper at Harrowhaven when he had been born, and would be the housekeeper at Harrowhaven until death came knocking.

"There, there, now," said Mrs. Forsythe, planting a motherly kiss on Henry's cheek and then pushing him away to maintain some sense of decorum. "What brings you to Sussex, young man?"

"Not my brother Rufus, certainly."

"Anyone could have guessed that much," said Mrs. Forsythe. While Henry bent down to pick up the ladles, she walked over to the counter in the kitchen and pulled out a dish of almond macaroons.

"You spoil me," said Henry, taking a handful of the small round sweets.

"I would have sent them up for tea had I known you would be there."

"Yes, and Robert would have eaten them all."

"Mr. Curtis is here as well? I'd best have all the rooms made up!"

"So it seems. And who are these other guests—the Malcolms?"

"Your brother the duke invited them. I was not informed as to the reason."

"It looks as if my mother was not informed either. Is something amiss between her and Rufus?" The strangeness of the situation had been perplexing him ever since he entered the drawing room. If he asked Adele, she would know nothing. If he asked his mother, she would tell him nothing. But if he asked Mrs. Forsythe....

The housekeeper pursed her lips. "They've had a...disagreement."

"And I'm sure you know all the details of it," Henry wheedled. He took a big bite of macaroon, knowing full well how much Mrs. Forsythe liked to see him eat.

"'Tisn't my place to say...."

"But you wouldn't want to leave me in the dark! I could be of some help to the situation."

The housekeeper snorted. "You, Master Henry? When was the last time you were in the mood to smooth things over with your brother? But I suppose if I don't tell you someone else will. The fact of the matter is that this spring your mother finally objected to his carryings-on."

"What sort of carryings-on?"

Mrs. Forsythe raised her eyebrows and gave a harrumph as if such things were better not mentioned by decent folk. "The same ones *you* objected to, Master Henry."

"Ah. And how did he take her criticism?"

"He told her he'd do as he pleased in his own house. She told him that, in that case, he could run the house himself."

Henry was not surprised. His mother had never taken any nonsense from his father, and he found it easy to believe she would not relax her standards for Rufus.

"And since that day, it's been his grace I take the menus to and the inventories, and the salaries, and the repairs—"

"How wretched!" exclaimed Henry.

"For him and me," said Mrs. Forsythe dourly. "I've asked him time and again to hire a new steward,"—she looked apologetically at Henry—"but he refuses. 'Taint gossip to say that his lordship has no mind or inclination for domestic matters. But unless he patches things up with her ladyship or takes a wife, there's no help for it."

"And that must be where the Malcolms come in."

"That's more than I could say," said Mrs. Forsythe, having led Henry by hand down the path to that very stopping point.

She looked discreetly over to the hallway where one of the maids had entered with a pail of dirty water and a scrub brush.

"Thank you, Constance. You can take some clean bedclothes upstairs now and make up two more rooms, one for Master Henry and one for Master Robert."

"Yes, ma'am," said the maid, bobbing a curtsey. Henry watched her take a blanket out of the linen closet and quickly fold it in halves then quarters.

"Your name's Constance, is it?" he said pleasantly. Putting the cover back on the dish of macaroons, he walked over to the maid. "And is this your first position as maid in a manor house?"

"Lord Henry!" said the housekeeper, a hint of thunder in her voice. She gestured the maid out of the room, and Constance scurried down the hall with the blanket in her hands.

"I won't have it again, I tell you!"

"Of course not, Mrs. Forsythe. Of course not," said Henry, doffing an imaginary hat to the offended housekeeper. "I'll be on my best behavior. Thank you for your macaroons and your conversation. I shall return to the other side of the house, and leave you to your domain."

4

OLLERTON CAME TO ELIZA'S ROOM FIRST THIS TIME TO HELP her dress for dinner. After laying out a shimmery dress of golden lace, the maid began to pull down Eliza's tresses to re-pin them for the evening. "Your mother did not know what to think, miss, with you disappearing like that this afternoon."

Eliza squirmed inwardly. An acquaintance in London had told her once that a lady's maid was the best sort of confidante, but Frances Ollerton, who had been Lady Malcolm's maid since before she was married, already had a mistress confiding in her. She was capable, she was motherly, but she was not a friend. Eliza was certain that whatever words passed between them at her dressing table would be repeated when Ollerton returned to her original mistress.

Eliza sighed. "I hardly know what to think myself, Ollerton." It was the truth. If that harebrained scheme of greeting the duke at the door had never entered her head, she would not have found herself involved in Henry Rowland's prevarications. She had no idea how to extricate herself now from the fib. She would just have to acknowledge the acquaintance as she had when the duke had quizzed her.

"And what does miss think of the duke?" asked Ollerton, quickly plaiting two braids on either side of Eliza's head to loop around the mass of auburn tresses.

"He is very kind," said Eliza. And he was. He had been. He had devoted his whole afternoon to showing them the house and the grounds. He had put up with her shy attempts at conversation. He had endured her father's sycophancy and her mother's severity. Was that not kindness?

"And handsome?" teased Ollerton, her lined face breaking into a smile.

"Of course," said Eliza, smiling a little as well. She had never preferred red hair, but that was rather hypocritical of her, seeing as how her own hair was halfway red or more. He was handsome enough, she supposed. He had to be. It was not as if she had another option.

Rising from her dressing table, Eliza stood in the center of the room as Ollerton lifted the golden gown over her head and then laced it in the back. The gossamer overlay was embroidered with flowers and birds. The rounded neckline was the lowest her mother had ever allowed her to wear, showing the delicate lines of her collarbone but still completely concealing her bosom. "Do you remember, Ollerton? I wore this to my first supper party after my coming-out ball."

"How could I forget, miss? You were a vision of loveliness."

Eliza sighed. It hadn't helped, of course. Her father's sunken fortunes and her own retiring nature were more than enough to deter any possible suitors. There had been no new dresses after her first season, just some extra ribbons and Ollerton's skillful needle to convert the old ones into the newest fashions. The sleeves on this one were different than when last she wore it. Eliza hoped that it would be enough to keep her from looking dowdy next to Lady Adele, who was certain to have her gowns made up by the best modiste in London.

Ollerton finished lacing the gown and stood back from her masterpiece. "You look even lovelier today than you did three years ago, child."

"Thank you, Ollerton." Eliza took the maid's hand and squeezed it. "Say a prayer for me tonight."

"I always do. Now hurry, miss! Can you find your slippers yourself? I must go lace your mother and the gong will sound any minute...."

⚜

WHEN HENRY WENT UP TO his room, the room he had occupied for most of his childhood and indeed up until three years ago, he found Frederick, one of the footmen, laying out an old set of his dinner clothes—shirt, cravat, coat, pantaloons, and shoes. "Mrs. Forsythe thought you might be wanting these, my lord," said the footman.

"How thoughtful of her," said Henry. "Give her my thanks."

"She said that an' you wish it, I'm to dress you."

"Mrs. Forsythe's foresight is astonishing. I do wish it."

Henry had packed very little in the one satchel he carried on his horse—at the time, he had not been intending to stay more than the afternoon. But then the jest with the calling card had turned into the jest with Miss Malcolm....

It was fortunate that his old clothes were still here, although he suspected that they would not fit the same as they once had. The years between the ages of twenty and twenty-three can have a great effect on a man, and Henry's chest and limbs had broadened considerably. He was no young sapling anymore, and the old pantaloons were far tighter than he preferred. Even with Frederick's help, he could barely shrug into the dinner coat.

"How long have you been a footman here?" Henry grunted, sitting down after the herculean effort of the coat so that Frederick could slide on his shoes.

"Two years, my lord."

"You seem very apt, very apt indeed. Have you ever aspired to greater things?"

"Like what do you mean, your lordship?"

"Like being the first footman at an establishment perhaps?"

Frederick whistled. "Can't say as I haven't dreamed. But there's others been here longer than me."

"Well, there's more places than Harrowhaven," said Henry, jumping to his feet and then regretting it as the tight shoes began to rub against his heels. "Just think on it, lad, and remember it, and maybe the opportunity will present itself."

Henry found himself first at the door of the dining room, although Stephen soon came to join him. "How was your garden adventure?" Henry asked insinuatingly.

Stephen's bare cheeks reddened.

"That delightful, eh?" said Henry. "Don't tell me about it. I don't want to hear."

"'Pon rep, Henry! Nothing untoward happened—"

"Please," interrupted Henry, plugging his ears with both hands, "spare my feelings as a brother."

The Malcolms were the next to descend for dinner, Miss Malcolm walking demurely in the shadow of her parents with eyes cast down and hands folded. Stephen engaged Sir Arthur in some small talk about the agricultural productivity of Sussex while Henry ceased plugging his ears and looked over at Miss Malcolm. The golden shimmer of her dress set off her skin far better than the dove gray she had worn earlier, and the slim lines of the skirt accentuated her slender figure. Henry considered complimenting her on her appearance but decided he should save his praise for a moment when Rufus was present.

The dowager duchess and Robert came down next, then Rufus with his friend Walter Turold. Henry had known the moment was coming, but he could not help quailing a little at the sight of Walter's glower. How many years had it been since he had earned Walter's disdain? Nearly a decade now, and he could still read the loathing in the other's eyes. Walter made no effort to speak to him, and Henry both resented it and was glad of it.

The gong sounded to bid them enter the doors for dinner. They all stood there a moment in awkward silence.

"For whom are we waiting?" asked Robert, delicately sniffing the flowers in the vase on the console table.

"For whom do you think?" replied Rufus, a little mean-spiritedly.

The answer soon swept into the room in a cloud of pink lace. "Oh, I didn't think I would be *last*," said Adele innocently.

"You are always last, my dear," said the dowager duchess. She had dressed in purple velvet, a fitting color for a dowager. Everyone looked to her, as the hostess, to sort out the seating arrangements, but she had her eyes on Rufus, and remembering what he'd learned from Mrs. Forsythe, Henry could see that they were full of challenge.

"Mother," said Rufus carefully. "Now that Adele is here, will you send us into the dining room?"

The duchess smiled grimly. "Very well." Henry knew that she would keep up appearances for the sake of the family's reputation, but her quarrel with her second son could not be resolved this easily. "Rufus, you must take Lady Malcolm in. Sir Arthur, please escort my daughter, Adele. Mr. Blount, please escort Miss Malcolm, and—"

"—and I will escort my dear Mama," said Henry, placing the duchess' arm in his and leaving Walter and Robert without a partner.

⁂

ELIZA FOUND HERSELF SEATED WITH Mr. Blount on one side and

Lord Henry on the other, a proximity that made her more nervous than she already was. The dinner party was small enough that talk need not be restricted to those on one's right and left, but still, she would have to let Lord Henry serve her food and thank him for refilling her cup. Across the table sat the duke's friend, Mr. Turold. He wore his hair long, in the old-fashioned style, pulled back into a neat queue at the base of his neck. Eliza felt a nagging sensation that she had met him before, but she could not recall the time or place.

As she had foreseen, Lady Adele's dress was stunning—a white dress of the finest muslin with an overlay of delicate pink lacework and a daring décolletage. "And how did you enjoy your tour of the house, Miss Malcolm?" asked Lady Adele from across the table.

"Very well, thank you," replied Eliza. She felt that she ought to add something, some comment about the cornices or the columns, but nothing came to her. She lapsed into silence, praying that she did not appear as inept at conversation as she felt. On the far end of the table, Rufus was explaining to her father just how many horses, hounds, and neighbors there would be at the hunt four days from now.

"May I offer you some fish?" said a voice in her right ear. Lord Henry was holding a large platter upon which a gargantuan boiled turbot was staring gruesomely at her.

"Yes, thank you," Eliza replied faintly, remembering only after he started to serve it that she did not in fact like fish.

"It's quite good with the anchovy butter," said her helpful swain, ladling some of that sauce next to the turbot on her plate.

"Excellent," murmured Eliza, the smell of the anchovies starting to waft into her nose. Determined not to engage Lord Henry in any further conversation, she looked to her left and saw Mr. Blount manfully attacking his piece of roast pheasant.

She wished he would dish some onto her plate, but he was paying her no notice and it would be impolite to ask.

The talk of the hunt was still going on, and now Mr. Curtis and Rufus' friend Mr. Turold had joined in. Eliza picked up her fork and made a halfhearted effort to spear a mouthful of turbot, but the piece of boiled fish disintegrated onto her plate.

"I have a new pair of hunting pistols," said Rufus, his voice rising with enthusiasm. "The cleanest action you've ever seen!"

"I would love to try them," said Robert. "If you don't need both, perhaps you'll loan me one for the hunt."

"Lud no, it would be wasted on you!" said Rufus. "Walter shall have it, for after me he is the best shot."

Eliza stared at her plate. She could not eat the fish. She could not do it.

"I am noticing your dress, Miss Malcolm," called Rufus' sister from across the table. She was clearly bored with the talk of guns.

"And I yours," said Eliza. She thought of what her mother would say if she ever attempted a neckline like Lady Adele's, and a smile nearly rose to her lips.

"I've seen nothing like it in town this season," continued Lady Adele. "Who is your modiste?"

Eliza blanched. It was no crime to wear a dress out of fashion, but it was a subject she had hoped to avoid over the dinner table. "Madame Lavelle."

"Do you know the shop, Mother?" said Lady Adele with interest. "I do not recognize the name."

No, she would not recognize it, thought Eliza, for Lady Adele had come out only this season, and this dress had been one of the last to be made before Madame Lavelle had closed her doors.

"I had a dress made by Madame Lavelle several years ago," said the duchess, setting down her wine glass thoughtfully. "The rose-colored crepe, Adele, but you may have been too young to recall." She turned to Eliza. "I was not aware that Madame Lavelle still plied her needle."

"Nor does she," said Eliza, seeing now that the awful truth must come out. "She made up this gown for me several years ago."

"Oh!" said Adele, clearly startled that such an enormity could happen or be admitted to. "Several years ago? I've never heard of such a thing." Her outcry drew the attention of the gentlemen at the table, and the hunting conversation, which had hitherto seemed interminable, now came to an unfortunate and untimely end.

Eliza knew that she ought to turn the conversation to some other subject, but she could not stop her face from flaming red or her tongue from sticking to the roof of her mouth. She glanced sideways and saw her mother sitting tight-lipped on the other side of Mr. Blount. No, it was too much to hope for rescue from that quarter.

"Miss Malcolm," said a cheerful voice on her right. It was Lord Henry again. She prayed that he was not about to ask her how she liked the fish.

"I must confess that you have just saved me from a very awkward circumstance. I was certain that over the course of this dinner Adele would point out to our esteemed company just how strange the cut of my coat is, but no, she has fixated instead on your dress and so I, for the moment, am safe."

"Why, Henry! It *is* strange!" said Lady Adele, a new monstrosity dangling in front of her like a worm on a hook. "What on earth are you wearing?"

"A dinner jacket, my dear," said Lord Henry. "And I *defy* you to guess how long ago it was made!"

"Last season?" asked Lady Adele, setting down her spoonful of pineapple cream.

"Wrong!" said Lord Henry. "I'll give you one more guess."

"Two seasons ago?"

"Wrong again! A pity we did not set a wager before I let you guess."

"Then when?" demanded Adele. "How old is it? It's positively ghastly!"

Mr. Curtis cleared his throat from across the table. "It's clearly at least three seasons old, Adele. Note the width of the lapels and the garish blue of the fabric. In fact, I doubt anything like that's been seen since Bonaparte crowned himself Emperor."

"Alas," said Lord Henry, with mock solemnity. "Would you not agree that the cut is excellent?"

"Oh, Henry!" said Adele as the whole table broke into laughter. "You'd better send up to London for your real clothes if you're planning to stay the week, for I think the seams of this one are about to explode."

They all laughed again, and talk turned once more to the amusements planned for next week. Eliza looked at her neighbor in his tight-fitting, unfashionable jacket, and felt, for just an instant, her tongue-tied shyness lose its grip.

"Thank you," she said softly.

"For what?" Lord Henry asked. "For the fish?" His eyes twinkled at her, and in that instant she knew that he knew how much she detested turbot. She laid her fork down on the edge of her plate—there was no point anymore in pretending to eat it.

"Yes," she said, "for the fish."

5

*H*ENRY WATCHED THE LADIES VACATE THE DINING ROOM with a distinct sense of concern. He hoped Miss Malcolm's spirits were fortified enough for Adele's intrusive questions. He also hoped his mother took things in hand and directed the conversation a little better than she had at dinner.

A quick look around the room reminded him that his spirits might need fortifying as well. He rose from his chair and walked over to the sideboard as soon as Hayward had decanted the port.

"Have you heard about this new invention involving locomotion?" Robert said, turning to Rufus.

Stephen abandoned his chair too and came to fill his glass. "A bit of a one-act show, your half-brother," he said quietly to Henry.

"Always," replied Henry. "Mark my words—he's speculating on this locomotive business and needs Rufus to back him."

"*You* could back him."

"Hush now." Henry looked around and saw Walter Turold eyeing them. "That's not exactly something I'd like to advertise." Henry turned his back on the table to curtail any eavesdropping. "And besides—how often has Robert been right about any of his gambles? He's deeper and deeper in dun territory every year—I expect Rufus holds the deeds to all his properties by now."

Stephen glanced back at the table and saw Sir Arthur listening with rapt attention to Robert's scheme.

"Perhaps he'll find a backer outside the family?"

Henry followed Stephen's eyes. "Sir Arthur? Come now, Stephen, do you really think the Malcolms have money to throw about?" He nearly alluded to Miss Malcolm's dress—three seasons old—but her utter embarrassment over the matter made him think better of it.

"I've never thought about whether they do or not. But maybe you're right." Stephen said. "And in that case, what exactly are Rufus' intentions in bringing Miss Malcolm here?"

"What are you saying? That everyone should follow your lead and be on the lookout for an heiress?"

Stephen reddened. "Is that what you think of me?"

"No, no," said Henry, clapping him on the shoulder. "I jest."

"What are you two whispering about?" demanded Rufus. He had grown tired of Robert's effusions and was looking for a way to escape.

"Just how incredibly dull it is to be in our own company," said Henry. "Why don't we rejoin the ladies? I know that Stephen, at least, will favor that idea."

"You seem to favor the idea as well," said Walter Turold. "Any particular reason why?"

Henry held his breath momentarily. It was the first time in years that Walter had addressed him directly. "A very particular reason," he said, forcing a smile. He would maintain his charade to the end. "The lovely Miss Malcolm and I are old friends. I can introduce you to her if you like."

"I fear you're behind the times in that regard," said Rufus with a smirk. "Walter's the one who pointed out Miss Malcolm to *me*."

"Oh?" said Henry. "And how did Miss Malcolm catch *your* eye, Walter?"

Stephen nudged his friend's arm.

"But perhaps a question better answered when the lady's

father is not present," said Henry, without any discomfiture. He gave a friendly bow to Sir Arthur. "Shall we, gentlemen?" And without waiting for a reply, he stepped out the dining room door and crossed the corridor to enter the drawing room.

<hr />

Eliza folded and unfolded her hands, rubbing her palms against the golden overlay of her skirt. As soon as they had entered the drawing room, the two older ladies had taken a seat on the sofa and begun to talk of events twenty or thirty years past, when France still had its king and when America still served the crown. It was the only thread that bound them together, their common age—and it was a thread that neither Eliza nor Lady Adele shared.

"Come, sit by the window with me," directed Lady Adele, and Eliza soon found herself secluded in an unexpected tête-à-tête with the duke's sister.

"What do you think of Mr. Blount?"

Eliza wondered if the question were a test. "He seems very polite."

"He's courting me, you know." Lady Adele took one of her brown curls in hand and began to twist it around her finger.

Eliza was not sure whether this last was a statement of fact, an exuberant boast, or a warning against trespass.

"I am...glad to hear it."

"I haven't decided yet, of course," continued Adele. "He's handsome and kind, but not exactly a catch...well, for me at least."

Eliza felt herself gaping and closed her mouth. She had never had a friend speak this frankly to her before. Her mother was forthright enough, but never on such a topic.

"Do you have a good many other suitors then?"

"Oh, Lud, yes," said Lady Adele. "Well, that is to say, I did after my coming-out ball earlier this year, but I may have put them off a bit by showing such a preference for Steph—that is, Mr. Blount. But if I should decide against him, I suppose they'll all come back again."

"It seems cruel to keep him in suspense," said Eliza, feeling genuinely sorry for anyone at the mercy of this pretty tyrant's whims.

"Oh?" Lady Adele's eyebrows lifted like a topsail catching the wind. "And are you not keeping my brother Rufus in suspense?"

Eliza's face reddened. The situation was not the same! She had never given him encouragement; he had simply shown an interest all on his own. And if, over the course of this visit, she learned that she could not return that interest, she would most certainly tell him at once.

The two women considered each other's faces, until Eliza became flustered and dropped her eyes. Lady Adele beamed like a child who has won her first hand at piquet.

"And what do you think of my brother Henry?"

"He seems a fine gentleman." Eliza had certainly not thought that at first, but over the course of the last half hour, she had decided that his intervention in the dining room more than made up for his rudeness in the saloon. But why Lady Adele should be asking this question, she was not at all sure. It was the duke who had invited her to Harrowhaven, not his brother!

"I am surprised that we never crossed paths while I was in town this season, with you and Henry being such particular friends." There was a sly look in Lady Adele's brown eyes.

Eliza floundered for a moment. It was hateful to have to maintain this fiction that Lord Henry had forced on her. However kind he may have been at dinner, he was still a scoundrel through and through. "You know your brother." She smiled wanly. "He keeps his own counsel about a good many things."

"Yes, that is true," said Lady Adele slowly.

Eliza breathed easier. Apparently she had said the right

thing. She looked over to where her mother sat talking with the duchess, anxious for this game of cat and mouse to end.

"And I am sorry for that," said Lady Adele, an air of decision in her voice, "for I should have liked to have met you before. You must call me, Adele." She took Eliza's hand and pressed it. "I think we shall be fast friends."

"Yes, of course," said Eliza, taken completely by surprise. She stammered out the necessary reciprocation. "And...and... you must call me Eliza."

"What's this? Sharing secrets?" asked a good-humored voice. Lord Henry was the first of the gentlemen to enter the drawing room, and he immediately approached the window where the two young ladies sat.

"I was simply telling Eliza that it was quite horrid of you not to bring us together during the course of the season. I could have used another friend at Almack's or one of those card parties Mother was forever attending."

"Horrid of me, was it?" Lord Henry seemed amused by the accusation. "Perhaps I was enjoying having Miss Malcolm all to myself." He put his hands behind his back and took up a stance in front of the nearby fireplace, an action formed by habit, not necessity, for it was much too warm indoors to even think of lighting a fire. His tight coat strained at the seams.

Eliza's pink lips opened with a faint cry of protest. It was the outside of enough for him to be claiming such things! "Perhaps I would have *preferred* meeting your sister, Lord Henry."

Her tormentor's face fell into a full grin. If she had not thought he was laughing at her, she would have appreciated how handsome he looked when a smile lit up its features.

"Oh, come now, Miss Malcolm! You were not so cruel the last time I saw you promenading in Hyde Park."

"And when was that?" demanded Eliza, determined to catch him out in his falsehoods.

"The fifth of April, the day after the fourth of April when you waved your hand to me at the opera. Do not tell me you have forgotten!"

"Sir!" said Eliza, astounded at the detailed nature of his fabrications.

"Upon my word, Henry!" said Adele, glaring at her brother. "You are embarrassing Eliza. Perhaps she would rather forget the things you mention."

"I beg your pardon," said Lord Henry. Stepping over from the fireplace, he reached for Eliza's hand. "It shall not happen again."

"No," said a cold voice from the doorway. "It shall not."

Eliza looked over to see that Rufus was entering the drawing room. His gray eyes were fixed intractably on his brother. She had never seen murder on someone's face before, but she suspected that this might be it.

Her right hand was still trembling slightly from the pressure of Lord Henry's fingers. She looked up at him and saw that, rather than being dismayed by his brother's entrance, he was, in fact, reveling in it. He had wanted Rufus to witness that exchange.

<hr>

HENRY WALKED BACK TO THE fireplace, a satisfied smile on his face. Rufus was angry. Well, let him be! He deserved to stew a little at the thought of another man taking something that belonged to him.

Not that Miss Malcolm belonged to anyone, thought Henry, casting an appraising eye back at the auburn-haired beauty. In that golden dress, she was a diamond of the first water. He had almost penetrated her reserve with that last round of banter. He wondered what it would be like to really have a conversation with her—uninhibited by convention, by prying eyes, or by her own reticence.

Rufus had walked over to her now. He rested his hand on the back of her zebrawood chair, a sign of ownership, of proprietorship. Henry watched Miss Malcolm return Rufus' pleasantries with a half-smile and polite response. What did she see in him, anyway? A dukedom, no doubt. Henry's jaw jutted forward.

There were women aplenty—and their parents—who were willing to put up with a scoundrel for the sake of a title or the accompanying fortune. Miss Malcolm's father, Sir Arthur, seemed quite taken by what Rufus had to offer. Was the mother the same? He doubted that Miss Malcolm would resist a suitor's advances if parental pressure was applied.

"Lord Brockenhurst," said Lady Malcolm, signaling Rufus from the other side of the room. "I was just asking your mother about the little white church on the edge of the forest nearby."

"Ah, yes," said Rufus. "A pretty building. It is part of the Brockenhurst estate."

"Is that the church we shall be attending for services tomorrow?"

Henry glanced back at the group in the corner and saw that Adele was barely suppressing a giggle. He could certainly understand why.

"Tomorrow?" said Rufus. "Ah, yes. I had forgotten that it was Sunday."

Lady Malcolm sniffed in evident disapproval. Apparently such a lapse in memory was unacceptable.

"Yes, we shall certainly attend there," said Rufus, trying to recover his footing on this new, unsteady ground. "Reverend Ansel will be pleased to see the Malcolms join us in the Rowland family pew."

"*You're* going to church?" asked Adele incredulously. Henry reflected that someone really ought to teach the girl the art of tact. Still, in this case, it was amusing to see Rufus caught out.

"As I always do when I am able," replied Rufus. There was an edge to his voice, warning their sister to mind her tongue.

Henry noticed Miss Malcolm looking over at the duke with a perplexed look on her face. She obviously valued piety, the same as her mother did. He wondered if she would see through the mask Rufus was donning before it was too late.

"And what about *you*, Henry?" asked Adele.

Now it was Henry's turn to squirm. "I am not fond of Reverend Ansel's preaching," he said curtly.

It was as good an excuse as any, and not too far off the mark. He would gladly attend a service in any church but that one. As long as Reverend Ansel—and his family—occupied the adjoining parsonage, he would keep his distance.

"Oh, come now, Henry," said Walter. It was the second time he had addressed him this evening. "Afraid of a little sermon?"

Henry gritted his teeth. Walter, out of all the people present in that room, knew exactly what he was afraid of. "You might say that."

He could see Miss Malcolm's eyes on *him* now. It was only too apparent what she thought of his refusal to attend divine services tomorrow. It vexed him to think that he was falling lower in her opinion. It vexed him even further to realize that the first matter vexed him.

What was wrong with him? He had commenced this foolery to torment Rufus, not to be tormented himself. He leaned an arm against the mantelpiece. He would *not* allow himself to be jealous.

"I think it's time we said our good-nights," said Lady Malcolm, rising to her feet. Her husband and daughter, apparently used to obeying, rose from their seats as well.

"Good night," said Rufus, giving Miss Malcolm a long look and taking her hand in his. Henry was disgusted to see his brother rub his thumb across the back of Miss Malcolm's hand. No, he was not jealous, he reminded himself. But all the same, it would be better if he left on the morrow.

When Ollerton came to Eliza's room to help her dress for bed, Lady Malcolm came as well. Eliza sat down in front of the mirror, and the maid began to unpin her hair. Lady Malcolm stood in the center of the room, lips pursed, hands folded. "You must be tired, Mother, from all the day's events," said Eliza.

"I'm sure we all are, child," replied Lady Malcolm. She took a seat on the bed and began tapping her foot against the floor. Eliza knew instinctively that her mother had something to say.

"Thank you, Frances," said Lady Malcolm, once the maid had helped Eliza slip into her dressing gown. "I will help my daughter brush her hair out tonight." And taking a comb, Lady Malcolm began to run it through Eliza's long auburn hair while Ollerton hung up the discarded dress and then disappeared down the hallway.

"My dear," said Lady Malcolm.

Eliza sensed that a criticism was forthcoming.

"Have you considered your behavior in encouraging Henry Rowland?"

"You mean Rufus Rowland, Mother?"

"I mean Lord Henry Rowland," said Lady Malcolm grimly. "The duke's brother. You were much too familiar with him tonight, and I think it gave the duke and his family concern." She began to brush her daughter's hair more vigorously.

"Oh...." Eliza colored as she felt pain shooting across her scalp. "I'm sorry, Mother. I didn't mean to do any such thing."

"Yes, well, you did." Lady Malcolm sniffed. "And I heard him claim an acquaintance with us, but I cannot recall in the least laying eyes on him before."

"It must have been at one of the balls this season or last," said Eliza, sickened by the idea of lying to her mother. "Perhaps I danced with him and he remembers it."

"No." Lady Malcolm dropped the brush onto the vanity. "I would remember it. I remember everyone you have danced with, my dear. That Mr. Turold stood up with you once, you recall."

"Did he?" said Eliza, delighted to turn the conversation away from Henry Rowland. "I thought he looked familiar." *He* had claimed no acquaintance, however—probably just as happy to forget a girl he had danced with once and would never speak to again.

"Consider your behavior tomorrow, child," said Lady Malcolm, walking over to the door of the chamber. "You would not wish to ruin your chances with the duke through over-friendliness to the wrong party."

Eliza grimaced. No one had ever accused her of over-friendliness before. "I did not think you cared for the duke or his suit, Mother."

"Perhaps I was over-hasty," said Lady Malcolm, her fingers pausing on the handle of the door. "He is courteous and well-spoken, and not so opposed to religion or godly living as I originally thought." She looked at her daughter with a wry smile. "Your father was not dissimilar when first we were married."

And not so dissimilar now, thought Eliza, but kept it to herself. She said goodnight to her mother and, left to herself, walked aimlessly over to the window, watching the sun begin to set over the forested horizon.

Ruin her chances with the duke? It was Lord Henry who was aspiring to do exactly that. And her mother was right—she must be more careful, for he was well on his way to succeeding. It was surely for the best that he was not attending church with them tomorrow, for she doubted whether she would be able to keep her mind on the sermon with Henry Rowland in the same pew.

6

*H*ENRY WENT TO BED IRRITABLE AND AWOKE EARLY THE next morning without his mood having improved. He stared up at the canopy over his bed. "I am not fond of Reverend Ansel's preaching." What a bumblebroth he'd made of things! He imagined Miss Malcolm's pretty, puzzled face curling into a sneer of derision. And the worst part was that it was about as far from the truth as Sussex from Northumbria. Reverend Ansel was a masterful preacher. He liked the man—he was simply afraid to face him.

Henry threw back the covers and kicked one of his pillows over the side of the bed. Why was he wasting his time playing games with Rufus? He should have gone back to the Blue Boar, shared a pint with Ned, and already been on his way at daybreak.

He found Frederick, the footman-turned-valet, waiting at his door with a freshly brushed pair of Hessians. Henry had packed one clean shirt, and the footman removed it from the cavernous wardrobe.

"Will you be breaking your fast before church, my lord?"

Henry yanked the white cambric shirt over his head and closed the buttons over his broad chest. "Yes, a quick breakfast and then I must be off." He refrained from mentioning that it was the metropolis, not the church, that was his intended destination. "Will you pack my satchel and send it downstairs? I'll not be back to the house."

"Of course, sir," replied Frederick with a hint of surprise in his voice. But he did not ask why—the mark of a good servant, noted Henry approvingly.

Still in a fit of blue devils, Henry fastened his cravat—a quick, serviceable knot—and shrugged into yesterday's jacket, a far more comfortable fit than the blue dinner jacket from last night. With Frederick's help, he slipped his Hessians on over his pantaloons, and snatching up his beaver, he headed down the hall and towards the stairway. The morning was young, and with any luck he would be out of the house before any of the other inhabitants had woken.

Voices behind one of the closed doors gave him pause. He glanced at the dark wood door—it was Rufus' chamber, but it was a woman's voice inside. Frowning, Henry put an ear to the door. "Please, your grace. Let go of me."

Henry stepped back in time to be a couple paces down the hallway when the door opened. A blond-haired girl stepped out in a dark dress with her apron somewhat askew. In one hand she gripped an empty porcelain pitcher and with the other she pulled the door closed.

She started at seeing Henry in the corridor, her blue eyes as panicked as a doe in flight. Putting a finger to his lips, Henry put his other hand under her elbow and steered her down the hallway towards the stairs.

"Constance, isn't it?" he asked, once they were a safe distance away from his brother's room.

"Yes," she said, her lip trembling a little. Henry let go of her arm, and she tried to put her apron back to rights.

"Don't be afraid," said Henry. "Is this the first time that my brother the duke has…bothered you?"

She hesitated. "No."

"Have you told Mrs. Forsythe?"

"No, but even if I did, what could she do, sir?" Her eyes began to mist a little, and Henry was afraid she would burst into tears.

"A very good deal, my dear." Henry pulled out his handkerchief and handed it to the maid. "She can send another maid to fill his wash basin, someone much plainer than you, and keep you out of his way altogether. Or if you fear for your virtue, she can give you a reference to find another position."

"Thank you kindly, your lordship," said the maid, "but I can't think where else I would go. And my parents need me to keep my place and earn my wages, for I'm the oldest with a dozen still at home."

"I might be able to help you there," said Henry, patting her arm encouragingly. She managed a smile and handed him back the handkerchief.

The sound of a footstep arrested them both, and looking behind them, they found they were being observed by another of the house's occupants. The blond maid bobbed a quick curtsey to Henry, and darted off with her porcelain pitcher, while Henry found himself a few yards away from a flustered Miss Malcolm.

"Good morning," said Lord Henry. Eliza saw him give a fleeting glimpse to the pretty maid making her exit.

"G-good morning," said Eliza. She had never witnessed a gentleman on such familiar terms with one of the domestics—the way he had touched her arm, and shared his handkerchief with her…it crossed all bounds of propriety!

Eliza looked down at the floral carpet of the corridor and forged ahead toward the head of the staircase.

"Going to breakfast?" asked Lord Henry. He had advanced as well and was now matching his own stride with hers as they came down the stairs.

"Yes," said Eliza, biting her lip. How dare he try to accompany her! Her mother had been right. She must keep her distance from this man.

"May I join you then?" said Lord Henry, offering her that same smile he had been giving the maid only a few moments earlier.

Eliza paused on the stairs. "Lord Henry," she said quietly, "I must confess, I would prefer it if you did not."

He stared at her, his brown eyes nearly on a level with her green ones. Then, lifting his beaver, he made her a slight bow. "I salute you, Miss Malcolm. You've finally found the courage to speak your mind. Don't let it desert you, for you'll need it in this house."

And with that, he turned his back on her and descended the stairs at a fast clip. Eliza watched him disappear through the saloon, and a few seconds later, the front door slammed, with far more force than was necessary.

∞

"Traveling on a Sunday, your lordship?" said Ned, eyebrows raised.

"Dash it all, yes!" replied Henry. Since the breakfast table at Harrowhaven—or rather, Miss Malcolm—had rejected his presence, he had stopped in at the Blue Boar to break his fast before he began his ride.

"What's back in London that's so urgent?" Ned asked. He leaned his elbow on the counter and placed his bearded chin in his hand. "A pretty young lady, is it?"

Henry scowled. "Hardly." He took a forkful of salt pork and thrust it into his mouth. Normally he liked to bandy conversation with Ned, but the morning's events had made him indelibly cross with the world. How had Miss Malcolm contrived to come upon him at exactly the wrong instant? She must think him a rake, through and through...and all when Rufus was really the one to blame.

He dropped his fork on the plate with a clatter. "Let me give you a piece of advice, Ned—where pretty young ladies are concerned, it's best to tip your hat and walk the other way."

"Ah," said Ned, scenting a story behind the foul mood. "Rumor has it there's a pretty young lady up at the big house...."

"I will neither confirm nor deny your rumors."

"So it's true then," said Ned. His eyes sparkled. "Blonde, is she?"

"Auburn."

"With blue eyes?"

"Green."

"And yea high?" Ned held his hand a little above the counter.

"Quite tall actually," said Henry. "Willowy. But you knew that already, I suspect."

Ned nodded. "I did have a description of her from Jimmy—the second footman, an' you'll recall. 'Twas his night off last night and he spent it here."

"And what else did *Jimmy* tell you?"

"That his grace's younger brother was most friendly with the young lady. It seems he knew her in London, and she was the reason he stopped in at Harrowhaven."

Henry laughed. One forgot how much the servants liked to talk. His little deception would have spread all over the village by now.

"Yes, well, the young lady was less than friendly with his grace's brother. And due to some unfortunate circumstances, she thinks him an irreligious libertine not worth associating with."

Ned whistled. "Seems the poor girl has the brothers a mite confused."

Henry took a swig of ale. "Seems that way." He slapped a coin down on the counter and stood up to take his leave.

"Aw, come now, your lordship," said Ned, stowing the money in his chest, "it'd be a pity to leave now and leave the poor girl in such a state of befuddlement."

"You know me, Ned," said Henry, snatching up his hat that lay on the counter, "always one to run rather than face the music." He looked away, his face a little pained.

"I don't know as I'd hold with that, your lordship. The measure of a man's not taken in one single moment."

Henry gave a noncommittal grunt and headed for the door. It was kind of Ned to say, but his own conscience knew better, and had known better for the last ten years.

∽·∽

Eliza had ample time to be alone with her thoughts at the empty breakfast table. She stirred her chocolate slowly, trying to recover from the unpleasant encounter upstairs. Lord Henry had not seemed embarrassed in the slightest to be caught with his hand on that maid's arm. And what did he mean when he encouraged her to continue speaking her mind?

She frowned. What did it matter? She must follow her mother's advice and stop thinking about that odious man.

The door opened and Eliza saw Mr. Blount entering the dining room.

"Good morning!" he said, helping himself to some eggs and bacon from the sideboard and sitting down diagonally from her at the large table. "How are you this morning, Miss Malcolm?"

"Very well, thank you." Eliza took a sip of her chocolate. Mr. Blount had barely spoken three words to her yesterday, but he seemed kind enough. "Will the rest of the family be down soon, do you think?"

Mr. Blount grinned. "Well, I should imagine that Lady Adele will take breakfast in her room."

Eliza smiled. Yes, she could not imagine Adele getting out of her bed any sooner than she had to.

"And I hear the duchess has been keeping to her room as well ever since…well, ever since she has been out of sorts. The duke was up 'til all hours playing cards with Turold and Curtis—I bowed out once the small hours of the morning began to chime—so it'll be no small feat to roll them out of their bedclothes. But Henry's an early riser, and I imagine he'll be down soon enough."

Eliza flinched. "Lord Henry has already come and gone."

"Oh?" Stephen popped a bite of eggs in his mouth. "Gone for good, you mean?"

"It seemed that way."

"Wish he'd stopped in to say good-bye, but no matter. Expect he has business back in town."

Eliza set her cup down carefully. "What business is that, Mr. Blount?" She felt unusually forthright asking such a question, but her curiosity had got the better of her, and besides, Mr. Blount seemed…safe.

Stephen looked up from his plate apologetically. "I'm sorry, I can't really say. He…doesn't like it talked of."

"Oh, of course," said Eliza with a blush. She might have known the question was too bold. Doesn't like it talked of? She wondered if it was something unsavory—like managing a gambling hell or…worse.

"But seeing as how you're such good friends, you should ask him yourself!" said Mr. Blount enthusiastically. "Next time you see him, that is."

Eliza murmured something non-distinct. She could sense no hint of sarcasm in Mr. Blount's voice—he was really very kind, and very trusting. "How long have you known the Rowlands?"

"I've known Henry nearly half a dozen years. We were at Oxford together."

"And…Lady Adele?" asked Eliza, having the pleasure of seeing someone else besides herself turn red in the cheeks.

"Just since the beginning of the season—nearly a year now, I suppose." Mr. Blount looked down at his plate with a bashful smile. "Has she mentioned me at all?"

"Yes, with the utmost consideration," said Eliza reassuringly—although she did not know how considerate it was to consider throwing someone over if a better match presented itself.

"It is rather a gamble," said Mr. Blount confidingly, "to aim for a star so high above me, but Henry gave me reason to believe that he would not frown on the match, unequal as it might be."

"And the duke?" asked Eliza, much more interested in *his* opinion than Lord Henry's.

"Well, I had thought Brockenhurst might quibble at my lack of fortune, but then again,"—Mr. Blount looked at Eliza in her plain pale blue dress—"perhaps he is not so opposed to an unequal match as I had thought."

Eliza did not know how to answer that, but fortunately, the dining room doors swung open and she did not have to.

"Ah, there you are, my dear," said Sir Arthur, with Lady Malcolm on his arm. Eliza's father helped himself to a full plate, the hearty fare much more plentiful than what they had to break their fast in London.

Lady Malcolm, on the other hand, contented herself with a muffin and some tea. "I hope they have already ordered the carriage," she said with a sniff. In town, the Malcolms always arrived at Sunday services with at least a quarter of an hour to spare. Lady Malcolm did not approve of being late.

"I am sure the duke will have everything in order, Mama," said Eliza.

"Of course he will!" said Sir Arthur, amidst a mouthful of

sausage. He eyed the sideboard lovingly. "He's a good man, Brockenhurst! A good man!"

◦⦿◦

HENRY MOUNTED HIS HORSE AND, setting his back to the Blue Boar, headed north up the main road. With fast riding, he would be in London before noon. He would stop in at Maurice's on Bond Street and make sure all was well and perhaps pay a visit to Mr. Maurice himself to assure him of the fact.

London would be dull now that the season was over, but then he was always used to spending his summers at Harrowhaven. Boyhood habits died slowly. A pity the old house was forbidden country for him now, except for the occasional visit he could steal behind Rufus' back or underneath his nose.

Was it only yesterday morning that he had walked through the entrance hall and found Miss Malcolm frozen there against a column like the statue of some virgin goddess? He had hoped that the clip-clop of his horse's hooves would drive that picture out of his head, but instead, it only seemed to set Ned's words to a regular rhythm in his memory: "It'd be a pity to leave now and leave the poor girl in such a state of befuddlement."

Yes, well, it was not his duty to mend matters that were none of his own making.

He urged on his horse with a flick of the reins.

"Please, your grace. Let go of me." He could hear the maid's voice echoing in his head now. The hair bristled on his arms and his jaw clenched at the memory. He had confronted his brother about this very behavior three years ago—and Rufus had thrown him out on his ear. Clearly, time had not improved his brother's morals.

What if Miss Malcolm had walked down the corridor a few moments earlier? What if she had been the one to overhear the exchange behind the closed door and glimpse the distraught maid trying to put her apron to rights?

What if the same scene was reenacted three months from now, when Miss Malcolm had been lured into becoming the new Duchess of Brockenhurst? What if she learned the truth about Rufus only after it was too late?

Henry let out a low growl. Sensing the tautness in his rider's body, his horse became skittish and he was forced to slow the pace. He had no special knowledge of the future, but he would wager a thousand pounds or more that matrimony would not rectify Rufus' rakish nature. And it was certainly not a love match if Rufus had the audacity to make love to a maid while his intended was in the house.

Henry pulled sharply on the reins and brought the horse to a halt in the middle of the road. Dash it all! Ned was right. Elizabeth Malcolm was a lamb going to the slaughter. He could not, in good conscience, leave now and leave her to her fate.

He turned his horse's head around. If that meant returning to Harrowhaven and enduring her ill opinion of him, so be it. And if that meant braving a service in Reverend Ansel's church—

He took a deep breath.

7

Much to Lady Malcolm's relief, the carriages came round the drive a full half hour before services were to start. The occupants of the house were a different story, however, and the Malcolms waited in the entrance hall with Stephen Blount for at least a quarter of an hour before the Rowland family descended.

Rufus and Walter Turold came down together, the duke's close-cropped red hair contrasting with his friend's light brown, shoulder-length locks. "Good morning," said Rufus, placing a neat kiss on Eliza's hand. His eyes had a hungry quality to them, and she blushed furiously. He had a gray suit on, the coat fitting perfectly over his strong shoulders and a light blue waistcoat that nearly matched the shade of her own dress.

"What a pair you make!" cooed Adele, coming down the stairs on the heels of her silent mother. "Eliza," she said, taking her new bosom friend's hands in her own, "you must let me lend you a bonnet to go with your dress. I have just the thing."

A footman was sent upstairs, and a few minutes later, Eliza found herself going out the front door on Rufus' arm in a straw poke bonnet festooned with white feathers and blue ribbons.

"It's such a beautiful morning," said Rufus, looking up at the sky, "I really ought to drive the phaeton. Miss Malcolm, will you accompany me?"

"Oh, I...." Eliza looked at her mother. She could not remember ever having ridden alone in a vehicle with a man. But then, it would just be up the road along the edge of the forest, with her mother and father in a carriage right beside them.

"Of course, of course!" said Sir Arthur waving the couple off with a smile. His wife set her lips into a firm line as he helped the duchess and her into the first carriage. Adele, Mr. Curtis, Mr. Blount, and Mr. Turold climbed into the second carriage, and Eliza saw that Adele contrived it so that she was sharing a seat with Mr. Blount, his leg pressed up against the delicate sprigged muslin of her Sunday gown.

She looked up at Rufus, her heart beating a little faster. In a moment *she* would be sharing a seat with him. The groom brought the phaeton around. Rufus escorted her down the front steps, and she expected him to hand her into the carriage. But instead, he put his hands around her waist quite unnecessarily and lifted her up into the seat. "I hope you don't mind," he murmured, sliding his hands away from her, stepping up into the seat, and taking the reins from the groom.

Eliza was speechless. She looked around to see if anyone else had glimpsed this impropriety, but the other carriages had already pulled forward around the circular drive. There was still the groom, however, and however many footmen were standing at attention by the door. She slid over as far to the edge of the phaeton seat as she could, putting more space between herself and her suitor. Rufus did not seem to notice. He whipped up the horses to catch up with the others, and Eliza soon found herself holding on to her ornate bonnet with one hand and the side of the phaeton with the other.

"How do you like Harrowhaven?" the duke asked, raising his voice above the pounding of the horses' hooves.

"Very grand," said Eliza. It was an intimate question she felt—the duke inquiring how she liked his most important asset.

"It's a little run down of late." The duke's brow furrowed as he turned onto the drive that led towards the church. "My mother has been…unable to manage it as she once used to. The housekeeper does her best, but it needs a mistress to take charge of it."

Eliza's chest tightened. Were these the opening lines to a declaration?

He sent her a sideways look. She kept her eyes fixed on the tops of the horses' ears. The church was in sight, its steeple cutting through the tree-lined horizon like a knife. Eliza could see that the other carriages were already disembarking at the church door.

The duke's eyes left her face, and within seconds he was whipping up his horses so that the phaeton could pull into the churchyard with panache. "A pleasure to have you ride with me, Miss Malcolm," he said, handing her down with more decorum than he had displayed earlier. Eliza could still imagine the feel of his strong hands around her waist—and was still unsure whether it had filled her with excitement or unease.

He offered her his arm and they joined her parents, the duchess, and the others to make their way into the church.

Henry slowed his horse to a walk before quietly turning into the churchyard. A dozen or more villagers were crowding around the entrance, and he could see the back of Miss Malcolm's figure going through the door on the arm of his brother. Henry set his jaw. If he had his way, she would not be walking into a church on Rufus' arm ever again.

The simple pale blue of Miss Malcolm's dress contrasted oddly with the feathery concoction on her head—he would not have suspected her to have such outré taste in hats. But still, the strange bonnet did not diminish her graceful carriage or elegant figure. She disappeared into the building.

Henry dismounted, tied his horse, and slipped in through the side door. No one noticed him enter—the villagers were too busy gawking at the full row in the Rowland pew up front. Henry nearly snorted. Apparently, Rufus' presence was creating quite the sensation. When exactly was the last time his brother had come to church?

Reverend Ansel had ascended the pulpit and was beginning the service. Henry slipped into a seat in the back corner. A gnarled old man looked up at him. "Master Henry!" he said in quiet shock. Henry put a finger to his lips. "But you should be up front, sir!" The old man's hands began to shake, and Henry put his own hand over them to steady them.

"I'm well enough where I am, Mr. Hornsby." He smiled. "Unless you don't care to share your seat with me?"

"Not at all, not at all, your lordship," said Ned's father hurriedly. He looked around to see if anyone else was noticing the signal honor the duke's brother was paying him. But the focus was all elsewhere. Henry could see half a dozen women whispering, no doubt trying to ascertain the identity of the young lady sitting near the Duke of Brockenhurst.

"Lord of all power and might, who art the author and giver of all good things…"

The collect had begun. Henry looked up at the pulpit. Reverend Ansel was tall and well-built, and his black cassock made him even more formidable. His big, bluff face resembled nothing so much as a Viking chieftain's, and Henry had no doubt that if he had lived in a different era, he would have happily preached God to the heathens with the blade of a two-handed axe.

"…graft in our hearts the love of thy name, increase in us true religion, nourish us with all goodness…"

Henry's eyes traveled uneasily from the pulpit to the first pew on the left, the one directly opposite from the Rowland pew. Empty. He choked down a sigh of relief.

"...and of thy great mercy keep us in the same, through Jesus Christ, our Lord. Amen."

Reverend Ansel's wife had died many years ago, and there was only one other person who had a right to sit in that pew. If the pew was empty, then where *was* she? Dead too? He had heard no word of such a thing. She had been alive three years ago, when Rufus had turned him out. Married? Impossible.

The homily had begun, and Henry was fidgeting like a dog with fleas. He saw Mr. Hornsby peer at him with questions in his old eyes, and he made a concerted effort to still his bouncing knee.

He took his eyes off the pew on the left and returned them to the pew on the right. Rufus was leaning over, whispering something in Miss Malcolm's ear. The intimacy was infuriating.

Just as he had known it would be, coming to this service was torture in more ways than one. But he would wait it out—if he was to influence Miss Malcolm where his brother was concerned, he would have to improve her own opinion of him first.

ELIZA HAD NEVER EXPERIENCED SITTING beside a suitor in church. Reverend Ansel was waxing eloquent about the various proofs for the existence of God, but it felt like nothing more than a wave of words washing over her ears. Rufus' knee was touching hers in the pew, and at one point he nearly buried his nose in her ear whispering that no one could concentrate on divine services when a creature so divine was sitting next to him. Her whole face was tingling at the impropriety.

When the service concluded, Rufus took her hand and placed it snuggly in the crook of his arm. The Duchess of Brockenhurst led the way down the aisle, greeting the stares of the villagers with polite nods of recognition. Sir Arthur, Lady Malcolm, and the rest of the Rowland party followed.

Eliza noticed that Rufus refrained from the friendly civility that his mother showed to the other congregants. Perhaps he was not as familiar with his tenants or the villagers—although he had been lord of the manor for three or four years now, and one would expect him to know a few faces at least.

As they moved towards the doors, she saw an old man in the back corner struggling to stand and a younger man—dressed like a gentleman—helping him rise. She looked more closely; the man's brown eyes met hers—Henry Rowland! She thought he had left Harrowhaven for good! And what about his protest that he did not like Reverend Ansel's sermons? Her brows knit together as Rufus' momentum carried her outside into the churchyard.

Reverend Ansel was there, greeting his parishioners as they filed out. The dowager duchess had given him her hand, and Eliza was just in time to hear Adele remark, "A very intellectual sermon, Reverend."

"Hopefully not too intellectual for you," said the Reverend. A smile played on the corner of his mouth.

"Not at all," said Adele, "although I do wonder if my brother was able to follow it all." She cast a pointed look at Rufus, bringing him to the Reverend's attention.

"Ah, Lord Brockenhurst," said Reverend Ansel, disengaging himself from the dowager duchess to speak to the duke. "It is good to see you here on a Sunday. And while I have your ear, I have not heard from you recently on that other matter...."

"I'm not sure what matter you're referring to," said Rufus. Eliza could feel his forearm clenching with irritation.

"About setting aside a portion of the woods near the church building for the common use."

"The answer remains the same as the last time you asked," said the duke stiffly. "I will not have trespassers in my forest."

Eliza felt a little dismayed at the duke's curt refusal. The churchman seemed genial and the request seemed reasonable—but perhaps it was some matter in which he was trying to take advantage of the duke. She would not judge on a matter she knew nothing about.

As Rufus began to steer Eliza and her parents out of the receiving line, she saw Reverend Ansel's face light up with real excitement.

"Walter, my boy!"

Mr. Turold had just exited the church. A strange sight followed as the large churchman enveloped the long-haired gentleman in a hug.

Rufus seemed as surprised as Eliza was. He cast a curious glance at his friend and halted momentarily to overhear the exchange.

"You must dine with us while you are here," said Reverend Ansel.

"Of course." Mr. Turold pressed the clergyman's large hand with what seemed genuine affection. "Give my regards to Miss Ansel."

"Give them to her yourself. Supper at five tomorrow!"

Mr. Turold nodded in agreement, and as he turned back to their party, Rufus pulled Eliza forward and began asking how she liked the silhouette of the church roof against the forest backdrop.

Eliza made a polite response but noticed that, although the duke was talking to her, his attention still seemed to be taken up by his friend. He was keen to know what had transpired between him and the Reverend and just as keen not to be seen eavesdropping.

∽∞∽

HENRY CONGRATULATED HIMSELF ON A lucky escape from having to speak with the Reverend. As the large man began to pump Walter's hand, he ducked around to the side and inserted himself into the little group of admiring females which had formed around Adele and Mr. Blount.

Stephen arched his delicate eyebrows, no doubt surprised to see Henry there at the church after his protestations of last night.

"I do declare," said Miss Ashbrook, one of the daughters of the country squire, "that bonnet is all the crack, Adele."

From the corner of his eye, Henry could see Miss Malcolm, tethered to his brother's arm. No doubt that hideous bonnet on her head was all the crack too. It must be Adele's. Everything he knew about Miss Malcolm told him that she would not have willingly purchased such a showy monstrosity from her hat maker.

Adele preened in acknowledgement of the praise piled on by her coterie of local worshipers. Henry had never known his sister to be self-deprecating about her appearance. "You are too kind, Miss Ashbrook. Mr. Blount was just telling me how much he liked my bonnet as well."

Henry grimaced at his friend, but Stephen seemed determined to ignore him.

"I have the most brilliant idea," said Adele, clasping her hands. "We shall have some entertainment tomorrow night at Harrowhaven. You must come, all of you." She waved a small hand roundabout to extend the invitation to Miss Ashbrook, Miss Bertram, and Miss Cecil.

"What sort of entertainment?" asked Miss Bertram, no doubt concerned about whether she should wear a frock suitable for dancing.

"Oh, I don't know," said Adele, as if the specifics were unimportant. "But I shall think of something diverting, and I shall send around some cards tomorrow morning."

Miss Bertram and Miss Ashbrook let out squeals of delight, while Miss Cecil's enthusiasm displayed itself at a more moderate level. Henry looked over their heads to see his brother leading Miss Malcolm over to the phaeton that they must have arrived in. It irked him to see that they were driving together unchaperoned. He looked over to his horse. Unchaperoned? He could solve that problem.

"And will you be there tomorrow night, Lord Henry?" said Miss Ashbrook, sending him a flutter of black eyelashes.

"Yes," said Henry, silently cursing the politeness that was detaining him from stepping into the saddle. He watched his brother hand Miss Malcolm up into the phaeton.

"How wonderful!" replied Miss Ashbrook. "It's been some time since you were...in the neighborhood."

"Quite," said Henry curtly. He had called upon Squire Ashbrook on matters of business regularly in the old days. He barely remembered Miss Ashbrook, but then, if she was Adele's age, she would have still been in the schoolroom.

Stephen noticed his friend's growing irritation. "I say, Miss Ashbrook," he said, physically placing himself between Henry and the overeager damsel, "what games are the young ladies of Sussex familiar with? Perhaps we can hit upon something that we all know to play tomorrow night...."

Henry seized his chance to disappear. He strode over to his horse and, climbing into the saddle, spurred the beast onward to catch up with the pair in the phaeton.

⁂

ELIZA HAD MADE UP HER mind. She was decidedly uncomfortable having Rufus Rowland take such liberties with her person. He was sitting far too closely on the phaeton seat, and squished up into the corner, she had no way of escaping him. She hoped her parents would be following soon in the coach...or Adele and Mr. Blount...or anyone.

As they turned the bend in the road, she heard hooves pounding behind them. It was a single rider, not a carriage. Within moments, the rider had come up alongside them, and there on her side of the phaeton was Lord Henry Rowland, doffing his beaver cordially.

"It looks like the road is wide enough for three here," he said, smiling broadly and reining in his horse to keep pace with Rufus' pair.

The duke slid over a little so his leg was no longer touching hers. "What the deuce are you doing, Henry?"

Eliza bit her lip. She was sure her mother would rebuke the duke if she ever heard him use such language.

"Keeping you company, of course."

"I already have someone to keep me company," said Rufus, his eyes glittering.

"Poor soul," said Lord Henry. He gave Eliza a wink.

"I did not expect to see you in church, Lord Henry," said Eliza.

"Yes, well, after I saw you in the hallway this morning, it occurred to me that it might be beneficial to attend the service."

Eliza's mouth fell open in disbelief. Was he actually alluding to the embarrassing incident with the maid that she had witnessed before breakfast? The man had no shame!

"Do you really mean to inflict yourself on us for the week?" demanded Rufus. His horses strained at the short rein he was giving them.

"Why not?" retorted Lord Henry. "It's not as if I have any sort of *occupation* to draw me away."

Eliza sensed a long history behind this fencing match. Why were the two brothers at odds? She was not vain enough to suppose that it had to do with her own person.

"Then send up to London for some proper riding clothes," said Rufus. "I'll not have you wearing some patched-up, three-year-old buckskins when we're following the hounds."

"Never fear," said Lord Henry, rolling his eyes at his brother. "I shan't spoil your hunt with my outmoded wardrobe. Will you be riding out with us on Wednesday, Miss Malcolm?"

"Oh, I...I don't know," faltered Eliza. Up until this point, she had not realized that she might be expected to trail along with the duke during his favorite pastime. She had no illusions about her own riding ability. Her mother had ordered her a riding habit for her first season, but she had not worn it more than once, and it was now woefully out of date.

Eliza's insides lurched. Was the duke *expecting* her to join him?

"Of course you will ride with us," said Rufus. "My mother and sister always do."

So. It was settled. Eliza's right hand clutched the side of the phaeton. Rufus seemed not to notice her discomfiture, but from underneath a veil of eyelashes, she saw Lord Henry's dark eyes look at her questioningly.

They were nearing the house now. Rufus turned the horses sharply as they entered the circular drive. "I hope our little country church was to your satisfaction, Miss Malcolm?"

"Oh, yes, indeed," said Eliza. "I thought Reverend Ansel a particularly gifted speaker."

Rufus looked at her with curiosity, as if he thought she might be shamming her approval. "I fear you'll find little to amuse you on Sunday afternoons at Harrowhaven."

"But Adele has knocked together some sort of amusement for tomorrow night," said Lord Henry brightly. "Some of the young people from the local gentry families, I believe."

Rufus snorted. "How tedious!"

"For you, maybe," said Lord Henry, "but Miss Malcolm might enjoy it."

"Oh, I'm sure I shall," said Eliza. She smiled wanly. Any activity would be preferable to one that required her to mount a horse.

It had been a quiet Sunday following their return from church. Lady Malcolm had a very strict view of Sabbath keeping, and she and her daughter spent the afternoon in the drawing room, reading aloud the sermons of Thomas Watson and others.

"Poor Eliza," said Adele, tiptoeing past the door with Stephen in tow, on their way out to the garden. "Henry, you should go in and distract her mother so she can escape."

"I'm afraid Miss Malcolm already thinks me impious enough," said Henry with a shake of his head. "Besides, I think I might do better to distract my own mother." He watched his sister lean in to whisper something to her lovelorn swain. "Don't get lost in the garden again," he called over his shoulder as he headed into the saloon.

"Oh, I think we can find our way about," said Adele archly. She tugged at Stephen's arm and drew him towards the exit.

Henry grimaced. Stephen really was a good fellow, and he hoped his sister was not simply toying with him. Whether Stephen would make a good husband for Adele, he was not entirely sure. The girl would indubitably lead him about by his nose—although Stephen seemed to have no objection to that state of affairs. He surmounted the staircase and went down the corridor to his mother's room.

"Come in," said the duchess, hearing his knock. She had changed into her dressing gown and was sitting in a padded rocking chair, her slippered feet propped up on an ottoman while she perused the latest Ackerman's. It would certainly not be approved Sunday reading in Lady Malcolm's estimation, but Henry refused to think less of his mother for it.

He planted a kiss on her cheek and sprawled out on the sofa a few feet away.

"Mrs. Forsythe told me you had left," said his mother. She turned a page idly in the magazine, as if Ackerman's were far more important than a tête-à-tête with her youngest son.

Henry knew better. "Yes, I thought I had. I decided to come back."

"Oh? Why is that?"

"I don't know."

"You mean you won't say."

"Yes, I suppose so." Henry rolled over to his side and propped up his head with his elbow. "I hear there's some trouble between you and Rufus?"

"Is there? I didn't know."

"You mean you won't say."

The duchess shrugged. "What do you think of this Miss Elizabeth Malcolm?"

"Too good for Rufus by far."

"He means to marry her, you know."

"I cottoned as much. And...where does that put you, Mother?"

The Duchess of Brockenhurst snorted. "In the Dower House as soon as I can pack my things."

Henry sat up on the sofa. "Is the Dower House empty then?"

His mother finally gave up the pretense of reading and dropped her magazine into her lap. "Oh, yes. I suppose you might as well know. I took matters into my own hands a few months ago. I went down to the Dower House and sent Rufus' Cyprian packing."

Henry whistled. He had never imagined that his mother suspected the existence of Rufus' many mistresses. But then, his mother was always taking him by surprise with the things she knew. "And Rufus took it...?"

"Not well. He took away my keys and told me he was master here. Since then, he's been having Mrs. Forsythe report to him instead of me."

"Yes, Mrs. Forsythe said it's been something of a...trial with Rufus in charge of the domestic arrangements. Enter Miss Malcolm, eh?"

"No doubt he wants someone more biddable than his dragon of a mother—someone to manage the staff meekly and dutifully without asking any questions. And with Miss Malcolm installed as the new duchess, that leaves me with nowhere else to go but the Dower House. Your father left it to me in his will...although Rufus has soiled my memories of the place with all his tawdry liaisons."

"What about Robert's estate?"

"Mortgaged up to the hilt. Rufus is his main creditor, and I wouldn't put it past him to call in his debts." The duchess scowled.

Henry leaned forward. "I'm sorry things have come to such a pass. I can't offer you quite the same luxuries as Harrowhaven, but—"

"Oh, Henry!" The duchess reached out a hand to grasp her son's. "I would never reproach you for that. You are not obliged to support me. I know the hand you were dealt."

"Yes," said Henry, "but what you don't know, is that even with my poor cards, I've had an extraordinary streak of luck." And he proceeded to outline in detail just how drastically his fortunes had improved over the course of the last three years.

ELIZA YAWNED. IT WAS HER turn to read now, and she was stumbling a little over the long sentences in this homily. She looked over at her mother. Lady Malcolm, who had been sitting quite erect for the past couple hours, had slumped a little against the back of her chair. Eliza paused. "Mama, I think perhaps we might finish this next week...."

There was no answer. Lady Malcolm had fallen asleep.

Setting the book down on the horsehair-stuffed cushion, Eliza walked quietly out of the room and took care that the door would make no sound as she closed it behind her. She looked right and left. Once again she was all alone in the Rowland mansion. There was the saloon, and the pillar she had leant up against yesterday afternoon while eavesdropping on Henry Rowland's entrance. She wondered where he was. And Rufus too. She had seen neither of them since Rufus had handed her down at the door of the house and Henry had ridden off to the stables to deposit his horse. Her father had disappeared as well, and she suspected the gentlemen were all off somewhere enjoying their Sunday afternoon in a way much different than Lady Malcolm approved of—shooting pool or enjoying a snifter of brandy.

She looked over at the new floral arrangement on the mahogany table. The yellow roses reminded her of the garden. She had not explored it thoroughly yet, and even though it was a Sunday, her mother would surely not object to such an activity. It would be much better to walk outside than to roam the hallways feeling like an intruder.

The afternoon heat was beginning to dissipate, and a soft breeze came whisking in from the edge of the untamed woods into the formal hedges of the Harrowhaven gardens. Eliza walked under a small bower of climbing vines and a little farther on found the bush that the yellow roses must have come from.

On one side of the path the high hedges of the maze stood up like a rampart, keeping out any except those who knew the secret of the entrance. Eliza heard giggles coming from behind the bushes. Adele. And Mr. Blount with her, no doubt. Eliza colored a little at the thought and kept walking. She had no desire to eavesdrop on that tête-à-tête.

A little farther on she found a bench and sat down, the stone pleasantly warm beneath her. She had been wrong. Even here in the gardens, she still felt like an intruder. And what is more, she still felt alone. She wondered if this would always be the case. If—as her father seemed to think—the duke of Brockenhurst did offer for her, was this what her Sunday afternoons held in store? To walk alone in the gardens while Rufus amused himself as he pleased and the rest of the family ignored her existence? She sighed.

But surely, to be the mistress of this house, of these gardens, was something, was it not? For that, one might reconcile herself to some of the infelicities of the match—or, at least, that was what her father would argue. Would her mother argue the same? Somehow, Eliza thought that whatever sermon her mother might give on the subject, it was invalidated by her mother's own actions. Had not the young Margaret Malcolm done the very thing the elder Margaret Malcolm inveighed against—betrayed her own religious convictions for a comfortable marriage with a man of weaker moral principle?

Eliza lifted her chin and surveyed the landscape in all directions. It was the Sabbath day, so there was not even the comfort of being surrounded by workmen spreading soil or gardeners trimming flowers. She was alone, and likely to be even moreso if she married Rufus Rowland and lost the small solace that her parents' company brought.

Henry returned to his room after a long chat with his mother. She had greeted his news with astonishment, and some pique that he had not told her of his success earlier. As for his offer that she come stay with him, she bid him wait until Rufus officially made a match with Miss Malcolm. Henry's jaw twitched. He had refrained from mentioning that the only reason he had returned was to ensure that such a match would never happen.

He sat down at the oak writing desk by the window. It felt smaller than when he had used it last. First, he penned a letter to Mr. Maurice explaining his extended absence. The old man would not care—the season had ended and there was little work to do after the people of quality had deserted London. Next, he penned a letter to his valet Biggs asking him to come down bringing a whole wardrobe of his clothing. He did not know how long he would be staying now, and it was best to be prepared for any contingency.

The window by the desk overlooked the gardens. His eye caught sight of a movement down below, and emerging from the path beneath the bower was a young woman in a pale blue dress. His pen paused on the paper, leaving a puddle of ink while his eyes were elsewhere. "Confound it!" he muttered, blotting up the spill as soon as he realized it. He put the pen in the inkwell and rose from his chair to get a better view.

She had paused now and, after looking about her a moment, settled on a stone bench outside the maze. Henry admired her carriage—even when sitting, her height gave her figure a natural elegance. He wondered what she could be thinking about. It was too far away to see the expression on her face, but he imagined that it looked pensive.

He dared not flatter himself that she was thinking of him. No, far more certainly, of his brother and of the events that lay ahead of her this week. Would Rufus propose marriage during this visit? Henry had no doubt that he would. The key then was to give her a true understanding of his brother's character before that moment occurred and fortify her with the strength she needed in order to refuse him.

Henry squinted and pressed his nose against the glass. Her face looked sad...or perhaps he was imagining things from this distance. But it had certainly held little joy this morning when he had found her cozied up against Rufus in the phaeton.

The talk of the hunt had seemed to terrify her. It was clear to anyone with an observant eye that she did not wish to ride out with the hounds. Henry wondered if she knew how to ride. That tall, supple figure would sit beautifully upon a horse. But her consternation at the thought made him suspect that she did not ride often. Her parents' straitened circumstances would hardly allow for a stable.

He stood musing a moment longer, and then turning abruptly, he found the bell rope to call for the servants. When Frederick materialized, he sent him back downstairs in search of the servant he really wanted.

In a few moments, the maid Constance had arrived. "Can I help you, my lord?"

Henry smiled winningly. "Constance, I have a small favor to ask of you."

"Of course! Anything!" The maid's face lit up. It was not the first time a maid had fancied Henry. The support he had offered her this morning had drawn them too close. He would need to purposefully add some distance to avoid unpleasantness—but first, he needed her help.

"Do you know which room Miss Malcolm is staying in?"

"Yes, your lordship." Her face had fallen a little. Perhaps this was not the favor she was imagining he would ask.

"Well, then, Constance, I was wondering if you might fetch me something from there. It must be our secret, though."

"Yes, your lordship. Of course."

Henry gave her a smile, and after explaining her mission, he showed her out the door. He returned to writing his letter. There was no reason that Biggs could not undertake a second commission besides retrieving his master's clothes.

9

When Eliza awoke the next morning, the sunlight was already peeking in through a gap in the curtains. Ollerton entered and opened the curtains all the way, letting in the whole flood of sunshine.

"Is Mother dressed already?" asked Eliza, covering her eyes.

"Oh no, miss," replied the lady's maid. "She went to bed last night with a well-seasoned sore throat, and this morning 'tis even worse, and with a cough too. I imagine she'll stay in her chambers all day, poor thing."

"Oh dear," said Eliza, her concern for her mother intermingling with her concern for her own situation. Being chaperoned by her parents in a strange house was bad enough, but being alone in a strange house was worse. "Is father ill as well?"

"Not that I know of, miss. He told your mother he was taking his breakfast with Mr. Curtis."

"I see." Eliza slipped out of bed and submitted herself to Ollerton's ministrations. She had no idea what the day would bring, but it was comforting to be dressed in one of her favorite gowns—a sprigged muslin with a green ribbon beneath the bust.

"Ollerton," she said, a thought coming to her. "Do you mingle much with the rest of the staff here?"

"I take my dinner with the duke's valet and the ladies' maids," said Ollerton. Her pursed lips voiced the question: "Why?"

"I assume they talk. People always do. Talk about other people, I mean. Have you...have you heard anything about Henry Rowland, the duke's brother?"

"What sort of things?"

"I...don't know exactly," said Eliza, unwilling to confide in Ollerton about the incident with the maid in the corridor. "Anything untoward, I suppose?"

"I can't say as I have," said Ollerton, "but I shall keep my ear to the ground." She gave her mistress' daughter a sharp look, but Eliza refrained from saying anymore on the subject.

"And what activities are planned for today, miss?" the maid asked, pulling the laces tight on the back of the bodice.

"I don't really know," replied Eliza slowly. "I suppose the duke will orchestrate some sort of amusement."

Ollerton grunted, her mouth holding several pins to use in pinning up Eliza's auburn hair. Within moments, a simple bun adorned the back of her head. "Well now, you look pretty as a picture, Miss Malcolm."

"Thank you, Ollerton," said Eliza. She looked into the mirror and put a hand up to touch her hair. It was vain to think too much of oneself, but she did hope that the woman staring back at her had the potential to be called a beauty. She flushed a little. Perhaps the Rowland brothers, or at least one of them, would think so as well.

The maid bobbed a curtsey and left the room. Eliza took a deep breath. She opened the bedroom door and headed down the corridor towards the stairs.

"There you are, Eliza!" called Adele. Mr. Blount and Lord Henry looked up from their eggs and bacon as Eliza entered the breakfast room. "Sit down," Adele said imperiously, "and submit your suggestions for what we shall do today."

"I thought you'd arranged for some friends to pay a visit?"

said Mr. Blount. His chair was quite close to Adele's, and Eliza almost suspected that their feet were touching beneath the table.

"That's tonight, you silly gudgeon," replied Adele, swatting his arm playfully. "We have the whole day in front of us. We must create a schedule!" Adele looked to Eliza for affirmation, but Eliza only gave her new friend a tentative smile.

She had been hoping that Rufus would be here to take control of events and steer her in the right direction. She saw Lord Henry's eyes upon her. He excused himself from the table and stepped over to the sideboard. He must be hungry this morning, thought Eliza, for he was filling a second plate.

"Perhaps," ventured Eliza, "the duke will have already created a schedule."

"Rufus!" Adele snorted in a most unladylike manner. She tossed a few unpinned tresses over her shoulder. "Don't be ridiculous. I daresay he won't awaken for another hour or more, and I'm sure he's hardly gone to the trouble to arrange *activities*."

"Well, that shall be *my* privilege then," said Lord Henry. He came back from the sideboard and set down the plate he had filled, heaped high with eggs, ham, fruit, and muffins, directly in front of Eliza.

Eliza colored. "Thank you." She picked up a muffin and bit into it.

"Now then," said Lord Henry, resuming his seat at the table, "I've a few letters and a parcel to post, so for the first order of the day, we shall drive into the village and show Miss Malcolm the local splendors. I warn you, however," he said, fixing his face on Eliza with mock gravity, "you must not set your expectations too high. There is little in the way of shopping."

"Oh, good heavens, no!" said Adele. "One cannot even buy a proper bonnet there."

Eliza dabbed at her mouth with a napkin. The eggs were

quite delicious. "I thank you for the warning, Adele. I shall endeavor to buy no bonnets on the excursion."

"Very good," replied Lord Henry. "From the village, we will set out west toward the lake. The air is cooler there on account of the water. I shall instruct Mrs. Forsythe to pack us a substantial hamper, and we shall picnic there on the shore."

"Upon my word, Henry," said Adele. "You would make an admirable tour guide or a butler."

"Or a steward even, perhaps," said Lord Henry dryly.

"Of course...well, yes...oh bother."

Eliza noticed that the usually irrepressible Adele had twisted her pretty face into a frown. Mr. Blount was looking uncomfortable as well.

Lord Henry's face, however, had grown a wry grin, and he did not seem in the least put out. "Well, Miss Malcolm, do you approve of our plan?"

"Oh, yes," said Eliza, taken aback by the direct question. Doubts assailed her a moment later. She laid down her fork and knife. What business did she have picnicking with Lord Henry when her sole business here was to explore the possibility of marrying his brother? She stared at the floor. "But perhaps we should see if your brother would like to join us?"

"I see *one* kind soul has spared a thought for me!"

"Speak of the devil," murmured Lord Henry as the duke strode into the room with Walter Turold on his heels.

Eliza flushed as Rufus approached the table, took her hand in his, and kissed it. "Good morning, your grace," she said.

"Good morning," the duke replied. He was wearing buckskins again and riding boots—it seemed to be his outfit of choice. His red hair was combed back carelessly and his freckled face lit up with enthusiasm. "Walter and I were just on our way out for a ride. Would you care to join us, Miss Malcolm?"

"Oh, I...." Eliza swallowed. She was already dreading the

thought of riding out with the hunt on Wednesday, and was she now to be subjected to mounting a horse even sooner?

"Lud, no, Rufus!" said Adele peevishly. "Eliza is to picnic with us by the lake! She doesn't wish to be jolted up and down all over the countryside on this hot day."

Eliza wondered if she would ever dare to contradict the duke the way his sister had.

"I'm sure Miss Malcolm can decide for herself," said Rufus, shooting a quelling look at his sister.

Eliza's heart beat a little faster. She would never be able to stand that look being directed at *her*. "I think," she said slowly, "that it would be better for me to rest today. My mother is taken ill, and I feel a bit of the headache myself. Perhaps if I keep to my room, I shall be well enough to join you all for dinner tonight."

She put down her napkin, and Rufus, seeing that she wished to excuse herself, pulled out her chair. She gave a quick bow to them all and then slipped out the door of the breakfast room.

༺ ༻

HENRY SIGHED. IT HAD BEEN a singularly tedious day. He had posted his letters and his parcel, visited Ned at the Blue Boar, and played the unwelcome third at the lake with his sister and her suitor. When he returned to Harrowhaven in the afternoon, he discovered that Miss Malcolm, true to her word, was still keeping to her room.

Allowing himself to be ruled by impulse, he attempted to dispel his ennui by knocking on her door. Alas, her lady's maid had answered it, a dragon of a creature determined to open the door no more than six inches wide while she spoke to him.

"How can I help you, my lord?" Her words said one thing, but her tone indicated quite the opposite intent.

"So kind of you to ask." Henry had encountered this type before and knew how to engage in battle. "I came to inquire how Miss Malcolm was feeling this afternoon? Is there anything she needs that I could have the housekeeper send up for her?"

"No, thank you, your lordship. Very good of you."

Henry smiled. The woman's face had a distinctively suspicious cast to it—he supposed that "good" was the antithesis of what she considered him. He wondered if Eliza had confided in her maid about the incident with Constance yesterday morning....

"I have a book here that perhaps Miss Malcolm would like to borrow—something to pass the time."

The maid took the book and held it gingerly. Henry hoped that she would not leaf through it. It was a novel, although the plain cover concealed that fact admirably, an older book that he had enjoyed many years ago. The title was *Pamela or Virtue Rewarded,* and he hoped that the second of those names would pass muster with the sergeant in charge of this camp.

"I look forward to seeing your mistress at dinner."

There was no response to that, so Henry retreated and allowed the maid to close the door. He snapped his fingers in frustration as he walked down the corridor. If only she had opened the door a little wider and let him catch a glimpse of the room's occupant. At breakfast Miss Malcolm's hair had been pulled up into a bun, with a few pieces falling down around her face. It was probably all unpinned now. He wondered if she really did have a headache—brought on by having to choose between Rufus' plan and his own.

The rest of the afternoon Henry whiled away playing billiards with his half-brother Robert and Sir Arthur. "So, Robert, I hear you're in deep waters," he said in an undertone while Sir Arthur was distracted with the decanter of brandy.

"Who says so? Nonsense," replied Robert. He squinted at

the table and knocked a billiard ball into a hole with more force than he had hitherto exerted.

"Mother says so. Rufus has your note? And it expires soon?"

Robert waved a hand dismissively. "He'll put a stay on the repayment—he has before. And with any luck, I'll get him to invest some more in this engine I've told you about—I've got a sure thing, this time!" He laid down his billiards stick and brushed an invisible speck off his lace cuffs.

Henry shrugged. "Suit yourself, Robert. But be advised that Rufus is by no means a benevolent philanthropist."

"I'm sorry, Henry," said Robert, reading more into the comment than Henry had intended. "I cannot think of a more unfair event than two inheritances and three sons. Your father's plan to provide for you made a mull of everything, and for that we must all be disappointed."

"Never mind that," said Henry, in no way desirous or deserving of his half-brother's pity.

"Another game?" said Sir Arthur, sloshing his drink down onto a table in the corner and seizing upon an unclaimed billiards stick.

"Of course," said Robert.

"Not I," said Henry. "I want to see if my valet has arrived with my clothes—perhaps I will have something presentable to wear for dinner tonight."

Robert and Sir Arthur waved Henry good-bye as they set up the billiard balls. Henry went down the hallway and started up the stairs. He had just reached the landing by his brother Rufus' portrait, when he heard Rufus himself in the entryway below. Rufus and Walter had been gone all day, either setting up the details of the upcoming hunt or shooting some fowl themselves.

"Plenty of time to dress for dinner," Henry heard Rufus remark. "I'll have a bath first, I think."

"Good plan," said Walter, giving a loud sniff and bursting

into good-natured laughter. "Could you give my regrets to your mother? I'll be dining elsewhere tonight."

"Oh?" said Rufus. Henry could not see the two men speaking, but Rufus' voice had an edge to it. "With whom?"

"Some friends from the village," replied Walter vaguely.

"You mean Reverend Ansel?"

"Why, yes, if you must know."

"Why so secretive about it?"

"I simply thought it would be of no concern to you."

"But of course it is a concern to me. That man's lobbying to allow public access to the strip of forest alongside the church. I won't have a bunch of farmers and village brats frightening off the game. What motive does he have for inviting you to dinner?"

"Friendship, I'm sure. I grew up around here, the same as you did, Rufus. You would not begrudge me a simple invitation to dine with the Reverend and his family?"

Henry could hear Rufus' foot tapping impatiently. "Hmm... well, all right. But I warn you, I shan't be swayed, no matter how much he tries to curry favor with you."

"Of course not," said Walter placatingly. "Now go, take your bath, your grace. You stink worse than one of those farmers you so desperately want out of your woods."

They had walked through the saloon now and were approaching the stairs. Henry took a deep breath, threw back his shoulders, and stood out of their way on the landing. Rufus walked past him without a word, but Walter paused, somehow aware that he had been eavesdropping. "How about it, Henry? Join me for dinner at the Reverend's?"

"No," said Henry evenly, "but you may give him my kind regards. And his family as well."

Walter shook his head slowly as if he could not believe the audacity of that remark. Then looking away, he spat vehemently on the flowered carpet covering the stairs.

HENRY WAS DELIGHTED TO DISCOVER that his valet had, in fact, expedited his pace to arrive at Harrowhaven with his luggage in time for dinner.

"You *ought* to have brought me along in the first place, my lord," said Biggs reproachfully. His bald head glowed with the exertion of hanging all of his master's coats in the wardrobe in this warm room.

"Yes, well, I didn't know I would be staying, did I?" replied Henry good-naturedly, aware that most men in his position did not bother justifying their actions to their valet. After stripping off his old clothes, he pulled a clean shirt over his head and reached for his waistcoat. "Did you complete that commission I sent you before you left London?"

"Yes," said Biggs, looking at his master's hessians with a frown. The abuse they had received in the last three days without their nightly cleaning was unconscionable. "Madame said she had just the thing, ready-made for a display piece, and would tailor it to your specifications."

"And can it get here tomorrow?" asked Henry, fastening the last button of the waistcoat. *That* was the essential question.

"It can, my lord. I made special arrangements for a courier."

"Good man, Biggs," said Henry, patting his valet on the back. He chose a gray suit to go with the rose colored pattern of the waistcoat.

A knock sounded on the door. It was Frederick, eager to help Henry dress for dinner. "Thank you, my dear fellow," said Henry, "but my man Biggs has arrived from London so I shan't have to impose upon you any longer."

"Oh, yes, Lord Henry," said the footman, crestfallen. "It weren't an imposition though. I hope I never implied as much."

"Not at all," said Henry generously. "If I could have two valets, I would."

"'Tis all right," said Frederick, putting a brave face on it, "and just as well, for I have the day after tomorrow on leave for my sister's wedding."

"Best wishes to your sister," said Henry, lifting his chin as Biggs adjusted his cravat. Must you travel far for it?"

"Nah," said Frederick, "just a morning's walk up the countryside. She's marrying the village baker—don't know as he's good enough for her, but he's a good baker, right enough."

"Ah," said Henry, his store of politeness nearly exhausted.

Biggs turned a quelling look at the younger man, his bald pate glowing with displeasure at the footman's presumption. "If you please, young fellow...."

"Oh, of course," said Frederick with a sheepish grin, and he ducked out the door to resume his other duties.

As Biggs tied the last knot in the neckcloth, a final question occurred to Henry. "Biggs, what color was the display piece at Madame's shop?"

"Green, sir."

Henry smiled as he shrugged into his tight-fitting jacket. Green was the best he could have hoped for. It would set off her eyes beautifully.

10

When Eliza finally gathered the courage to leave her room, the gong had begun to sound. Her mother was still ill, but her father met her on the stairs and gave her a cheerful smile and a pat on the arm. "How are you doing, my dear?"

"As well as can be, Papa." There was no time to elaborate further on the subject. And besides, the smell of alcohol on his breath did not encourage confidence.

Mr. Curtis took her in at dinner, and she was happy to note that she would be on the opposite side of the table from Lord Henry. This precluded him talking to her in an over-familiar manner, but it did not preclude him from staring. She self-consciously dropped her eyes every time he tried to catch them—by the end of the dinner she had vastly improved her acquaintance with Harrowhaven's dishes and cutlery. She did manage to notice, however, that Lord Henry's suit was of as smart a cut as she had ever seen in London, a far cry from the tight blue jacket he had worn two nights ago. His valet must have arrived. She looked down at her plate once again. It made her feel even dowdier in her re-worked green silk.

The duke sat at the head of the table as far from his mother as possible. He did not speak much throughout the course of the dinner—indeed, the brunt of the conversation was left to

Adele and Mr. Curtis, who seemed only too happy to oblige—and Rufus seemed impatient, agitated. He gestured for the footman to refill his wine glass several times, and as soon as it was full it was empty again.

"Our guests will be here soon," Adele tittered as the ladies rose to remove to the drawing room. "Don't be too long with your port, gentlemen."

"Of course not!" said Mr. Blount gallantly, giving the ladies a bow as they disappeared.

"I'm going for a ride," Eliza heard Rufus say curtly just before the doors swung shut. So he would not be joining the party this evening? She was not sure if she was feeling a pang of disappointment or a pang of guilt at her lack of regret. It seemed to fit, however—she could not quite imagine the duke enjoying himself with amusements Adele had devised.

"Eliza!" Adele was calling her from across the room. "Have you ever played Buffy Gruffy?"

"No," said Eliza, instantly apprehensive. Her mother had never allowed games to be played, and the few times she had observed them at the homes of acquaintances, she had never wished to join in.

"Well, it's time you learned," said Adele. "Stephen, that is to say, *Mr. Blount* suggested it, and I think it is a marvelous idea."

"Be kind to Miss Malcolm," said the duchess, retiring to the corner with a book to provide the requisite chaperonage for tonight's entertainment.

"Oh, but of course, Mother," said Adele. The sparkle in her eyes did not fill Eliza with reassurance.

The gentlemen—Mr. Blount, Mr. Curtis, and Lord Henry, sans the duke and Eliza's father—rejoined them just as Adele's friends from the local gentry were arriving. Adele presented Miss Ashbrook and Miss Cecil to Eliza. Miss Bertram was indisposed and unable to attend, but Miss Cecil's brother Edward Cecil had accompanied them, making it four couples exactly—a fact that was disturbing to Eliza. Her mother had always warned that even numbers of young people boded ill.

Mr. Blount had never met their visitors before, but Mr. Curtis and Lord Henry were already acquainted with them.

"You're looking very modish tonight," said Miss Ashbrook to Lord Henry. "I love a well-tied cravat."

"Then I'm certain you would prefer Robert's to mine," said Lord Henry with a hint of irony in his voice. He gestured to his half-brother who was across the room conversing with the Cecil siblings. "That Oriental knot he's sporting is the *pink* of fashion."

"Oh, well you know, it all matters how one wears it," said Miss Ashbrook, lowering her voice to a murmur as if her words were only meant for Henry Rowland.

Eliza, standing a few feet away, found herself suddenly curious just who this Phoebe Ashbrook was. She cast an appraising eye over the young lady and saw a brown-haired girl of average height, with an average figure, and an average countenance. There was nothing remarkable about Miss Ashbrook, at least not at first glance. But then, Eliza had never flattered herself that *she* was a particularly remarkable character either. Beauty, as the old saying went, was in the eye of the beholder. Eliza found herself transfixed by the beholder's eyes, trying to fathom how much of Miss Ashbrook's beauty they were appreciating.

"I suppose one might say the same of a lady's gown," said Lord Henry with a wry smile. Miss Ashbrook simpered at this no doubt expecting a compliment, but Eliza saw Lord Henry's eyes dart in her direction instead. "Miss Malcolm wears her green gown remarkably well, don't you think?"

"Oh...yes, of course," replied Miss Ashbrook, disappointment registering in her face.

That disappointment only increased as Lord Henry sidestepped her to address himself to Eliza.

"I trust your headache has dissipated, Miss Malcolm?"

"Yes," said Eliza. "For the most part." She had forgotten about the headache's existence. She lightly pressed her fingertips to her temple to add some verisimilitude to her malady.

"In all the time I spent with you in London, I never recall you suffering from a headache." Lord Henry's eyes gleamed.

He was teasing her, perpetuating that odious falsehood he had created on the first day of their acquaintance. It was as plain as day to him that she had feigned the headache to avoid the difficult decision between riding with Rufus or picnicking with him. Not that it had been a difficult decision—she would choose a picnic over mounting a horse any day of the week. But she had not wanted to offend the duke—or cause her mother more grief by encouraging the wrong man.

"Perhaps I'm not used to all this wholesome country air," replied Eliza. She felt strangely emboldened in this room full of strangers. "But surely you must remember the time I went home ill from the opera—I had a most decided headache then."

"Ah, how could I have forgotten?" replied Lord Henry, not missing a step in this farcical dance. "*Artaxerxes*, was it not?"

"Indeed." Eliza inclined her head.

Miss Ashbrook, who would not be ignored any longer, advanced to Lord Henry's elbow. "Everyone is here. Shall we choose a game to play?"

"I know!" said Mr. Cecil, a pleasant-faced fellow with black curls. "Let's have a round of Musical Magic, yes?"

Adele, the empress of the evening, agreed to his suggestion, and the young people swiftly set up a circle of chairs. Eliza saw the Duchess of Brockenhurst look up from her reading briefly and then return to her book once she saw that the young people were beginning their entertainment. Miss Ashbrook took the seat directly to the right of Henry Rowland, and Eliza found herself seated between Miss Cecil and her brother, Mr. Cecil.

Mr. Cecil had chosen the game, so it was his prerogative to go first. The group banished him from the drawing room and, in his absence, selected a goal for him to achieve. He must snuff the large candle sitting on the table by the door. When he returned, Adele began to hum a popular Irish air and the rest joined in. Eliza was relieved to find that she knew the song. She looked over to Lord Henry and saw that he was merely observing the scene with an amused look. Apparently he was content to let the ladies make the music.

As Mr. Cecil returned to his chair and moved farther from the candle, the humming grew softer. He stood up again and walked back to the door. The humming crescendoed with every step. Unsure of his object, he knocked once on the door. The ladies shook their heads and continued humming.

He stepped sideways and found himself directly in front of the table as the humming increased to a frantic pitch. He opened a book that lay on the table. Again the ladies shook their heads, their lips continuing to buzz out the Irish air like an angry swarm of bees.

The only other item on the table was the candle. "Aha!" said Mr. Cecil, and with a swift pinch of the fingers he snuffed the wick.

The humming ceased immediately. "Bravo, Edward!" said Mr. Cecil's sister. "Shall we have another round?"

Eliza's stomach tightened. She hoped no one would propose her as the next participant—or rather, the next victim—for this game. To be the center of attention in front of this group… her stomach turned somersaults inside of her and her knuckles tightened around the arms of the chair in which she sat.

When Miss Cecil offered to go next, Eliza's fingers relaxed and she breathed a sigh of relief. Miss Cecil was a proficient player. She approached the stool by the fire without much difficulty and promptly sat on it when the music cued her to do so.

Eliza faced another moment of uncertainty and creeping dread until Mr. Curtis offered to be the next sacrificial lamb. The group decided that he must pull his pocket watch out of his vest and open it, a difficult maneuver to execute with only the volume of the humming to instruct him. After nearly ten minutes of trying to understand his goal, Mr. Curtis returned to his chair, lifted his coattails, and sat down testily, averring that he had had *enough* of this silliness.

"Oh, come now, Robert," said Adele, wrinkling her nose. "You will ruin all our fun with your peevishness." She turned to the gentleman next to her. "Mr. Blount, shall we put *you* to the test and have one more round? Leave the room, and no listening at the door while we discuss!"

"As my lady commands," said Mr. Blount.

Eliza thought it was remarkably good-natured of him to stomach being ordered about in such a manner.

"Now then," said Adele, dropping her voice to a stage whisper, "we must choose an action for Mr. Blount to accomplish. What do you suggest?"

"Let him open that window," said Miss Cecil, gesturing toward the far wall of the drawing room.

"Too simple," said Adele dismissively.

"Let him stand on one leg," said Mr. Cecil.

"Even simpler."

"Perhaps he should kiss one of the ladies' hands?" offered Miss Ashbrook slyly. Her suggestion was met with giggles.

"But whose?" said Miss Cecil, affecting an innocent gasp.

"Adele's?" said Miss Ashbrook. "It is *her* party." She smiled at her friend complicitly, and Adele returned the smirk.

Eliza reddened around the cheekbones. No wonder her mother disapproved of parlor games.

"I object!" said Lord Henry. "If this were my party, I would most certainly *not* want Mr. Blount kissing my hand. A simple bow to my sister should suffice, should it not?"

Adele snorted. "Henry!" She tapped her foot in annoyance, and Eliza noticed that her face, when irritated, looked markedly similar to her half-brother Robert's.

The duchess looked up from her solitary book reading in the corner of the room. "Adele, my love. This game is played out. Choose something else."

It was not a suggestion.

Adele huffed momentarily, then called in a firm voice for Mr. Blount to return.

"Have you selected my task?" he asked, surprised to hear no music being hummed.

"We're changing the game," said Adele curtly. "What was it you asked to play earlier? Buffy Gruffy?"

Eliza squirmed in her chair. The name of the new "amusement" sounded no more promising than the last. What embarrassments lay in store with this next game? At least the duchess was a vigilant chaperone—perhaps *some* decorum might be maintained....

∽∂∾

HENRY ROSE FROM HIS CHAIR as Adele took the floor to explain the new game to everyone. He watched Miss Malcolm touch her hand to her head—either this activity was causing her some distress, or her fictitious headache had returned to her in earnest.

"How amusing!" said Miss Ashbrook. "If Mr. Blount does not mind, I shall go first."

"Of course not," said Stephen.

Henry saw Miss Ashbrook's brown eyes sparkle with a hidden purpose.

"You must cover your eyes," said Adele, looking about for a suitable blindfold.

"I shall use my shawl," said Miss Ashbrook, shrugging the long piece of fabric off of her shoulders.

"Are you sure," asked Mr. Curtis, squinting to see better, "that it is not too sheer?" Henry had been thinking the very same thing.

"Oh, no," replied Miss Ashbrook, tying it over her eyes. "I cannot see a thing, I promise you."

After Miss Ashbrook was effectually blinded, Adele signaled the rest of the group to rise to their feet, and in a disorderly jumble of whispers and giggles, they rearranged themselves so that Miss Ashbrook should not know their locations.

Henry managed to place himself next to Miss Malcolm. "Hello," he whispered. She gave him a nervous smile, her hands folding and unfolding. It did not take an Oxford scholar to understand that Miss Malcolm did not like games of this sort.

"Are you all ready?" demanded Miss Ashbrook, and hearing nothing to the contrary she spun around thrice in the center of the circle. Then, putting her hands in front of her, she slowly walked forward till her slippers trod upon the toes of the person in front of her—Henry's toes.

Yes, thought Henry, that scarf was decidedly too sheer. Miss Ashbrook could see straight through it and had homed in on him on purpose. And now, she had the opportunity to ask him three questions to "guess" his identity.

"Where do you hail from?" she asked.

Henry affected an accent but answered truthfully as the game required. "Och, London, but Sussex originally."

"What brings you back to Sussex?" Her pink lips curved up into a smile.

Henry debated how much to reveal. "A bonnie lass, I reckon."

Miss Cecil and Adele sent out a peal of laughter while

Stephen and Robert shook their heads at his audacity. Henry sent a sideways glance at Miss Malcolm, but she was looking in decidedly the other direction, head held high, cheeks scarlet.

"How long are you planning to stay in the neighborhood?"

"As lang as I am wanted," replied Henry promptly. Miss Malcolm would still not look his way. *Was* he wanted? It was difficult to tell.

"I will guess who you are then," said Miss Ashbrook, putting one hand on her hip. "You are Lord Henry Rowland, are you not?"

"Indeed I am, Miss Ashbrook," said Henry reverting to his normal voice. He rose from his chair. "And now that you have solved my identity so admirably, I shall beg leave to take your place." He held out his hand for the shawl that she had removed from her face. "Another round, ladies and gentlemen?"

Miss Ashbrook hesitated, then handed him the shawl. Henry wrapped the soft material around his head and—as he had suspected—was still able to make out the surrounding faces with little trouble through the semi-sheer fabric. He would not call a lady out for cheating, however. And besides, he was quite happy to do a little cheating of his own.

"I am ready. Change places!"

Henry held perfectly still as the guests scurried about and scuffled over the chairs. Alone of the group, Miss Malcolm remained seated. Perhaps she thought to throw him off by maintaining her position. He spun around three times and then walked forward until his knees grazed another pair of knees beneath a green silk skirt.

<hr />

ELIZA'S EYES WIDENED IN HORROR as she saw the blindfolded Lord Henry walking her way. This, of all things, was what she had hoped to avoid. And now here he was, his hessians nearly toe to toe with the slippered feet she was hiding under her chair, his knees pressing against her own insistently. Everyone's eyes were upon her, and she now had three questions to answer.

She wished she could see his eyes to know what he was thinking.

"Do you enjoy staying in London?"

Eliza's lips parted in surprise. "Yes," she said in a low voice, "I do." She *did* enjoy London. She much preferred it to the country. Not the parties or the intrigues, but simply the city-ness of it.

She took a deep breath. That question was not so bad...but perhaps the embarrassment was still to come.

"Do you have any brothers or sisters?"

"No, I do not." The thought struck her that Adele had brothers, and Miss Cecil too. That answer must needs give her away, if he did not already know whose chair he stood in front of.

"And for my last question—do you like fish for supper?"

The way that his mouth curled up into a little smirk, she could almost swear that he was looking at her straight through that blindfold. Yes, he knew it was her. There could be no other reason for such a question.

"No, Lord Henry, I detest fish, especially turbot."

"Ah, I see." He clasped his hands behind his back, feet spread apart. "I think that I have your measure then. You are Miss Ashbrook!"

"Henry, you gudgeon!" said Adele, breaking in before Eliza could say a word, while across the circle, Miss Ashbrook let out a little squeak. "It is Miss *Malcolm*, of course!" The younger sister leaped from her chair and tore the flimsy scarf off of Henry's face so he could witness his mistake himself.

"Why, yes, so I see," said Lord Henry, looking down at Eliza where she sat. The closeness, which had been bearable only because of the blindfold, became unthinkable now that their eyes had met without the veil. Eliza's face grew red as fire, and Lord Henry himself took a quick step backwards. "I beg your pardon, Miss Malcolm, for my slow wits."

"You've lost, Henry," said Adele disapprovingly, "and now you must pay a forfeit. Come, give something to Eliza in penance for your stupidity."

Lord Henry looked more amused than downcast at this command. He reached into the pocket of his waistcoat and pulled out a small white card. "Your servant, Miss Malcolm," he said with a bow.

Eliza took the calling card and glanced at it. "Henry Rowland, Duke of Brockenhurst." Startled, she looked up.

The rest of the crowd had turned their attention to selecting the next player. Lord Henry met Eliza's eyes and gave a little wink. He had somehow contrived to get her through a parlor game with little to no humiliation—an unheard of feat. But what on earth was the meaning of this calling card, assigning him a title so patently untruthful? Henry Rowland had seemed her friend more than once during her sojourn at Harrowhaven, yet why must she always be suspecting that he was up to no good?

11

ADELE WOULD HAVE CONTINUED THE GAMES FAR INTO the morning, but just before midnight, the Duchess of Brockenhurst intervened, kindly but firmly bidding farewell to the guests who must go home by carriage and saying goodnight to those who must retire to their rooms upstairs. Instead of following directions, Stephen and Robert tiptoed away for a game of billiards, while the duchess pulled Adele aside for a tête-à-tête.

Henry watched Miss Malcolm leave the room and, after waiting until the door had closed, got up to follow her. His larger stride caught up with her as she entered the saloon. It was the room where he had first caught a glimpse of her. He had frightened her then. He would tread more carefully now.

"Good night, Miss Malcolm," Henry said, intending it to begin a conversation, not end one.

Miss Malcolm pulled up sharply and looking around. "Good night, Lord Henry."

"I trust your headache has abated?"

"Yes, thank you." She smiled shyly. "I am sorry I could not join you and your sister for the picnic."

Henry waved his hand dismissively. "It is no matter. Did your maid give you the book?"

She colored at that. "Yes, thank you."

"And...?" He could not resist pressing the question a little further.

"I am not accustomed to reading novels."

"Ah." He might have known that her mother would have forbidden that sort of reading material. It was a hard thing, though, that a young woman of one and twenty should not be allowed to choose her own books. A married woman would have more freedoms. "Perhaps, some day," he said, imbuing his voice with understanding.

"Perhaps," said Miss Malcolm. It did not sound hopeful. "Good night then, your lordship." She turned toward the staircase.

"Miss Malcolm," said Henry with insistence. He would not let her escape so easily. "Since your headache has abated, I have another activity to propose for tomorrow."

She waited.

"Would you care to go riding with me, early, before the heat of the day?"

Her dismay registered on her face, but Henry forged ahead before she could object. "I am aware that you do not approach equestrian pursuits with enthusiasm. Perhaps the chance to familiarize yourself with one of Harrowhaven's horses, at a slow pace and out of the eye of public scrutiny, might be to your liking?"

She took a deep breath, her bosom rising and falling beneath her green silk dress. He could tell she was considering the merits of his proposal.

"Would it be...proper?"

Henry grinned. She wanted to come. She was on the verge of accepting.

"Certainly. After all, you must remember that we've ridden together several times in London." He gave her a wink.

Her lips tightened into a straight line, but the brightness in her eyes seemed to indicate that she enjoyed the jest.

"I shall bring a groom with us. Two grooms, if you like."

"I think one groom will be sufficient. Good night." She reached the stairs and began her ascent.

"Good night," Henry said, his gaze lingering on her until she reached the top of the grand staircase and disappeared down the corridor. Her tall, willowy figure was designed for such a house—the staircase a perfect setting for this jewel. She would make an admirable duchess, the perfect hostess for Harrowhaven—and *that* was what he was determined to prevent.

True, said a part of him, but it is only right to do so, for she would not be happy with Rufus. Ah, said his wiser self, but that is no guarantee that she would be any happier with you....

✦

"A LATE NIGHT, MISS," SAID Ollerton, who had been waiting up for her lady's daughter.

"Yes, I beg your pardon," said Eliza, closing the bedroom door quietly behind her. "I did not mean to keep you up."

"Oh, it is no matter to me," said Ollerton, in a tone that belied the truth of her statement. "As long as you enjoyed yourself."

Eliza offered no comment on how the evening had gone—in truth, she had not yet decided whether she had enjoyed herself. The duke's absence, Lord Henry's presence, the overly intimate games, the fear of embarrassment, the elation of escape, and then, at the end, Lord Henry's invitation to go riding.... He seemed to mean well. She hoped it had not been improper of her to accept.

She could not remember the last time she had perched on a saddle—it would be very good to practice before she humiliated herself in front of the whole company at the hunt. Of course, now there was the nagging fear that she would humiliate herself in front of Henry Rowland. But somehow, that seemed a much remoter possibility—he had carried her through the blindfold game with as much consideration as he had used at the awkward dinner two nights ago. Even if she were to fall off her horse, she suspected that somehow, he would be able to make everything...all right.

She wished that she had not stumbled upon that scene with him and the housemaid. In every other particular he seemed so gentlemanly, it was unfortunate to have to view him in that light. Perhaps she had misunderstood the situation? But no, she knew what she had seen—and what good reason could possibly be given for such familiarity between a young man and a servant girl?

Ollerton unlaced Eliza's dress and carried it over to the wardrobe to put away. "That reminds me, miss. Do you know where your golden gown is? Did you give it to one of the maids to have it cleaned?"

Eliza's forehead puckered. "No, I gave no instructions about it. It is missing?"

"Yes. I turned this wardrobe inside out and it was nowhere to be found."

"How strange!" said Eliza. She unpinned her tresses and shook them out.

"Suspicious is more like it," said Ollerton with a snort. "I'll take it up with the housekeeper—some light-fingered housemaid needs to be sacked. It's at the bottom of her trunk and we'll never find it, I wager."

Eliza said nothing. It would be unfortunate to lose that dress with so many memories attached to it. But she refused to worry about it. Ollerton had been wrong about things before.

She slipped into a clean chemise while Ollerton's back was turned and folded down the bedclothes.

"Would you like me to brush your hair, miss?" asked Ollerton, taking the comb in hand.

"No, thank you," said Eliza, climbing into the bed. "I am tired now. My hair can wait till the morning."

Before she dismissed Ollerton, she remembered something essential. "My riding habit is not missing, is it?"

"No," said Ollerton, "I will make sure it is laid out for the hunt on Wednesday."

"I shall need it laid out for tomorrow morning."

Ollerton's eyebrows rose. "As you wish, miss," she said pulling it from the wardrobe.

Eliza could sense that Ollerton was hoping for an explanation, but she had no intention of divulging whom she would be riding with in the morning. She did not want her maid going straight to her mother with that story. The thought of hiding such a thing from her mother gave her some unease, but she deflected the guilt and suppressed the thought. It was simply an innocent excursion to help her practice her equestrian skills.

Ollerton's fingers felt the brown fabric of the riding habit. "It has been so long…there is a little damage from the moths. But perhaps if we pin a ribbon here." She pointed at the shoulder of the garment.

"Thank you," said Eliza. She had never liked this article of clothing—her father's tailor had made it, since riding habits were more properly the province of men, and she felt uncomfortably masculine in the military cut of the jacket—but it was the only riding habit she had, and it would have to do.

She snuffed the candle as Ollerton left and pulled a light quilt over herself. She had almost drifted off to sleep when the unfortunate memory came to her that the duke had invited her to go riding with him this morning. What would he think if he learned that after declining his invitation, she had agreed to go out riding the next day with his younger brother?

Eliza grew uncomfortably warm and threw off the quilt. Her mother would not be the only one annoyed that she had chosen to go riding with Henry Rowland.

THE EARLY MORNING AIR WAS pleasantly cool as Henry went to consult with the head groom Gormley about the best mount for Miss Malcolm. He yawned as his quick stride covered the ground between the house and the stables.

He had slept fitfully for most of the night. Shortly after falling asleep the first time, he had awoken to the sounds of arguing in the hallway. There were two voices, both male. It was not hard to identify Rufus. Henry swung his legs over the side of the bed and walked silently to the door to get a better listen.

"You've been hiding something from me!" the duke said, in a tone halfway between a hiss and a snarl.

"I don't know what you're talking about," said the other man in a more measured voice. Was it Robert? No. Less urbane, more gravelly. Walter.

"Don't play games. You know what I mean."

The voices quieted now and Henry strained for a moment to hear more than a collage of mumbles.

"How dare you follow me!"

"How dare I? Oh, that's rich. I'll do more than follow you next time...I'll get there first."

"Stay away from her or—"

"—or what?"

There were more growls and mumbles, and then—"For God's sake, calm down! I've never seen you get so worked up about anything in the petticoat line."

The pair had taken themselves off then, presumably to resolve their quarrel or continue it in a more secluded setting. Henry had paced his room a while.

It was gratifying to hear those two at each other's throats. But, at the same time, the topic of their conversation filled him with the gravest concern. What woman were they speaking of?

Whom had Walter been concealing from Rufus? Even after Henry had calmed himself enough to go back to bed, he had still tossed and turned the night through.

In the morning, his mind pushed away his midnight worries and returned to Miss Malcolm. They had not set a time for their ride, but Henry's experience on Sunday morning had taught him that she was an early riser. He had risen early himself and, after changing into the buckskins and riding boots that Biggs had laid out, taken himself off to the stables to prepare for the outing.

Miss Malcolm did not disappoint. Not fifteen minutes later, he saw her step out onto the front porch in a fitted brown riding habit trimmed with orange braid. Her hair was swept up in a twist with a little hat perched on the pile of curls at the top. The style of the jacket was not altogether flattering, but it still made an appealing scene—her slender figure framed by the columns of the entrance with the train of her skirt draped over her arm.

"Gormley," said Henry, without taking his eyes off Miss Malcolm. "Do you have a groom you can spare to accompany me? Someone discreet."

"Aye," said the head groom, looking from Henry to Miss Malcolm and then back again. He scratched his beard thoughtfully. "Martin can go with ye."

As the straw-blond undergroom saddled up a mount, Henry raised a hand to hail Miss Malcolm and led his chosen pair of horses over to where she stood. His own gelding that he had ridden down from London pulled at the loose reins, while Marigold, the docile mare he had selected for Miss Malcolm, showed much less spirit.

Miss Malcolm came down the stairs.

"Enchanted, Miss Malcolm," said Henry, doffing his hat.

"Good morning," she replied tautly.

Henry saw that he would have some ground to regain again

this morning. Must he do this each time he saw her afresh—make a concerted effort to dispel her wariness?

Martin, the groom, approached at a respectful distance, already seated on his own mount.

"This," said Henry, nodding his head at the mare, "is Marigold. She's a pretty, gentle little thing, and I think you two will get on splendidly."

"I suppose first I must get on her, though?" said Miss Malcolm, wrinkling her forehead. Her fingers tightened around the train of her skirt, crumpling it instead of just supporting it.

Henry signaled for the groom to come over and take the reins of his own animal. "Come here, Miss Malcolm," he said. She obeyed. "Now, if I may...." He took her hand in his and brought it near to the mare. "Good darling," he said, placing Miss Malcolm's hand upon the horse's side and moving it over the horse's coat to stroke it gently. "Sweet darling."

Slowly, her fingers relaxed themselves underneath his own.

Marigold whinnied and turned her head. Henry lifted Miss Malcolm's hand to the horse's face. "Easy, girl."

Miss Malcolm remained perfectly still, but Henry saw the hint of a smile on her face when the horse nuzzled her fingers. "Now that we are all friends...." said Henry. "Allow me." Kneeling down he cupped his two hands and waited for her to step up. "Other foot, my dear," he said, as she lifted the wrong half boot, and blushing, she placed the opposite foot into his hand.

In less than a second she was up, Henry's hands steadying her waist and then immediately letting go. Marigold had been well trained, and she barely moved a muscle as Miss Malcolm's weight dropped into the side-saddle.

"Now," said Henry, "we walk." Taking the reins in hand, he started leading the mare around the circular drive. Martin fell in behind, leading Henry's horse behind his own.

"Are you not going to ride?" asked Miss Malcolm in a tone of apprehension.

"When you are ready to take these reins yourself, I shall."

They proceeded onward. Glancing back every few minutes, Henry could see her struggling to maintain her seat in the saddle as the horse's back shifted with each step. It was no mean feat to ride as a lady ought; it was far harder than riding astride.

Gradually, her seat grew more secure, and Henry thought that something more difficult might be attempted. "How do you feel?" He slowed his step and looked around.

"Like a lapdog stuck on the skinny branches of a tree," said Miss Malcolm, "which is to say, better than I usually feel when on a horse."

Henry laughed at that, and she rewarded him with a smile in return. "May I pass you the reins?"

"Yes," she replied, her teeth clenched. Slowly, carefully, Henry placed the loops of leather in her hands.

"Now," he said, "a gentle pressure with your heel, here." And reaching for her half boot, he showed her how to indicate forward motion to the horse. Marigold started forward again, and Henry walked alongside. "Turn her head to the right," he said, nodding at the bend in the road.

Miss Malcolm's nervous fingers pulled the reins far too sharply, but Marigold was a placid beast and took no offense.

"*Brava!*" said Henry after a spell of five more minutes walking. "You are a horsewoman, Miss Malcolm."

"You are far too kind," she replied, her body still as taut as the rope on a pulley.

Henry looked back and saw that Martin was still following at a respectful distance, leading the extra mount. "My horse, if you please!" he called, and giving Miss Malcolm an encouraging smile, he climbed into the saddle as well. "Now, then—shall we?"

ELIZA COULD NOT REMEMBER EVER having been shown how to ride by someone with such patience. Her father had put her on a horse when she was but a half-grown girl and seemed surprised—and put out—by her reticence. No one had followed up that effort with regular instruction, and every time she was called upon to mount a horse, her ineptitude was only greeted with confusion and annoyance. The last time she had ridden, the horse had spooked, and when a groom had caught up with her, she had lapsed into a fit of hysterics and declared that she would never go near a horse again.

But she could not exactly refuse to ride out with the Duke of Brockenhurst's hunt tomorrow—she had already feigned one headache. And the hunt, it seemed, was the focal point of Rufus' pastimes and enjoyments.

"Ready?" asked Lord Henry with a smile.

"Ready," she replied. But her horse did not move.

"A gentle pressure with your boot."

"Oh yes," she said, embarrassed again. "I am sorry that I am so stupid about this."

"Not at all," he replied gallantly. "I am stupid about a great many things myself."

"That I can hardly believe." The horse was moving now. Her hands shook as she held onto the reins.

"Shall I give you examples?"

He sat so easily in the saddle, his broad shoulders rising and falling in perfect rhythm with the animal's hooves. She reminded herself to keep her eyes on her own horse. It seemed calm now, but in her experience, equestrian mishap was always lurking at every corner.

"I cannot draw worth twopence. My mother asked me to

sketch the house once, and when it was finished, Adele said it looked like a bizarre temple surrounded by a stunted forest."

"I'm sure she was exaggerating."

"Not at all," replied Lord Henry. "It was very bad." While he was speaking, he had, almost imperceptibly, increased the pace so that their horses were now moving along at a fast walk. "I am also quite stupid at writing letters."

"How so?" Eliza's fingers relaxed a little. The horse seemed to know exactly what to do.

"Give me a report to write about expenditures, or repairs, or improvements and the ink will flow onto the page. But to write a personal letter of daily happenings and social events? My thoughts tie themselves into knots. My mother will tell you quite readily that I have not written her one letter in the past three years."

"If you see her often, perhaps there is no need to write?"

"Ah, but I do not." He looked at her fixedly and then seemed to make up his mind about something. "I do not know if you have observed this, Miss Malcolm, but I am not a welcome visitor here at Harrowhaven. And that is not my mother's doing."

It was the ideal moment to discover just how deep the animosity between Rufus and Lord Henry went. "Your brother…?"

"Quite," said Lord Henry. "He has forbidden me the house. I see my mother occasionally for an hour or two—never an extended visit."

A whirligig of thoughts ran through Eliza's head. What could Lord Henry have done that would cause Rufus to forbid his visits? Did the duke know about his behavior with the servants?

"And yet you are here now?"

"Only by pretending acquaintance with you. He did not want to appear the despot to your family, so he was obliged to let me stay."

She did not know what to say to that, and so she said

nothing at all. He seemed so kind, so patient—and yet, he was taking advantage of her presence to countermand his brother's wishes. Why had she agreed to ride out with him? If the duke was so set against his brother, he would be furious when he found out.

Her companion was watching her with his dark eyes, trying to read her opinions, no doubt. Her hands tightened up on the reins once again and her face flamed red.

Without warning, Lord Henry slowed his horse and, leaning across the divide, checked the reins of her mount as well. They came to a stop, their horses standing so close that his riding boot nearly brushed against her leg. "Have I offended you with my disclosures?"

"Oh, not at all, your lordship." Her answer was more well-bred than truthful. Her heart began to race. She looked around to make sure the groom was still following them.

"I can see that I have. I am sorry. I simply want to warn you to be careful of my brother. I know why he invited you here, and I beg you, do not do anything rash without a proper knowledge of his character. He is not everything that he seems."

"I thank you for your warning," said Eliza frostily, looking away into the distance. She disliked it that he would assume so much about her. "It is superfluous, however, since I have no intention of betrothing myself to a man that I know so little." Her green eyes met his dark ones. "I think that he is not the only one here who is not everything he seems."

Lord Henry bowed his head. "I am not certain what you mean by that, but I shall take it as a compliment. I should very much like to be friends, Miss Malcolm."

Eliza did not know how to answer that. She had never had a friend of the opposite sex before, and she still felt like a pawn in the Rowland brothers' mysterious game of chess. He was waiting though—he expected a response.

"I am...not sure if I can offer friendship."

He gave her a mischievous smile. "It is *I* who am offering."

He waited, but she made no response.

"Very well, if we cannot be friends, then I must go back to being your riding instructor. You have mastered the walk quite admirably, Miss Malcolm. It is time to move on to the trot."

"Oh," gasped Eliza. "I hardly think that is necessary."

"It *is* necessary. They will all ride out at a trot tomorrow for the hunt, and not on the road either."

Eliza took a firm grip on the reins. "Well then, if I must, I must." Following Lord Henry's guidance, she turned her horse's head until it faced away from the road and toward the surrounding forest. There were tall oak trees here, with space between them to ride, but Eliza—used to traveling in one direction—was dismayed at the idea of trotting and changing course at the same time.

"Don't be afraid," said Lord Henry calmly. She was surprised to hear that he had both sensed her fear and acknowledged it openly without taking the opportunity to belittle her. "Your horse no more wants to run into a tree trunk than you do. Encourage her with both your heel and with the reins, and she will understand your wishes. I will go first and set a path for you."

Eliza took a deep breath. Trotting through a forest seemed more terrifying than her first ball, her first card party at Almack's, and her introduction at court all rolled into one. But somehow, with Lord Henry leading the way, it also seemed... surmountable. "I am ready."

She saw the quick flash of his spurs as he flicked the reins of his horse, and then they were off. Her own horse seemed to know what to do almost without her urging. They had left the road entirely and were surrounded by tree trunks on every side, a leafy canopy filtering the sunlight over their heads. The air, which had been close and turgid earlier, now blew pleasantly past her ears.

If this quick pace was a trot, she imagined a gallop must feel like flying. She kept her eyes firmly fixed on Lord Henry's back as his horse zigged and zagged through the forest obstacles.

And then, of a sudden, he pulled up on the reins, and Eliza, unprepared, went sailing past him.

"Pull hard on the reins and lean back!" he shouted, and despite her panic, she was able to complete his instructions.

In a moment he was at her elbow. "Are you all right?"

"Yes!" She was breathless, but she was whole and unscathed, and what is more, she had kept her saddle and her control of the horse throughout. "Thank you, your lordship."

"Henry."

"But we are not friends," objected Eliza.

"Of course not," replied Lord Henry, "but I instruct all my riding pupils to call me by my Christian name."

"You are incorrigible, your lordship."

"Henry."

Eliza shook her head, but she could not resist smiling.

How long had they been gone from the house? It was hard to see the position of the sun from underneath the trees, but Eliza suspected it was now late morning. They had not ridden too far from Harrowhaven, probably no farther than the little church, and if they went straight back, perhaps no one would notice their absence.

"Shall we return to the house?" asked Eliza.

But Lord Henry's face had frozen as he stared beyond her into the woods.

"What is it?" she asked, alarmed at his expression.

"Nothing, nothing," he said, shaking the unusual look off his face. "Yes, let's return to the house immediately. Do you see our groom? Ah, there, the road is in that direction."

He maneuvered Eliza's horse around and then bade her lead the way. A walk seemed as easy as a slow minuet after their exuberant trot through the trees. When they reached the road, Lord Henry spurred his horse forward until he was even with her, but he remained as silent as the groom that was trailing behind them. *Preoccupied* was the word for it.

Eliza glanced over at him periodically and saw his brow furrowed, his jaw set. When they had rounded the circular drive and were only a few paces from the house, she made up her mind to speak. "I hope I have not offended you, your lordship."

Lord Henry's face relaxed immediately. "Not at all, Miss Malcolm. My apologies for my rudeness. Apparently one of my other stupidities is to become lost in thought instead of enjoying a beautiful woman's presence."

"Please, my lord, nothing obliges you to pay me compliments."

They had reached the front of the house now, and Lord Henry dismounted. "Nothing except your beauty and my excellent eyesight."

He reached up to lift Eliza down. For the thousandth time in her life, she wished that she did not blush so easily. "I hardly think friends speak to each other in such a manner." She was relieved to find that his hands did not linger on her waist after he had deposited her on the ground.

"Ah, but you rejected my offer of friendship, if you remember. That makes our relationship something else entirely." He handed Marigold's reins to the groom that had accompanied them and gave Eliza his arm to walk her up the steps.

"My lord—"

"Yes, I would like to discover just exactly what that relationship is too. But I regret that that will have to wait, as I have a pressing matter to attend to." He opened the door and ushered her inside. Then, taking her hand, he bowed over it. "Your servant, Miss Malcolm."

"Th-thank you," Eliza said as he let go her hand and disappeared into the saloon. It had been a most educational morning, but even though her knowledge of horsemanship had vastly improved, she felt that her knowledge of Lord Henry Rowland still left something to be desired.

12

As much as he regretted deserting Miss Malcolm in the entrance hall, Henry knew his errand could not wait. He could tell that Miss Malcolm still had qualms about trusting him,—curse that incident with the housemaid in the hallway!—but he hoped that she trusted him enough to heed his warnings about Rufus' character.

His own opinion of Rufus' character had sunk to the depths of the abyss during their excursion into the forest. The horror of looking over Miss Malcolm's shoulder and seeing Rufus in the distance alongside a white dress and a head of blond curls had shaken him. He had gathered his wits and retreated from the woods as soon as possible. The plan had been for Miss Malcolm to gain some insight into his brother's defects, but not that way—not that way.

But still—as jarring as that discovery was—it did imbue him with a new sense of purpose. Hitherto, he had felt a sturdy sense of determination to keep Miss Malcolm safe from entanglement with his brother. Now, his interest in the matter had warmed to a feverish obsession. Rufus, it seemed, would descend to any depth of depravity, and Henry would do everything in his power to stop Miss Malcolm from shackling herself to such a rogue.

He spotted the housekeeper in the saloon near one of the

pillars. "Mrs. Forsythe, could you tell me which room you've put Walter Turold in?"

The housekeeper frowned and looked up from the large vase she was filling with flowers. "I'm assuming you're having a good reason for asking, Master Henry. No childhood mischief?"

"Of course not," Henry assured her. "I need to speak with him."

"*That* is a change," she remarked. How well the servants knew the relationships of the higher class.

Henry tried disarming her with a smile. "Please, Mrs. Forsythe."

"Oh very well then. He's in the red room upstairs."

"Thank you," said Henry, planting a kiss on her old cheek.

"Oh, get on with you!" said the housekeeper, swatting at him as he darted for the stairs, but her wrinkled face melted into a smile as she returned to her flower arranging.

It was not yet noon, and judging by the midnight quarrel he had overheard, Henry knew that Walter had had a late night of it. He knocked on the door of the red room.

"Who is it?"

"Henry."

There was a pause, and then the door opened a few inches, Walter's long hair still tousled and his shirt unfastened. "What do you want?" he asked gruffly.

"I need to speak with you."

"Then do so." The door opened no further.

Henry decided to mince no words. "I saw Rufus in the forest today arm in arm with Catherine Ansel."

There was a slight pause, and then the door swung open. "Since when do you care about Catherine Ansel?"

It was the retort Henry had been expecting. "Since that wretched day ten years ago."

"Hmm...well, you've done a fine job of showing it." Their eyes locked and Henry refused to flinch. Walter finally softened. "Best come in then and we'll talk about this disaster. I'm afraid I put Rufus' back up last night by letting on that she mattered to me...."

◈

Eliza stood in the entrance hall for a few moments uncertainly until it became apparent that Lord Henry's errand was of a lengthy nature and he would not be returning. She decided to go to her room and change out of her riding habit. Some tea would also be in order and a muffin, for she had forgotten to breakfast before they left this morning.

"Ah, there you are, Eliza!" said a happy voice. It was her father, coming out of the drawing room.

"Good morning, Papa," she said, giving him a filial kiss on the cheek. "Is Mama better today?"

"A little," replied Sir Arthur, "but I think she will still keep to her rooms to be fully rested for the hunt." Eliza supposed that to be her father's interpretation of events—she imagined her mother cared very little whether she attended the hunt or not.

"But darling girl, I have news for you," continued Sir Arthur, throwing an arm around her.

Eliza's eyes opened wide. Her father was never this affectionate. "What is it, Papa?"

"The duke invited me to his study early this morning about a very important matter."

"Oh, yes?" Her lungs felt like they were collapsing.

Sir Arthur turned to face her, placing both hands on her shoulders. "He asked permission to marry you, Eliza."

"What did you say?" She could hardly manage more than a whisper.

"Why, what else would I say but *yes*! You will be happy to hear that your mother has overcome her aversion to him and now views him merely with indifference."

Eliza did not consider indifference to be identical with a glowing enthusiasm. "Were you thinking of consulting me?"

"Have I not already done so?" Her father sounded hurt. His hands dropped to his sides and his shoulders stooped a little. "I am quite sure that I did in the carriage ride to Harrowhaven. You said that you did not know him well enough yet, but now that you have improved your acquaintance with him, I can fathom no reason why not to proceed."

"Papa!" One of the housemaids was scurrying by, and Eliza, afraid to speak so publicly, grabbed her father's hand, dragged him into the empty drawing room, and shut the doors. "Now that I have improved our acquaintance, I have discovered that I don't wish to wed Rufus Rowland."

He blinked at her in incomprehension.

"Papa, I am wholly and utterly opposed to the notion."

He threw himself down upon the sofa and pounded a fist against the cushion. "But how can this be, Eliza? And why have you said nothing to me on the subject before? I gave the duke assurances that you were amenable to his proposals."

"How could you, Papa?" A few tears streaked down her face. She sat on the sofa opposite him.

"But, my dear...what is there to object to? Perhaps you do not love him yet, but that can come in time."

"No, it is not that—although, certainly, I do not love him. It is his character, Papa. He is not considerate of his mother or his sister. He is not considerate of me. He puts his own amusements before everyone else's. He takes liberties that I would rather he did not—"

"Oh, pish," said her father. "A young buck in love. You understand very little of men."

"Perhaps so," said Eliza, her courage rising, "but I don't think it is asking too much for one's husband to be courteous... and kind."

"Listen here, my girl," said Sir Arthur, leaning forward. "I am sorry that it comes to this, but I must be quite plain with you. You are one and twenty with no other prospects than the Duke of Brockenhurst. The Malcolms have more creditors than you can count on your fingers and toes, and if we are to avoid retrenching to a tiny cottage in the country, you must make an advantageous marriage—*this* marriage. Would you sentence your mother and me to penury?"

Eliza began to sob. "Of course I do not wish that, Papa. But think what you are sentencing *me* to!"

"Nonsense. It's hardly a hardship for you to be a duchess with lots of pin money and pretty gowns. What does it matter if the duke likes hunting better than conversation—you'll have plenty of other consolations."

Eliza's whole body was trembling. "And does Mama feel the same?"

"She would not put it in so many words, but I know she acknowledges the prudence of the match."

Eliza remained silent for the space of a minute, her father's eyes boring holes into her. She should have known it would come to this—should have known it from the moment her father had grasped at the duke's resolution to come calling. But somehow, Eliza had assumed that it would all be for naught—that Rufus Rowland would cry off as soon as he knew her better and that she would not be obliged to make any decision concerning him.

Her father had got his hopes up now, and it was too cruel of her to disappoint him. It was only her future she was giving up. It was only the rest of her life.

Eliza brushed the tears off her face and, folding her hands meekly in her lap, said, "Very well, Papa. I shall do as you bid me."

"Good girl," said Sir Arthur, exhaling in obvious relief.

"Where is the duke now?" Eliza asked faintly.

"Out for his morning ride," said Sir Arthur, "but I'm sure

he'll be back before long. Perhaps you should go change out of... that dress"—he waved a hand at her brown riding habit—"and put on something more appealing."

"Yes, Papa." She brushed the tears from her face one more time and, exiting the drawing room, hurried up the stairs to her room. As she went, she said a little prayer that she would not meet Henry Rowland again until all was said and done. It was not that she necessarily preferred him to his brother—but to see herself fall in his estimation? That was something she could not bear.

∽

WHEN HENRY CAME DOWNSTAIRS AGAIN, he found his sister, along with Stephen and Robert, standing by the dining room windows that looked out to the garden.

"Is there some exotic bird in the hedge?" he demanded.

"More of an exotic event," replied Robert smugly. "What think you, Hal? Our dear brother has taken Miss Malcolm outside to offer his hand and heart."

"Miss Malcolm is far too sensible to make that mistake," said Henry briskly. His stomach lurched inside him, however, and he prayed that the lady in question would substantiate his claim. She had *seemed* set against Rufus when he broached the subject earlier, but other forces might come into play besides her personal inclinations.

"I am sorry to disappoint you, Henry," said Adele, her nose pressed against the glass, "but the proposal is happening as we speak, and...she appears to be agreeing." Adele shrieked and put a hand over her mouth. "He is kissing her! No, not on the lips—she turned her face away—merely on the cheek."

"Come away from the windows," said the duchess. "There are some things that should be done in private."

"And some things that should not be done at all," said Henry shortly. His brows turned into thunderclouds. What kind of man proposes marriage to a gentlewoman directly following a tryst with another woman? He growled under his breath and sat down heavily on the sofa, beating his fist into one of the cushions.

"Don't be jealous, Henry," said Adele. "You had your chance in London, didn't you? I suppose Eliza must simply prefer redheads...or dukes." Adele smiled at her own witticism, but Stephen sent Henry a look of quiet sympathy.

Henry's mother came over and sat down next to him. "My dear," she said quietly, "is it true that you fancied Miss Malcolm?"

"I had rather not answer that."

The duchess looked at him gravely. "I am sorry, Henry." She glanced over to the window. She was a strong woman, beautiful, but with a hard cast to her face, made stern by the vicissitudes of life. "Perhaps he is actually fond of her too. She could reform him, you know."

Henry pushed himself up from the sofa and, bending down, planted a kiss on his mother's cheek. "I wouldn't count on it, Mama."

Her eyes grew sad. "A mother can hope, can she not?"

Henry opened his mouth to say something, but then thought better of it. He would not vent his spleen on his mother.

He saw Robert abandoning the window and heading toward him with a simpering smile. He could bear no more questions. Turning sharply, he made to escape the dining room and nearly collided with Sir Arthur.

"Pardon me! Have you seen my daughter?" said the older man.

"I believe she is otherwise occupied at present," said Henry, "with becoming a duchess."

"Ah!" said Sir Arthur, his eyes shining. "Capital! Capital!"

And in that moment, Henry—who had hitherto only considered him weak—found Eliza's father to be utterly despicable. "I suppose congratulations are in order, Sir Arthur," he said, forcing a smile. He was too well-bred to say what was really in his mind.

"Thank you, thank you!"

"Here they come!" shrieked Adele.

Henry cringed and backed toward the door. He was more than adept at dissimulation, but this was one well-wishing he did not wish to be part of. He needed a moment to himself. Later, he could put on a brave face and decide what was to be done.

∽⦿∾

ELIZA WAS TREMBLING ALL OVER by the time she came in from the garden on Rufus' arm. It had all seemed like a swirling dream of inchoate events. She had known what he would say before they stepped out of doors. And when he had said it, she had not hesitated…but she had felt, for all the world, like a painted marionette, stiffly playing the part the strings assigned it.

"Yes," she had said, rubbing her dry lips against each other. "I will be your wife."

And then he had tried to kiss her—an action not horribly improper at the scene of a betrothal—but Eliza had panicked at his proximity, twisting away so that his lips only grazed her cheek.

He had not liked that, she could tell, but he did not express his displeasure beyond a slight stiffening of his upper lip. "Come, let us tell the others the happy news," he said. Was it only her imagination that he dwelt overlong on the word "happy"? Was he being ironic? Did he know how unhappy this engagement was making her?

"Miss Malcolm has done me the honor of accepting my proposal," said Rufus, leading her into the circle of his family. They were all there—sans one, but it was the one person she had resolved *not* to think about—the dowager duchess, Mr. Curtis,

Adele, and her admiring Mr. Blount. In the corner stood Eliza's father, beaming his approval.

The dowager duchess bestowed a kiss on Eliza's cheek, and while her words were not effusive, they also did not seem unwelcoming.

Adele squealed with delight and pressed Eliza to her bosom. "We shall be sisters! Just think of it!"

"Steady on there, Adele," said Rufus. "You would not want to frighten Eliza into calling off the match before I've got it into the banns."

Everyone laughed at that, save Adele, who gave her elder brother a petulant scowl.

"Never fear that!" said Sir Arthur, and walking forward, he planted a kiss on Eliza's cheek. She looked at him reproachfully. No, she had committed herself to the course her father had laid out in front of her. She could not call off the match now.

"I must tell your mother the glad tidings," said Sir Arthur, clapping his hands together. He took Eliza's hand in his and pressed it.

"Yes, do," said the duchess, "and tell her I hope she will be recovered enough to join us this evening to celebrate."

Sir Arthur bowed to his hostess and departed from the dining room.

"Come, Eliza," said Adele, drawing her away from her brother. "We must discuss a whole new bridal wardrobe for you. And your wedding trip! You and Rufus *must* go to Italy."

Eliza looked over at her intended and saw his brow furrow. He cleared his throat. "Italy is a little far, don't you think, Adele, with things being so unsettled on the continent? And I would not wish to leave the estate. Better to stay close to home, I think."

"Oh, how dull!" said Adele. "When I get married, I shall certainly wish to travel. And not just to Italy, but to Greece and Spain as well."

Eliza could not help but look at Mr. Blount. He looked a little worried himself—Eliza wondered how well his finances could afford the extensive traveling that Adele had in mind.

She did not mind that Rufus did not wish to travel abroad, but perhaps they could take a wedding trip to the north of England or to Scotland. If she was to marry a man she barely knew, it would be nice to become acquainted with him when it was only the two of them—rather than in a large house full of servants with the duke's family always waiting in the wings.

"...and you must have a veil of Chantilly lace," Adele was saying. Eliza murmured something polite, but her mind was not really on the subject. Rufus, bored with the conversation, had drifted over to where his brother Robert stood. Eliza could not hear the gist of their exchange, but within moments, they had both headed for the door, looking as if they had some business to discuss—either that, or a particularly excellent glass of brandy was calling their names.

The rest of the day passed by in a blur. While the other gentlemen made themselves scarce, Mr. Blount soldiered manfully through the nuptial planning well into the afternoon, offering helpful affirmations to queries about flowers and candles. A few times Eliza suspected that Adele was far more interested in Mr. Blount's opinion than in hers, perhaps making mental notes about a different wedding that might one day come to pass.

It was not until dinnertime that the dreaded moment occurred—the moment when Eliza must see Henry Rowland again, after flouting—so blatantly—his well-meant advice that morning. Rufus met her outside the dining room and led her in for dinner. He attempted no more displays of affection, for which Eliza was grateful.

She half expected Lord Henry to ignore her or else to glower at her, but whatever annoyance he might be feeling, he was concealing it admirably. When Rufus seated her beside him, Lord

Henry contrived to take the chair on her other side. Eliza swallowed hard and tried to maintain her composure.

"I hear you've had an eventful day," Lord Henry murmured, holding out the platter of veal cakes.

Eliza's hand shook as she laid her fork down on the side of her plate and took a small veal cake. "Yes, so it seems."

Rufus, who had been resting against the cushioned back of his chair, lips pursed in thought, leaned forward at this. "Are you not going to congratulate me, Henry?" He took Eliza's hand in his. It was hard and rough from handling the reins of his horses, and Eliza felt her own hand dwarfed by its size.

"Yes, I believe congratulations are in order," said Lord Henry, clearly and confidently, "to one of the parties at least. Congratulations, Rufus." He raised a glass to his brother and took a sip.

"Thank you," said Rufus smugly. He left his hand atop Eliza's, like an explorer's flag on some newly claimed piece of territory. "I am excited that I will soon be able to install my wife as mistress of this place." He looked around the table, and Eliza—if it was not her imagination—noticed that his gaze halted when it came to his mother.

"I am sure you will wish to make some changes as most brides do," said the duchess, addressing Eliza in an even tone. "And I am sure that *I* shall not stand in your way."

"Of course not, Mother," said Rufus, "and I applaud your decision to move out to the Dower House following the wedding."

There was a pause following that statement, until Adele broke in with a little cry of indignation. "The Dower House! Why should you wish to move into that moldy pile, Mother? I was told I must never go near it on account of it being in such poor repair."

"Oh, is that the story going around about it?" said Lord

Henry innocently. "I was not aware that the Dower House was dilapidated…or vacant."

"It has been for three months or more," Rufus snapped.

"How trying for you," replied his younger brother.

Eliza began to feel that she had fallen headlong into some tangled family quarrel and could find neither head nor tail of the string.

"But who was living there?" demanded Adele.

"Caretakers," said Rufus shortly. "They are gone now."

"How many do we expect for the luncheon tomorrow?" asked the duchess, deftly deflecting the topic. As the details of the next day's hunt filled the air, Eliza was able to retrieve her hand from underneath the duke's large paw.

13

AFTER DINNER, THE LADIES ADJOURNED TO THE DRAWING room, and after a suitable interval, half the gentlemen made their appearance—the duke, Mr. Turold, and Lord Henry were absent. Eliza endured three quarters of an hour of hearing her father discuss business ventures with Mr. Curtis—acting for all the world as if he had money to scatter about—then pleaded a headache and deserted the drawing room. Did he really think Rufus would be so full of largesse to his newly acquired relations?

The summer sun was just beginning to dip behind the horizon, and instead of retiring to her rooms, Eliza sought solitude outside in the gardens. The roses were inviting at this time of day, the low sun bathing them in a gentle glow. Eliza admired the scent of a few of them before turning down the path that led past the garden maze. She would find her bench and sit and think.

But the solitude she craved was not to be found tonight. She had no sooner sat down and smoothed out her skirts than she heard men's voices from the maze behind her.

"Why her?" asked a surly voice. "There could be so many others."

"Why not?" replied his companion. She recognized the duke's voice. "She's beautiful, and in just the style I like. She's unassuming. She's vulnerable."

"She's a simpleton," said the other man.

Eliza nearly gasped aloud but instead put a hand over her mouth.

"And what of it?" replied the duke.

Eliza did not think she would ever be able to forgive him for that. She knew that she was painfully shy, awkward even—but that he should think her a simpleton? An imbecile? Her hands balled into fists.

"A clever girl would not come along with me so easily. I suppose what I should do is thank you for the introduction, as it were. I would never have noticed her if it had not been for you."

Eliza's fingernails dug into her palms. What was it that her mother had remembered? That she had danced with Walter Turold at some assembly? It must have been he that set the duke on her scent. It must be he conversing with her betrothed behind the hedge.

A stir of movement from somewhere nearby caught her by surprise. Someone else was there outside the maze—a second eavesdropper.

She stood up quickly and felt a rush of dizziness and sent up a silent prayer that she would not faint. Her ankle turned slightly on the uneven grass, and in a moment Lord Henry was at her side, one hand supporting her arm, the other with finger pressed against his lips enjoining her to silence.

Time seemed broken as Lord Henry led her quietly down the path. Eliza felt hot tears running down her face. She could not look up. Which was more awful—that the man she was to marry thought thus of her, or that Lord Henry had overheard the shameful words?

They had half circumambulated the house now and put the building between themselves and the hedge maze. In another couple moments they would come round to the porch between the columns and the front door of the house. The yellow twilight was turning to purple and blue, and shadows were all around.

Lord Henry stopped, pulling Eliza to a halt as well. He turned to face her without loosening his grip on her elbow. A quick glance through her own wet eyelashes showed his dark eyes full of concern. "Eliza..."

She tried to pull away.

"What you heard—"

"Please! As you are a gentleman, I beg you not to speak of it."

His lips parted in protest, but no argument came forth. She had disallowed him the office of friend, and he was too kind to force the intimacy upon her.

"May I escort you back to the house?" He had let go of her and was offering his arm properly now.

Eliza wiped the back of her hand over her tear-stained cheeks. "As long as you leave me at the door to enter on my own." She did not want to be seen in his company—not while in such a state.

"As you wish."

They rounded the corner of the house and climbed the steps. Eliza needed to be rid of him then, before the butler or the footmen took notice. "Good night, your lordship."

"Henry," he reiterated. "I believe the familiarity is justified now that you have agreed to become my sister."

Is that what she had agreed to? At the thought of such a consequence, she began to sob uncontrollably. Pulling the door open, she ran into the house, through the saloon, and up the stairs to her room where she fell on her bed and wept until the summer's night went black.

⁓⁂⁓

HENRY PAUSED BY THE DOOR, his brow knit in consternation. A

wretched business, this. What exactly had Eliza overheard? She must have heard enough to know that Rufus—on the very day he was proposing marriage to her—was pursuing another woman. Whatever she had heard, it had cut her to the core. Her face was absolutely stricken, her body trembling with shock. Henry was torn by conflicting emotions of rage and pity. He wanted to strike Rufus across the face and call him out with a brace of pistols. He wanted to fold Eliza Malcolm in his arms and still her shaking until she felt safe again.

But first there were other affairs that must be handled. He stopped staring at the door behind which Eliza had disappeared and returned to the maze. The voices behind the maze were silent now. Rufus was nowhere to be seen, and Walter was pacing beside the entrance. He looked up at the sound of Henry's footfalls, his long hair falling around his face in lank curls. "Well, did you hear it?"

"Not all of it," answered Henry. "I was...interrupted."

"He threw it in my face at first, said it was my fault he had even noticed her, but when he came to see that I was in earnest, he changed his tune. Said he'd stay away from her and not so much as lay a finger on her—an especial favor to me."

"And you believed him?"

"Like I believe the devil! He'll search her out again at his first opportunity."

"Did you part quarreling?"

Walter snorted and kicked the ground with the toe of his boot. "No, I let him *think* he'd convinced me. Thanked him for his grand gesture." He spat on the ground. "But what now? How do I stop him?"

Henry felt a peculiar rush of pleasure at the question—could it be that Walter respected his opinion?—but also a poignant sense of loss. Ten years gone of nothing but silence between them. Ten years of friendship wasted, or even worse, ceded to

Rufus, for after that awful event, Walter had turned to his older brother for companionship. Perhaps Walter still respected his opinion on this matter, but it was as certain as rain in spring that he no longer respected *him*.

"You should warn the Reverend," said Henry. It was the only reasonable course of action.

Walter scowled and did not respond.

"Is there any reason not to?"

"He has a...weak heart."

"Truly?" Henry remembered the Reverend's sturdy physique. "He does not look it."

"It's true though," growled Walter, "and it'll startle him badly to hear of this. She's the apple of his eye. His only jewel."

"I do not doubt you," said Henry placatingly. "Well then, have you a better idea?"

"I must watch Rufus. All the time. Never let him out of my sight till we're back in London."

"Is that...possible?"

Walter shrugged. "It will have to be."

⁓⧅⁓

ELIZA'S EYES BLINKED OPEN. THEY felt puffy and dry after her tears last night, and her body craved another hour of sleep. But a noise in her room had awakened her. She saw a blond woman in a dark dress hovering over the small couch at the foot of the bed.

It was certainly not Ollerton.

"Excuse me, what are you doing?" asked Eliza, sitting up abruptly as her sleepy eyes focused on the intruder's white cap and apron.

"Beg your pardon, miss," said the maid, bobbing a curtsey. She turned to leave the room. It was the same blond maid that

Eliza had seen "conversing" with Henry—no, *Lord* Henry—in the hallway three days ago. Eliza could not help feeling an instant dislike towards her, coupled with the knowledge that such a dislike was unworthy of her.

"Wait," said Eliza, throwing back the bedclothes and sliding out of the bed. "What is this?" Clad only in her chemise, she walked over to the Roman couch where a green dress—somewhere between the green of the grass and the green of the forest—lay spread out with care. Eliza stroked the fabric and found it soft as lambskin.

"If you please, miss," said the maid with another curtsey, "it is a riding habit."

"But there must be some mistake. It is not mine."

The maid gestured to a little white card posted like a placard on the green landscape of fabric. Eliza picked it up and turned it over.

To Miss Malcolm, with my warmest regards

There was no signature. But even so, Eliza was almost certain who had written those words. Did the maid know as well?

"Could you please tell me who sent this?"

"Oh...." The maid's eyes turned wary. "I couldn't say, miss."

"I'm sure you must know who gave it to you."

There was no reply.

In normal circumstances, a newly-engaged lady might expect an anonymous gift to come from her betrothed. Eliza steeled herself to pretend that all was normal. "It must be from the duke," she remarked innocently.

Again, there was no reply, although Eliza detected a sneer rippling across the pretty maid's nose. She contemplated sending for the housekeeper and questioning the maid in front of her—that would get some answers—but then again, it might also have negative repercussions for the maid. As much as she disliked the maid, Eliza did not wish the girl to be let go on *her* account.

"Thank you. You may go."

The maid disappeared within seconds.

Eliza could see the hem of her golden gown peeking out from the door of the wardrobe. The maid must have returned that dress as well.

She looked at the little white card again. "With my warmest regards." No, it was not from the duke. Never mind the fact that it was too thoughtful of a present for him to give—it had probably never occurred to him whether she owned a riding habit or not—it was also too ambiguous a note. She could not imagine him giving a gift without claiming ownership of it. Rather than favoring an anonymous card, he would have had his name embroidered on the dress itself.

But if not from the duke, then from whom?

Eliza's mind danced around the obvious possibility. Who was the one person who knew the outdated style of her old riding habit? Who was the one person on cordial enough terms with that blond maid to enjoin her to silence?

She took a deep breath, unsure how she felt about such a gift from…him.

Picking up the green habit, she held it out full length. The elegant lines of the bodice were a marked contrast to the boxy shape of her old brown habit. How had he been able to order such an exquisite garment to be made on such short notice? A longing fluttered inside of her to put on her mysterious present, to feel the bodice fitting tightly over her breasts and the skirt cascading smoothly over her hips.

Even alone in her chamber, her cheeks began to redden. She dropped the garment guiltily. A knock sounded on the door, and without waiting for a response Lady Malcolm stepped into the room. "Good morning, daughter," she said crisply, walking over to give her daughter a kiss on the cheek.

Eliza was surprised at the unusual display of affection.

"Your father told me about yesterday's events. I must confess, I had hoped you would visit me in my rooms to tell me yourself, even though I was indisposed." Lady Malcolm sniffed the sniff of undeserved persecution.

"I am terribly sorry, Mama," said Eliza in dismay. In truth, it had been most remiss of her—she ought to have been able to overcome her own distress enough to do the duty of a daughter. But then, it was doing her duty that had occasioned the distress in the first place.

"It is no matter now," said Lady Malcolm, magnanimously setting aside her own wounded feelings as a mother should. "Your father tells me you are not as happy about the match as some young ladies might be."

"No." Eliza stared at the floor.

"I am sorry, my dear. Marriage of any sort is a trial that a woman must bear up under. The Apostle Paul himself recommended that it were better to remain unwed since the unwed virgin cares more for the things of the Lord. But in this current world and with your father's financial affairs being what they are...." Lady Malcolm sighed and then continued. "I suppose the brevity of the acquaintance must give you pause. However, the duke seems eager to tie up the matter quickly, and your father does as well. One must hope that love will come later for you, or if not, then at least felicity and companionship."

"Yes, Mama." Eliza bit her lip. Felicity...that was what her parents had—or if not always felicity, then at least companionship. Perhaps it was foolish to hope for anything more. Perhaps it was enough to have a husband who admired his wife's appearance...while deploring her intellect. Eliza shuddered.

"What is this?" Lady Malcolm picked up the green riding habit and held it out with a puzzled stare.

Eliza handed her mother the unsigned card.

"Ah, from the duke," Lady Malcolm surmised. It was clear that her mother had scant knowledge of the character of her future son-in-law. Lady Malcolm handed the card back to Eliza. "A romantic gesture, surely"—Eliza's lack of enthusiasm must have registered on her face—"but perhaps it is not in your temperament to appreciate such things."

"Oh, certainly it is!" said Eliza, losing some of her restraint.

Lady Malcolm frowned. "I am not sure I entirely approve of such a gift, but I suppose it will do little harm to have you wear it." She opened the door where Ollerton was waiting for the conclusion of the conference between mother and daughter, and together they helped fit the new riding habit onto Eliza.

When they had finished, they stood back and looked at her. Neither said a word.

"Well?" asked Eliza, a little apprehensively, taking hold of the train to allow herself greater ease in walking.

"You are beautiful, Miss Eliza," said Ollerton, her old eyes shining. Eliza's mother nodded a silent but unqualified approval.

There were other preparations to be made—Eliza's hair must be twisted up into a suitable frame for her face and her half boots buttoned into place, but it was not more than a quarter of an hour before she was ready to go downstairs.

"I shall pray for you, my child," said Lady Malcolm, "that you do not suffer any mishap in the saddle."

It was only then that Eliza remembered that the primary purpose of a riding habit was for *riding*. But somehow, in light of everything that had transpired since yesterday morning, staying atop a horse seemed one of the smallest worries clouding her future.

14

Henry paced the checkered floor of the saloon. He had been awake before sunrise, alert and anxious and angry. He had seen his brother ill-use his tenants and his servants, he had been ill-used by his brother himself, and the knowledge that his brother was about to ill-use two innocent women—whose lives had been inextricably tangled with his own—filled him with incandescent rage. Walter would attempt to stand guard over one—could he stand guard over the other?

Eliza's face surfaced in his mind—he could never imagine it without seeing a sadness there—and he wanted, oh so much, to see what could happen if that sadness were exchanged for joy. She reminded him of a shy woodland flower, needing tender shade and gentle rain to flourish—and Rufus was neither of those things. He was a thick-soled boot, treading indiscriminately on any plant that stood in his path.

Henry paused by the staircase, one hand on the banister. He could not stand by and see her trampled by abuse or withered by neglect. How if he spoke to her father and warned him of Rufus' character? His teeth clenched. Somehow he could not imagine Sir Arthur taking his concerns seriously, especially when they stood in the way of such an advantageous alliance. The man was too deeply dipped, and the Rowland fortune promised a way out. He would never consider ending the understanding with Rufus unless another opportunity—equally lucrative—presented itself.

Henry's heart thudded like a drum. Why did he hesitate? He knew that he was able to offer the sort of advantageous alternative that would appeal to Sir Arthur—that was not the sticking point. Was it fair, though, to have Eliza freed from one undesirable match only to be coerced into another match that was also distasteful to her? Nothing that had transpired so far could lead him to presume that he had gained her goodwill. Was there enough time still to earn it?

A sound at the top of the staircase drew his eyes upward. There she was, exquisitely beautiful in the gift he had given her. He would not call her a goddess—that was for statues of marble and granite—and Eliza was a woman of flesh and blood, and tears and blushes, and someday trust and love.

Did she love him a little? Would she trust him enough?

It was clear as sunlight that he was waiting there only for her. She came down the stairs slowly, her fingers gliding over the same banister where his hand was rooted. He held his place at the bottom of the stairs, and she came to a stop one step above him, her hand only a fingerbreadth away from his own on the railing.

"Eliza," said Henry in a low voice. "Do not marry my brother."

"Good morning to you too, your lordship," she said, clearly pitching her voice over his head.

Henry swiveled around and saw his half-brother Robert entering the room. He was dressed to ride, but somehow, his slight frame still looked every inch the dandy. "Hal, I need to speak to you. In private." There were spots of color on Robert's cheeks, peeking out from beneath his sideburns.

"Of course," said Henry, so annoyed at the inopportune interruption that he did not even wonder at the reason for it. "I will join you in the morning room presently." Henry's eyes followed Robert until he disappeared. The room was safe, but it might be invaded again at any minute. He must unburden his heart quickly.

His eyes returned to Eliza and drank in her beauty once again. "That color suits you even better than I could have imagined. And I don't recall wishing you a good morning. It will only be a good morning if you decide not to marry my brother."

"I must." Her voice was quiet but intense.

"Your father?"

"You are perceptive, Lord Henry."

"How if another candidate were to present himself?"

"It would depend on the candidate."

She stood one step higher than him, and his eyes were on a level with her perfect lips.

"How if *I* were to present myself?"

"I fear my father would not consider you suitable."

Henry noted that she said nothing about whether *she* considered him suitable. She had not blushed at the suggestion though—which led him to believe that she had already been mulling over the idea in her own head.

"Is it a matter of money?" he asked, sliding his fingertips up the banister until they were touching hers.

"Yes," she whispered, and she did blush now, her cheeks as pink as a summer sunset over London.

"Then it is not a matter at all." His hand covered hers and he pressed it gently.

"Hal!" said Robert's voice urgently from the door of the morning room.

Eliza snatched her hand away, but she did not offer any words of rebuke.

"Do not marry my brother!" repeated Henry, and sending back a long, lingering glance, he disappeared down the hallway to see what was agitating Robert so greatly.

"Oh, Eliza!" said Adele. "What a charming riding habit! If I had not had this blue one made up just last month, I think I should be jealous. Shall we go out to the stables?"

Many equestrians had already congregated in the stable yard, those from the house as well as from the surrounding neighborhood. Eliza recognized the black-haired Mr. Cecil, who had come to Adele's parlor games and beside him his sister, Miss Cecil, and their friend, Miss Bertram.

"Will Miss Ashbrook be coming as well?" asked Eliza.

"No, she says she is indisposed," said Adele, "but I think it is really a fit of pique that Henry would not fall for her lures. I sometimes think that half my friends are really not my friends at all and only angling to be my sister-in-law."

Eliza blinked at this sudden confidence.

"I do not mean *you*, of course," said Adele hurriedly. "Good Lord, no one could imagine that *you* were angling."

"Thank you," said Eliza faintly. No, she was not angling. But somehow, she seemed to have caught both brothers through no fault of her own.

The head groom saw the ladies nearing the stable and led out a milky white mount for Adele. "This is Serafina," she said proudly, stroking the horse's muzzle. "And perhaps since my mother does not mean to ride out today, you may ride her horse."

The head groom cleared his throat. "I'm under strict orders that Miss Malcolm is to only ride Marigold."

"Oh, well, if Rufus says so then you must," said Adele with a shrug of the shoulders. "A pity though. Marigold is so…dull."

Eliza and the groom exchanged a glance. The strict orders had certainly not come from Rufus.

The groom brought Marigold and helped Eliza mount.

Many of the other horses were stamping impatiently, but Marigold stood firm as a rock.

Mr. Turold was seated nearby on his own horse, holstering the pistol that was part of the matched set that Rufus owned. When he saw Eliza looking at him, he tipped his hat, and Eliza, as much as she wanted to cut him, was compelled to nod her head. Odious man with his effeminately long hair! She much preferred the closely cropped brown hair of...another gentleman.

Rufus stood a little way away from the main group in careful conference with the undergroom who had accompanied Eliza and Henry on their ride yesterday morning. Eliza felt an uncomfortable tightening in the chest as she wondered whether the groom was relating the story of that ride to her fiancé. She studied Rufus' face. No, there was no irritation there. They were not speaking of her. Her apprehension diminished completely as she saw that the undergroom was not speaking at all.

But even if the undergroom were a rattle and a gossip, Rufus would probably have never thought to ask about her. He doubtless would not even notice her presence in the excitement of his precious hunt. At least she was "beautiful in the style he liked," she thought bitterly, even if he considered her good for nothing else.

What had Henry—yes, she would call him Henry—meant when he had said that money was no matter? She had strong doubts that Henry had received any inheritance from his father. There was no possibility that he could possess a fortune comparable to his brother's. He should be searching for an heiress to better his condition not the daughter of a penniless baronet.

But if, as he said, one could pretend that money was no matter...she allowed herself to daydream. What would it be like to wed someone who had compassion on her weaknesses, who considered her opinion, who respected her character? She remembered the feel of his hand on hers on the banister, and her cheeks grew warm again.

She stopped herself. She must not think thus. It was a fool's errand and a sure road to breaking her own heart.

There was Henry now, walking at a fast clip down from the house to the stable yard, with Mr. Curtis several steps behind him. But instead of the tender look he had given her earlier, there was thunder now on his brow. She saw him stride up to Mr. Turold.

"Walter, a word!"

She wondered briefly, what heinous deed Mr. Turold had done—besides introducing her to Rufus Rowland—that should make Henry so angry.

The longhaired Mr. Turold dismounted, and the two men disappeared into the stable.

⁂

IT WAS A FULL TEN minutes before Henry resurfaced. He was astride his horse. The scowl on his face had lessened, but Eliza sensed that something still troubled him.

She willed Marigold to move towards him, and as if by magic—aided by a slight tug on the reins—the horse complied.

"You seem vexed, Henry," she said as her horse sidled up to his.

His face broke into a smile at the sound of his Christian name. "I can assure you, it is very vexing to have the woman one loves betrothed to marry another."

Eliza's heart skipped a beat. She looked around quickly to make sure no one else had heard. Did he really mean that? Would he really try to break off the engagement and win her for himself?

"I fear you are poking fun at me, my lord."

"I should never presume to do so...at least, not upon such a topic."

Adele directed her horse over to them and shook her riding crop at her brother in disapproval. "Henry, now that Rufus has the matter all sewn up, you really must stop flirting with Eliza."

"Oh, *must* I?"

Eliza's eyes widened. He really was incorrigible. But whereas his attentions had initially mortified her, she found that now she was beginning to enjoy them.

"He's not serious," said Adele, sending a glare in Henry's direction.

"Of course not," murmured Eliza.

Henry dropped her a wink, and she had to remember to take her next breath. "Lud, Adele," he said, "why don't you find some other poor soul to pester? Where's Stephen?"

"Being useful." Adele wrinkled her nose as if she disapproved of the notion of usefulness. "Rufus has him in charge of the luncheon for later. He's giving instructions to the village lads."

"Lads" was hardly the appropriate descriptor since some of the men unloading barrels were nearly twice Mr. Blount's age. They were dropping off hogsheads from the local tavern and sweets from the bakeshop.

"Ho there, Ned!" Henry called out suddenly, and Eliza saw one of the villagers wave a hand and come over. Henry dismounted and shook hands with the bearded fellow. He did not forget Eliza, however, and soon pulled his friend over to make introductions. "Miss Malcolm, may I present Edward Hornsby, proprietor of the Blue Boar?"

Eliza bowed her head and Mr. Hornsby expressed the appropriate sentiments of pleasure at making her acquaintance.

"Ned and I grew up together in these woods."

"That we did," said the bearded tavern keeper with a gleam

in his eye. "There's many a story I could tell about young Master Rowland—"

Henry cleared his throat. "But naturally you'll keep them to yourself unless they redound to my credit."

"Hello, Ned," said Adele, interjecting herself into the conversation. Eliza supposed she was used to inserting herself unasked as the youngest child in a family of brothers. "You may have heard that Miss Malcolm is just lately engaged to be married to Rufus."

"Is that so?" said Mr. Hornsby, giving a whistle and eyeing Henry thoughtfully.

"Come now, Adele," said Henry. "There's no need to spread rumors about."

"Rumors? Henry Rowland!"

"I'll believe it when I read it in the papers and not before." Henry clapped his friend on the back and stepped back into the saddle. "Good to see you, Ned! I'll look forward to a pint of your finest at the end of the chase."

Adele followed Mr. Hornsby over to the wagon full of hogsheads—doubtless to keep an eye on Mr. Blount's activities. Henry urged his horse back to where Marigold stood placidly. "And now, my dear, do you remember your riding lessons?"

"I believe so," said Eliza, taking a deep breath. "I shall do my best and strive not to embarrass you."

"I shall never be embarrassed by you, Eliza."

"That is kind of you to say."

"I mean it."

Eliza stared back at him and forgot to blush, for something within her whispered that Henry Rowland was sincere.

⁓⁕⁓

WITHIN THE NEXT HALF HOUR, everyone had found their horses.

The dogs had been released from their kennels and were straining at their leashes. Rufus addressed the company of two dozen riders, reminding them that they would not come home without a pair of antlers.

"He says this every hunt," said Adele with a yawn.

"But he always succeeds," Miss Cecil said with a little smile.

"Yes, well, Rowlands always do," said Adele matter-of-factly.

Eliza wondered what happened, then, when two Rowlands opposed one another. They could not both be successful....

She herself had no further ambition than to ride beside Henry Rowland for the whole of the hunt. Adele, however, had other plans. "We ladies," she said, "shall ride along the road until we come to the grassy knoll that overlooks the eastern part of the forest. It will be far more agreeable than chasing about after the hounds."

Miss Cecil and Miss Bertram acquiesced, as was their wont, to their high-ranking friend's desires. Eliza followed and soon found herself bringing up the rear of the party on sure-footed Marigold. They rounded the circular drive and turned onto the main road heading towards the little church.

"How strange!" said Adele in surprise, noticing one of the Rowlands' carriages parked neatly on the side of the road. Eliza saw the undergroom, Martin, sitting in the box, chewing on a blade of grass.

"Why is the carriage waiting here?" Miss Cecil asked, but Martin either did not hear her or disregarded the question.

"He can't speak," said Adele in an undertone. Eliza recalled that he had said nary a word during her ride with Henry yesterday morning.

The ladies rode past, and Eliza gave Martin a shy smile. He stared back at her like an inmate behind the bars of a cage. She dropped her eyes. Poor man—it must be a heavy affliction to be dumb.

The steeple of the church was just in sight when Adele pointed to the side of the road. A grassy hill rose up on the left. The other ladies directed their mounts off the road, and Eliza, trying to keep pace, gritted her teeth as she urged Marigold up the climbing slope. She angled her sideways body forward, willing herself to stay in the saddle. She was sure that she did not look at all elegant right now, even with her new green riding habit, and she was rather glad that Henry Rowland was not there to see her. But then again, he probably would have just given her an encouraging word, stripping away her self-consciousness like a maid pulling dust cloths off the furniture.

From the top, they could see on one side the summer fields of the Sussex countryside, plotted and pieced like a brown and green quilt. On the other side ranged the tangled limbs of the forest, the stage set for the players in today's hunt. Here and there a small clearing in the woods gave them a view of the forest floor.

"Look there!" said Miss Bertram, her hand shooting out like an arrow towards the south. They caught a glimpse of a half dozen riders before they disappeared into the leaves again. "I think I saw your brother," she said to Miss Cecil.

"The wish is father to the thought!" said Adele with a smirk, and Miss Bertram colored at that sally. "I cannot make out a single one of those figures—they're too far off. Could you tell if Rufus was with them, Eliza?"

"Oh," said Eliza, "I'm not sure...." His red hair would certainly stand out, but then, he had been wearing a beaver. This was to be her lot in life now—surveying the forest and waiting for Rufus while he pursued his pleasures.

From the distance came the baying of hounds. The riders were moving closer. The ladies scanned the woods for more traces of the hunting party, but saw nothing. A half hour later, they were still searching the tree line. "How tedious this is growing!" said Adele. "I thought we should have better sport than this."

"Oh, look there," said Miss Bertram. "Mr. Cecil!"

This time it was not just the young lady's wishful hope. Mr. Cecil was emerging from the forest with Eliza's father, Sir Arthur, beside him. Adele hailed them and the ladies came down from the hill to meet them at the road.

"Did you sight a stag?" Miss Cecil asked her brother.

"Yes, right away, but we lost our bearings once we all started for it. Rufus is normally two lengths ahead of everyone when the chase is on, but he disappeared as soon as the hounds started baying."

"How peculiar," said Adele. "Did you carry on?"

"Why yes! We took off after the buck until the hounds lost the track, and then the whole party fell to pieces. Henry went off one way and Turold the other. And here we are come to look for you ladies."

"Your loss is our gain," replied Miss Bertram smoothly.

"Do you think the others are gathering back at the house?" Eliza asked.

"That is a logical assumption," said Sir Arthur, "and perhaps we ought to return as w—"

A shot rang out in the forest farther down the road from where the six horses were standing.

"Tally ho!" said Mr. Cecil, lifting his beaver off his curly black hair with excitement. "Someone's picked up the trail."

"Let's go on," said Adele, "and see if they hit him."

Eliza felt a twinge of pity for the poor creature. She rather hoped that they *hadn't* hit the stag, and that he would escape into the underbrush to live another day.

The horses felt the excitement in the air, and it took barely any encouragement to move them from a walk to a trot. Eliza held on determinedly.

When they had gone a couple hundred yards, the church came fully into view. "Over here," said Mr. Cecil, waving at a spot where the trees thinned, a natural entryway into the wooded kingdom. They were just about to enter the forest when another shot sounded, this one deeper into the trees.

"Wounded the first time," conjectured Sir Arthur. "They must have finished it off."

Eliza shuddered and reined in Marigold. She did not know if she wanted to come across the freshly killed body of the stag.

"Hold here, ladies," said Mr. Cecil, misunderstanding her reticence for confusion about which path to take. He stopped everyone near one of the great oak trees. "I'll find the others then bring you to them." His horse bounded away, stepping nimbly over tree roots.

"Any wagers," said Sir Arthur, "on who the lucky shot is?"

"It would surprise me greatly," said Miss Cecil, "if it were anyone other than the duke."

Eliza did not know whether to feel pained or proud at that statement.

"But perhaps the second shot was Henry's," said Adele. She tossed her brown curls in Eliza's direction. "He always *has* enjoyed poaching his brother's game."

Eliza's cheeks flamed. It was not so amusing when she herself was the target of her future sister-in-law's wit. Fortunately, her father was too oblivious to notice the double meaning.

"And here is Mr. Cecil returned to us!" said Miss Bertram with enthusiasm.

"Stop!" said their black-haired guide. A look of panic was on his face. "Stay there. Don't go any farther."

"Whatever is the matter?" demanded Adele.

"There's been an…accident. Stay there."

The forest air erupted with a cacophony of feminine cries and queries.

"Merciful heavens!"

"What sort of accident?"

"Who's hurt?"

"Why can't we see? We might be able to help!"

"Sir Arthur!" said Mr. Cecil. "Take these ladies back to the house."

"Why? What do you mean to do?"

"Go to the church. Get the Reverend. Send someone for Doctor Selkirk. And Constable Cooper too."

"The constable!" echoed Miss Cecil. "Why, Edward, how bad is it? Do you mean…?"

"Yes," said Mr. Cecil, his voice a little overwrought. "I do mean that. Now, ladies, please, back to the house, and I will tell you all when I know more."

PART TWO

15

ELIZA SAT DOWN CAREFULLY ON THE SOFA IN THE DRAWING room and breathed deeply while the other ladies congregated in the hallway expressing their confusion and dismay in hysterical tones. Mr. Cecil had refused to tell them the nature of the accident, but the matter could not long remain a secret. The first of the stragglers coming back from the aborted hunt shouted something about "the duke" as he dismounted and ran up the steps. A frowning Hayward begged him to step aside and lower his voice, but after the butler had learned the particulars, he ascended the stairs with a rapidity never before seen, on a quest to find the Duchess of Brockenhurst.

A quarter of an hour later, the carriage which had been driven by the silent groom Martin wheeled into the driveway with a flurry of riders surrounding it. Eliza swallowed and rose from the sofa, hurrying to the window with the other ladies. Henry was up in the box alongside the groom, and it was he holding the reins. He pulled the horses to a stop and then jumped down, waving aside the footmen and yanking open the carriage door himself. "Hayward, a blanket!" he called out, and within seconds a large wool coverlet had materialized.

Mr. Cecil stepped down, along with Mr. Turold, and together they lifted an inert figure out of the carriage. The blanket was covering the head and most of the body, but Eliza knew, even without catching a glimpse of the red hair, that it was Rufus. And she knew, even before the doctor arrived a half hour later, that the doctor would be no help. Rufus Rowland, the Duke of Brockenhurst, was dead.

The constable arrived shortly after the doctor and took a look at the body laid out in the morning room. The Duchess of Brockenhurst was sitting beside Rufus, holding his lifeless hand, her face as gray as ash. Most of the men had gone back outside and were talking together loud and fast. Miss Cecil and Miss Bertram stared at each other like frightened deer uncertain where to run. Adele seemed frozen, ever since the body had crossed the threshold. Eliza put her arms around her and settled her on a bench in the hallway. Tears began to streak down Adele's cheeks, and Eliza laid the girl's head against her bosom and let her sob out her grief. Mr. Blount, standing nearby and fidgeting anxiously, offered his handkerchief.

There was no time for Eliza to examine her own feelings. No, that would come later, in the quiet of her room. But now, she must remain unshaken, a pillar of strength for those who needed her.

Henry and Mr. Cecil re-entered the house as the constable exited the morning room.

"An accident, you say?" said the constable gravely. His bushy gray sideburns reached almost to the sides of his mouth.

"I believe so," said Mr. Cecil. "Here is the weapon." Using two hands, he presented a pistol to the constable. From across the hallway, Eliza recognized it as the same pistol Mr. Turold had been holstering in the stable yard.

"Oh dear," said the constable, clucking underneath his breath. "Oh dear, oh dear. And of course there is the possibility that it was *not* an accident...."

"What is to be done now, constable?" Henry inquired forcefully.

"Normally I would carry the case to the magistrate to start an investigation, but the magistrate is…." The constable waved a hand to the door of the morning room.

"Quite," said Henry. "But old Cecil was the secondary magistrate in my father's time, which means that you"—he turned to Edward Cecil—"are next in line to investigate the matter."

"Yes, Lord Henry, that is as it should be," said the constable.

Mr. Cecil raked a hand through his black curls. "I fear I have never been involved in such an undertaking before. I hardly know where to begin."

Mr. Blount, who had been listening quite earnestly, cleared his throat and took a step towards the trio. "If I might be so bold, I know a man—or rather, I know *of* him—a Bow Street Runner who came from London and was able to sort out some business for my father this past winter."

"You mean that business with the Earl of Anglesford?" said Henry.

"Yes, that," replied Mr. Blount. "The man's name was Pevensey. Jacob Pevensey."

"Well," said Mr. Cecil, "there could be no harm in calling in some reinforcements. I daresay Constable Cooper and I would be glad of the help. Henry, could you arrange it?"

"Of course," said Henry. "I'll send my valet to town with a message, and perhaps the man can even be here by nightfall."

Mr. Blount returned to take up his position as auxiliary comforter. When Adele reached out for his hand and pulled him down to the bench on her other side, Eliza found that her ministrations were no longer needed. She folded her hands and gazed quietly at the three men across the hallway.

"I'll need to take his statement," said Constable Cooper, fumbling in his pockets for a notebook.

"Henry," said Mr. Cecil. "I'm sorry." He clapped the broad-shouldered man on the back.

"Thank you," said Henry, "but we were not exactly...close."

Mr. Cecil shook his head. "I think we all know that. But still, man, he was your brother. One feels such things, no matter the level of estrangement."

"Certainly," said Henry. His eyes flicked over to where Eliza sat and met her own. "One feels such things. Most deeply."

Eliza looked away. She could not decipher *what* she felt. She was numb. She was dreaming. They were bringing in a Bow Street Runner to unravel the events of the day. A pity he could not also unravel the tangled web of her heart.

HENRY SHOWED THE CONSTABLE OUTSIDE to where Walter was waiting, arms folded and brow furrowed. "This is Walter Turold," he told the constable. "Walter, he wants to take your statement."

"In private?" asked Walter in a guarded tone. His long hair had come out of its queue and hung in lank strands about his face.

"If you wish," said Henry coolly, "but I must confess that *I* am eager to hear your statement as well." What he felt about his brother's death was of little consequence, but what Walter felt? That would tell volumes. He had already asserted in the forest that the shot had come from his gun. That was *not* the plan they had discussed in the stable.

"I have no qualms about stating it in front of you. It was an accident. I saw movement. I thought it was the stag. I fired my pistol."

"Indeed, sir," said the constable, jotting down notes as fast as his pencil could write. "I've had the same happen myself. Almost clipped the wing of my cousin one day—thought he was a pheasant!" He started to chuckle at the thought, then seemed to think better of it. "And was there any ill feeling between yourself and the duke?"

Walter looked at Henry. "No."

Henry's nostrils flared. He would not call him out on that lie. Not yet.

"That's all I need then," said the constable, closing his notebook. "The Runner will doubtless want more from you. It goes without saying, I think, that you must not leave the premises."

"Of course," said Walter, inclining his head. "I shall keep to my room until I'm needed. I am truly sorry for this regrettable accident." That last sentiment was directed to Henry. "He was my friend, you know."

The constable drifted away to consult with the housekeeper about where the body should be kept prior to the inquest.

"I am aware of that," said Henry dryly. "I also know that if I were to accidentally kill my friend Stephen Blount, I would be doubled over vomiting until the shock of it passed, and then on my knees before God begging His forgiveness."

"Not everyone handles tragedy the same," said Walter in a monotone voice.

"Or perhaps not everyone believes that Rufus' death *was* a tragedy."

"I can only assume you are speaking for yourself."

"You can assume all you like—I have a letter to write."

Henry walked back inside. Eliza had disappeared. What was she thinking right now? What was she feeling? Relief that she was freed from marriage to a rake? Shock at the suddenness of the event?

In truth, Henry did not know what he himself felt. Rufus was dead, and under very suspicious circumstances. Did he believe Walter's claim that it was an accident? Not at all. And yet, he had never known Walter to be a dishonorable man. A hard man, an unforgiving man, but not a liar.

And what if Walter *was* lying? Did Henry even care? Whether intentional or unintentional on Walter's part, Rufus had been struck down by the hand of God. The mills of God had not ground slowly this time.

Henry strode into the study. The sight of the dark leather chair, the mounted stag's head, and the bearskin rug brought back a surge of memories that he thought had ebbed for good. He remembered pulling up a stool to sit beside his father at the desk while he went over the books with the steward. "You've a good head for numbers, Hal. A good head!" It was a piece of praise that Henry had treasured, for it was always Rufus who was the best wrestler, the best horseman, the best shot, having earlier grown into those physical qualities that William Rowland so much prized.

"Very good, Master Henry," the old steward had echoed—Mr. Hodgins was his name. "You must come collect the rents with me next time so you can see the faces that go with each number."

"What a bore!" Rufus had said when he heard Hodgins' idea. "Visiting some sad-faced old men in their hovels? No thank you!"

But Henry had gone, and he had listened, and he had learned....

The Brockenhurst seal was lying there on the desk among the papers, a ring that Rufus had rarely, if ever, worn. Henry picked it up and traced a fingertip over the stylized "B" and the symbol of the oak tree. He had used this seal many times, closing letters on all the business he had transacted in Rufus' name. And now it would no longer be Rufus' name connected to that seal. He turned it over in his palm. It would be his.

He set the seal down and scanned the desk for a clean piece of paper to write his letter. Underneath the most recent issue of *The Sporting Magazine*, he found a signed document with both his brother's and half-brother's signatures on the bottom. It was a promissory note, a loan of fifty thousand pounds to Robert with his house Fontbury as collateral in case he could not repay the loan in two years' time. Henry's eyes flicked over to the date of the document. The loan had come due last month. It was exactly as Robert had told him earlier that morning.

Underneath that document was the blank paper. Henry scrawled a quick note to Jacob Pevensey, the Bow Street Runner that Stephen had recommended. He signed his name—Henry Rowland. He looked in the drawer of the desk where he knew pocket money would be kept and pulled out ten pounds to enclose with the letter for travel expenses. He folded in each side of the letter and tucked the bottom piece into the top.

The seal still sat on the desk, beckoning him. Was it too soon for him to use it? No, it was his right. He melted a few drops of blood red wax onto the folded ends of the letter and stamped the ring into it with unnecessary vigor.

He rang for Hayward and asked him to send down his valet.

"Biggs, I need you to ride back to London for the afternoon. This letter"—he handed the sealed message to his valet—"goes to Bow Street. And then stop also at Maurice's, and beg pardon from the old man. I must tarry a few more days in the countryside. If he has any urgent business for me, he can send it back with you, and I will transact it here."

16

Jacob Pevensey stepped into the warm office of the Bow Street Magistrate. He was a Londoner, born and bred, and a good thing too, else he might resent the heat, and the fog, and the smell that meant summer in England's largest city.

He had just finished an inquiry into a theft—a pretty piece of jewelry that a doting doctor had bought for his young wife. The concerned husband had found it missing and blamed servants, tradesmen, even guests. It had never occurred to him that his darling wife, having run through her pin money, might sell the emerald necklace to finance her amusements at the gaming table. Pevensey, who had uncovered the real reason for the necklace's disappearance, felt a little sorry for her. He was glad she was out of the house when he came to reveal the truth to her formerly indulgent husband.

Pevensey had written up his own report of events to place on Sir Richard's desk. The head magistrate liked to be kept apprised of all cases solved and unsolved. It was the only document that Pevensey had composed about the affair; he was notorious for storing all his notes for a case in the one place where nobody else could find them—his head. He had hoped to slip the report onto a vacant desk and edge his way back out of the office for an early end to the day's work, but the desk chair was decidedly and masterfully occupied.

"You have a letter," said Sir Richard, exchanging the paperwork Pevensey handed him for another piece that threatened more work.

Pevensey put a smile on his face, but inwardly he was groaning at his bad luck. "Who is it from?" He turned the folded packet over in his hands.

"By the seal, I would say the Duke of Brockenhurst." Richard Ford knew everyone in London, from the peers in Parliament to the actresses at the Drury Lane Theater. It stood to reason that he would recognize every seal that came across his desk.

"Could you inform me of the contents as well?" said Pevensey, his freckled face lighting up with mischief.

"Cheeky fellow," said Sir Richard, leaning back in his chair with his hands behind his head. "Read it yourself and tell *me* what Brockenhurst wants."

Pevensey examined the contents of the letter. "Brockenhurst is dead."

"Strange that he should write you a letter then," said Sir Richard, his lined face appreciating the irony of the matter.

"It's from his brother. The duke was killed during a hunt. Purported to be an accident but needs investigation. The local magistrate and constable are inexperienced and asking for reinforcement."

"Why *you*, Pevensey?"

Pevensey had been asking himself the same question. "I suppose word's got out about the Anglesford case. But that was a one-time affair. London's my jurisdiction, Sir Richard. I can't be gadding about Sussex when I have work here."

"But haven't you just finished your last case?" said Sir Richard, looking pointedly at the report freshly placed on his desk. "The death of a peer is a serious matter and certainly deserving of a qualified investigator."

Pevensey cocked his head, his red sideburn nearly touching his neat collar on the left. "Are you ordering me to take this assignment, Sir Richard?"

"Yes," said Sir Richard, leaning forward and reaching into a drawer. "And I'll even supply your travel expenses up front." He handed Pevensey a bank note. "If you change horses, you can be there by nightfall."

Pevensey took a deep breath and made one last effort for a quiet evening. "Surely, tomorrow morning would be adequate."

"Nonsense," said Sir Richard, waving Pevensey away as a signal that he desired no more argument. "It's not as if Harrowhaven is all the way to Brighton."

"Of course, Sir Richard," said Pevensey, forcing a smile and giving a curt bow on his way out of the office.

As he turned into the corridor, he deposited Sir Richard's bank note in his waistcoat pocket. Then, reaching into the letter, he pulled out a ten pound note and placed it in his pocket as well. It was always nice to be doubly reimbursed for travel expenses. But somehow, it did not quite make up for the prospect of an afternoon ride to Sussex in the wilting summer heat.

⁓⊚⁓

WHEN ELIZA WENT UPSTAIRS, SHE found her parents hidden away in their private sitting room discussing the impact of the day's awful turn of events.

"It was not the will of God," said Lady Malcolm grimly.

"Yes, Margaret. Clearly!" Sir Arthur threw his head back and sighed. "Apparently, it's His will instead that we all beg for pennies outside the workhouse."

"Arthur! Don't blaspheme."

Eliza's father muttered underneath his breath.

"Eliza, my dear," said Lady Malcolm, rising from her seat. "You must be overwhelmed. Sit down."

"Thank you, Mama," said Eliza. She was still wearing her green riding habit, and she adjusted the side train to drape properly on the seat of the wingback chair.

"We should leave as soon as we can," said Lady Malcolm, pacing the room with her hands behind her back. "Tomorrow."

Eliza's heart took a little jump. It would be unfortunate to leave Harrowhaven so soon. But then, of course, it might not be pleasant for the family to have them stay.

"Not possible," growled Sir Arthur. "There's to be an investigation."

"I thought you said it was an accident!"

"It was. But when a duke dies, they do things thoroughly. We'll be lucky to leave here by the end of the week."

Eliza rubbed a hand against her ear. Three more days here—maybe four. She wondered if the investigation meant that all the other houseguests would be staying on as well? Mr. Blount, Mr. Curtis, Henry Rowland....

"How tedious," said Lady Malcolm, "now that there's nothing here worth staying for."

"Indeed," said Sir Arthur. "Why couldn't that blasted Turold have fired a foot to the right? He's shot a hole in our fortunes, that's certain. Unless...unless...." Sir Arthur fingered his chin and looked over at Eliza. "Eliza, does it seem to you that the younger Rowland brother has eyes for you?"

"I don't know, Papa." Eliza's voice quavered. It was quite clear what scheme her father was hatching now.

"I think he does. He seems quite smitten, in fact. I wonder if our protracted visit might be for the best."

"What foolishness is this, Arthur?" Lady Margaret gave a

chilly sniff. "Whatever notion you have clamoring in your head, silence it immediately. The younger brother is not at all suitable."

"He'll be duke now," said Sir Arthur, leaning forward eagerly. "That makes him very suitable. And I think that Eliza has already got his goodwill."

"A ridiculous notion."

"Nonsense, Margaret. It's a splendid idea, and very biblical too, if I'm not mistaken—the younger brother marrying the bride of the elder who perishes prematurely. Eliza? You shall do your best. Be friendly to him, yes?"

Eliza crushed a handful of green fabric inside her right hand. "Of course, Papa. As you wish." It took all her willpower to keep from smiling.

"No," said Lady Malcolm, the intensity in her quiet voice replacing the volume. "I forbid it. It was enough that you made us come here, Arthur, to throw our daughter in the way of...these people. And look what good came of it! It is *not* God's will. He has shown that plainly. We shall keep to our rooms and bide our time and leave at the earliest opportunity. Eliza, you are to have nothing to do with the younger brother. Do I make myself clear?"

"Perfectly, Mama," said Eliza, but the light refused to leave her eyes. She looked at her father, but he voiced no argument and merely hunched back in his chair, his shoulders expressing his frustration. As for herself, she had not given up hope quite yet. There was still time for her mother to change her mind regarding Henry Rowland.

※

HAYWARD AND MRS. FORSYTHE PRESENTED themselves together at the door of the study. "Your grace," said Hayward hesitantly.

At the unfamiliar address, Henry looked up from the account

books—old friends that he had not visited these three years or more. "Come in, both of you. What can I do for you?"

"It is late afternoon now, your grace." Hayward hesitated. "It is not a matter of great importance, but the luncheon for today after the.... It was never served."

"And no matter the event, people must eat," said Henry, understandingly. "You are quite right. Set out a sideboard of cold meats in the dining room, and send up a tray to everyone who has retired to their rooms."

He stood up from the desk.

"What can we get for *you*, your grace?" asked Mrs. Forsythe.

"Nothing, nothing," said Henry. "But I shall bring the tray up to my mother when it is ready."

"If you please," said the housekeeper, "she's had some tea already and has fallen asleep. I sat with her until she did."

"Thank you," said Henry. He pressed Mrs. Forsythe's wrinkled hand. "Then in that case, I shall take up the tray to Miss Malcolm."

"Of course, your grace," said Hayward without batting an eye.

Henry sat back down with the account books while he waited for the tray to be sent in. He felt a gnawing in his stomach, but it was not hunger. It was something else.

He had not been able to convince Eliza to stand up against her father and reject his brother, but circumstances had intervened, and now, she was free. That was why he had remained at Harrowhaven—was it not?—to save her from the indignity of marriage to a scoundrel. But was that the only reason? No, honesty compelled him to admit to himself, there was more to it than that.

He thought of her tall, willowy form at the top of the staircase, her shy spirit with far more strength to it than an observer might suppose. He remembered her stricken face from yesterday evening and the silent cry of despair coming from her eyes. Those beautiful green eyes that a man—the right man—could lose himself in. He wanted Eliza Malcolm, wanted her desperately for himself.

Rufus was gone now—his presence would not stand in the way of Henry's plans. But his absence might. Henry could not imagine Sir Arthur rejecting an offer to continue the betrothal in Rufus' place. But Eliza? Would she concur? The past five days had set in motion a chain of events each more tumultuous than the last. Perhaps her heart was not ready. Perhaps he should bide his time.

Hayward brought the tray of cold meats, cheese, and bread, and Henry carried it to the stairs. There would be no biding. He must see her. He followed the ribbon of floral carpet to the door of her room and knocked.

"Come in," said a quiet voice.

Henry balanced the tray on one hand to turn the doorknob with the other and then taking the tray in two hands again, pushed the door open with his elbow.

Eliza was seated on the sofa in the little room adjoining her bedchamber, her legs curled up under her and a book on her lap. The presence of the tray must have registered before his face did, for with barely a glance in his direction, she said, "Thank you. You may put it on the table."

He stepped inside.

"Oh!" The book snapped shut in her lap. "I beg your pardon—I did not realize."

"No apologies necessary," said Henry with a smile. "I rather enjoy having you order me about." Before she could blush at that, he introduced the object of his visit. "I am sure you are hungry…we have here a little cold ham, and some roast beef, and a lovely goat cheese I think you will enjoy along with bread ordered up from the village this morning."

"Very thoughtful of you," murmured Eliza. She made no move to touch the food.

Henry stabbed a fork into the contents of the tray and filled a small plate for her. Then, after handing it to her, he began to fill the second plate which Hayward, with the prescience of a skilled butler, had provided.

"Are you dining here with me then?"

Henry saw Eliza casting an eye towards the door which he had purposely left open. It was a calculated risk to tarry in a lady's sitting room, but with the door wide open, it was not entirely indiscreet.

"I thought you could use the company. Am I wrong?"

Eliza hesitated. "No."

Henry noticed she had swung her feet down to the floor and straightened her skirt into a more formal position. Her arms folded over themselves like a fence between him and her.

"Now then," said Henry, determined to overcome the barriers she had set up. "I am famished. Take a bite, my dear hostess, so that I can begin as well."

She stared back at him.

"Come, you owe me something at least for not bringing you cold fish, yes?"

She smiled a little at that, and unfolding her arms, tried a morsel of bread and cheese. Between the two of them, they soon decimated the luncheon tray. But as much as he tried to engage her attention, she steadily averted her eyes. How could he recreate that moment of sincerity that they had shared at the bottom of the staircase this morning? How could he restore the camaraderie that she had shown in the stable yard?

※

Eliza tried to keep the cover of her book hidden under the folds of her dress. The somberness of circumstances demanded serious reading. She ought to have been meditating on Fordyce's sermons or some such edifying literature, but instead she had picked up *Pamela* as soon as she had come back to her room.

Her mother had forbidden her to have any connection to Henry Rowland. The only thing left to her was to read the novel he had loaned her. How mortifying to have him come upon her now with such frivolous reading resting in her hands!

"Feeling better with a full stomach?"

Eliza put her empty plate back on the tray. "Yes, thank you."

She waited for him to speak, but it seemed as if he was waiting too. The awkwardness grew until she could bear it no longer.

"What…happened today? I overheard that Mr. Turold mistook Rufus for the stag and fired too hastily."

"Yes, that is what they are saying," replied Henry. He leaned forward to put his own empty plate back on the tray as well and then, sitting back, crossed one leg over the other as if he meant to stay a while. Eliza uttered a silent prayer that her mother—or Ollerton—would not decide to visit her rooms.

"Is that true?"

He hesitated. She marveled at how his hesitations always seemed to radiate strength while her own hesitations were the product of painful shyness and self-doubt.

"I don't know for certain. That's what Turold is saying. There is an investigator from London coming up to sort things out. Hopefully it will take no longer than a day or two. He'll ask questions of all the necessary parties and recommend what must be done at the inquest."

At the term "necessary parties" Eliza blanched. She took a few quick, shallow breaths. "He would not need to interview me, would he?"

Henry regarded her thoughtfully. "I'm afraid he might. You *were* engaged to him, after all."

"Oh," said Eliza miserably. "I don't know what I would say."

"I don't suppose it will make much difference," said Henry

with arched eyebrows. "He will simply want to know if Rufus had any enemies, anyone who wished him ill."

Eliza looked up from the hands clasped tightly in her lap. "I wouldn't be able to help much on those matters. I barely knew him. He didn't, did he? Have anyone who was his enemy?" Eliza stopped there and looked earnestly into Henry's dark eyes.

For the first time since she had met him, he was the first to drop his gaze.

"That's the investigator's job to find out. I certainly don't envy him the position."

Eliza shifted in her seat. She had been hoping for a firm denial, but Henry's response left matters open to speculation. A whispering thought came into her mind that perhaps Walter Turold was not the one who had aught against Rufus, but Henry himself. She had overheard Mr. Turold urging Rufus not to marry her, but it was hardly a heated argument—and what man would kill his friend to prevent his friend from making a foolish marriage?

But Henry, on the other hand, had far more at stake. And he had even offered—how long ago it seemed!—to present his own suit for her hand. There was no great affection between the brothers—she had seen as much when she witnessed their first encounter in the saloon. Was there enough jealousy for Henry to act out of premeditated hatred?

"H-Henry, are you saddened by your brother's death?" Her words tumbled over each other. "Surely you must be, even though you do not show it. You are simply bearing up well under the grief?"

Henry's lips twisted up into a wry smile. "You are delightfully transparent, my dear. Yes, I am saddened by Rufus' death— though not as much as some brothers would be, I suppose. My brother was a scoundrel—you do not know half of the black marks against him. They say that one should not speak ill of the dead, but I have never been one to give convention place over truth. But no, to answer your unspoken question, I did *not* shoot him. I am a law-abiding man and a God-fearing one. I would never presume to take justice into my own hands in that manner. If someone else did just that today...well, let us just say that I shall ensure he does not go unpunished."

Eliza's cheeks reddened. Of course he had seen through her questions—she hoped that he did not think she was accusing him of anything. It was just the smallest sliver of a doubt that had made her ask.

She shifted uncomfortably on the sofa and felt the hard spine of the hidden book pressing against her leg. She really ought to return *Pamela* to him, but she was mid-chapter on one of the most engrossing scenes. The wicked Mr. B. had dressed up as a housemaid and had sneaked into Pamela's chamber—it was wholly unedifying to read such things, but she could not end the story now. And besides, when she finished it, it would give her an excuse to see him again.

He stood up from his chair and deftly picked up the tray from the table. "Can I send a servant up with anything else for you? Tea? Coffee?"

"No, thank you."

He was so solicitous of her comfort, almost as if he himself were her host.... As he stepped into the corridor, the realization of how matters stood swept down on her like a cavalry charge. He *was* her host now. He was the new owner of Harrowhaven. Henry Rowland had succeeded his brother as the new Duke of Brockenhurst.

17

Pevensey glanced up at the tall oak trees, their shadows looming over the road like the dark fabric of mourning dress. The last sliver of the sun was still visible over the horizon, and by its light he could make out the stately manor house up ahead.

The journey had been shorter than he had anticipated, and had he left directly from Bow Street, he would have arrived with plenty of light to spare. As it was, however, he had decided to go home and pack a satchel of clothing and make a few inquiries in London about both the man who had written the letter and the man whom the letter was about.

To the left of the house, he saw the dark outline of the stables and, turning his horse's head, walked the beast over to the building. The door cracked open at his approach. "Who is it?" asked a gruff voice, and Pevensey caught a glimpse of a small, wiry man, much the same size as himself but a couple decades older.

"Jacob Pevensey, at your service, attached to the London magistrates' office, come down to Harrowhaven on business."

"Aye, I know what business that'll be," said the man. He opened the door wide. "I'll take your horse, Mr. Pevensey. They'll be wanting you up at the big house right away."

Pevensey dismounted and handed the reins to the groom.

"Did you witness the event?" he asked as he loosened his luggage from the back of the horse's saddle.

"Naw, I was too busy seeing every beast was saddled and every man was horsed."

"Ah, you are the stable master then, Mr....?"

"Gormley's the name. John Gormley."

"Did you hear the gunshot?"

"Can't say as I did, but my hearing ain't the best. I certainly heard the hue and cry, though, when the hunters came back in."

"What were they saying?"

"Not much fit to repeat in decent company, but the main of it was that the duke had been shot and that Mr. Turold was the man as had pulled the trigger."

"Did you see Mr. Turold with the men?"

"Aye, he was there, well enough, all Friday-faced after causing an accident of that kind."

"So it *was* an accident?"

Gormley scratched his head. "I wouldna think it could be otherwise, Mr. Turold and the duke bein' bosom friends for ten years or more."

"And there was no falling out between them?"

"Not that I heard tell of."

"Thank you, Mr. Gormley," said Pevensey. "You've been most helpful." He watched Gormley lead his hired nag into the stable and hand him over to a younger man, his hair the same color as the straw on the stable floor. "Ah, I see you have help here," he called out. "Might I ask your fellow groom some questions while I'm here?"

"Who, Martin?" Gormley grunted and pointed a thumb in his fellow groom's direction. "The man's tongue-tied. Dumb since birth."

Martin's eyes narrowed into a glower, and he pulled the horse's head a little more sharply than was necessary as he led it into its box. He might be mute, but he was clearly not deaf, and Pevensey could see that he did not like to have his deformity discussed.

Pevensey wandered away from the stables, pulling out a small notebook from the inside pocket of his jacket. As he neared the steps to the house, he sketched a rough picture of the silent groom with a menacing look in his eye like a boxer about to plant a facer and a thick black "X" over his mouth. In Pevensey's experience as an investigator, it was always the ones who couldn't speak who had the most to say.

~~~

DINNERTIME HAD COME AND GONE without any formal gathering in the dining room. Once again, Henry had ordered trays be sent up to each of the rooms so that the family and guests could grieve—or not grieve—as they each saw fit. He took his own dinner in his mother's rooms, although in truth, neither of them ate much.

The duchess swayed back and forth rhythmically, her dry eyes having already cried all their tears. "Perhaps it is not something a mother should say, but sometimes, almost, I would rather it had been you than him."

"Might I inquire why?" asked Henry, his *amour propre* a little wounded.

"I can hardly explain it...it's not because he was a better person than you—no, quite the opposite. He was a selfish man with little control over his passions. I take no pleasure in saying that, and I blame myself that I did not curb his nature more while he was still a child. But he was on the cusp of something—marriage. And if marriage and children cannot change a man, then what can? It was my one hope that his union with Miss Malcolm would bring about a reformation in him. But now...too late."

Henry pressed her hand. "I am sorry, Mother." He cleared his throat. "I suppose I can take that as a compliment then, that you do not consider me in need of a reformation."

She sighed. "I'm sure we're all in need of reforming in some way. But no, you're not in *dire* need." She planted a kiss on his forehead.

A knock sounded on the door, and one of the footmen entered. "My lady, your grace—the investigator from London is here."

"Investigator?" The duchess' dark gray eyebrows crinkled in concern. "Why? I thought Rufus' death was an accident?"

"Just a formality," said Henry, rising to leave the room. He paused, leaning one arm against the door frame. "It is possible, though, that he may want to ask you some questions, Mother. Are you well enough to speak to him?"

"Tomorrow I will be."

And Henry knew that was true. She had buried two husbands, and soon, one son, and she would carry on, her head held high, and do whatever was required of her.

Henry's boots beat a tattoo on the stairs. He found the investigator waiting in the entrance hall.

"Mr. Jacob Pevensey, your grace," said Hayward.

"Thank you for coming on such short notice," said Henry. "I admit, I did not expect you until tomorrow morning."

The slight, red-haired man smiled. "Sir Richard Ford at the London magistrates' office was eager for us to assist, and so I came on right away."

"Hayward, ask Mrs. Forsythe to ready a room," said Henry. He looked at the visitor appraisingly, trying to decide if the man was as competent as Stephen's father had claimed. "You must forgive me—I am not familiar with the normal procedures in such matters. Now that you are here, what do you need to do first?"

"Normally, I would speak with the magistrate and constable

in charge of the case. Your letter mentioned a Mr. Cecil. Is he still here?"

"No, I regret he has returned home for the night. He will come back in the morning."

"Then the morning will be the best time to get started." Pevensey cocked his head. "Or perhaps I might ask you a few questions tonight to familiarize myself with the people involved?"

"Yes, of course. Let us go to the study."

Henry led the way through the saloon and over to the dark-paneled study that was now his. The investigator sat down lightly in the chair opposite the desk and crossed one leg over the other.

"Well?" Henry did not mean to be abrupt—he simply thought it better to dispense with the pleasantries and relate to Jacob Pevensey as a man of business.

"Please acquaint me with the members of the family."

"There is my mother, the Duchess of Brockenhurst, in residence. My father, as you must know, has been dead three years or more."

Pevensey gave a slight nod and folded his hands in front of him.

"There is Robert Curtis, my mother's son by her first marriage."

"And Mr. Curtis is in residence?"

"Not permanently. He is here on a visit. And then there is my sister Adele—a permanent resident until such time as she weds." Henry paused. "That is the extent of the family."

"You leave out yourself," replied the investigator.

"I believe my existence is implied since you are speaking with me."

"But your residence is not, I think, permanent?"

"No, no, I reside in London."

"And you are here, as your brother Robert, on a visit to the late duke?"

Henry hesitated. "Yes." There did not seem to be any point in explaining that it was not the *duke* he had been visiting.

"Are there others visiting?"

"Yes, there is Walter Turold, whom I mentioned in my letter. There is Stephen Blount, a friend of the family. And there are Sir Arthur and Lady Malcolm and their daughter Miss Malcolm."

Pevensey's hands were still folded in his lap. Henry marveled that the man was not pulling out some notebook to jot down the details.

"You said in the letter that Mr. Turold takes responsibility for the shot that killed the duke?"

Henry inclined his head. "Indeed. He says he mistook the movement for a deer and fired unawares."

"And you believe him?"

They had moved out of the realm of fact into a scrutiny of Henry's insides. "I'm sure my belief is of no consequence. It is for you to discover whether his statement is true."

"I should not like to conjecture," said Pevensey, leaning forward in his chair a little, "but such an answer leads me to suspect that you do *not* believe him. *Why* not?"

Henry frowned. "You are very precipitate, Mr. Pevensey. I assure you I am simply keeping an open mind on the matter. It could very well have been an accident, as Turold says."

"Ah."

That single monosyllable made Henry feel as if *he* were on trial here. "Is there anything else you need to know tonight?" he demanded, trying to take charge of the conversation.

"Could you explain the relationship of the guests to the family? Why were they visiting?"

"Walter Turold was a friend of my brother's. They were inseparable—Walter always visited Harrowhaven anytime my brother did."

"Is Mr. Turold a man of property?"

"No, his late father lived roundabout on a small parcel of land, but I believe Walter converted it to ready money many years ago and has been living off of it ever since."

"And Stephen Blount."

"A friend of the family, as I said."

"Of which member of the family?"

"Of mine."

"But as you said, you are not in permanent residence here. Did Mr. Blount come down from London with you?"

"No. He is courting my sister, Adele, if you must know. Although I do not see how that is pertinent to your investigation." Henry was beginning to view these questions as an invasion of his family's privacy.

"Every detail helps to give me a fuller picture," said Pevensey smoothly. "And the Malcolms? Why were they visiting?"

Henry's collar felt much too tight around his neck. "They were visiting Rufus."

"Were they longstanding friends like Mr. Turold?"

"No." Such prying was beginning to be insufferable.

Pevensey paused. "Was this their first visit to Harrowhaven?"

"I do not know. I believe so."

"Is there anything you can tell me about the family?"

"No, I was not acquainted with them prior to last week."

Pevensey rose from his seat. "Thank you for your thorough explanation of the matter."

Henry could not tell whether there was a hint of irony on the word *thorough*.

"I will conduct interviews with the family and the guests in the morning. And might I also have your permission to interview the servants?"

"Of course," said Henry, rising from his own chair and walking toward the door. "One of the footmen can show you to your room."

Pevensey bowed. "Thank you, your grace." He lifted an eyebrow "It *is* 'your grace,' isn't it?"

Henry nodded, maintaining perfect control of his features. "Yes, the title devolved on me at my brother's death."

"Of course," said the investigator with a smile, and he disappeared down the corridor leading back to the saloon.

Henry clenched his right hand into a fist and hit it against the side of his leg. Stephen's father had been right—this fellow was good at his work. He would certainly get to the bottom of whether Rufus' death was accidental or intentional, but Henry feared he would also get to the bottom of other things as well....

———

PEVENSEY LAID OUT HIS CLOTHES for the next day across the back of the chair in his room. The housekeeper had ordered up a tray of chilled soup and cold meats for him, a kind gesture. He placed an exploratory hand on the bed and found a generous pile of down over the straw ticking. In his profession, he was used to being treated on the level of a tradesman, but here they were feting him almost as if he were a guest.

The footman who had brought him to his rooms, a friendly fellow by the name of Frederick, had proven remarkably more loquacious than the new duke. Pevensey, with very little trouble to himself, had learned the names of all the servants as well as some further information about the inmates of the house. The most startling piece of news? Miss Malcolm, the daughter of the family that Henry Rowland had mentioned, had apparently just entered a betrothal with the now-deceased duke.

Pevensey sat down on the edge of the chair and removed his boots, his feet enjoying the freedom after the long day in London and the hot ride to Harrowhaven. Why had Henry Rowland omitted this? What other matters had the new duke withheld from his attention? He was beginning to think that he ought to confront Henry Rowland regarding this misinformation before proceeding with the rest of the investigation.

Pevensey stood up to take off his jacket, taking care to remove his notebook and pencil from the pocket before laying the garment out neatly. There was a small table beside the chair, and he settled down to sketch. A picture of Henry Rowland soon materialized—dark, broad-shouldered, broad-featured, handsome in a way that women would find attractive. There he was leaning back in the chair behind the desk, masculine, confident, secure, as if the study in which he sat had always belonged to him.

From what the footman had said, Rufus Rowland could have been depicted in much the same manner, save for the fact that his hair was red, not brown. Two masterful men, little more than two years apart in age, yet divided by the vast gulf of primogeniture. Pevensey's inquiries in London had unearthed some interesting stories surrounding the Rowland inheritance—and the ill-feeling it occasioned. One brother, with the sole advantage of being born two years earlier, had obtained the title, the land, and the money that accompanied them. The other, nothing but the remote expectation that he might inherit if his brother died childless.

And Rufus *had* died childless—yet, seemingly, on the road to producing an heir. His marriage with Miss Malcolm would reportedly have taken place in short order, and if the lady were fertile, an heir might not have been far behind. Had Henry Rowland tried to catch the nearest way to wealth by eliminating his brother before it was too late?

Pevensey closed his notebook and laid it on the table. It was too early to tell. But as he fell asleep, his last thought was that there might be far more to this shooting than the word "accident" conveyed.

18

ELIZA DEBATED WHETHER TO COME DOWNSTAIRS FOR BREAKfast. Henry had said that an investigator was coming... surely, it was too early for him to have arrived already? She decided to chance it, and after Ollerton had laced up her blue morning dress, she glided down the corridor to the top of the stairs.

She remembered yesterday morning, when *he* had been there, waiting for her. She remembered her hand traveling down the banister toward his, and stopping just short of contact with him. She remembered his fingers reaching up to close the distance. "Do not marry my brother!"

There was no one standing at the foot of the stairs today, but Eliza caught her breath sharply to see a man standing on the landing. His back was to her, as he stared at the portraits on the wall. His bright red hair was the same color as Rufus'. For a moment she thought she was staring at a ghost. But no, he was smaller, much smaller—two of him could have fit inside of Rufus' frame.

The stranger turned around. He had seen her. She could hardly retreat quietly to her room now. Swallowing hard, she placed her hand on the banister and began to descend the stairs.

"Good morning!" said the intruder, his freckled face splitting into a smile. "You must be Miss Malcolm."

"I'm afraid you have the advantage of me, sir," she said, reaching the landing and finding herself an inch taller than him.

"Jacob Pevensey at your service. Attached to the magistrates' office in London."

"Oh, I see. You must be the investigator H—his lordship spoke of."

"Yes, exactly. I am especially hoping to speak to you this morning. I realize that it is a difficult time, but your words might be able to shed some light on this dark tragedy."

Eliza opened her mouth to reply, but a firm voice from the bottom of the stairs preempted her.

"Any questions can wait until Miss Malcolm has had her breakfast."

She looked down to see that Henry had entered the saloon.

"How thoughtless of me," said the investigator. "Of course, you are eager to break your fast. May I escort you to the dining room, and perhaps we can talk there? I will be taking the witnesses' official statements later, but there are just a few preliminary questions I wanted to ask you."

Flustered, Eliza took the arm that Mr. Pevensey offered and continued down the staircase with him. She could see Henry's eyes narrowing, but he turned and led the way to the dining room, throwing open the doors and pulling out a chair for her to sit down. Mr. Pevensey walked around the table and sat opposite to her while Henry walked over to the sideboard to fill a plate with food.

Eliza could see the investigator watching her, studying her. She dropped her eyes to the glaring white of the tablecloth. If only he would ask his questions and get it over with. She had nothing to hide except her fear of strangers. Henry gently placed a full plate in front of her, complete with fork and knife, and returned to the sideboard to fill another plate. Eliza's palpitating heart hoped that he was planning to sit down as well.

Whatever she was going to say to Mr. Pevensey could surely be said in front of Rufus' brother.

"Bacon, Pevensey?" Henry asked.

"Yes, thank you."

Eliza's face fell. Apparently, he was merely serving breakfast to the investigator. She watched him slide another full plate to the place across from her.

But then, instead of leaving the room, he pulled out a chair for himself and sat down. He was not eating, but he was also not leaving. He would not abandon her to face the investigator alone. "Well then, Pevensey?"

Mr. Pevensey's thin red eyebrows lifted, but he made no objection. It was surely not normal to have a chaperon of this kind, but he did not deny her the comfort of Henry's presence.

"Miss Malcolm, as I investigate the cause of the late Duke of Brockenhurst's passing, I must ask questions to everyone on the premises that day. Please answer me to the best of your ability."

"Oh, yes, of course," Eliza murmured. She gripped the handles of her fork and knife, having forgotten to take a single bite of her breakfast. She saw Henry place his right arm on the table and look intently at the investigator.

"How long have you been acquainted with the duke?" said Pevensey.

"About one month."

"Where did you first make his acquaintance?"

"In London, at a ball."

"And how quickly did your acquaintance progress?"

Eliza blushed.

"What I mean to say"—the inspector corrected himself—"is how well did you come to know him during the past four weeks?"

"I...I only knew him slightly. My father talked with him more than I did."

"Why did he ask your family to visit him at Harrowhaven?"

Eliza set down her silverware, hands shaking. Surely, he must already know the answers to these questions—otherwise, why would he ask them?

"Miss Malcolm?"

"I believe he wanted to improve our acquaintance."

"What day did you arrive here?"

"On Saturday."

"And how would you characterize the time that you spent with his grace during the past five days?"

How would she characterize it? Difficult. Uncomfortable. Demeaning. She glanced over to Henry, her green eyes begging for help.

Henry leaned forward. "Perhaps you are not aware, Mr. Pevensey, that my brother proposed marriage to Miss Malcolm the day before the sad event. They were engaged to be married."

"Oh, I beg your pardon, miss," said Pevensey, a glint of something inscrutable in his eyes. He looked at Henry. "Your grace failed to mention as much last night."

"It must have slipped my mind." Henry's voice was unapologetic.

The investigator's eyebrows lifted again. He took several bites of his eggs and bacon. "Miss Malcolm,"—he paused a moment to swallow—"now that we've reviewed your acquaintance with the late duke, perhaps you might enlighten me as to your acquaintance with the new duke. How long have you known this gentleman?" He pointed a fork at Henry.

Eliza's heart raced. How ought she respond to that? Under the table she felt a gentle pressure on her right slipper as Henry touched it with his boot.

"Oh! Mr. Rowland and I met in London ages ago." She smiled wanly.

"Ah, how interesting!" The investigator's eyes flicked back

and forth from Eliza to Henry. "I think, Miss Malcolm, that I shall postpone the rest of our interview until a time when we can be less encumbered by an audience."

Henry's lip curled up into a devilish smile, but Mr. Pevensey was no longer looking at him. He stood up and carried his plate, still half full, back over to the sideboard and placed it on the shelf below for dirty dishes. "Until later, Miss Malcolm." The redheaded investigator departed from the dining room to take his interviewing elsewhere.

Eliza and Henry sat in conspiratorial silence until they were sure that Mr. Pevensey had moved far out of earshot.

"Did I say the right thing?" Eliza asked anxiously.

Henry laughed. "Well, considering that I told him we had just met last week, probably not."

"Oh, Henry, how awful! He will think me a liar. I suppose I am one...."

"Not at all, my dear. I'm certain he thinks *I'm* the one telling taradiddles. Ah well—what does it matter? It's not as if this has anything to do with his investigation." He took her right hand in his and began to rub his thumb over the back of it.

"No, of course not," said Eliza. Her face turned pink all the way up to the roots of her auburn hair. She nearly drew away her hand, but the feel of his skin against hers was too compelling.

She *hoped* that his interest in her had nothing to do with the investigation....

"Elizabeth Malcolm!"

Standing in the open doorway was the stern and angry figure of Lady Malcolm. Eliza gasped and snatched her hand away from Henry's. Her mother advanced to her chair and pulled it back so she could rise from the table. Henry stood as well, a look of seriousness suffusing his face.

"Mr. Rowland," said Lady Malcolm, inserting herself between the offending gentleman and her daughter. "Please be aware that we are not interested in any further connection to your family. We will be leaving this place directly following the inquest—perhaps sooner if this kind of behavior continues."

"I beg your pardon, madam."

Lady Malcolm sniffed. "I forgive you, as I must, but do not think this means that I shall relax my vigilance. Come, Eliza, we shall read together for the remainder of the morning."

⁘

HENRY SAT DOWN AT THE table and raked his hands through his hair. He had been counting on Sir Arthur's avarice to advance his suit, but it seemed that Lady Malcolm might be the more formidable of Eliza's parents. And she—for some unexplainable reason—had taken a pet against him. He chided himself for losing control of his hands. How foolish of him to touch Eliza, and how unfortunate that her mother should enter just then. He had been forbidden—perhaps permanently—from entering Eliza's presence, and all his racing blood could think about was how much he desired to touch her skin again.

"I could not help but overhear...."

Drat! It was Pevensey again.

"Of course you couldn't," said Henry sharply. He frowned as the investigator entered the room and resumed his chair opposite him. He had hoped that the man would be off questioning the servants and viewing the scene of the death, but instead, he was skulking around the house and eavesdropping at the most inopportune moment.

"Your grace, I think it is time for plain speaking between us."

"I have always appreciated candor," said Henry, aware that he had exercised very little of that virtue in their previous conversation.

"I am aware that you were not on good terms with your brother."

"Who is your source for such information?"

"London."

"London is a very loud-mouthed woman. And you must be aware that her rumors are not always true."

"But in this case I find her information very persuasive. You received no inclusion, I think, in your father's will, while your brother received the title and the whole of the estate—"

"As is customary in our country," Henry interjected.

"Surely, it is more customary for the father to set aside something for a second son—perhaps money to buy an officer's commission in the cavalry, or money to secure a living in the church. Was your father so uncaring?"

Henry felt his craw stick in his throat. He had asked himself the same question more times than one, but he would not let his father's memory be demeaned by a stranger.

"My father *did* provide for me in the way he thought best. He established me as steward at Harrowhaven over the Rowland lands in Sussex with a substantial income that he thought would be enough for my needs."

"And yet, you are no longer steward here?"

"My brother and I had a falling out"—that term "falling out" hardly described the rage Rufus had shown when Henry confronted him about the matter of the Dower House—"and he elected to dismiss me from the post."

"And so you have even more reason to resent your brother. Penniless, cast off—"

"One could imagine so, but no. I fell on my feet." Henry refused to elaborate any further.

"There is still, though, the matter of Miss Malcolm. Your brother was about to marry her."

"Indeed."

"While you, it seems, have nursed a partiality for her for months."

"I have only just met Miss Malcolm."

"And yet she seems to be under the impression that she has known you for ages—and your own conduct not ten minutes ago would seem to confirm the...familiarity."

"What are you suggesting, that jealous of my brother's inheritance and his bride, I took the opportunity to murder him in the forest?"

"You must grant that you have the motive and, since you were a member of the hunting party, the opportunity."

Henry's fingers balled into a fist—he stopped his hand from pounding against the table. He had never entertained the notion that he himself would be considered a suspect in the case. But then, he really ought to have known—it was the first direction Eliza's mind had jumped when he visited her yesterday afternoon.

"And what of the fact that Walter Turold has confessed to shooting him?"

"Yes, that is the rub, isn't it? Is Mr. Turold such an inexperienced hunter then, that he would fire wildly at some movement in the bushes?"

It was Henry's previous falsehoods that had placed him in this precarious position, and as much as he wanted to say yes, he resolved to stick to the truth from now on. "No. He is an exceptional hunter. I would not expect him to make that sort of mistake."

"And does *he* bear any resentment towards your brother?"

Henry was silent. That subject—the subject of Catherine Ansel—was not a place where he was willing to let Pevensey tread about with his muddy boots and muck-raking fingers. "Why don't you ask him yourself?"

"I intend to," said Pevensey, "after I confer with the magistrate in charge about the case."

⁂

Pevensey went to the windows in the entrance hall where he could see Cecil's approach. After the Banbury stories the new duke had been telling him, he was eager to speak with an impartial witness—presuming that Cecil, as magistrate, was indeed impartial.

"Mr. Cecil gave me to understand that he would return at ten o'clock this morning, sir," said Hayward, the butler.

"Yes, very good. And is Mr. Cecil a punctual fellow?"

"I have never known him to be unpunctual."

Pevensey appreciated the butler's professionalism. "And would you describe him, Hayward, as especially friendly to the Rowland family, in particular to the new duke, Henry Rowland?"

Hayward pursed his lips. "No, I would not say so. They are much of an age and grew up here in the same part of the country, but Mr. Cecil had a sickly childhood, and he kept to his home while Master Rufus and Master Henry roamed the woods and the countryside."

"Whom did Master Henry play with then? His brother?"

"No, Mr. Pevensey. Master Rufus was often with his father, the old duke William Rowland. Master Henry, in his younger years, played with Mr. Turold and another boy from the village, a tavern-keeper's son."

Pevensey felt a jump of excitement at this new piece of information. "Are Mr. Turold and Henry Rowland still close?"

"No," Hayward put his hands behind his back. "They grew apart when Master Henry went to Eton. Mr. Turold is now closer...or should I say, *was* closer to Rufus Rowland. They shared certain proclivities...." And then, as if suddenly aware that he was sharing too much of the Rowland family business, the butler grew quiet and placed his hands behind his back.

Pevensey felt the trail had gone cold and did not press any

further. A few moments later he saw a slim young man dismounting near the steps. "This must be Mr. Cecil."

The man bounded rapidly up the stairs, rapped three times on the door, and was soon handing his beaver and gloves to Hayward.

"Jacob Pevensey at your service," said Pevensey with a nod.

"Excellent!" said the man, his enthusiasm as springy as the black curls covering his head. "I must tell you, Mr. Pevensey, I am delighted to learn from your expertise in this matter. Where do we begin?"

"I thought we might begin by taking your statement," said Pevensey, motioning towards the empty morning room. "You were there, were you not?"

"Indeed," said Cecil. "I was on the scene almost directly." He found a chair and, lifting up his coattails, sat down with alacrity.

"And dealt with the aftermath, I understand?" Pevensey took a seat opposite the young magistrate.

Cecil shrugged. "I was alarmed, as were the others. But someone had to manage the women...and deal with the body."

"Could you start at the beginning of the day yesterday, when you arrived for the hunt?" Pevensey pulled out his notebook, and Cecil had hardly begun his tale before his profile materialized on the page.

"Rowland organized a hunt and invited the whole neighborhood. I suppose I should specify *which* Rowland—it was Rufus. He's mad about hunting. Always has been. And when he sets up a shooting party, one goes, even when it's not one's favorite sport."

"As in your case," said Pevensey with a smile.

"Exactly. My sister Edwina was keener on it than I. She wanted to spend time with Lady Adele, I suppose, who's been in town all season—"

"So there were women who rode out with the hunt?" interrupted Pevensey.

"Yes. You'll want to know their names, to be sure." Mr. Cecil began to count off on his fingers. "There was my sister, Edwina Cecil, and then Miss Bertram, a neighbor, and Lady Adele, and Miss Malcolm. The Duchess of Brockenhurst, I believe, was indisposed and did not ride out that day. The ladies climbed aboard their mounts in the stable yard, but when we rode out into the woods, they took a different route—along the road, I believe—since none of them were armed, and their sole purpose was to watch."

"Which gentlemen attended the hunt?"

Mr. Cecil began to count on his fingers again. "There was myself, Rufus, Henry, Robert Curtis, Walter Turold, Sir Arthur Malcolm, Squire Ashbrook, his two sons, and...." He listed off three or four more gentlemen from the neighborhood. "We left the stable yard all in a pack with the hounds in front. There was a good deal of shouting and jesting about who would see the stag first."

"And did you continue in a pack?"

"No, and that is the queer thing. Usually, Rufus is up there at the front, and nine times out of ten, the kill is his. But yesterday, I lost sight of Rufus almost immediately. The hounds picked up the scent and we were all caught up in the thrill of the chase. I sighted a goodly pair of antlers up ahead, but he must have doubled back at the stream, for the hounds lost his scent there, and that is when we all split up, Henry off one way, Walter Turold off another. Squire Ashbrook and a few others decided to follow the water with the dogs, and Sir Arthur and I struck north to the road where we met up with the ladies."

"Go on," said Pevensey. It was a curious story, this tale of the scattered hunters, for if all was as Cecil said, then there would be more than one man without a confirmation of his whereabouts.

"We met the ladies at the road, and that is when we heard the first shot."

"There were more than one?"

"Yes, there were two."

"How far apart?"

"Five minutes, I would hazard. At the time, we conjectured that someone had wounded the stag and then fired a second shot to finish him off."

"And what do you conjecture now?"

Mr. Cecil sighed and rubbed the palms of his hands on his buckskins. "I'm not sure. Perhaps Rufus saw the stag, fired, and missed. And then Walter, thinking he saw the stag, fired and hit Rufus."

"Hmmm...." said Pevensey. His pencil had completed the black, corkscrew curls, and the frank, open eyes. "What did you do after hearing the shots?"

"The ladies were eager to see the kill—the stag, you understand, not the duke—and we headed into the woods after the first one. The second one came from farther away, and I bade them wait while I found the others so I could show them the proper trail."

"And when you came upon the scene?"

"Walter Turold was in a clearing, seated upon his horse looking down at the duke's body. The duke's horse was standing nearby. Turold's pistol was in his hand, and he looked over at me with a stare of absolute wretchedness on his face. 'I've shot him, Cecil,' he said. 'I thought he was the stag.'"

"And those were his exact words?"

"As far as I can recollect."

"Was the duke lying on his back or his front?"

"His back. His eyes were all glassy...I was certain with one look at him that he was dead."

"Did you get down from your horse and check?"

"Certainly, that was my first instinct. He had no pulse."

"Did Turold dismount as well?"

"No, Turold remained on his horse. He seemed to be in shock. I told him to give me his weapon, and he handed it over without a word. Curtis rode up then, and Ashbrook with his sons. And Henry came after a minute. I left the body with them and went back to warn the women away. Sir Arthur accompanied them to the house. I went back to the clearing. Henry had already sent Ashbrook to ride for the village to find the doctor and the constable. The church was nearby and I checked there and at the parsonage, but neither Ansel nor his curate were there."

"Did anyone answer?"

"No, nobody. Their housekeeper must have had the day off. I returned to the clearing then and Henry said that we must bring Rufus' body back to the house."

"Before the doctor or constable had seen it?"

"Yes. Was that wrong of us? I hope we did nothing improper. We laid the duke over the back of his horse and led the beast out to the road. And there was the carriage from Harrowhaven. Sir Arthur must have sent it when he returned to the house with the ladies. The groom helped us put the duke inside, and Henry drove the carriage."

"I see," said Pevensey. He wondered how many clues had been lost by this hasty shuttling of the body to another location. This Mr. Cecil certainly had zeal, but it was without adequate knowledge. "Where did the bullet hit the duke?"

"The back. The body is still here, I believe. It was in this very room yesterday, but no doubt they moved it somewhere more convenient. Would you like to see it?"

19

The servants, under Mrs. Forsythe's directions, had placed the corpse in the cellar—a rather macabre addition to the pickles and preserves but necessary given the summer's heat. The plan, Mrs. Forsythe told Pevensey, was to have it removed tomorrow for burial, but for now, it was under lock and key down below the house—the housekeeper being the one to hold the keys lest giddy housemaids become too curious.

Mrs. Forsythe stood solemnly at the door while Pevensey and Cecil examined the corpse. He was naked, except for a white sheet that had been thrown over him. The dead duke's skin was just as white as the sheet, a ghastly, uncanny whiteness that contrasted blindingly with his red hair. Pevensey motioned for Cecil to roll the body forward a little so he could see the wound.

The bullet had entered jaggedly beside the shoulder blade, at an angle it seemed, for after piercing the heart, it had come out through the side of the duke's pectoral muscle. "A well-positioned hit," said Cecil with a whistle.

Someone had taken the trouble to clean up the blood and dirt from the body. "Mrs. Forsythe," said Pevensey, "do you have the clothes that the duke was wearing?"

"I've sent them down to be laundered and mended," said the housekeeper, "and if his valet doesn't want them, they'll go to one of the footmen."

Pevensey's lips compressed into a thin line. Any clues the clothes could provide had probably been irrevocably destroyed. Nevertheless, he did not forget the wonders a polite smile could produce, and his face soon radiated friendliness once again. "Mrs. Forsythe, your industry is remarkable. I wonder, though, if perhaps you could send to the laundry and discover whether they have been thrown in the lye yet. I would love to see the stains if I might."

"Of course, Mr. Pevensey," said Mrs. Forsythe, surprised. She stepped outside the cellar to say a word to one of the staff.

"First rule of investigations," said Pevensey, giving a wink to Cecil. "Always get the housekeeper on your side."

"And second rule—never let the domestics tamper with the evidence," said Cecil. "My apologies."

"You're a fast learner, Cecil." Pevensey eyed the young man thoughtfully. In his experience, most gentry folk had as much common sense as a popinjay, but this fellow seemed determined to listen and learn.

"Is the shot consistent with Turold's story?" asked Cecil.

"Possibly." Pevensey eyed the exit wound one more time. "Although it has the appearance of something fired at closer range and not at a distance through a stand of brush and trees."

"The constable took a statement from Turold. He should be here shortly, and I've instructed him to bring both the statement and Turold's pistol."

Pevensey smiled. "I never use another investigator's notes. I'll need to take the statement again."

"Do you think his line of questioning will have been inadequate then?"

"Maybe. The important thing is to *see* the one you're questioning. It's not so much the things he says as the way he says them."

"Ah," said Cecil. "Well, I've cleared my schedule for the day—postponed meetings with tenants and tea with the

Bertrams—so if it is all the same to you, I would like to sit in on the statements."

"Commendable of you," said Pevensey with a twinkle in his eye, "for in the end, it's *you* that will have to recommend at the inquest whether there's enough evidence to send it up to the county assizes."

"Indeed," said Cecil gravely. "Where do we begin?"

"Servants first," said Pevensey. "They see and know far more than your class gives them credit for."

"*My* class." Cecil smiled. "And what class do *you* consider yourself, Mr. Pevensey?"

"Me? I am part of no class. I am invisible—only here when you do not want me and likely to be forgotten again as soon as I leave."

"I doubt that very much, Mr. Pevensey." Cecil adjusted the sheet over the corpse as they prepared to leave the cellar. "And after the servants?"

"The least likely suspects to the most likely."

"Why that order?"

Pevensey shut the cellar door behind them as they waited for Mrs. Forsythe to return with her keys. "Because by the time you get to the end, you'll know which questions are the ones you ought to be asking."

⁂

"I THOUGHT I MADE MYSELF clear," said Lady Malcolm stiffly. Eliza had been herded into her mother's sitting room and made to sit.

"Yes, Mama, you did."

"Apparently not clear enough."

"I was not intending to encourage him," said Eliza miserably.

"Not *intending*? Did he force you to take his hand?" Lady Malcolm's voice was cynical. "No, I thought not. A lady can always find a way to refuse unwanted attention. You did not. So clearly, the attention is not unwanted."

"Mama, that is unfair—"

"What has come over you? In London, you were as shy as a primrose. And now? You make eyes at men over your fiancé's dead body."

Eliza turned white with anger. "How dare you!" She jumped up from her seat. "I never wanted to marry Rufus Rowland. It was all Papa. And you! You said it would be for the best, and I went along with it, despite my heart."

"And where is your heart?"

"With Henry Rowland. Oh, Mama! If only you could come to know him. He is kind. He is gentle. He understands me as no one ever has."

Lady Malcolm's face was as taut as the strings of a violin. "Child," she said, "sit down and listen to me. When I was your age, I thought the same. I met a man who was warm, and tender, and more wonderful than any I had ever known. I had no mother's counsel to guide me, and what do you think I did? I married him."

Eliza fell back against the cushions of the chair and stared. Was this her father that her mother was speaking of?

"I married him in haste, and repented—yes, repented—it at leisure. Your father is faithful to me now, and we rub along together after a fashion, but our early years…oh, our early years were difficult. There were many dark nights of the soul where I did not care whether I lived or died. I would not wish that on you, child, and so I counsel you with all my soul against this Henry Rowland."

Eliza clutched one of the cushions convulsively. The revelation of her father's infidelities was astonishing to her, but so was the comparison that her mother was trying to draw. "How do you know that Henry is like Papa? He is not! He is nothing like him."

Lady Malcolm gnawed her lower lip. "Ollerton has made some inquiries among the staff about him. Something you said spurred her on to do so. It seems that the housekeeper has forbidden the maids to speak to him. They did not say why, but they mentioned a girl named Jenny with whom he was friendly on his last visit. After he left, she disappeared suddenly and took a coach for London. She has not returned."

Eliza's breath came more quickly. "A coincidence!"

"Is it?" said Lady Malcolm. She gave a sniff. "I can think of only one explanation for such an occurrence, but perhaps you are too innocent to understand. Now is not the time for innocence but for shrewdness. Think back to all you have observed of him—is there nothing that gives you pause?"

It was Eliza's turn to gnaw on her lower lip. It was almost as if her mother knew—knew about that nagging doubt in the back of her mind, that sordid memory of Henry Rowland stroking the blond maid's arm and giving her his handkerchief. It was a memory she had dismissed—a memory too inconvenient and inconsistent with her own desires to be true. But now, with this further news from Ollerton, her suspicions seemed to be instantly and irrevocably confirmed.

"Oh, Mama!" she moaned and, without offering an explanation, burst suddenly into tears. It was a complete and utter surrender.

"There, there, my child," said Lady Malcolm, coming near and putting her arms around Eliza. She lifted Eliza's chin and brought her eyes on a level with her daughter's. "Then we are agreed, yes? You will stay clear of Henry Rowland until we can remove ourselves from this house?"

"Yes," said Eliza dully. "I will do as you say, Mama."

"See that you do this time," said Lady Malcolm, and letting go of her daughter's chin, she leaned over to the table and found a book of sermons for them to read aloud.

Pevensey arranged three chairs around a table in the morning room while Cecil secured some ink to take notes in a little book on the process about to unfold.

The servants came in by turn, with either feigned trepidation or obvious curiosity. "Where were you yesterday morning?" was the first question Pevensey asked each of them. "And who can corroborate your story?"

Three of the footmen had been engaged in laying out the luncheon tablecloths and centerpieces under the temporarily erected pavilion near the rose garden. The butler Hayward vouched for their presence since he had been directing them.

"Did you know of any unpleasantness between the duke and Mr. Turold?"

None of the three had seen or heard anything of the kind. Pevensey expected that when it came time for the housemaids, they would prove more imaginative.

A fourth footman, the loquacious Frederick, informed Pevensey that he had been absent the day of the hunt. He had gone a half a day's walk north of the village to his mother's house to celebrate his sister's wedding. She had married the baker from the village, and Frederick was looking forward to free buns from his new brother-in-law.

"And was this your usual day off?" Pevensey asked.

"No, sir," said Frederick. "I had special permission from the duke to be gone on Wednesday. I heard the sad news on the road late last night while I was on my way back to Harrowhaven."

"Prior to this, had you heard of any unpleasantness between the duke and Mr. Turold?"

"With Mr. Turold? No."

Pevensey caught Cecil's eye. Here was something to be explored.

"Perhaps some unpleasantness between the duke and someone else?"

Frederick shuffled his feet. "I might have been listening when I oughtn't, but when I walked past the study on Tuesday night, I heard voices arguing."

"Whose voices?" asked Cecil, leaning forward with interest.

"The duke, for one."

"And the other?" said Pevensey.

"I wouldn't stake my mother's life on it, but I think 'twas Mr. Curtis."

"And what did you overhear?"

"The man who sounded like Mr. Curtis was saying, 'By God, you have to give me more time. This is unfair!' And the duke said something like, 'You've had time enough. I intend to take possession of the place tomorrow.'"

"And did Mr. Curtis say anything else?"

"I couldn't quite hear it all, but I thought he said something about how even a Jew would be kinder."

"And then?"

"And then I heard Mr. Hayward coming and took to my heels so he wouldn't see me neglecting my duties and eavesdropping on my betters."

Cecil was scribbling notes furiously while Pevensey, notebook close to his chest, sketched a cheerful profile of the footman with his ear against a door. After discerning that Frederick had no more information, they dismissed him and bade the butler in the hallway wait a moment before sending in the next servant.

"What do you make of that?" asked Cecil. His black eyes were alive with interest.

"Robert Curtis is the half-brother, you said?"

"Yes, the Duchess of Brockenhurst's son by a previous

marriage. He's not at all like the other brothers—a preening peacock if I've ever seen one."

"Was the duchess' first husband untitled?"

"Yes, untitled, but he left Robert a pretty estate in Kent, a few hours' ride from here."

"Was Mr. Curtis indebted to his brother Rufus?"

"*That* is the question, isn't it?" Cecil rubbed his chin thoughtfully. "It looks like we are beginning to see *which* questions we ought to ask."

Pevensey beamed. "We'll make a detective out of you yet, Cecil." He was still irritated with Sir Richard for forcing him to ride out to Sussex in the August heat, but he must admit that this case was proving more interesting than he had expected, and he had never realized before what a pleasure it would be to disciple such an apt pupil in his unusual trade.

⁂

HENRY RETREATED TO THE STUDY to take his mind off the events of the past hour. Not only had Lady Malcolm forbidden him to go near her daughter, but the investigator also suspected him of involvement in Rufus' death! Growling under his breath, he began to tidy up the papers on the desk. This was his room once again, and here at least he could have things the way he wanted them. He squared up the inkwell and a neatly trimmed pen on the right corner of the desk. Next, he found the seal with which he had stamped the letters only yesterday and placed it on the middle finger of his left hand.

"Your grace," said Hayward with a gentle knock on the open door. "Reverend Ansel is here to see you."

The soft syllables of the Reverend's name came as a sharp surprise. Henry started visibly before recovering control of his countenance. "I'm not at home, Hayward."

"Yes, your grace," said the butler. It could have been Henry's imagination, but he thought he glimpsed a fleeting glance of disappointment on the old retainer's lined face.

Henry swallowed. Not at home? It was the excuse Rufus would have used to avoid being harangued by the minister about his responsibilities to the parish. Henry had made enough of his own excuses while he was steward at Harrowhaven to avoid encountering Reverend Ansel. It was time to be done with such folly. He was the duke of Brockenhurst now. He must take his fears and look them in the face.

"Hayward!"

The retreating butler turned around. "Yes, your grace?"

"I was mistaken. You may show him in."

Hayward bowed his head perfunctorily, but Henry could see that he was pleased.

Within seconds, Reverend Ansel came barreling through the study door, the energy in his red face permeating the room like the heat from a fire. He sneezed a few times into his sleeve, great, herculean sneezes that shook his large frame, and blinked back the tears forming in his eyes, the product of a summer's cold.

"Henry!" he said, pumping the young man's hand. "It has been too long. My curate tells me you were at services on Sunday, but I missed seeing you."

"Yes, a pity," said Henry, his voice catching in his throat as if he were still a young lad growing into a man. "Won't you have a seat?"

"I'm so very sorry, my boy," said Reverend Ansel, taking the chair opposite the desk. "So very sorry about your brother."

"Thank you," said Henry.

"Do they know what happened?"

"Walter Turold asserts that he fired accidentally, mistaking Rufus for a stag in the bushes."

The Reverend pulled a handkerchief out of his pocket. "Dear me." He blew his nose loudly. "What will happen now?"

"There's an investigation pending—a man up from London to help Cecil and the constable look into things. They need to evaluate if it was in fact an accident. If so, I expect things will go no further, and the matter will be laid to rest with Rufus."

"And…Walter?"

"Will simply have to carry the burden of mistakenly ending my brother's life."

"Poor soul," said Reverend Ansel, shaking his head. He blew his nose again. Henry noted that the clergyman seemed deeply distressed about the matter—that, or deeply distressed by his malady.

"The shooting took place quite near the church," said Henry. He leaned forward on his elbows.

"Yes, that's what I hear," said the Reverend. "I went up the road to Dealsby Cross to perform a wedding there yesterday. I preach there once a month since the post is vacant. My curate is hopeful the living will fall to him, but we shall see…."

Henry's curiosity finally got the better of his reticence. "I hope no one else in your household was too alarmed by the shot?"

"No, no, not at all," said the Reverend. "We hear poachers shooting quite often in our part of the woods…although I probably ought not to be saying that to you, the new duke!"

"Never fear. I am not as jealous of my sport as my brother was. It is rather fitting, in a way, that he should leave this world while riding out to hunt."

"May the Lord have mercy," said the Reverend quietly. He rose from his chair. "I shall offer my condolences to your mother, if I may. And then…is it permitted that I visit Walter Turold? The man must be beside himself with grief."

"He is keeping to his room, but he is not in confinement. His grief, if it exists, must be a stoic one, for he shed no tears yesterday following the event."

"The absence of tears does not necessarily mean the absence of sorrow," said the Reverend. "A heart can brim with remorse on the inside while the outside man remains silent."

"Very true, Reverend," said Henry, a catch in his throat. He stood up in respect as the Reverend quitted the study. Then, alone again in his sanctum, he sat back down in his chair and leaned back to stare at the ceiling, acutely aware that Reverend Ansel's last statement could have been talking about him just as much as about Walter Turold.

20

As the maids entered to be interviewed one by one, the housekeeper stood by the threshold of the room to exhort each maid to mind her tongue and answer the gentlemen's questions with no silliness.

"If you please, sir," said the first maid, a pretty, young blonde, "Mrs. Forsythe asked me to give you these." The girl handed over a wrinkled pile of clothes to Pevensey.

"Not been through the lye yet?" said Pevensey with excitement.

"No, sir, though I did put some lemon juice on the bloody patches."

Pevensey gave the girl a rewarding smile and walked over to a small table to spread out the clothes. "Mr. Cecil, if you would be so good as to conduct the interview while I examine these."

"Certainly," said Cecil. Pevensey had been afraid that he would hem and haw over being thrust into the helm so soon, but the man was a quick study and confident in his own powers. "What is your name, miss?"

"Constance," replied the maid.

Pevensey examined the dark spots on the clothing where the blood had seeped onto the shirt and the jacket. There were no powder burns on the jacket, indicating that the bullet had been fired from at least a few yards away. The majority of the blood was on the back of the clothing, but when Pevensey saw the front, he noted something curious.

"Did you notice anything unusual on the morning of the duke's dea—"

"Cecil!" Pevensey interrupted. "Did you drag the body on the ground when you moved it to the carriage?"

"No," said Cecil, his black eyebrows lifting in surprise. "There were plenty of men there by that time. They lifted him onto his horse and we led it to the road."

"Hmm...very interesting," said Pevensey. He pulled out his notebook and began a sketch. "Carry on, carry on," he said to his assistant.

"Of course," said Cecil, recovering his aplomb. "And now, Constance, was there any unpleasantness between the duke and...well, and anyone?"

The maid hesitated. "I don't know as I could say, sir. But I'm sure if there was, it was entirely the duke's fault."

Pevensey's ears perked up as Cecil continued the questioning. "It seems that you did not care for your master, Constance. Any particular reason why?"

There was a pause. "No, sir," said the maid, her tone verging on sullenness.

"Very well then," said Cecil. "Anything else from you, Mr. Pevensey?"

"No," said Pevensey, "that will be all. Thank you, Constance." He watched the maid bustle out of the room and drew a quick sketch of her profile. She was a pretty young woman— the kind that sometimes attracts too much attention from an employer. Pevensey drew a shadow lurking behind her.

"Was there something important about the clothing?" asked Cecil, breaking in on Pevensey's thoughts. He was fingering the jacket and had stuck his finger through the bullet hole in the back of it.

"I'm not sure yet," said Pevensey, his eyes looking back over the dead man's garments. While the back of the coat was covered with only a soft spray of dust, the front of the coat was caked with a thick layer of red dirt.

◦◦◦

DISMISSED FROM HER MOTHER'S ROOM at last, Eliza returned to her own room. She sat down hard on the sofa and felt a book beneath her. From underneath her skirt, she pulled out *Pamela* and threw it against the wall. It fell open on the ground, its pages fluttering in the air like a wounded butterfly. Eliza turned her face away. She would not indulge in self-pity. She must control herself.

From the door came a timid knock. "Eliza? Are you there?"

Eliza choked back the tears that were starting to form and, instead of weeping, opened the door. Adele was standing in the hallway, her own face streaked with tears. "Oh, dear! Come in," said Eliza, putting her arm around the girl. Apparently the shock of losing Rufus had not worn off yet.

Eliza led Adele over to the sofa where they sat down together. "I am so sorry, Adele. It must be horrible to lose a brother...."

"Oh, yes...." Adele sniffed back some of her tears. She looked away from Eliza.

Eliza swallowed. Perhaps this intrusion was the grace she needed to distract her from her own misery. "Do you want to talk about it?"

"Well, I don't know...the thing is...."

Eliza waited.

"It's just that Rufus dying is so horribly inconvenient!"

Eliza blanched. "Inconvenient?"

"Yes! I shall be in blacks for six months or more—no parties or balls once the season starts up. And if Stephen *did* propose, we should have to postpone the wedding till we were out of mourning. And even more horrible—perhaps I won't be allowed to marry him now? Rufus never cared what I did, but Henry will be much stricter. I don't think he approves of me and Stephen."

"I thought you weren't sure yourself about Mr. Blount?"

"Of course I'm sure about him. But it wouldn't be ladylike to say such a thing until he actually offers for me, would it? Anyhow, Mother told me it's horrid to be thinking about such things right now, but I can't help it." Adele blew her nose on her handkerchief. "I'm sorry to turn into such a watering pot. I suppose Rufus dying is inconvenient for you as well."

"I had not exactly thought of it in that way." Eliza reflected that it had actually been the other way around. Rufus' death had seemed entirely fortuitous since it left her free to look elsewhere—and she had, until her mother had made her examine Henry's character more deeply.

"Oh, you know," said Adele, "the chance to get new dresses and get away from your fusty parents."

Eliza flinched.

"But, dear me! I am a rattle-trap. Did you love Rufus?"

Eliza saw no harm in telling the truth. Indeed, nothing she said could be as indiscreet as Adele's emotions. "No, I didn't love him."

"I didn't think so. You seemed so...scared around Rufus. I could hardly imagine you eating breakfast across from him every day. Or having children with him!"

"Adele, please!" Eliza stood up from the couch and walked over to the window, her face as red as the late August roses in the garden below.

"Oh, Eliza, I'm sorry!" Adele jumped up and hurried to her side. "I did not mean to vex you." Her pleading brown eyes could almost make Eliza forget her outrageous comments. "Was there someone else?"

Eliza hesitated. Someone else? Only the phantom of someone that had never truly existed except in her own mind. "No, no one else."

"Are you certain?" Adele took Eliza's hand and pressed it. "Because I thought perhaps, maybe, you might have had a *tendre* for Henry before Rufus came along. There seemed to be something between you, the same something that there is between me and Stephen, a *je-ne-sais-quoi* that was not there between you and Rufus."

"Or perhaps, your brother Henry is simply a prodigious flirt." Eliza felt warm all over. She seized a fan off of the end table and waved it briskly in front of her face. She did not want to hear about him anymore.

Adele threw her head back and laughed. "Henry? 'Pon rep! I should think not. Did you see him give Miss Ashbrook a set-down the other night when she would not leave him alone?"

"Yes, well, even so...perhaps he is different when he is in town."

"Unlikely," said Adele. "He attended my coming-out ball at our house in Grosvenor Square, even though Rufus refused to allow me to send him an invitation, and I can tell you he was in no way popular with the ladies. I think he spent more time talking to Mother's friends than he did mine!"

"Why were matters so strained between your brothers?"

"I don't know exactly. I was still in the schoolroom when the big quarrel happened. I believe it had something to do with the Dower House though. And whatever it was, I know that Mother took Henry's part."

"So it was nothing untoward on Henry's part?"

"Goodness, no. The servants were very upset at his banishment. Hayward and Mrs. Forsythe went about all tight-lipped for nearly a month, and the whole house felt shrouded in gloom."

Eliza's brow creased. Here was a very different picture of

Henry's relationship to the servants than what Ollerton's inquiries had painted.

"Eliza! Look!" Adele pressed her face against the glass.

Eliza's room was on the side of the house facing the garden, but from the window, they could see part of the circular drive and the stable yard. A coach had just pulled up to the stables tethered to a fancy pair of perfectly matched blacks.

"Who is that?" asked Eliza, unsure as to the significance of the apparition.

"I don't know," said Adele, "but we must find out!"

Following in Adele's footsteps, Eliza walked, rather more quickly than was elegant, down the corridor and the staircase. As they entered the saloon, they could hear Hayward in the entry way speaking in stern tones.

"I am sorry, madam, but you are not welcome here."

"Oh, Hayward, don't be ridiculous," said a woman's voice, both sultry and snide at the same time.

Adele and Eliza halted and exchanged glances.

"Run along and tell your new master that I am here."

"I regret that the duke is not at home."

"The duke!" The mysterious visitor burst into a peal of laughter. "I suppose he *has* moved up in the world."

Adele started edging closer, eager to get a glance at this uncouth intruder. Eliza saw someone entering the saloon from the opposite door, however, and put her hand on her friend's shoulder to stay her progress.

Henry walked past the two girls without acknowledging their presence. "Hayward," he said. "It is all right. I will receive Mrs. Flambard in the study."

"You heard the man," said Mrs. Flambard, laughing again, and in a few seconds she was traipsing through the saloon in Henry's wake. Eliza had expected an imposing woman but was surprised to see that Mrs. Flambard was a girlish blonde with large blue eyes and an innocent, heart-shaped face. She was dressed in a very low-cut blue muslin, with a small hat mounted atop her blond curls. She looked over at Eliza and Adele, where they stood frozen against the wall of the saloon, and dropped them a wink. Then, without a word, she disappeared down the hallway, following Henry.

"Come in, Mrs. Flambard," they heard Henry say.

It was followed by a trilling laugh. "Oh, please, Henry! We know each other far too well for such formalities. Do you remember these pearls? You paid the bill for them...." The study door shut on the voices, and the two girls looked at each, wide-eyed.

Eliza exhaled, finally remembering to breathe. "Who *is* that?"

"I have no idea," said Adele, "but I'm dying to find out."

Eliza's own curiosity could not outweigh the sinking feeling in the pit of her stomach. A mysterious woman with pearls from the new duke? Here was yet another proof that Henry Rowland's character was far more enigmatic than upright.

THE OTHER HOUSEMAIDS HAD PROVIDED little more information about the events of yesterday; however, they did provide some curious insights into household affairs at Harrowhaven. "His grace used to disrespect Mrs. Forsythe all the way to Brighton and back," said one bright-eyed brunette, "when she came to him with the menu or a change in staffing."

"Was not the Duchess of Brockenhurst in charge of such things?" asked Pevensey.

"Well, she were...but, I don't know exactly when it happened, but then she weren't anymore."

"I see," said Pevensey, although the picture was still not entirely clear. There must have been a falling out between mother and son. He had already established a falling out between Rufus and his elder half-brother and a quarrel between Rufus and his younger brother. The whole family was seemingly at loggerheads.

After the brown-haired maid left, Pevensey queried Cecil. "Did you know anything of this, a rift between the duke and his mother?"

"No, not at all," said Cecil. "But then the duchess is hardly one to air such things in public. A true lady if I've ever seen one."

They sat down to partake of a luncheon and fortify their spirits for the next round of questioning. It was at this point that the constable, for whom they had been waiting all morning, finally arrived, a gray-haired man in a gray suit, carrying a satchel.

"This is Constable Cooper," said Cecil, motioning to a nearby chair. "He took Turold's statement and his weapon yesterday."

"Goodness, yes," said the constable. "Would you like to see it?" He dug into his pocket and brought out his notebook.

"The weapon, yes," said Pevensey. "I can guess what lies in the statement well enough."

"Oh, well, in that case...," said Constable Cooper, crestfallen. He opened the satchel and took out a pistol. It was made of walnut with a single chamber, silver fittings, and the engraved initials "R.R."

Pevensey picked it up and examined it. "It's clean."

"Of course!" said the constable. "My old father brought me up to take care of my firearms."

"Yes," said Pevensey, trying to stem the flood of growing irritation welling up in his breast, "but the point is that this is not *your* firearm. It is evidence. Had this pistol been discharged when you received it?"

"It certainly had been." He proffered the notebook again. "You can see in Mr. Turold's statement that he says—"

"Quite." Pevensey handed the weapon to Cecil. The black-haired gentleman offered him an apologetic smile. Pevensey suspected that the young magistrate might be learning to curb Constable Cooper's enthusiasm in future cases.

"What does the engraving mean on this weapon?"

Cecil ran a finger over the initials. "I suppose the 'R.R.' must stand for 'Rufus Rowland.' Perhaps Turold borrowed one of Rufus' pistols for the hunt."

Pevensey pulled out his own notebook and made a quick sketch of the weapon.

"If this weapon was taken from Mr. Turold, where is the duke's pistol?"

Cecil and the constable looked at each other. The constable scratched his head. "I couldn't rightly say, Mr. Pevensey."

"It was not on the body?"

"No," said Cecil, thoughtfully. "It was not. I did not think to look around for it at the time."

An interesting possibility began to form in Pevensey's mind. "And you are certain there were two shots?"

"Yes, with a few minutes elapsing in between." Cecil looked at him pointedly, but Pevensey was not ready to elaborate.

"That gun has only one chamber," the constable pointed out.

"Indeed," said Pevensey, "so one of the shots was fired by somebody else. We must scour the forest, Cecil, to search for the missing weapon. And do not publicize the lack beforehand. It's possible there's a reason that the duke's pistol was not with his effects."

༺⁂༻

HENRY GRITTED HIS TEETH. HIS brother had barely been dead twenty-four hours before the carrion crows were descending. Mrs. Flambard had been friendly—too friendly—at first, but when he refused to give her an advance on the bequest she was expecting, her girlish face turned ugly. "I shall make such a scene that you'll be sorry!"

"Do as you must," Henry said, and taking her arm firmly, he escorted her down the corridor, through the saloon, and to the entrance hall. "Hayward, please see that Mrs. Flambard makes it to her carriage without mishap."

Mrs. Flambard's blue eyes narrowed into slits and Henry would not have been surprised to see a forked tongue shoot out between her perfect pink lips. But the promised scene did not materialize, and Hayward managed to herd her out the front door with the aplomb of an experienced butler.

Henry turned around to see that he was under scrutiny from more than one individual. Adele and Eliza were exhibiting a feigned interest in the pictures on the walls of the adjacent saloon, and the Bow Street Runner, Cecil, and the constable, had just exited the morning room and were coming down the corridor.

"Where are you off to?" asked Henry, seeing Cecil pick up his beaver.

"A ride. Care to join us?"

Henry glanced over to the saloon where Adele was tensing like a housecat ready to pounce. There would be a barrage of questions coming from that quarter. Right beside her was Eliza, studiously looking away from him, her face as grave as an undertaker's. Henry wondered if it were best to take cover for the present.

"Certainly I will join you." He beckoned for one of the footmen to fetch his own beaver.

Out on the steps, the gentlemen saw the visiting carriage with its blond occupant pulling away around the circular drive.

Cecil's dark eyes squinted. "Is that—?"

"Yes," said Henry. He saw Pevensey looking at him with that uncanny, measuring stare of his. "My late brother's bird of paradise," he said gruffly.

"She didn't seem particularly distraught," said Pevensey. A hint of a smile played beneath his freckles.

"They parted ways several months ago. She came to see if there was anything for her in the will."

"And is there?"

"I don't know. It's still with the solicitor in London. But I imagine not. Rufus was never sentimental about his Cyprians."

"She made good time," said Cecil, going down the steps two at a time. "The news has traveled fast." Pevensey and Henry followed suit, with the constable trailing behind them at a slower pace.

At the nearby stables, Gormley and Martin were sitting outside in the shade of the overhanging roof. The sun had approached its summit, and the day had just begun to reach an uncomfortable level of heat. The gentlemen entered the stables and let their horses out of the boxes to saddle them.

"Where are you off to, your grace?" asked Gormley, standing up in confusion. Henry could see that he was agitated to have the gentlemen leading out their beasts themselves.

"A good question!" said Henry with a shrug. "Cecil?"

His curly-haired neighbor grinned and gave a vague wave in the direction of the church. "The woods!"

Gormley grunted and returned to his chair. Silent Martin, mending a harness that had frayed, never looked up from his work.

They departed in the same direction the hunt had taken, Cecil leading the way, Pevensey falling in beside Henry, and Constable Cooper bringing up the rear. The trees had grown from when Henry was a boy, but he could still recognize all the pieces and paths of the forest with no more than a cursory glance.

They reached the fork in the path where Rufus had first disappeared from the group and where the nagging fear had first begun to claw at Henry's throat. They passed the gulch where the stag had dipped his feet in the water, a deep ravine that always made Henry's skin crawl cold even in the heat of August. It was here that Henry had noticed that Turold had split off from the others too, and it was here that Henry had struck out on his own to find the missing riders.

Cecil continued to advance. Henry could see now that they were going to the clearing, the place where Rufus' body had been discovered. He ought to have expected as much. The red-haired Runner was nothing if not thorough—he would want to view the location.

"I'm keeping a sharp eye out for it," called the constable from the rear.

"Very good, Mr. Cooper," said Pevensey. Henry had the uncanny feeling that Pevensey's sharp eyes were more on himself than on the woods. He straightened his back and clenched his knees against the saddle.

They were at the clearing now. Pevensey urged his horse forward into the middle of it. He looked around. "Where exactly did you find the body?"

Cecil's horse nosed forward as his rider hesitated. The grass in the clearing, shaded from the full sun by the surrounding trees was uniformly green. There was no stain of dried blood to identify the death, no cross to note the passing of a soul. Even the grass blades crushed by Rufus' bulk had recovered their spring. Cecil scratched one of his black sideburns in puzzlement.

While Cecil cudgeled his memory, Henry took charge of the matter—much as he had yesterday when there was a dead body to be dealt with. He dismounted and walked about a third of the way into the clearing. "The body was here when I arrived. You hadn't moved it, had you, Cecil?"

"No, not at that point."

Pevensey dismounted as well, and walking over to where Henry stood, he knelt down on the green carpet and ran his hands over it. Then, standing, he bent down to brush off his trousers, but the clean grass had left barely a speck of dust upon them. He pulled out his notebook, and Henry saw his pencil make wide, swooping strokes as he noted his observations.

Then, closing the book, the Runner lifted his chin and raised his voice. "Constable Cooper, Mr. Cecil, let us make a perimeter and search for the weapon." They spread out, about two yards apart, and began to methodically comb the clearing. A few minutes' search yielded no results, and they expanded their examination to the trees surrounding the clearing.

Henry, feet planted apart, watched their endeavors with a creased brow. "I thought Turold turned over the gun already."

"That he did," said Constable Cooper, "but it's the other gun we're looking for. The duke's. Mr. Pevensey pointed out that it was missing from the body."

"They were a matched set," said Henry. "Rufus said at dinner that, for the hunt, he would give one to Turold and keep the other for himself."

"Indeed?" said Pevensey, from about twenty yards away. His head popped out above a stand of bushes. "Then we know exactly what we're looking for."

But despite this knowledge, the search proved uneventful. Henry added his eyes to the expedition, and between the four of them, they covered a large swathe of ground surrounding the clearing. But after two hours, the only objects they had found lurking on the floor of the forest were stumps and roots.

"And now, Mr. Pevensey?" asked Cecil, as they returned to their horses, shirts damp from their exertion in this heat.

"Now," said Pevensey, "we promulgate the news that the gun is missing." The others acted disappointed at the fruitless search, but Pevensey's freckled face seemed almost pleased that the pistol had failed to materialize. His eyes twinkled in Henry's direction. "You wouldn't mind sharing the word with Mr. Turold, would you, your grace?"

Henry wiped the beading sweat off of his brow. "Certainly." This Runner was up to something, but he could not quite put his finger on what that something was. "I take it that since you're soliciting my assistance, you no longer suspect me of doing away with my brother?"

"Oh, I've ruled nothing out yet." Pevensey's smirk bordered on supercilious. "But all the same, I'd be obliged for your help."

21

Vexed that her quarry had escaped, Adele waited in the entrance hall for a full quarter of an hour in case Henry should return.

Anxious to avoid any further encounters with Henry Rowland, Eliza begged her friend to come away to the drawing room, but Adele would not be dissuaded. When it became apparent that Henry's return was not imminent, Adele summoned the butler and began to ply him with questions.

"Who was that woman, Hayward?"

"A Mrs. Flambard, my lady."

"Yes, but who *is* she?"

"I am not certain of her social standing."

"Come now, Hayward. You cannot cut shams with me. I know you have seen her before."

"I regret I have no further information to share." Hayward's face hardened like concrete.

"Oh, very well then," said Adele in a huff. She murmured something about a proper butler being more of a disappointment than an advantage. Eliza blushed for her friend and dragged her off to the drawing room.

It was not long before Stephen Blount joined them. "Would it be improper to suggest piquet?" he asked, no doubt sensing that distraction was needed.

"Not at all," said Adele. She had made it abundantly clear that it would take more than a death in the family to sate her appetite for amusement. Or perhaps that was too harsh a judgment. Some people's way of coping with grief was to ignore it so it would not tear them apart.

Adele took a seat at the table as Stephen prepared the deck of cards for the two-player game. "You do not mind, Eliza?"

"No," said Eliza, grateful that Mr. Blount had relieved her from her duty of consoling Adele and delighted that an interest in piquet had replaced Adele's interest in Mrs. Flambard. "I shall be happy to sit and watch."

Mr. Blount dealt the cards and the game began. It did not take more than one round to see that the distraction was less than perfect. "Have you ever met a Mrs. Flambard, Stephen?"

"Hmm...." He exchanged a pair of cards for better ones. "I don't think I have. Friend of yours?"

"Not of mine," said Adele, laying down her hand and claiming victory. "Of Henry's. You don't know her?"

"Can't say that I do." Stephen tallied up her points on a little sheet he was using to keep the score. "Henry moves in far more circles than I do."

And what circles would those be? Considering Mrs. Flambard's provocative appearance, Eliza was not sure that she wished to know.

"Show your cards," said Adele, ready to see who had won that round. Mr. Blount smiled at her impatience and obliged. Eliza noticed that his smooth face was actually quite handsome when he smiled. Not in the same dark, masculine way that Henry Rowland was, but.... She dug her fingernails into her palms. She must stop thinking such thoughts.

The game of piquet progressed slowly. And when it was finished, Adele suggested another. After an hour or more, Eliza excused herself and slipped out into the corridor. It was afternoon now—she would retire to her room and take a rest. She heard voices in the entrance hall once again, and tiptoeing closer, she saw Hayward conversing with a bearded man who had just entered and removed his hat.

"What do you mean coming round to the front, Ned?" Hayward was as stern as a night watchman.

"No barrels to give ye today," said Ned. "I've a message for Master Henry."

"The *duke* is not at home."

"Not at home, or *not at home?*" asked Ned, a twinkle in his eye.

"Both."

"Well, God's bones, Hayward, I'll sit and wait for him." And without receiving an invitation, Ned plopped down on the bench, leaned back against the wall, and crossed his arms over his chest.

Eliza saw Hayward give a lengthy frown and then, folding his hands behind his back, walk away towards the kitchen. He might disapprove of Ned Hornsby's presence in the entrance hall, but he was not going to take measures to forbid it.

She headed for the staircase at the end of the saloon, but the swish of her skirt must have caught Ned's eye. He jumped up from the bench and, hat in hand, hurried over to intercept her.

"Miss Malcolm! A pleasure to see you again."

Eliza halted. "Thank you, Mr. Hornsby."

"Have you seen Henry?"

Eliza swallowed. It was presumptuous of this fellow to assume she knew or cared about Henry Rowland's whereabouts. But all the same, she could not lie to him. "I believe he went riding with Mr. Cecil and the constables."

Ned scratched his beard. "Well, here's a to-do. I've some news he needs to hear. But I can't stay long, for my father's not well enough to manage the tavern by himself. Could I give you a message for him?"

"Oh, I...." Eliza flushed, a feeling of panic seizing her ribcage. A message meant that she would have to convey it—that she would have to speak to Henry Rowland again.

"It's quite short," said Ned reassuringly. "Just that Mrs. Flambard is staying at the inn. He'll want to know. Thank you kindly."

Eliza opened her mouth and closed it again. What was this bearded fellow doing? Acting as go-between for Henry and his paramour? And how dare he involve her in such a thing!

Before she could answer back, she saw the innkeeper heading for the door. He let himself out.

She clenched her fists and headed to the staircase. Surely, this was a message she had no obligation to deliver....

HENRY CLOSED THE FRONT DOOR quietly. He was not looking forward to spending time with Walter Turold. The years he had spent dreading Walter's disdain and deploring his own cowardice still stood in stark relief to the strange rapprochement that had occurred between them this past week. They had re-forged something between them, a chain that had broken long ago. But in the process something else had fractured—the bond between Walter and Rufus.

Henry was not sure whether Walter *had* murdered his brother, and if he had, Henry felt a certain complicity in the matter since he alone knew the motivation behind the action. Still, Jacob Pevensey wanted Turold to know about the missing gun, and it was a message Henry had agreed to deliver. He had not agreed to do it straightway, however....

Perhaps Eliza was still downstairs with Adele. If he could separate her from his sister, he might be able to apologize for his forwardness at breakfast. Lady Malcolm's displeasure had seemed severe. He hoped it would not prejudice Eliza against him further, just when he seemed to be making progress in their friendship.

He opened the door to the drawing room. The man and the woman on the settee sprang apart, guilty looks on both their faces. Henry's jaw set. They might have been doing nothing more than holding hands, the same offense he had committed at the breakfast table, but he decided to take stern measures to discourage any sort of clandestine activity.

"Careful, Blount," he said darkly. The joking tone he had used with the two of them this past week was entirely absent from his voice. Henry was head of the Rowland household now, and no one, not even a friend, would take liberties with his sister. Besides, a firm hand might be the push Stephen needed to come up to scratch.

"You're needed in the morning room for questioning." Henry tried to make the summons as ominous as possible.

"Right ho," said Stephen with a weak smile. Standing up, he straightened his coattails and departed with an apologetic look in Adele's direction.

"Hen—" began Adele, but he raised a finger to stop her.

"We'll speak of this later. Rufus paid far too little attention to your antics. That will change."

Adele let out a cry of protest.

"Later, Adele."

Henry left the room and shut the double doors behind him. His face broke into a wry smile. A firm hand with Adele as well might stop her from toying with Stephen—and help her make up her mind about whether she really wanted him.

He followed the path of floral-patterned carpet up the stairs and down the corridor to Walter's room. Inside he heard voices. Apparently, Walter already had another visitor. Curious as to who it could be, he rapped on the door. Walter opened it, his haggard face and uncombed hair sending the message that Henry was not welcome there.

"Can I talk to you?" Henry braced himself for a refusal.

Walter hesitated and looked back over his shoulder. Henry followed his glance and saw, through the crack in the door, a small piece of Reverend Ansel seated in an armchair.

"Still here, Reverend?" Henry called out. It had been a good three hours since Henry had taken leave of him. What had they been speaking about? The perennial wave of guilt occasioned by the Reverend's presence swept over Henry. His reluctance to speak with Walter had trebled. He straightened his broad shoulders and reminded himself that he was the Duke of Brockenhurst. Harrowhaven was his home, and he would hide from no man who came through its doors.

"Yes, still here—although I was just leaving," said the Reverend, pulling out a damp handkerchief to stay the stream flowing from his nose. Walter let the door swing wide as Reverend Ansel pushed himself up from the chair.

The Reverend patted Henry's shoulder as he passed into the corridor. "Do let me know if I can be of any use."

"You can let me know if you run across Rufus' pistol in your piece of the woods."

"His pistol?" The Reverend looked confused.

"Yes." Henry turned his eyes to Walter. "It wasn't with the body and the investigator is looking for it."

Walter's eyes darted away like a pair of minnows. "Probably knocked it loose when they put him on his horse to take him to the carriage."

"We just searched the clearing...." Henry shrugged. He omitted to mention that they had searched the surrounding woods as well.

"Ah, well, if I see anything, I'll be sure to let you know," said

Reverend Ansel. He looked back through the door at the long-haired man. "God bless you, Walter."

Walter bowed his head.

The Reverend disappeared down the corridor. Henry leaned against the doorframe and folded his arms.

"What was it you wanted?" Walter growled.

"Oh," said Henry, having already delivered his message, "I just came to see how you were getting along."

"Miserably. I've no one to play at cards with except Robert, and there's little sport at faro when both players are dipped so deep that they're handing each other vowels."

"I forgot that was Rufus' chief quality—his ability to spread around his blunt. No wonder you are missing him so terribly."

Walter reached for the handle to pull the door closed, but Henry put his foot in the way. "Did you tell the Reverend about Rufus' interest in Cat—"

"No! I already told you his heart was too weak for such a shock. I beg you, do not mention anything of the matter to anyone."

Henry's lips hardened into a thin line. The "anyone" Walter was referring to was of course Jacob Pevensey, the man in charge of finding out the truth. And if he discovered Walter's story of an accidental shooting to be dishonest, then Rufus' intentions toward Catie Ansel could prove particularly pertinent to the investigation.

Walter's piercing eyes focused on Henry's face. "You asked something of me once, a promise to conceal a matter in which you were at fault. I kept that promise—have kept it for ten years and will keep it to my grave. And now I am asking you to make me a similar promise. Will you conceal this matter?"

"Are you at fault?" demanded Henry. He could not promise to keep the matter quiet if Walter had murdered his brother. But if he were innocent?

"I swear to you, by all that is holy, I have no bloodguilt on my hands."

Henry breathed deeply. "Very well then. I promise you that, come what may, I shall say nothing about the matter of Rufus and Catherine Ansel."

◦◈◦

PEVENSEY WAITED IN THE STABLE yard for Cecil to turn his horse over to the groom and then fell in beside him as they walked back to the house. "What next?" asked his young protégé.

"More interviews," said Pevensey, "this time with the guests and the family."

"I hope you do not mind that I dismissed Constable Cooper." Pevensey snorted. "Not at all. I was going to suggest it myself."

They were about to enter the front door, when it opened to allow egress to a large man wearing the collar and black coat of a clergyman.

"Good day, Reverend Ansel," said Cecil, shaking the man's hand.

"Good day to you," responded the clergyman. His eyes began to water, and he held up a hand to signify that he was about to sneeze. A second passed, then another, and then the good Reverend bent over double with four successive sneezes as powerful as a gale in the Caribbean.

"This is Jacob Pevensey," said Cecil, raising his voice above the noise, "down from London to help me investigate the death of Rufus Rowland."

Pevensey was not normally squeamish, but he omitted offering his hand to the moist Reverend. "You live by the church, Reverend?"

"Yes, in the next door parsonage," said Reverend Ansel, recovering himself.

"Were you part of the hunting party yesterday?"

"No, no," sniffed the Reverend. His large chin jutted out

defensively. "The duke was not accustomed to include me in such things. And in any case, I was asked to marry a couple up at Dealsby Cross that day."

"So you were not home when the shots were fired."

Nostrils flaring, the Reverend raised a finger again, and shook his head in answer before the storm of sneezing broke.

"What about any family members or servants?"

The Reverend shook his head again. He pulled out his handkerchief. "I'm sorry, gentlemen. I must ask you to excuse me. This cold refuses to leave my head, and I think I must go home and put myself to bed."

"Sleep is the best medicine," Cecil called after the retreating Reverend. He raised an eyebrow at Pevensey as the two entered the house. "Curious he said there was no family there, but I daresay he just wanted to be left in peace. He has a daughter, the same age as Lady Adele—not quite right in the head—who rarely leaves the house, and a housekeeper of sorts, who is tasked with taking care of her."

"Ah!" said Pevensey. "And being so nearby, perhaps they might have seen or heard something that could help us. The servant, at least, is in her right mind. Perhaps we can pay a call at the parsonage tomorrow."

The two men headed for the morning room where they would resume their interviews. As soon as he opened the door, Pevensey saw a light-haired young man sitting in one of the armchairs near the window, his knee vibrating nervously.

"Mr. Blount!" said Cecil. "We did not realize this room was occupied."

"Oh, I beg your pardon," said Mr. Blount. "Is this not the right room? Henry told me I was to come here for questioning."

"Did he indeed?" said Pevensey with a slight smile. The new duke had anticipated his plans quite accurately. "Then you are in just the right room at just the right time." He pulled out his notebook to render the sneezing Reverend. "If you would be so good, Mr. Cecil, as to conduct the questioning."

Cecil settled himself in the armchair facing Mr. Blount while Pevensey took up his position by the window which would afford him the best light for sketching.

"Where were you during the hunt?"

"With the main party of hunters. You know that—you were there yourself."

"Indeed. And did you ever split off on your own?"

"No, I followed Squire Ashbrook's sons throughout. You can ask them if you like."

"Was there any unpleasantness between you and the duke?"

"No, not at all."

Pevensey looked up. It was better to cut to the quick. "How did the duke respond to your interest in Lady Adele?"

Mr. Blount started. "He had no objections that I know of."

"And who is Lady Adele's new guardian? Henry Rowland?"

"Yes."

"How does he look upon your suit?"

"I...am not sure."

Pevensey fixed Mr. Blount with a knowing stare. He had already proven his omniscience with his first question. Let the man squirm a little until he told the truth.

"That is to say...he is not enthused about the match. It is an added difficulty."

"Or in other words"—Pevensey allowed his freckled face to relax into a smile—"you had little reason to wish the late duke ill."

"Yes." Mr. Blount breathed a sigh of relief. "Exactly as you say."

⁂

HENRY WALKED BACK TO HIS room. On the floor directly in front of his door was a small rectangle. He bent down and saw that it was a book. A few of the pages were bowed as if the volume had been marred by poor handling. He turned it over and looked at the cover—*Pamela*.

Henry frowned. He cared little about the bent pages, but he had hoped Eliza would return the book in person.

Jutting out from between the pages was a slip of paper. He pulled it out and unfolded it.

Your Grace,

Thank you for the loan of the book. I am at present fully occupied with other reading, so I am returning it to you unfinished.

E. Malcolm

P. S. Mr. Hornsby called to inform you that a lady friend of yours, Mrs. Flambard, is staying at the village inn should you desire to visit her.

At the sight of that last line, Henry cursed underneath his breath. What had Ned said to her? Whatever it was, Eliza had clearly drawn the wrong conclusions. He groaned and pressed his forehead against the closed door. A surprised footman lifted both eyebrows as he walked by with a pair of freshly polished candlesticks.

Henry opened the door to vent his annoyance and despair in a more private setting. He sat down on the side of the bed and read the letter over again. A slight smile formed on his lips. He had to admit, she was quite bold with the pen. Much bolder than she would have been face to face. How she would have blushed to say the word "lady friend" to him!

He read it a third time. His smile disappeared. Looked at from her perspective, circumstances were certainly damning.

First, she had witnessed him consoling the maid in the hallway and then, she had overheard Mrs. Flambard's seductive language. Her mother, Lady Malcolm, had no doubt added fuel to the fire, convincing Eliza that he was a libertine through and through, and only dallying with her at the breakfast table as he had with a hundred other women.

He folded the letter thoughtfully and placed it beneath his pillow. A hundred women? Ha! That was the irony of the situation. There had not even been five women in his life—just one. And before Eliza Malcolm, no one. Certainly the pretty face, here and there, had caught his eye, but no one had ever captured his heart like Eliza Malcolm. No one had ever captivated his imagination and filled his dreams of what *could be*.

And now the whole thing was a tangle that might never come undone. He lay back on the bed and closed his eyes. Even if Jacob Pevensey sorted out the real story behind Rufus' death, there was no one to sort out the knotted ball of misunderstandings and mistrust that seemed likely to keep him from Eliza Malcolm forever.

***

PEVENSEY LOST NO TIME IN coming straight to the point with Robert Curtis.

"I am aware that you had a quarrel with your late brother."

The dandy's lace cuffs fluttered nervously. "I'm not sure what you mean."

"Come now, Mr. Curtis," said Pevensey. "I have it on good authority"—he did not mention on whose authority—"that there were high words exchanged. When was it? Yesterday morning before the hunt?"

"The evening before," Mr. Curtis admitted grudgingly.

"What were the circumstances?" Pevensey crossed one leg over the other.

Mr. Curtis glanced anxiously at Cecil, who was sitting nearby, pencil poised to write in his notebook. "It was because... because...dash it all! One doesn't like one's affairs to be spread all about the neighborhood, or all about the ton."

"I assure you," said Cecil, his black eyes radiating gravity, "both Mr. Pevensey and I are adept at discretion."

"Very well." Mr. Curtis coughed delicately. "A few years ago I borrowed a substantial sum from Rufus."

"What was the purpose of the money?" Pevensey's pencil recreated the paisley pattern on Mr. Curtis' waistcoat.

"I needed it for a speculation in...." He named an enterprise now defunct.

"Ah," said Pevensey knowingly. "And the money was lost."

"Indeed," said Mr. Curtis sadly. "The term of the loan came up recently. I expected Rufus to extend it—it would have been the brotherly thing to do. But he summoned me to his office after dinner that night and told me he intended to call in the loan."

"Had you the wherewithal to pay?"

"No, certainly not. I am in the middle of financing another project certain to bring great returns, but until then, I have nothing but a small allowance from the rents on my estate. And as you can see,"—he waved a demonstrative hand across his fashionable ensemble—"after my tailor and haberdasher are paid, there is barely enough left over for the cobbler."

Mr. Cecil leaned forward in his chair. "What was the security for the loan?"

"My estate. Rufus informed me he meant to take possession of it immediately."

"What did he want it for?" demanded Cecil.

"I don't know!" Mr. Curtis' tone was all frustration. "He

already has Harrowhaven and his house in Grosvenor Square. What could he want with a third residence?"

Pevensey and Cecil exchanged a glance. The red-haired detective resumed the questioning. "Had your brother shown any animosity towards you in the past?"

"No, not at all. He was cordial, friendly."

"Was he a spiteful man?"

"Yes, I suppose he could be on occasion. But he was never spiteful to me."

"On whom would you say he exercised his spite?"

"Oh, on Hal, I suppose. They were close in age, and always at each other's throats growing up. I had no expectation that he would do such a thing. That fellow Walter Turold was always borrowing from him, and he never called it in."

"Hmm...." Pevensey finished his sketch and snapped shut his notebook. "I think that is all, Mr. Curtis. Unless, of course, your dismay was so great at losing your estate that you felt compelled to shoot your brother."

"Good heavens, no!" Robert Curtis looked truly alarmed. "Utterly impossible. I was with the main hunting party the whole time."

"Not to mention the fact that your fraternal affection would never for a moment consider murder." Pevensey's freckled face lit up with good-natured mockery.

"Indeed," said Mr. Curtis. "And as long as Cecil will forbear from spreading it around, I'll admit that I'm far too poor a shot to attempt such a thing." He lifted a long finger and tapped his temple. "Bad eyesight."

"Ah," said Pevensey, standing up to signal that the interview was at an end. "One might consider a pair of spectacles."

"One might." Robert Curtis shrugged. "But they look such a fright, I'm afraid I'd rather take my chances with wandering about half-blind." He nodded his head. "Good day, Cecil. G'day, Pevensey."

Pevensey watched him out the door, then turned to his black-haired apprentice. "What did you make of that?"

Cecil whistled. "It seems Rufus wanted that estate for something."

"Yes, but what?" Pevensey pursed his lips. "We must investigate the matter further. My intuition tells me it is connected to the duke's death."

"Then is Curtis lying about his whereabouts during the hunt?"

"No, I hardly think he would have the stomach for murder. And besides,"—Pevensey's upper lip twisted into a wry smile—"he might dirty his clothes."

22

ELIZA CLASPED AND UNCLASPED HER HANDS AS SHE SAT ON the bench in the hallway. Mrs. Forsythe had knocked on her door a quarter of an hour ago to let her know that the man from London wanted to see her again. Her aversion to seeing the investigator had increased immeasurably since this morning at breakfast when he had trapped her in a lie. And of course, this time, there would be no Henry Rowland to assist her if she floundered.

She stiffened. There was no time for such foolish thoughts—she had no need to rely on Lord Henry. She was a woman grown and could speak for herself. Her fingers began to rhythmically twist the fabric of her skirt.

She had looked at Lord Henry's door on her way downstairs and noticed that the book was gone—and the letter with it. If it had still been there, she probably would not have had the courage to let it lie. She would have retrieved the letter that she had so hastily written. As it was, the letter was most probably already in his hands....

Adele bounced into the hallway. "Eliza! There you are! That Pevensey fellow is with Mother now, but I think he means to speak to you next. I've just come from my interview."

"How was it?" asked Eliza, trying to steady her words.

"Oh, nothing to worry about," said Adele, flouncing over

to sit by her friend. "He just wanted to know whom Rufus had quarreled with and why—and of course, I knew nothing about that. They don't tell me such things, you know. And then he asked what I did the day of the hunt. So I told him we went up the road. Quite dull, really. I was hoping he would have something more interesting to talk about."

Eliza gave a small smile. "I think *you* are supposed to be the one telling *him* interesting things."

"Oh, well, I did that too," said Adele. "I hope you do not mind—I mentioned that Henry was quite taken with you."

"Adele!"

"Well, it's true! And he asked about it."

The Duchess of Brockenhurst entered the room at just that moment. She took a look at Eliza's stricken face and walked over to claim her overly loquacious daughter. "Your turn, my dear." She placed a graceful hand on Eliza's shoulder. "There is no harm in simply speaking the truth. It is what the duke—both the dukes—would want."

"Yes, my lady," said Eliza, swallowing hard. She stood up and went into the morning room.

◦◦◦

As the willowy Miss Malcolm glided into the room, Pevensey saw her cast an apprehensive look at Cecil. He supposed it would be awkward, talking about personal details in front of a gentleman one had just recently met at a social gathering.

Pevensey directed Miss Malcolm to a chair and watched her sit down.

That was the advantage of *his* position, of course. He was a nobody. He was invisible. There was no chance that any of these ladies would encounter him later, sharing their opera box or drinking punch at Almack's.

"I am sorry to summon you so close to dinner," said Pevensey, "but I am nearing the end of my inquiries and hope to finish by nightfall."

Miss Malcolm murmured something non-distinct.

"Before we talk about the hunt, there is one thing I wish to clear up. You have indicated that your acquaintance with Henry Rowland is of a longstanding nature, but the gentleman himself said that he had only met you since your visit to Harrowhaven."

Pevensey watched Miss Malcolm's face turn as red as his own hair. "I hardly know what to say, Mr. Pevensey. I am embarrassed for the untruth I told earlier. It is as Lord Henry says. We first became acquainted less than a week ago."

Pevensey saw Cecil out of the corner of his eye doing an admirable job of not registering surprise. Inexplicably, the curly-haired young man had managed to turn himself into an inanimate piece of the morning room's furniture. Pevensey was grateful—it might lead to greater candor on Miss Malcolm's part.

"Could you explain the nature of the misunderstanding?" Pevensey asked gently.

"Yes, I...I suppose it came about because"—Miss Malcolm's fingers were toying restlessly with the fabric of her light dress—"when I first arrived, I had not seen the duke yet—Rufus, I mean. And when I came downstairs I came across Lord Henry in the saloon. And then the duke came in, and Lord Henry pretended that he and I were old friends, and I...I did not correct him."

Pevensey's fingers itched to pull out his sketchbook and preserve the long lines of Eliza Malcolm's face and figure in art, but he had begun to gain her trust now, and like a trainer with a skittish colt, he did not want to startle her with any sudden movements.

"Why do you think Lord Henry might have said that?" he asked soothingly—hypnotically he hoped.

"I suppose he wanted to make his brother jealous."

"And was the duke jealous?"

"I...I don't know. I believe he might have been."

"Do you think there was already a pre-existing rivalry between the two men?"

"Oh, yes! It was clear to everyone."

"Why do you think that was? Was Lord Henry jealous of his brother's position?"

"His position? No." Her shoulders tensed. "Or...I don't know. Maybe he was?"

Pevensey wondered if there was something here—a piece to the puzzle that she was reluctant to share.

"Please, Miss Malcolm, what do you remember?"

"Lady Adele held a party a few nights ago with"—she glanced over at Cecil—"some of her friends from the country. We played a game and Lord Henry paid a forfeit. He gave me...a calling card."

"What did the card say?"

"It said"—she breathed deeply—"Henry Rowland, Duke of Brockenhurst."

Pevensey raised an eyebrow. "Almost as if Lord Henry was prescient, yes? To have such cards made up before he left London?"

A pained look came over Miss Malcolm's face. "Oh, no, I ought not to have told you! I am certain it was a joke of some kind. It is impossible to think that Henry had anything to do with the accident. It *was* an accident! Mr. Turold has said as much and admitted to firing the shot."

"Of course," said Pevensey, afraid he had pressed her too far. He decided to return to a safer, although just as unpleasant, subject. "Did you see the duke on the day of the hunt? The former duke, I mean."

"From afar, yes, but we did not speak."

"That is strange, is it not, considering that you had just become betrothed the day prior?"

He could tell that Miss Malcolm did not know what to say.

"Did you see him during the course of the hunt?"

"No, Adele and I and the other ladies went along the road. We saw the riders once or twice from a hill, but they were so far away I could not make out who was who."

The rest of Miss Malcolm's story confirmed everything he had heard from Cecil and Lady Adele—until a small detail at the end.

"And after Mr. Cecil warned the ladies away from the tragedy, your father escorted you to the house and sent the carriage?"

"No. Yes. That is to say, he did escort us to the house, but the carriage was already there."

"Already there?"

Miss Malcolm nodded her head emphatically. "We passed it on our way down the road. It was just sitting there on the side."

"Was it occupied?"

"No, the groom was sitting up in the box, but there was no one inside. He seemed to be waiting for something."

Pevensey sent a sideways glance at Cecil who was now sitting forward, hands on knees, no longer blending in with the furniture. Miss Malcolm was looking nervously between the both of them, unaware of the import of what she had just said.

"Thank you, Miss Malcolm," said Pevensey, rising from his chair to escort her to the door. "I hope you will forgive my impertinent questions. You have been more than helpful."

As the door clicked shut, Cecil's black eyes came alive. "The carriage was already there!"

"So she says."

"It makes sense! We did not have to wait for it at all when we brought the body to the road."

"Did the groom say anything when he saw you with the duke's corpse?"

"He seemed as shocked as the next man, but I don't remember any specific exclamations. A visit to the stable is in order!"

"Agreed," said Pevensey. He headed into the hallway in search of his hat. Hopefully the groom would be forthcoming about who had instructed him to wait there with the carriage and why. At that point Pevensey would know which upcoming interview was more important: the one with Walter Turold or the one with Henry Rowland.

✦

After an hour or so of quiet reflection, Henry rang for Biggs and allowed his valet to dress him in a clean shirt, new jacket, and pressed cravat. He headed for the billiards room. There was still time to play a game before dinner—not that dinner was to be any great affair tonight. He had told Mrs. Forsythe that they would serve it in the dining room as usual, but it was not certain how many of the family or guests would attend.

Entering the billiards room, he found Sir Arthur just finishing a game with his half-brother. Robert took himself off almost immediately, needing ample time to dress for dinner, even an informal one. "Another game?" said Henry brightly, taking the cue in hand. He had come into the billiards room looking for distraction, but he appeared to have stumbled upon a golden opportunity.

Sir Arthur looked around nervously. "If we have time...."

Henry took that for a yes, and without further comment, arranged the three ivory balls—two white, one red—on the green table. He was a fair hand at billiards, but he sensed that this afternoon would not be the time to show that. He made a quick and inexpert shot, grazing Sir Arthur's ball with his cue ball, but failing to strike the red one as well. Sir Arthur smiled and immediately scored hazards, driving the red ball into one of the pockets.

After a few plays—and a glass of brandy liberally poured by

Henry—Sir Arthur was in a far more jovial and garrulous mood. "Excellent game, billiards," he said, having scored the requisite twenty-one points and leading the way for a second game.

"Excellent to have someone around to play it with," replied Henry. His ivory ball bounced off the padded wall of the table, missing the red ball entirely. "You know, you needn't leave once that Runner fellow finishes his investigation. Why not stay on a little longer into the summer? There's more hunting to be had here and nothing happening in London until the season begins."

The uneasiness returned to Sir Arthur's face. "Very kind of you, Lord Henry, but afraid it wouldn't do. The old frigate is eager to make sail for home, if you take my meaning."

Henry decided it was time to be frank. "I know the timing is unfortunate, but I was hoping to improve my acquaintance with your daughter, Miss Malcolm. From what I have seen of her, I think she and I would deal admirably together—far better than she and Rufus would have."

Sir Arthur hemmed. "Maybe so. Maybe so. Lady Malcolm is not of that opinion though. The recent events have set her nerves on edge, and there'll be no peace from that quarter until we put Harrowhaven behind us."

Henry made one last attempt. "May I call on your family when you return to London?"

Sir Arthur hesitated again, scratching his gray sideburns with both hands. "Don't know how long we'll be staying in London. Naturally, we wish you all the best, your grace."

An awkward silence reigned until the next game of billiards finished. "Will you and Lady Malcolm be joining us for dinner?" Henry asked, as he put the ivory balls away in their wood case.

"I shall be there," said Sir Arthur. He made no promises regarding his wife.

Pevensey and Cecil found the head groom crouched on a stool and applying some ointment to the legs of one of the horses.

"I'll be with you gentlemen in a trice," he called behind him once he realized he was being waited for.

"Gormley, isn't it?" asked Cecil as the older man turned around and wiped his hands on his apron.

"Yes, sir," said Gormley, feet planted, arms folded. "What can I do for you?"

"Yesterday, before the hunt," said Pevensey, "did someone order the carriage readied?"

Gormley frowned thoughtfully. "Yes, must have, for I remember the carriage going out. But it weren't I who heard the directions or harnessed it. I was tending to the ladies' and gentlemen's mounts. It would ha' been Martin who done it."

Gormley bellowed the other man's name into the recesses of the stable, and within seconds, a gangly fellow, wearing the same leather apron Gormley had on, came out and stood before them. Remembering the fellow's infirmity, Pevensey fell silent to determine how best to wring the needed information from him.

Cecil, unaware, launched into the same questions that Pevensey had just asked. Martin stared back at him in stony silence.

"He's tongue tied," interjected Gormley, jerking a thumb at his undergroom.

"Now, see here, Martin," said Cecil. "There's nothing to be afraid of. We just need to know the answers to our questions."

"Not afraid," said Gormley. "He's mute. Can't speak more than a grunt."

"Can he understand us?" asked Cecil, a little taken aback.

"To be sure," said Gormley. "He understands as well as you and me."

"Then he must be aware who asked him to lead out the carriage yesterday morning," said Pevensey. He pursed his lips thoughtfully. "Does he know his letters?"

"Nah," said Gormley. "He canna even write his own name."

Martin's sullen glare turned ferocious at that comment and confirmed for Pevensey that the groom knew exactly what was being said.

"Martin," said Pevensey, "I am an investigator attached to the magistrates' office in London. A man may have been murdered here." It was the first time in this case that Pevensey had used the gravity of a murder accusation to impress a witness. "It is essential that I know who asked you to lead out the carriage yesterday morning and wait alongside the road. Was it Walter Turold?"

There was no reply.

"Was it Henry Rowland?"

The groom's scowl deepened.

"Was it Rufus Rowland?"

The groom looked away.

One by one, Pevensey patiently listed the butler, the housekeeper, the dowager duchess, and all the other inmates of the house, but the names failed to elicit even the smallest of grunts from the mute undergroom.

"Now, see here, Martin!" said Gormley, catching at the straw-haired man's sleeve with a wrinkled hand. "You tell the gentlemen what they need to know!"

But not even his superior's exhortation could compel his cooperation.

Gormley's face began to grow red with expostulating until Pevensey held up a hand. "It's all right, Mr. Gormley. No doubt young Martin here has a good reason for concealing why he was waiting on the road with the carriage—haven't you, Martin?"

The sullen face split with a smile that could only be described as sly.

"I thought as much," said Pevensey, returning the smile measure for measure, "and I hope you won't be landing in the gaol when I discover what that reason is."

23

"The family is eating dinner," Hayward informed Pevensey as he and Cecil returned from the stables and re-entered the house. It was not an invitation to join them, but an injunction to stay away until dinner was over.

Cecil, who had no doubt dined dozens of times at Harrowhaven, looked a little dismayed. After all, investigations were hungry work, and the prospect of no dinner was a dismal one.

"Well, since we are not invited to table," said Pevensey, "have you the stomach for one more errand?"

"Where to?" asked Cecil. Pevensey noticed that he did not acquiesce immediately.

"To find where the carriage was sitting and examine the ground for clues."

"Very well," said Cecil, "although do you think Brockenhurst's Cook would be good enough to pack us a hamper?"

"I hardly imagine she would care to do so while she is in the middle of serving dinner to the family. Perhaps we can wend our way through the kitchens and snag a crust of bread on our way out."

Cecil balked at that idea. He probably rarely visited the kitchens at his own manor, and never at the house of another gentleman. In the interest of furthering the investigation, however, he agreed to tighten his belt and press on until food should present itself.

The two men returned to the stable for their horses. Gormley led out Cecil's mount with alacrity and cuffed his sullen assistant when he was slow to saddle Pevensey's.

They followed the circular drive at a medium pace and then slowed as they turned onto the road. The summer evening's light was still good, and they scanned both sides of the road carefully for anything unusual.

"What's *your* guess as to who wanted that carriage sitting on the roadside?" Pevensey asked.

Cecil's stomach grumbled. "Not the slightest sliver of an idea. But perhaps the best way of figuring it out would be to think why each person would want the carriage there."

"A valuable experiment. Well then, Walter Turold? Why would he want a carriage standing ready on the road?"

Cecil nudged his horse nearer to a dark shape on the side of the road, but moved along when he saw it was only a rock. "Perhaps the shooting was premeditated. The carriage was to be his means of escape afterwards, but he did not count upon others reaching the clearing so quickly."

"What was his motive in the shooting?"

"Money? Curtis told us that Turold had given vowels to Rufus too. Perhaps Turold was feeling the stranglehold of debt and needed a way out. Or perhaps Curtis didn't want to dirty his hands, and paid Turold to do it for him."

"Hmm." Pevensey patted his horse's neck. "It's possible. Let's try another. Henry Rowland?"

"Do you really think Lord Henry a suspect? I mean, Turold admits to shooting the duke."

"But how many shots were there?"

"Two."

"Is it not possible that the duke died from the first bullet before Turold fired the second one?"

Cecil's lips parted. "Yes, I suppose it might be. I had not thought of it that way. Perhaps the movement Turold saw in the bushes was actually the murderer escaping. He thought it was the stag, shot, and missed. Then, when he came through the underbrush, he saw the duke's body and thought he had killed him."

"Yes, so in that case, why would Henry Rowland want a carriage waiting on the road?"

Cecil frowned. "Not to escape in—that would give everything away. If Henry Rowland fired the shot, his main ambition would be to remain undiscovered. Becoming the new duke would be small reward if he were to hang a few weeks later. So the carriage must have been because…because…. No, I give up. You've lost me there."

"And lost myself as well," said Pevensey with a grin. "It's impossible to tell where the carriage was parked on this dry ground. Perhaps the carriage was not connected to the death. Perhaps Rufus ordered the carriage himself?"

"I can't see why he would do such a thing. He was mad about hunting—could keep nothing else in his head when it was time to follow the hounds. And if he had wanted a vehicle to carry the deer back in, he would have ordered the dogcart, not a velvet-cushioned carriage." Cecil narrowed his eyes and looked into the distance. "Pevensey, perhaps we are on the wrong tack altogether. Perhaps Martin was using the carriage for his own purposes and refuses to tell us why for fear of a reprimand."

"You know the country better than I," said Pevensey. "Could he have been meeting someone here on the road?"

"The closest building to this spot is the church," said Cecil, "and the parsonage next door."

"The Reverend and his curate were away that day. And you

said that Ansel has a budding daughter?" Pevensey looked at Cecil meaningfully.

"Yes, but she is a lady!"

"And a simpleton," Pevensey reminded him.

Cecil's forehead wrinkled. "As much as I hate to entertain the notion, I suppose that she and Martin might have had something...in common. Perhaps there *was* a meeting arranged between the two of them."

"Then perhaps the carriage had nothing to do with the duke's death," said Pevensey. He saw a white building in the distance. "But in any case, I think we should stop by the parsonage to inquire further."

"Of course!" said Cecil. "And who knows? They may invite us to join them for supper."

✧

THE SOFT LIGHT OF THE evening had just begun to filter through the trees when Pevensey and Cecil pulled their horses to a stand at the iron fence surrounding the churchyard and the next door parsonage. They dismounted, and Pevensey felt a puff of red dust cover his trousers as his boots hit the ground. There had been no rain in this part of the country for some time, and while the shaded areas under the trees were still green, the open ground was parched.

Cecil led the way to the door and rapped upon it with polite, but hungry, knuckles. An elderly woman with a white cap and an apron opened the door. "Hello, Mrs. Hodgins! Is the Reverend at home?"

It was long past calling hours, as evidenced by the flustered look on the housekeeper's face. "Well...yes...he is, but just about to tuck into his dinner."

"Oh, goodness me," said Cecil, feigning a look of distress.

"Is it that time already? I do beg your pardon, Mrs. Hodgins. We would not have called had it not been so urgent. Regarding the murder...I mean the death of the duke yesterday."

At the mention of murder, Mrs. Hodgins' face looked quite frightened. "I don't know anything about that, Mr. Cecil."

"Of course not," he said reassuringly. Pevensey noted approvingly that the young man was using the right touch. "We just need to speak with the Reverend."

It did not take much more persuasion before Mrs. Hodgins showed them inside and had them wait while she went into the small dining room. The tone of the muffled voice inside implied that they might not be entirely welcome, but a man of the cloth is used to intrusion, and in less than a minute, Reverend Ansel had appeared beside Mrs. Hodgins in the hallway.

"How can I help you?" Reverend Ansel had shut the dining room door behind him, but in the brief moment that it had been open, a delicious savory smell had wafted out into the entry hall. Pevensey could hear Cecil's stomach grumbling again. The Reverend removed his handkerchief from his pocket and blew his nose.

Pevensey took the lead. "We learned that the carriage from Harrowhaven was seen parked on the road near here yesterday morning. Did anyone from the house see it?"

Reverend Ansel looked at Mrs. Hodgins. She shook her head. "I was away very early yesterday," said the Reverend, "and I saw nothing when I departed."

"But you came back," said Mrs. Hodgins.

"Of course I did," said Reverend Ansel. "But by then, it was of course much later, and there was nothing of the sort on the road."

Pevensey eyed the dining room door. "Was there anyone else in the house who might have seen something?"

The Reverend looked instantly uncomfortable, as if his clerical collar might be choking his large neck. "Yes, there is my daughter Catherine, but Mr. Pevensey, she is given to flights of fancy and not entirely...."

Cecil laid a hand on his sleeve. "Mr. Pevensey is aware of your daughter's unfortunate condition."

"Ah, yes." The Reverend seemed mortified to have it spoken of. "Well, if you think it important to ask her about the carriage, we could try."

"I do," said Pevensey. Since the Reverend remained stationary, he moved toward the dining room door and led the four of them inside.

Seated at the small table was a girl on the cusp of womanhood. Blond ringlets framed her face, and soft blue eyes stared calmly at the invaders. Her slender figure, dressed all in white, could have been the model for a neo-classical painting. Pevensey wanted quite badly to draw her himself, but he suppressed the urge. He did not want to frighten her by pulling out his notebook.

"Catie, child," said the Reverend gently. "These men need to ask you a few questions. Can you just answer what they ask you? You need not worry to say anything else."

She blinked and smiled. Pevensey was reminded of a porcelain doll.

"Miss Ansel," he said, "there may have been a carriage parked on the road yesterday morning. Did you see it?"

"No, I did not," said the girl. "I never see any carriages except on Sundays."

"Did you see anyone walking about in the woods near the parsonage?"

"Sometimes I see people in the woods. But not yesterday. Did you see anyone?"

Her eyes were frank and trusting. Pevensey smiled gently. "No, I did not. Did you go out yesterday, Miss Ansel?"

"No, I wanted to go out, but Papa would not let me."

Reverend Ansel took his daughter's hand and patted it. "Of course you could not go out, my dear, since I was not here in the morning to go with you. If that is all, Mr. Pevensey?"

"Just one more question. Miss Ansel, do you know a man named Martin?"

"No, I do not. Who is he? Is he your friend?"

"He is a groom at Harrowhaven. I did not expect you to know him, but I wanted to make sure."

"I know where Harrowhaven is!"

"Yes," said Pevensey, signaling to Cecil that it was time for them to take their leave. "It is quite close to here." He turned to Reverend Ansel. "Thank you for letting us invade your supper hour."

"Of course," said Reverend Ansel, sneezing into his sleeve.

"And if you should happen to run across the missing weapon, do let us know."

Catie Ansel's head jerked upright. "I saw the gun. Papa had the gun."

Reverend Ansel blushed, doubtless unused to exposing his child's infirmity to strangers. "Mrs. Hodgins, could you take Catie to the kitchen with her dinner?" The girl picked up her plate and docilely followed the housekeeper out of the room.

Reverend Ansel went to the door and closed it behind them. "Yes," he said, turning back to his visitors, "I found the gun this afternoon. I remember you saying that you were searching for the gun in the clearing. I took a walk over there and found it right nearby in the trees roundabout and brought it home to give to you."

"Excellent!" said Pevensey. "May I have it?"

"It is in my study," said the Reverend, and he hurried out of the room to retrieve it. "Here it is," he said, returning to place a familiar-looking pistol in Pevensey's hands.

"And you found it just outside the clearing?"

"Yes, in the underbrush."

Pevensey examined the chamber of the weapon. "Did you clean it?"

"No, no," said the Reverend hastily. "I found it like this."

"So, it was never fired?" said Cecil with a wrinkled brow. He exchanged a glance with Pevensey.

It was something Pevensey could hardly credit. Then how had there been two shots? "Thank you, Reverend Ansel. We shall take this with us and be on our way."

They left the house, walked through the church yard, through the iron gate, and back to their horses. "Well?" asked Pevensey, as he stepped up into the saddle. "What do you think?"

Cecil laughed. "I think that Hayward would not allow us to intrude upon the family's dinner. But surely the ladies must have retired by now, and perhaps we can join the gentlemen over some nuts and sweetmeats and avail ourselves of the duke's sherry or port."

⁂

HENRY WATCHED THE LADIES DEPART from the dining room with an inward sigh. The brief moment of delight he had experienced at seeing Eliza come down for dinner was curdled by the subsequent appearance of Lady Malcolm. His mother had recovered her spirits enough to join them as well, and as an insightful hostess—albeit a grieving one—she had not made the mistake of asking Henry to take Eliza in to dinner. No, that honor had fallen to Robert, and Henry was left to fume inwardly while he sat a whole table length away. He fruitlessly tried to catch Eliza's eye at regular intervals throughout the two courses, but the auburn-haired beauty would barely look up from her plate, her long eyelashes veiling her expression and shutting him out.

Desultory conversation about the weather and Adele's reminiscences about her London season kept complete awkwardness at bay, but the dinner still dragged on interminably. Barely three words came out of Eliza's mouth. The only blessing of the evening was that Walter had had the grace to stay in his room. No one would have denied him room at the table, but no one wanted to sit down to dinner with the man who had shot Rufus when they were all still coming to terms with his death.

The ladies were departing now, and the duchess warned the gentlemen that as they would likely all retire to their rooms the gentlemen need not worry about rejoining them. There was his last chance to see Eliza—gone. Henry growled beneath his breath and walked over to the decanter of brandy on the sideboard.

"Ho there, Brockenhurst!" said a voice at the dining room door. "Do you mind if we join you?"

Henry looked up to see Cecil and Pevensey poking their heads around the corner. The last thing he wanted was to find himself under inspection right now, but he managed to smile and play the gracious host. Cecil lost no time in procuring a glass of spirits for himself and for the Bow Street Runner and helping himself to the sweetmeats on the sideboard. Henry noted, however, as he filled a second glass, that Pevensey was drinking his own beverage sparingly. Abstemiousness was an admirable quality in a constable. Henry wondered if the man ever went "off duty" when he was on a case, or if his mind was continually watching, observing, evaluating.

"Well, Pevensey," said Henry, abruptly. "Have you brought any new information to light?"

The red-haired Londoner fixed his eyes on him. "That I have, my lord. The question is whether any of it is pertinent to the case."

Sir Arthur set his glass down with a clink. "Surely, it is a simple enough matter! Turold says he shot the duke—albeit in error. You must have heard of a hunting accident before now!"

"It is a possibility," said Pevensey. "Mr. Turold's gun certainly *was* fired. But I am not prepared to certify it was that bullet which killed the duke, and I am not prepared to swear to the fact that it was an accident."

"Good Lord, Cecil!" said Robert. "Has this fellow actually convinced you to turn the matter into a murder investigation?"

Cecil shrugged. "If the evidence warrants it...."

Henry returned to his chair at the table and sat down. Wasn't this what he had wanted, an investigation to determine whether Walter Turold had acted out of ill fortune or ill will? Yes, but he had not anticipated the suspicion of foul play to fall on himself as well. The Runner seemed to actually consider his ill-disguised interest in Eliza as motive for murder.

"What are your plans, my lord," Pevensey asked, "now that you've inherited the title and the estate?"

"Plans?" Henry frowned, unsure whether this question was filled more with guile or bad taste. "I've hardly had time to make any."

"No?" Pevensey seemed amused. "I thought you had been mulling over the idea for some time, considering the calling cards you had made while you were in London."

Henry's mouth fell open. He had forgotten about those blasted cards. After the events that had transpired, they were quite macabre—macabre, and maybe even damning. And where had Pevensey got a hold of one? Had he been searching his room? The only card he had given out had gone to...Eliza.

"Oh, those?" Henry waved a hand casually. "Those were simply a jest between me and my brother. I never thought there would be any truth in them."

"God moves in mysterious ways," said Pevensey, and the glint in his eyes hinted that he did not think the Almighty was the only one who had been moving. Henry could feel Cecil's black eyes staring at him as well.

"What calling card, Hal?" asked Robert, his interest piqued. Sir Arthur put down his drink, ready to listen.

Henry's jaw jutted forward. There was really no good way to explain it.

"Oh, it was all a joke," interjected Stephen. "A jest to poke fun at Rufus' dignity. Henry showed them to me at the club before we came down here to Harrowhaven."

"Well, what did they say?" asked Robert.

"They merely had Henry's name on them with the Brockenhurst title." Stephen looked around, dismayed at the silence. "Quite amusing at the time...."

"And quite convenient considering the recent turn of events," said Pevensey brightly. "Excellent forethought, my lord. You will not have to order new cards now."

Henry saw Sir Arthur give him a look of confusion and disgust—there was hardly any hope now that he would reverse his opinion regarding Henry's suit. Robert also seemed perplexed, and the two of them took themselves off a moment later for a game of cards in the billiards room.

It was just the four of them now—Henry, Stephen, Cecil, and the red-haired investigator. Henry stalked over to the sideboard and removed the lid from the decanter. "Thank you, Mr. Pevensey," he said, as he poured himself yet another drink. "It was very kind of you to bring that up in front of my future father-in-law."

"What?" Stephen started. "Are you engaged to Miss Malcolm?"

"No." Henry downed the glass of spirits. "Nor am I likely to be as long as this fellow wants to see me hanged for murder."

"I do not believe that is his intention," said Cecil. "We are simply trying to unravel some suspicious circumstances surrounding the death."

Henry set his glass down with more force than was necessary. "Have you even spoken to Walter Turold?"

"No." Pevensey's tone was unapologetic.

"And why not?"

"I have already heard the gist of Mr. Turold's story. What I should like to hear is yours."

"Devil take it! I already told you I had no quarrel with Rufus. Yes, he threw me out without a penny, but I have done quite well for myself in London."

"Then what quarrel did Walter Turold have with your brother?"

Henry took in a large mouthful of air. He had promised to say nothing about Catie Ansel. And Walter had promised, in turn, that he had no blood on his hands. Should he conceal the matter from the investigator? Tell a lie, point blank, to this direct fire of questioning?

He recalled that it was the little lies and foolish deceptions of a week ago that had put him under scrutiny now....

Henry looked Pevensey squarely in the eyes. "I know nothing that I am at liberty to share."

Pevensey rose from his chair. "Then I think it is time for Cecil and me to pay your friend Walter Turold a visit."

24

When Pevensey and Cecil knocked on Turold's bedroom door, there was a slight delay. Then Walter Turold opened it, dressed in his shirtsleeves and a pair of buckskins. He had not bothered to dress for dinner, and Pevensey suspected he had not bothered to dress at all for the past day and a half. His breath smelled strongly of spirits, and his long hair was lank and greasy.

"Hello, Turold," said Cecil. "This is Jacob Pevensey, the inspector from London. We'd like to ask you some questions if we may."

Turold grunted and let them come in. It was a small room, and there were not enough chairs for them all. Turold sat down on the side of the bed while Cecil took the wingback armchair and Pevensey stood before the empty fireplace. The only other piece of furniture was a desk, on which a large book lay open. Apparently, Turold had been spending his time of solitude in reading.

"I already gave the constable my statement," said Turold. His tone was not exactly belligerent, but it was not friendly either.

"Yes, but we should like to have it again," said Pevensey. He extracted his notebook from his pocket and began to sketch that wild, unkempt face—the wary eyes and sharp nose reminding him of a rat in a trap.

"As you wish," said Turold. "I was separated from the others while chasing the stag. I thought I saw him in the bushes. I fired. When I rode up into the clearing to see if I had hit the beast, I saw Rufus lying on the ground, with his horse nearby. And that's when Cecil here came upon me."

Cecil nodded in confirmation of that last detail.

Pevensey had finished the face and was moving on to the shoulders. The man was a wiry, muscular build, much less broad in the shoulders than the Rowland brothers, but still certainly a sporting enthusiast. "Are you an experienced hunter, Mr. Turold?"

"Yes."

Of course he was. The man had grown up in these woods. He had probably hunted the deer near Harrowhaven every summer of his life.

"Then why would you make the error of shooting at movement in the bushes, knowing full well it could be a fellow hunter?"

Turold shrugged. "I thought I saw the stag. I was mistaken."

"Did you hear a shot a few minutes prior to yours?"

"No, I don't remember another shot."

Cecil coughed into his hand, concealing his astonishment at this denial. "Several other witnesses have mentioned a second shot," said Pevensey, eyebrows raised.

Turold offered no further information, and so Pevensey pressed on. "What was your relationship to Rufus Rowland?"

"He was my friend."

"But you were not equals." It was a calculated jibe.

Turold's brow turned ugly. "Equals? Of course we were. We were both gentlemen."

"Yes, but he had a title, and you did not. He had an estate, and you...?"

Turold looked away. "I sold the land my father left me."

Pevensey did not know the man from Adam, and yet he felt a twinge of sympathy. To be born without land was no disgrace, but to be forced to sell away one's patrimony—it humbled one.

"Was there any quarrel between you and the duke?"

"No."

The answer came almost too quickly. Pevensey saw Cecil's knees tense and could tell that he felt the dissonance as well.

"Yet you owed him money? From card-playing perhaps?"

"Some. He did not care when I paid it." His voice had fallen back into its normal speech pattern, and Pevensey was almost certain that this was truth.

"And yet he had called in Robert Curtis' debt the day before the hunt...why not yours too?"

Turold sighed exasperatedly. "Rufus did not *need* money. If he called in Curtis' debit, it was for other reasons than needing ready cash."

"Do you know what reason that might be?"

"No."

There was something peculiar about this fellow. Whether the death had been accidental or not, he expressed no remorse about the passing of his friend. What had bound him to Rufus in the first place? And what had sundered those bonds? Pevensey finished his sketch and shut the notebook.

"Were you often in Rufus Rowland's company?"

"Yes."

"Both in London and at Harrowhaven?"

"Yes."

"And besides cards and hunting, what sort of interests did you share?"

"I don't see how that's pertinent, inspector." Turold's eyes narrowed.

Pevensey could see that he would get no further with this line of questioning. "Perhaps it isn't." He left his position at the fireplace and walked to the door. "I think that's all I have to ask you tonight. Good night, Mr. Turold."

Cecil rose as well and offered his hand to the disheveled

Turold. The long-haired man held back for a second, then rose from the bedside and shook Cecil's hand briefly.

※

Pevensey and Cecil exchanged a look filled with meaning as the door closed behind them.

"What do you make of that?" whispered Cecil, as they headed down the corridor to the staircase. "I know I didn't imagine the first shot. The ladies and Sir Arthur heard it too. But Turold says he didn't hear one, and Reverend Ansel showed us that Rufus' pistol had not been discharged."

Pevensey waited until they had crossed the saloon and entrance hall and were standing near the front door. "I think it's clear that Turold is either lying or mistaken. There *were* two shots. But who fired the first one, I do not know."

Cecil located his beaver and put a hand on the doorknob. "It's getting late. I'm for home, Pevensey. Home, and a very late supper. Shall I meet you back here tomorrow? I think I'm more perplexed about this case at the end of the day than I was at the beginning. And the inquest must be tomorrow so the body can get below ground. I will call it for tomorrow afternoon."

Pevensey clucked his tongue against his teeth. "I think I shall go into the village tomorrow morning. I may find more information from the local folk about the relationship between Walter Turold and the late duke. It seems clear from Henry Rowland's evasions that there was some rift there. But until we know what it was, it is hard to judge Turold's motives."

"Very well then," said Cecil. "I'll meet you at the Blue Boar at nine o'clock." He looked around the entrance hall to where two footmen were standing at attention. "We can eat breakfast and perhaps talk more discreetly about our next plan of action."

"Very good," said Pevensey, bidding the young magistrate

goodnight and heading towards his own chamber. As of this evening, he had no information to present at the inquest besides the likelihood of accidental death. The case would probably go no further, and Turold would never have to stand trial at the county assizes.

And yet, something about that verdict niggled him. There were too many loose ends that kept fraying further the more he questioned. Why was the carriage waiting there on the road? Who had fired the first shot? And why had Turold denied hearing it? Why had they not found Rufus' pistol the first time they searched when Reverend Ansel came across it so easily on the outskirts of the clearing? If Rufus' gun had not been discharged, then which gun had been? He toyed briefly with the idea of Walter Turold firing two shots and reloading his pistol in between.

And besides the questions surrounding the scene of the death, there were also all the questions surrounding the motives of the main players in the drama. Why had Rufus Rowland decided so suddenly to call in Robert Curtis' loan and evict him from his estate? Why had Henry Rowland refused to tell him about the disagreement between Turold and Rufus? And why had Henry Rowland created those calling cards and tried to obfuscate his relationship with Miss Malcolm?

Pevensey opened up his notebook and flipped through the sketches he had made. The last page on the left showed the tense, guarded face of Walter Turold. The man had been less than forthcoming with his answers, and Pevensey remembered the other thing that bothered him. Next to Walter Turold he quickly sketched a desk and an open book. The man had been reading when Pevensey and Cecil had entered. And Pevensey was willing to wager that that large volume open on the desk was nothing other than a copy of the Holy Bible.

Walter Turold was not given to personal piety—that he

would also wager. Pevensey remembered the butler's comment that Turold and Rufus Rowland had shared "certain proclivities." Wenching was one of them, Pevensey imagined. The visit from that cast-off mistress confirmed it, on Rufus' part at least. And the pretty housemaid's aversion to the duke—that might well be due to improper advances.

Had the two men fought over a woman? That would be a quarrel as old as the world. But was it over the duke's new fiancée? It would be remarkable if Miss Malcolm had attracted the attention of three men all in the same house party. But then, perhaps interest breeds interest—another time-tested trope.

The pages of the book looked fresh and new, as if the Bible was in its virgin reading. Pevensey recalled that Reverend Ansel had visited Turold earlier that day. Had Turold confessed his crime to the man of the cloth and received the Bible to find the path to salvation in its pages?

Pevensey sighed and removed his boots. The soles had been brushed off on the carpet at the front door, but the upper parts of the leather were caked with dust. He ran a curious finger over them. It was the same red dirt that had covered Rufus Rowland's clothing.

He stripped off his clothes, and reaching into the nearby wardrobe, extracted a nightshirt and pulled it over his white shoulders. He blew out his candle and lay down on the bed, already aware that the wheels of his mind were turning too quickly to allow him any rest. A few minutes later he sat up. There was something he needed to do before he slept.

Retrieving his notebook from the pocket in his jacket, he found the empty page facing the likeness of Walter Turold and began to pencil in the picture he had missed drawing that day. Slowly, carefully, the ethereal features of Catherine Ansel began to take shape on the page. There was something about the girl—that poor, simple creature—that intrigued him. He drew her hair, her lips, her nose. He finished the curve of her eyes—trusting, biddable, without the capacity to contravene any instruction she was given.

And then, with the portrait of Catherine Ansel completed, a weight seemed to slip away from Pevensey's mind. He sank back against the bedclothes and rolled over onto his side, certain that tomorrow's events would provide some clarity to today's.

✦

"Up early, Mr. Pevensey?" said Gormley.

"Yes," said Pevensey with a smile, as he threw one leg over the saddle of his mount. He looked around the stable yard for Gormley's subordinate. "Any more communication from our friend, Martin?"

"No!" Gormley scowled and made a fist, implying a desire to beat an explanation out of his surly undergroom. That action might not be prudent, considering their respective ages.

"Ah, well," said Pevensey with a shrug. He leaned down conspiratorially. "If he's not about today, you might check where he keeps his gear."

"An' what should I be looking for, Mr. Pevensey?"

"Anything unusual," said Pevensey. He could see from the light in the groom's eyes that the suggestion was not a wasted one.

Pevensey gave his horse some rein and headed down the road toward the village. The Blue Boar provided a favorable impression as he rode into sight. It was not a large inn, but the outside looked well-kept, and the sign—with its porcine mascot—had been recently painted.

The proprietor was a smiling fellow with a large brown beard, and he cheerfully served Pevensey a tankard of ale while the sausages he had ordered were cooking.

"Ah, you're ahead of me," said a cheerful voice. Cecil's curly black head came in the door.

Pevensey raised his tankard in salute. "Have you breakfasted?"

"Yes, but it would not hurt to do it again," said Cecil. He took a seat next to Pevensey and asked the innkeeper for a full plate of whatever was available. "Well then, where are we at?"

"We have all the pieces," said Pevensey, "but somehow we must fit them together."

"Let me see if I have the same pieces you do," said Cecil. He pulled out his notebook and squinted as he tried to make out his own handwriting. "Item 1: the quarrel between Rufus and his half-brother Robert Curtis over the expired loan and the forfeiture of the estate."

Pevensey crossed his arms over his chest and wrinkled his nose. "Rufus Rowland wanted that estate for some reason. Either that or he wanted to spite his older brother. He didn't need the money."

"What does one want an estate for?"

"Presumably to live in. Although, given that he already had Harrowhaven and a house in Grosvenor Square, it seems superfluous."

Cecil thought hard. "He was about to be married. Perhaps it was to be a gift to his new wife."

"Perhaps," said Pevensey, "although he hardly strikes me as the gift-giving kind." He pursed his lips. "How far away was Curtis' estate?"

"Several hours' ride. Why?"

"Just the distance a man would want to separate his wife from his mistress."

"Lud, I think you might be onto something there! The need was pressing since he'd just become engaged. And did we not see his light skirt in the neighborhood just yesterday?"

"His *former* light skirt, according to Henry Rowland."

"Oh, pish, these dalliances with high-flyers are always

on-again, off-again affairs," said Cecil, waving a hand dismissively. He stopped himself and grinned. "Not that I would know from personal experience."

Pevensey laughed. "Of course not. Next item?"

"Item 2: the carriage on the road."

"Come now," said Pevensey, "given our previous conjecture about Curtis' estate, you should be able to solve the mystery of the carriage easily enough."

It only took Cecil a moment to fathom out what Pevensey meant. "It was for the mistress! To take her out of the way to the new location."

"Exactly," said Pevensey, pleased to see his pupil so apt.

"Item 3: the second shot?"

"Why is that a question?" asked Pevensey. "You are certain yourself that there were two shots, yes?"

"Indeed. But Walter Turold denies hearing two. I know I asked you this last night, but I'm asking it again: why?" Cecil took a swig of ale to wash down a large bite of sausage that was clogging his throat.

"An error on his part," said Pevensey. "He ought to have admitted hearing the first shot if he wanted us to believe that the shooting was accidental."

"What do you mean?" Cecil forgot to take another bite. "Who fired the first shot?"

"Possibly Turold himself, but not in the clearing, I think—"

"I can tell you who fired the shot!" a girlish voice interrupted. Both men's heads jerked around sharply to see a diminutive blond woman standing behind them, hands folded, eyes bright.

⁂

For the briefest of moments, Pevensey thought that the figure confronting them was Catherine Ansel—the build and fair features of the woman were so similar to that of the clergyman's daughter. But no, this woman's carriage was much more certain, and there was an alluring quality to her stance that would never have occurred to the Reverend's daughter.

Cecil rose from his seat instantly, the manners of a gentleman indelibly engrained in him. "Good morning, Mrs. Flambard," he said, nodding his head.

"I don't believe I've had the pleasure," said Pevensey, rising a little more slowly with a question in his eyes.

"Ah, yes, Mrs. Flambard, may I present Jacob Pevensey, attached to the London magistrates' office." Cecil turned to Pevensey. "Mrs. Flambard is...." Here his manners faltered as he struggled to come up with a suitable introduction.

The lady smiled coyly. "I think what Mr. Cecil is trying to get at is that I am—I was—a special friend of the Duke of Brockenhurst."

Pevensey had guessed as much already. "You seem to have overheard our conversation, madam."

"I could not help overhearing in such a public place." She cast down her eyelids with a counterfeit demureness that only drew attention to the décolletage of her dress. "The innkeeper informed me that you are investigating Rufus' death, and I..."— she gave an attractive little sob—"I could not remain silent, knowing what I know about the matter."

"And what might that be?" asked Pevensey. He saw Cecil offer Mrs. Flambard his handkerchief, and he hoped that his protégé was not about to be taken in by this sharp-witted minx.

"There was someone—someone quite close to him—who had quarreled with Rufus. It's a very delicate situation, you understand." She dabbed the handkerchief against her eyes. "I almost hate to mention it since the quarrel was...oh, how can I say this? The quarrel was over me! But, please, gentlemen, if this could just stay between us."

"Of course," Cecil murmured. "A lady cannot be too careful of her reputation." Pevensey caught the note of irony in the young magistrate's tone and knew that all was well.

"Are you referring to Walter Turold?" asked Pevensey, coming straight to the point.

"Lud, no!" said Mrs. Flambard, forgetting to ply the handkerchief. "To Rufus' brother—Henry! He was quite jealous of Rufus, you know. Resented the fact that his brother got the estate, the money, the woman he wanted for himself."

"You refer to yourself?" Pevensey had encountered this type far too often in his investigations.

"Oh, I am being much too open with you, far too bold," simpered Mrs. Flambard, fluttering her eyelids down at her neckline once again. "But I must speak out—for Rufus' sake!"

"So Henry quarreled with Rufus over property, money, and *you*," said Pevensey. "Go on."

"It all came to a head the last time Henry was here," said Mrs. Flambard. "They quarreled so violently, and in my presence! I thought that Henry was about to throttle Rufus then and there, but Rufus threw him out of the room. And then Henry stood at the door and swore—such terrible oaths!—that he would have his revenge on Rufus. I tremble to remember the scene." She put her hand on Cecil's sleeve to steady her nerves.

"So, you believe that Henry shot his brother during the hunt on Wednesday?"

"Oh, yes! I am certain of it."

"Walter Turold is not. He has confessed to it." Pevensey wondered how she would counter that piece of evidence.

"From what I have heard, he simply fired at random into the bushes. And there was another shot, they say. Someone else fired first. I think if you examine the matter, Mr. Pevensey, you'll find that Rufus was dead before Mr. Turold even fired." She still had not let go of Cecil's sleeve.

"I have considered the notion," said Pevensey dryly.

"And when I went to Harrowhaven the following day," said Mrs. Flambard, "his brother as good as admitted it to me!"

Cecil patted her hand gently and removed it from his arm. "Henry admitted to shooting Rufus?"

"Yes, he was disgustingly proud of himself. As if I would ever care for him after that!"

Pevensey saw Cecil's forehead wrinkle in perplexity. He decided to take the matter in hand. "Thank you for this new information, Mrs. Flambard. We shall, of course, take it into consideration as we continue our investigation. I do have one question for you."

She tilted her chin at an attractive angle and waited.

"Since Rufus Rowland was engaged to be married, he undoubtedly would have been severing all connection with you. Is that correct?"

She laughed. "Mr. Pevensey, you disappoint me. Surely, you understand the ways of the world. That redheaded giraffe would never have satisfied him in the arts of love. She wasn't at all the type of woman he admired. She was simply the quiet little mouse that Rufus needed to keep his house for him. He would never even have noticed her if a friend had not pointed her out."

"And how do you know that?" asked Cecil.

"I have my sources," Mrs. Flambard replied archly.

"I see," said Pevensey. "Good day, then Mrs. Flambard." He resumed his seat. "Oh, and I hope you weren't kept waiting too long for the carriage on Wednesday?"

"The carriage?" Her face had a look of bewilderment.

"Never mind," said Pevensey, waving her away with the bare minimum of civility, and coolly resuming his seat. "Cecil, do sit down. Your breakfast is getting cold."

25

The two men waited for Mrs. Flambard to leave the room before they continued their conversation. Cecil had hardly opened his mouth to speak, however, before they were interrupted again. "I couldn't help but overhear...." said the bearded innkeeper.

"Is that so, Ned?" said Cecil.

Pevensey merely smiled and took out his notebook. There was quite a rash of eavesdroppers in a village like this, eavesdroppers who did not mind being discovered and sharing their own opinions on the matter. And in Pevensey's experience, when he had not yet solved a case, it was best to continue gathering as many clues as possible. Who knows? Perhaps this young innkeeper might hold the key to unlock the mysteries that still plagued them.

"Yes, it is so, Mr. Cecil," said the innkeeper. The twinkle seemed to have gone out of his eye. "And what that Mrs. Flambard said to you—don't know as to why she calls herself *Mrs.*, for I can guarantee to you there weren't never any *Mr.*—what she said is a raggedy, patched-up bag of moonshine."

"Which part?" asked Pevensey. He could see that the innkeeper felt very strongly about the players in this tragedy.

"Master Henry never would have entertained such a thought as murdering his brother. And as to the quarrels they had—faugh!—they certainly weren't over the likes of her. I mean, they were, but not in the way she says."

"Why don't you tell us what the quarrels were about then," said Pevensey. "And perhaps a little bit of background as to how you know so much about what goes on at the big house."

"Master Henry and me go back a long ways," said Ned.

Cecil nodded in confirmation of this fact.

"When the old duke died, he left the estate to Master Rufus, and Master Henry was the steward. It was a fool's arrangement, but there you have it—it's what the old duke wanted. It didn't take long for Rufus to set up with some harlots from town in the old Dower House. Henry objected, and Rufus quieted down his riotous living for a time. But then not a few months had gone by and he imports this Mrs. Flambard—and she preening it like a peacock all over the village, letting it be known that she was the duke's favorite. Master Henry couldn't stand no more of it, and he told his brother to stop dragging the Rowland name into a swamp of lechery. But Rufus wouldn't listen, and he was the one who went into a rage. He stripped Henry of the steward's job and tossed him out on his ear. Master Henry made his way up to London—he comes down on occasion to visit his mother—but he don't hold no grudges. Leastwise, none that would end in murder."

"Hmm...quite a different narrative of events," said Pevensey. "Did Mrs. Flambard remain in residence following Henry's expulsion?"

"Aye, for a right long time. But something happened in the spring of this year. Maybe she grew too greedy, or else Master Rufus just grew tired of her. But one day she was preening about the village, and the next day she was gone. The Dower House went empty, and a little later Master Rufus went up to London and stayed there for a few months until just a fortnight or so ago."

"I see," said Pevensey. He looked over at Cecil. "So just

about the time he started showing interest in Miss Malcolm." He drummed his fingers on the table in front of them. An idea was forming in the recesses of his brain. He pulled out his notebook. "Cecil," he said. "Who is this a picture of?"

"Why, Mrs. Flambard," said Cecil, leaning closer to examine the notebook page. "No, wait! It is similar, but not quite her. It is—"

"—Catie Ansel," said the innkeeper, looking over Cecil's shoulder.

"Yes, exactly," said Pevensey, snapping the notebook shut. "The resemblance is uncanny, don't you think?"

"I suppose so," said Cecil, "but what does it mean?"

Pevensey ignored the question for the time being, and asked another one of his own. "Cecil, on the evening you visited Harrowhaven—Monday, I think—was Walter Turold there with the other guests?"

Cecil pursed his lips as he cudgeled his brain. "No...I don't believe he was."

"Did anyone mention where he was?"

"Not to my knowledge. Er...yes! Someone mentioned, I think, that he had a dinner invitation elsewhere."

"At Reverend Ansel's?"

"Possibly. I know that Ansel was a mentor, of sorts, to Turold after his father died. But Rufus was also absent. Could they have both dined at the Reverend's?"

The bearded innkeeper shook his head. He had given up all pretense of working to focus on the conversation. "The duke and the Reverend weren't exactly on friendly terms. Land disputes."

"Ah," said Pevensey, his fair skin lighting up behind his freckles. "Better and better."

"But what does it mean?" asked Cecil. "And what does Catie Ansel have to do with it?"

Pevensey pushed back in his chair and stood up. "I think

it's time to head back to Harrowhaven, Cecil. If you've finished your breakfast, we have a murderer to catch."

※

HAYWARD HAD BROUGHT THE MORNING post on a silver salver, and Henry had just begun sorting through it when he heard voices entering the saloon.

"Twenty pounds?" said a shocked voice. "Where on earth would he get something like that?"

"Gormley thinks he stole it," said a calmer voice that Henry recognized as Jacob Pevensey's, "but I'm inclined to think otherwise. I think it was payment."

"Oh, yes, of course!" said the first man. Henry now recognized the voice of Edward Cecil. "For the carriage and keeping quiet. From Rufus?"

The Bow Street Runner must have either nodded or shook his head, for Henry heard nothing of a reply. There was a letter on the tray from Mr. Maurice. He pocketed it for later reading and left his study to discover what was afoot.

"Ah, Brockenhurst!" said Pevensey as Henry came into view. "We were just coming to look for you."

Henry preempted him. "What's this about my groom?"

"It appears," said Pevensey, "that Martin is in possession of a large sum of ready cash. I believe that your brother Rufus paid him this money on the day of his death. Do you have any guess as to why?"

A sick feeling came over Henry. "No, not at all."

"Perhaps Mr. Turold knows why. With your permission, I will send for him."

Henry nodded and listened dully as Pevensey instructed a footman to usher Turold down to the morning room. The three men entered the morning room themselves, took seats on the sofa and chair, and waited. Henry's face set into a grim look of resignation. Cecil offered him an encouraging smile, but he did not reciprocate. He knew what was about to come.

Turold entered the room. He had dressed hastily, by the looks of it. His hair was pulled back into a tangled queue and he was missing a cravat.

"Thank you for joining us, Mr. Turold," said Pevensey, waving a hand towards the empty armchair. He acted as if he were the owner of the house, thought Henry. No—more than that. He acted as if this room were his court and he was the all-powerful judge.

Turold obeyed, sitting down on the edge of the seat, his slim body leaning forward, alert, taut, like a fox scenting the air for signs of danger.

"What was the relationship between Rufus Rowland and Catherine Ansel?" asked Pevensey. There were no preliminary pleasantries. The Runner had cut right to the core of the matter.

Henry licked his lips. He could feel Turold's eyes locked on him, willing him to remember his promise. Why had he ever given such a promise, and to the murderer of his brother? He closed his mouth, said nothing, and waited.

"Neither of you will tell me?" said Pevensey, his red eyebrows lifting into arches. "Very well. Then I shall tell you. Rufus Rowland was attempting a seduction of Catherine Ansel."

His eyes flashed back and forth between them. "What do you say to that?"

They said nothing, more fully united in their silence than they had been in the last ten years of their separated lives.

"*Cum tacent, clamant*," murmured Cecil.

"Neither of you denies it?" said Pevensey. "Good. Then I shall tell you more. He was attempting a seduction of Miss Ansel, and on the day of the hunt, he had paid his groom Martin to wait in the carriage on the road near the church. While the rest of the household was distracted with the hunt, he headed for the church building. He knew that the Reverend was away for the day to conduct a wedding. The timing was perfect. Miss Ansel is a simple and trusting young woman. She would be easy to lure away from the house and into the carriage. The well-paid groom would lock the carriage doors and transport his prisoner to Fontbury, the estate the duke had just recently acquired from his half-brother. The duke would return to the hunt and, with any luck, still be the one to shoot the stag. A week or so later, after the hue and cry over Miss Ansel's disappearance had receded, he would venture out to examine his new estate and complete the seduction of the clergyman's lovely daughter."

Turold let out an oath and slammed a fist into the arm of the chair. Henry kept quiet by sheer force of effort. It was a story he had refused to rehearse in his mind, but he knew that it was all true—and that Pevensey's dramatic description of the event was having the desired effect.

"Unfortunately, for the duke, someone got wind of his plan. Someone knew he had the intention of carrying off Catherine Ansel that day. Someone followed him to the church." Pevensey paused and looked from Henry to Turold and then back again. "That someone could have been either of you two gentlemen."

Again there was silence. Henry shifted in his chair. "I admit it. I noticed that Rufus had left the main body of the hunting party. I split off from the group to look for him. But when I reached the clearing by the church, he was already dead and others were there before me."

"Not I," said Turold hoarsely. He glared at Henry as if he were guilty of the greatest betrayal. "I followed the stag. I shot at the stag."

"Interestingly," said Pevensey, "there were two shots fired that day. Multiple witnesses recall it. The two shots were about five minutes apart. One of the shots took place in the clearing.

That was the second shot. But the first shot took place several hundred yards away, in the dusty churchyard where Rufus was readying himself to ride off with Catherine Ansel."

Henry was taken aback. In his imaginings, he had always seen Walter Turold stalking Rufus through the woods, and taking a coward's shot in the clearing before his brother ever reached the parsonage. "How do you know that, Pevensey? The body was found in the clearing."

"The clearing is full of soft, clean grass," said Pevensey. "And yet, the front of the duke's clothing was covered with a thick layer of dirt, the same kind of red dirt kicked up by carriages and hay carts all over the yard outside the church and the parsonage. When he first fell to the ground, it was not in the clearing."

Cecil nodded and finished Pevensey's explanation. "We believe that the body was moved afterwards to the nearby clearing where a second shot was fired to give verisimilitude to the ploy."

Henry let out a soft sigh and sat back in his chair. Had Catie Ansel actually been on Rufus' arm when Turold fired? Had Turold demanded that Rufus release her, and then fired only as a last resort? He closed his eyes. Would he have done any differently? He opened his eyes and stared at Walter Turold. What agony of the soul he must be suffering—must have already suffered, ever since that fateful decision to pull the trigger was taken!

Pevensey had not yet finished applying pressure to the thumbscrew. "It is clear to me that both of you gentlemen knew of the duke's plan, and that both of you gentlemen considered it to be immoral. It is also clear that both of you struck out alone from the main hunt and have no alibi as to your whereabouts during the time of the shooting. I know that you have admitted to firing the accidental shot, Mr. Turold," continued Pevensey, "but what is not clear to me is whether you were working alone or in concert with—"

"Yes!" said Turold, the word exploding from him like a cannonball. "I admit it. It was I, all alone. I shot Rufus in cold blood. No one else had anything to do with it."

Henry's heart accelerated. There it was—the confession from Turold's own mouth. And instead of recalling past grievances and claiming him as an accomplice, the man had exonerated him. He felt a surge of overwhelming elation mingled with sorrow.

"Surely not *cold* blood," Cecil urged. "Your desire to protect Miss Ansel's virtue must provide some extenuating circumstances."

"Please," said Turold, swallowing. "Please. I will give you a written confession. But I don't want Catherine Ansel's name brought into this. I don't want her talked about across the countryside as a flirt and a strumpet. She didn't know what she was doing. How could she?" Turold looked around the room. "How could she?"

Henry gripped the arms of his chair. It was true. The poor girl might never outlive the whispers and the calumny. But if she was not mentioned, if that part of the story was left untold….

Pevensey looked Turold squarely in the eyes. "I'll make no bones about it, Mr. Turold. If Catherine Ansel's name is *not* brought into it, it's very likely that you'll hang."

Surely, he must understand that!

"Then so be it," said Turold. "Fetch me pen and paper, and I'll write out my confession."

⁂

ELIZA AND ADELE FINISHED THEIR walk through the garden maze just before the morning sun became unbearably hot. For Eliza, the maze was full of unpleasant remembrances, but Adele had insisted on guiding her through every hidden corridor in the greenery.

"Dear me," said Adele, fanning herself as they entered the

French doors at the back of the house. "It is a good thing I wore my bonnet, or I should have as many freckles on my nose as you."

"And what a misfortune that would be," said Eliza dryly. She was surprised to find that Adele's comment failed to mortify her as it certainly would have a week ago. Could it be that the two were becoming friends?

"I'm parched!" said Adele, tossing the previously touted bonnet onto a little mahogany table by the entrance. "Let's have some ratafia and rest a bit."

"Lemonade," said Eliza, the voice of wisdom. She was not about to drink alcohol-laced punch at eleven o'clock in the morning.

Eliza followed Adele down the hallway to the morning room. Adele threw open the doors, only to discover that most of the seating was already taken—Mr. Pevensey and Mr. Cecil on the sofa, Henry in one of the wingback chairs, and Mr. Turold at the table, signing his name at the bottom of a lengthy letter.

Four pairs of eyes turned in their direction, and Eliza had the distinct impression that they were intruding on some sort of solemnity that was forbidden to the fairer sex. The gentlemen rose to their feet perfunctorily, Walter Turold taking the opportunity to fold his letter in quarters and hand it to Mr. Pevensey.

"What now?" asked Henry.

"Now we wait for Constable Cooper," said Pevensey.

"Shall I send a groom to the village to summon him?"

"No, we were just at the village a half hour since, and I told him he'd be needed at Harrowhaven this morning."

"Do I have your leave to go up to my room and pack a portmanteau?" asked Mr. Turold. Eliza's lips parted. Apparently, Rufus' friend was preparing to leave the house.

"Of course," said Cecil. "You give your word you'll not try escaping, yes?"

Mr. Turold pulled at a piece of hair that had fallen out of his queue. "Where would I go?"

At the word "escaping," Eliza's eyes opened wide. Had there been some new development in the investigation? Adele stared openmouthed at Turold. He turned on his heel and exited the room. The curly-haired Mr. Cecil followed him out.

"Lud, what is happening here, Henry?" demanded Adele.

Henry's jaw set into a hard line. "Walter has confessed that the shooting was no accident."

Adele let out a shriek. "He murdered Rufus? Whatever for?"

Eliza saw the red-haired investigator and Henry exchange a glance. Neither of them responded.

"I say, what's going on here?" asked Stephen Blount, peeking around the door of the morning room and seeing the somber gathering.

Adele breathlessly explained the new information. Stephen's eyes bulged, and he rubbed his invisible sideburns in disbelief. "But we still don't know why he would do such a thing." She stamped her foot. "They were friends!"

Stephen offered her his arm, and she took it. It was probably the closest thing to taking hands that they could do with Henry in the room. Eliza found herself staring at Henry's hands. She blushed and looked away. She was certainly *not* going to allow him to take her hand again.

The butler's form materialized. "Mr. Pevensey, the constable is here to see you." The investigator disappeared without a word.

"I'll tell Mother," said Adele, and within seconds she and her escort had disappeared, leaving Eliza alone in the morning room with Henry.

Henry walked over to the door which had swung shut and opened it half way. For a moment, Eliza thought he was leaving the room too—but no, he was simply lending a little more propriety to their tête-à-tête.

"I am very sorry about your brother," said Eliza. She stood

uncomfortably, refusing to sit down and thereby signify that she wanted a conversation to take place.

"So am I," said Henry. His stern face lifted into a wry smile. "But at least the investigator no longer believes that *I* murdered him." He gave her a direct look. "Nor you either, I hope."

"Oh!" said Eliza, taken aback. "I'm certain I never believed such a thing, my lord."

He seemed pained to hear her return to formal address, but he did not insist that she call him Henry.

"You are not as curious as Adele," he remarked, "demanding to know why this happened."

"It is not for lack of interest. I can see you do not want to say. Or perhaps it is not fitting for gentlewomen to hear."

"Both of those things are true. And yet"—Henry gave a slight gesture of his hand and she found herself sitting down without a shadow of protest in a nearby armchair—"I think it only right that you should know. I would prefer you not to share these details with Adele."

He took a seat opposite her, leaning forward and looking at her intently. "Rufus," he said, "was a scoundrel. I know you may not believe me—I know it seems that I have every reason to try to tarnish his reputation with you—but the fact of the matter is that he was a libertine through and through. That woman you saw here yesterday was his former mistress, and on the day of the hunt, Rufus was actually hunting something else besides a stag. He was attempting a seduction of a young woman in the neighborhood."

"Which young woman?" asked Eliza. It was an uncomfortable question, but she felt that—as the late duke's betrothed—she had the right to know.

"Catherine Ansel, the Reverend's daughter." Henry paused. "I think you overheard him discussing her with Turold in the maze that one evening."

"Oh...yes," said Eliza, swallowing. She had thought they were discussing her own self. Perhaps she was not the simpleton Walter Turold had referred to. And perhaps she did not have just the style of beauty that Rufus Rowland preferred. "She was not quite right in the head, Adele said." Eliza shuddered at the thought of Rufus taking advantage of the poor girl. "Why? What happened to her? Was she born like that?"

Henry stood up and paced over to the window. A moment passed. "I suppose the polite thing to do would be to say that I don't really know and pass on from the subject—but I find myself unable to give half-truths to you, Eliza. I have never shared this with anyone before, but since you ask...Catie Ansel's condition is entirely my fault. Several years ago, when she was really little more than a girl, I encountered her in the forest, and—"

Eliza's face drained of color. She stood up from her chair. "Thank you for your frankness, Lord Henry, but please, go no further. I understand that you consider me to be of greater maturity than your sister, but I have no desire to hear such tales." The half-open door called to her like a beacon in a hurricane. She darted toward it and disappeared into the hall, hurrying breathlessly through the saloon, and up the stairs to her room.

What horror had he been about to confess? Rufus was a scoundrel, he had said.... "But what about you?" her heart demanded. "What about you?"

26

PEVENSEY WALKED PENSIVELY OVER TO THE ENTRANCE hall. The confession from Walter Turold had been unexpected, and somehow...incomplete. There were so many details still unresolved. But perhaps it was best to take the man into custody and sort those details out later.

Constable Cooper was waiting in the entrance hall, his bushy gray sideburns nearly doubling the width of his round face. "Ah, Mr. Pevensey," he said. "I thought I'd come round this morning before the inquest and see if you have made any progress."

Pevensey could tell that it would delight the man to no end to find that no progress had been made. He kept quiet.

"I still have that statement by Mr. Turold," said the constable helpfully, "should you be needing it."

"Very kind of you," said Pevensey brightly, "but I've taken a new statement from Turold this morning, and he's confessed that it was no accident. He murdered the duke."

"Dear me!" said the constable, his jaw falling open in shock. "Oh dear, oh dear, oh dear. Are you sure he's quite sure?"

"The confession was made of his own free will."

"Well then," said the constable, "I suppose you'll be wanting me to hold him for the time being."

"Yes, exactly so. He's upstairs packing his things as we speak. Mr. Cecil should be bringing him down shortly."

Pevensey took a seat on the bench in the hall, and Constable Cooper followed suit. Out of the corner of his eye, Pevensey saw Miss Malcolm heading through the saloon, a look of distress on her face. Henry Rowland emerged from the morning room half a second later, his eyes on Miss Malcolm, but as soon as she disappeared, he stalked away in the other direction, presumably to his study.

Pevensey shook his head. There was clearly an attraction between these two, but also an impediment that stood in the way. The girl's mother was not in favor of the match—he had overheard as much yesterday—and the girl herself seemed undecided about something, hesitant to trust. He snorted. But who was he to fault someone for that? He had never been one to lower his defenses for anyone....

Constable Cooper initiated some small talk, and Pevensey reluctantly exercised his conversation about the weather in Sussex, the condition of the roads, and his opinion on the Prince Regent's diet. What on earth could be keeping Cecil and Turold? It was not as if they were packing a woman's trousseau.

After a quarter of an hour had elapsed, Pevensey signaled for one of the nearby footmen. "Could you show me where Mr. Turold's room is?"

It was the loquacious footman who had gone on leave the day of the hunt for his sister's wedding. He responded with alacrity and even a little show of excitement. Apparently, word of Turold's confession had already spread through the domestic staff. When they reached the door, the footman stood back at a discreet distance.

Pevensey knocked, but there was no response. He tried the door—locked.

"Who has keys to this?" he demanded.

"Mr. Hayward, Mrs. Forsythe—"

"Get them now!" said Pevensey, his tone clipped and urgent.

The footman broke into a run, making for the servants' staircase. It was not more than two minutes before he returned, thrusting an iron ring of keys in Pevensey's hands. The butler—stately Mr. Hayward—was only ten steps behind, his lined face glistening with the exertion of ascending the stairs so rapidly.

"This one," said the butler, reaching for the correct key. Pevensey put it in the lock.

He entered the room slowly, with the two domestics peering over his shoulder. There was no sign of Turold.

A man's body was lying prone on the floor near the bed. Pevensey knelt down and turned it over. Cecil!

He was still breathing, but unconscious. Pevensey saw something wet on his black curls and touched his head. His fingers came away red. Turold must have struck him with something hard.

The fireplace poker lay nearby.

While Pevensey examined Cecil, Hayward and Frederick searched the small room.

"The window is open, Mr. Pevensey," said the butler.

Pevensey wiped his hand on a handkerchief and stood up. Hayward was right, the window had been opened and propped up, the space large enough for a man—especially a lithe, athletic one like Turold—to slip through.

How far was the drop? Pevensey walked over to the window sill and looked down. It was a goodly distance, but there was grass below, and if he had lowered himself down by his arms first, it might have done no more than jar him. But then again, perhaps the open window was only a ploy—perhaps Turold had exited the bedroom through the door and hidden himself somewhere in the house.

"Have you notified all of the staff about Mr. Turold's confession?" asked Pevensey.

"No, sir," said Hayward. "I was never instructed to—although tongues wagging as they will, it may have spread to most of the downstairs servants by now."

"But probably not to the stables," said Pevensey. If Turold *had* left the house, Gormley would have had no warning to deny him the use of his horse. The fellow could have twenty minutes' start on them.

He looked back at Cecil, torn between running to the stables to give chase and looking after the needs of the fallen. Friendship won out. "We need a doctor. Now."

"Yes, Mr. Pevensey," said Frederick. He darted out of the room and ran down the corridor.

"Help me, Hayward," said Pevensey, and together they lifted Cecil onto the bed.

HENRY SAT DOWN HEAVILY. He had tried—for the first time in ten years—to bare his breast about that awful day. And Eliza had not even stayed to hear the whole of it. He took a deep breath. He had never considered the fact that he might someday find the woman he wanted to spend the rest of his life with and fail, through no fault of his own, to gain her good opinion.

He stretched and rolled his shoulders. What was he doing here anyway? The investigation was over. Once Rufus was in the ground, he could return to London. That was where his life was now.

The letter from Mr. Maurice was still in his pocket. Taking it out, he slid a finger under the flap and broke the seal. No doubt this was a summons to return to his duties.

An urgent knocking sounded on the door of his study. Without waiting for his answer, Mrs. Forsythe threw open the door.

"What is it?" asked Henry, standing up from his desk as he read the concern on the housekeeper's face.

"Oh, Master Henry!" she said, reverting to his childhood name. "Mr. Turold's attacked Mr. Cecil and run off."

Henry dropped the letter on the desk and made for the door. "Where's Pevensey?"

"Here," said Pevensey, just coming from the saloon into the corridor. "Cecil has a serious head injury. I've sent your footman for the doctor. Mrs. Forsythe, if you could tend to him until then—Hayward's putting some bandages on him to stop the bleeding. Brockenhurst, I need *you* to help me with the search."

Henry did not take time to mince words. He reached for the bell rope in the study and rang it sharply four or five times. Several of the staff came scurrying, and Henry sent them back to call the others for an emergency assembly in the saloon.

Meanwhile, Pevensey ran out to the stables, presumably to check with Gormley about the status of the horses. By the time he had returned, the caps of the maids were fluttering around the saloon like a bevy of white butterflies.

As the servants gathered on the floor below, the family and guests congregated on the staircase above. Adele and Stephen came down with Henry's mother. Lady Malcolm and Sir Arthur were not far behind. Robert poked his head out from the top of the stairs to see what all the commotion was about. Henry noted that only Eliza was missing.

Pevensey ascended a few of the steps in the grand staircase so that he could project his message into the crowd. In short order, he explained about Walter Turold's confession, his attack on Cecil, and his disappearance. "He has not taken a horse, which means he is either hiding here in the house"—a gasp went up from the maids—"or has escaped through the window and is making for the woods on foot. I shall need every able-bodied man to help with the search."

Henry heard Constable Cooper clear his throat from the

back of the crowd. "Excuse me, Mr. Pevensey, the gentlemen should be arriving for the inquest quite soon."

"It's not an inquest anymore," said Pevensey. "It's a manhunt. I'm sure we can use the extra help. My lord?"

Henry stepped forward to sort the male domestics into pairs and sent them off to search different quadrants of the house. He told the maids to stay in the kitchen with Hayward and asked his mother and sister to step into the morning room with the Malcolms. "Stephen," he said, "go out to the stable with Robert and have Gormley saddle our horses."

"I say, Hal," said Robert, "I think it would be better if I stayed here to guard the ladies." He blinked his poor, shortsighted eyes.

"Suit yourself," said Henry. The crowd started to disperse, each to his own assigned location. "I'll be with you momentarily, Stephen." Taking the stairs two at a time, Henry reached the top and strode down the corridor. He reached Eliza's door and knocked sharply.

"Who is it?" The thick wood of the door deadened her voice.

"Henry. I need to talk to you."

"I don't think there's anything more to say." He could hear her voice closer now, as if she had moved directly in front of the door.

He took a chance and turned the door handle.

"Lord Henry!" she said, affronted at the imposition. Later on, Henry would have no memory of what she was wearing or how her hair was arranged, but he did remember how lovely she looked when she was angry.

"Listen to me, Eliza," he said, overruling her objection. "Turold has escaped. He's injured Cecil—badly—and he could be hiding in the house still. I need you to go downstairs with your parents. Immediately."

She hesitated.

He held out his hand. "Please."

She placed her hand in his, removing it to the more proper position of the crook of his arm as they went down the corridor. Despite the macabre circumstances, Henry's mind could not help seizing on what might have been....

As soon as they reached the hard floor of the saloon, she took her arm away. Henry felt an acute sense of loss. "They are in the morning room," he said—because he was unable to say what he really wished to say.

"Thank you," she said crisply, and headed in that direction without a backward glance.

∞

It was nearly nightfall when Pevensey dismounted from his horse outside the small stone manor belonging to the Cecil family. He tied the horse to an iron ring and knocked on the door.

A suspicious housekeeper answered the knocker and was about to shoo him away when he inquired after Cecil until a clear, feminine voice floated towards them from an adjacent room. "It's all right, Mrs. Potter. He can come in."

Pevensey was shown into a small sitting room where a young lady sat at her embroidery, working away at an intricate pattern of flowers and leaves on a large hoop. Her curly black hair hinted at her identity right away.

"Good evening, Miss Cecil," said Pevensey with a bow. The lady's black curls, half of them unpinned, fell forward over the shoulders of a pale blue day dress, a slightly softer shade than the blue of her eyes.

"Good evening, Mr. Pevensey," the young woman said, gesturing toward a nearby chair. He sat down. "Any luck in the search?" She laid her embroidery hoop in her lap.

"Nothing worth mentioning," said Pevensey. It had been a

grueling day of searching the woods on foot and on horse with a pack of bloodhounds that never picked up the scent. "I heard your brother was transported here by carriage. Is he...?"

"Quite well," she said reassuringly, "or at least as well as one can be after such an ordeal. I believe he came to his senses before the doctor even arrived at Harrowhaven. He has a good-sized bandage and a splitting headache, but he may be walking about in the morning."

"Is he asleep now?" asked Pevensey. They had never had the chance to speak together after Walter Turold's confession, and Pevensey dearly wanted to know what had transpired upstairs directly before the suspect's flight.

Miss Cecil smiled. "Probably not. He wanted to come down for dinner, but I insisted that he follow the doctor's orders and stay in bed for at least one day."

"I hope you at least sent him up a tray."

Her eyes twinkled. "Of course. I hardly think I could have enforced fasting, even if the doctor had required it." She stood up, laying her embroidery down on a small table. Pevensey rose to his feet as well. "Shall I show you upstairs?"

"Yes, please." Pevensey fell in behind her as she left the sitting room.

They went up a narrow staircase, and she opened a door leading off the top landing. There was Cecil, his black hair wrapped round with a strip of muslin. He was propped up in bed with half a dozen pillows, a tray of cold meats and soup on his lap. "Pevensey! I hoped you would come."

"How did it happen? Did you turn your back on him?"

"Regrettably, yes. We had no sooner walked into the room than he walked over to the fireplace. I went over to the wardrobe to open it, and within seconds, there was a very large bump on the back of my head. But enough about me. What news? Did you apprehend him?"

"Regrettably, no," said Pevensey. He walked over to the bed and took the nearby chair. Miss Cecil stayed farther back, leaning her black head against the frame of the door. In keeping with human nature, she would want to know what events had transpired today. "He's gone to earth somewhere," continued Pevensey. "We couldn't trace him, even with bloodhounds."

Cecil frowned. "Did you try the parsonage?"

"It was the first place I looked, but the Reverend swore on his Bible that he hadn't seen so much as Turold's whiskers today."

"Did he seem…surprised to learn of the confession?"

"In my estimation, no," said Pevensey. "At the same time, though, he made no admission of prior knowledge. He acted doubtful when I told him the shooting had taken place just outside his home." He cast a sideways glance at Miss Cecil, for whom this information might be too detailed. Turold had wanted them to leave out Miss Ansel's involvement in the sordid affair—but then Turold had also bludgeoned Cecil on the head and fled the premises. It was perhaps not necessary anymore to honor that request.

"He must have known!" said Cecil, showing no such restraint. His knees nearly overturned the dinner tray onto his bed. "Rufus was in the middle of abducting that girl. She would have told her father. Or at least the housekeeper, Mrs. Hodgins, would have known—where was she in all of this?"

"Locked in a closet, I imagine. And told to say nothing about it later. Miss Ansel would have given us some clues, I think, but her father forestalled her."

"So they are accomplices—although I think I can sympathize with their reasons for silence." Cecil lay back against his pillow. "Where do you think Turold will go?"

"The coast," said Pevensey. "Hastings perhaps. He will take ship as soon as possible."

"France?"

"Or America."

"And if he makes it, what happens then? The case is over?" The cutlery on the tray clattered on the plate as Cecil's knees moved again.

"Essentially—unless he has the folly to return to England someday. We will publish his name in the *Hue and Cry*, but there is no hope of retrieving him if he has gone abroad—France and America are not exactly friendly to us at present."

Miss Cecil entered the room and removed the tray from the bed, placing it on a small table. "I hope you do not mind, Mr. Pevensey, but my brother has discussed the case with me."

Pevensey raised his eyebrows. Seduction and murder were not usual topics to discuss with well-born females. "I hope it did not distress you unduly, Miss Cecil."

"Not at all." She folded her hands in front of the pale blue skirt of her dress. "I was quite impressed with your skills in piecing it all together. But I must confess there is one aspect that puzzles me still. Why would Turold fire a second shot? The clearing was so close to the house that there was no reason for it. Everyone at a distance would have assumed that the first shot took place in the clearing. And it was impractical. He would have to have gone to all the trouble of reloading."

Pevensey stared at her. This same question had been niggling at him just this morning, but he had suppressed it in all the excitement of the chase and the worry over Cecil. Apparently this young woman's mind was as sharp as her embroidery needle. "You are exactly right, Miss Cecil. It *is* befuddling."

They all stared at each other then, but no one had any answers to give. A few moments later, Pevensey said his goodnights and Miss Cecil followed him downstairs. The formidable housekeeper had disappeared. They paused in the entry hall. A large vase laden with giant blooms stood on the console table, filling up too much of the narrow entryway for comfort.

"I will try to call again tomorrow," said Pevensey.

"As will others," said Miss Cecil, nodding at the floral arrangement. The Bertram family name was written in flowery script on the card, one of the neighbors that lived nearby and—if Pevensey remembered correctly—a family with an eligible daughter who had attended the hunt. "But there may be no need. He swears he will be out of bed and ready to mount his horse in the morning."

Pevensey was surprised to feel a small sense of disappointment, as if a part of him wished to call on the Cecils again in the morning. But then, who was he fooling? He was a London constable who provided assistance to local magistrates about a given case. He was not the sort of man who made calls on gentlemen and their sisters. "Then perhaps he will wish to meet me in the village. I shall be there tomorrow making inquiries and expanding our search for the fugitive."

"I shall tell him," said Miss Cecil, and she opened the door to let Pevensey out into the summer night.

27

Eliza awoke to the noise of Ollerton's industry as the maid busily packed her dresses, slippers, and jewelry away in her brass bound trunk.

"What is this?" asked Eliza, climbing out of bed. "Are we leaving?"

"Just so, miss," said Ollerton. "The inquest is over, short as it was, and with the murderer having confessed, the investigator said there's no need for us to be imprisoned here any longer."

"I see," said Eliza. She turned her face to the window where the bright sunlight was streaming in with the unfamiliar sound of birdcalls. It would be good to get back to London, to the hustle and bustle of town life that she missed, the crowds of people that she could so easily blend into without calling attention to herself. But at the same time, the idea of leaving Harrowhaven was bittersweet. There was something here that still felt unfinished.

She shook herself, replaying her mother's admonitions in her own head. That was nonsense. There was nothing here for her. And however kind Henry Rowland had been to her, it made no difference when his true character was taken into account. No, she was just another pretty face for him to dally with, like the Harrowhaven housemaids, that blond courtesan, and the imbecile daughter of the clergyman.

She rose from bed and dressed for travel, hoping that the carriage ride would not be as stifling as the journey here. It was best to get an early start on it—no wonder Ollerton was hurrying so. She knocked on her parents' door. "Good morning, Eliza," said Lady Malcolm, further ahead in her toilette than Sir Arthur and trying to spur her husband on to quicker progress. "Yes, yes," she said to Eliza, "go down and see that the footmen put everything in the carriage correctly. And tell the housekeeper to send up a tray." She sniffed. "The least they can do is feed us after everything that's been put upon us during our stay."

Eliza went downstairs to follow her mother's directions. Mrs. Forsythe, noticing the commotion, had already thought to send up some breakfast, and she tried to press some on Eliza as well. The prospect of eating made Eliza queasy, however, and she continued outside to gain some fresh air and see to the loading. A footman, whom Ollerton had pressed into service, followed her out the door bearing her trunk. The post chaise they had hired for the journey—at an exorbitant and now unrequited expense—had pulled round in the circular drive and was waiting to be filled.

She went down the steps and stood nearby the coach.

"Eliza!"

At the sound of her name she turned instinctively. It was Henry Rowland, striding toward her with a purposeful look in his eyes. He was in riding dress, his dark hair already windblown by an early morning ride.

Eliza's lips parted but no sound came out. She looked away. He pressed forward, undeterred by such an ineffectual snub.

As the coachman hoisted Eliza's trunk onto the top of the carriage, Henry Rowland took hold of her arm and led her around the corner of the house out of sight of the carriage and the front door.

"Unhand me, sir!" she said, working up the courage to show affront at this treatment.

"Eliza, please," he said, releasing her arm, but then seizing her hand in his when she turned to go. "Please! I know I ought not to speak to you on this subject without your father's blessing, but—I cannot help myself. Please." He let go of her hand as she grudgingly forbore her flight and allowed him to say his piece.

"Eliza, I have loved you from the first—from the rosy blush of your cheeks to the freckles on the tip of your nose."

The words washed over her like a waterfall. Her hands balled into fists as her spirit fought against being overwhelmed.

"I cannot pinpoint the exact moment I first knew it—when I served you turbot at dinner, when I visited the church just to see you once more, when I asked you questions through that flimsy blindfold. Believe me when I say that it nearly killed me to imagine you in the arms of another. You are, and have always been, the only woman for me."

At this last protestation, Eliza shrank away. He seemed so sincere in that last statement, and yet how well she knew it for a lie. Was that how all these rakehells worked?

"I do not ask you to decide now," he continued. "I simply ask you to allow me to win you over, to gain your good opinion. Our acquaintance has been short and attended with too many unfortunate events. Please, let me call upon you in London. Perhaps, in time, you will come to regard me with affection, and—dare I hope it?—love."

Eliza swallowed. For receiving a declaration like this she had no experience to draw on, and a tide of emotions was threatening to sweep her off her feet. She could only rely then on the resolves she had made when her head was clearer and when her heart had not been beating in such a fashion. "Sir, I thank you for the sentiments you have expressed. Regrettably, the interest is not mutual,"—she felt the lie as soon as it rolled off her tongue—"and I must ask you to refrain from renewing the acquaintance in London. It is better, I think, that we go our separate ways and see nothing of each other in the future."

His face looked so stricken that she almost recanted then and there. But the thought of her mother's revelations steeled her—if her parents' marriage was an example of two people with diametrically opposing moral principles, then she wanted no part of such a thing.

She was afraid that he would turn angry, but in this, it seemed, he was not like his brother. He simply looked on her for a moment, his dark eyes filled with pain, and then turned away and walked towards the house.

Eliza watched him go, knowing that this was the last image of Henry Rowland that would ever appear before her. And her mind could barely quench that unreasoning part of her heart that was bidding her to forsake all reason and blindly run after him.

⁓⊚⁓

Henry entered the house and walked mechanically down the corridor to his study. It would have been easier if there had been some reason for Eliza's refusal—if he had been too poor to support her, if she had loved another man. But there was nothing, nothing that he knew, keeping her from accepting him except her mother's opposition. It was especially galling that not one week ago, despite all his brother's shortcomings, she had accepted *his* proposal.

What a fool he had been to approach her today! He should have waited till her nerves had time to calm and called on her later in London. And now she had forbidden him to attempt to renew the acquaintance.

He sat in his chair and waited listlessly until he heard carriage wheels in the drive. There. She was gone.

He looked down at the desk. The letter from Mr. Maurice lay there still unread. He unfolded it, scanning the page. His eyes widened a little and his lips parted. Here was news indeed—something to make London a little more palatable despite his too-recent disappointment.

A knock came on the door.

"Enter!" said Henry, looking up from the letter.

Stephen poked his head into the room. "I say, are you busy? Could I have a word?"

Henry wanted nothing more than to be alone right now.

"Of course. Come in." He set the letter down on the desk.

Stephen sat down on the chair opposite the desk and began to pull at his invisible sideburns with his left hand. Henry waited for him to begin, but after a minute had passed, he realized that he would need to initiate the conversation himself.

"What can I help you with, Stephen?"

Stephen cleared his throat. "Well, it's a rather delicate matter, you see..."

Henry stifled the urge to yawn.

"...regarding a lady."

"I hope the lady is my sister."

"You do?" Stephen's countenance brightened considerably. Henry could tell that he had been expecting more gruffness.

"You've been dangling after her for months, and if I find that you've been playing her false for another, I might have to call you out with pistols."

"Never," said Stephen. "She is most certainly the lady in question. I have come to apply to you for permission to seek her hand in marriage."

Apparently there were to be two proposals of marriage at

Harrowhaven today, although it was likely that the second one would fare better than the first.

"You seem nervous," Henry remarked. He could not let Stephen attain his prize *too* easily. "Perhaps you are afraid she will reject you."

"No, I am quite certain of Adele. It is someone else I am not altogether certain of."

"You mean me."

"In point of fact, yes. And I realize it is not the most fortuitous of times to ask...."

"Are you referring to the fact that my brother has just been murdered or the fact that Miss Malcolm has declined my proposal of marriage this morning?"

Stephen's jaw fell open. "Oh, dear lord, Henry—I *am* sorry. A most unseemly time for me to put forward my own suit." He half stood up from his char. "Shall I wait a week or two? Or a month even?"

Henry manfully resisted the temptation to add some company to his misery. "Certainly not. Whatever disappointments I may have had, there is no reason for you to share them. As long as my mother has no objections, I give you my blessing. Although I warn you, Stephen, you will be a henpecked husband."

"I am looking forward to that eventuality," said Stephen, both recklessly and resolutely.

"Get to it then," said Henry, dismissing his friend with a wave. Stephen stopped to say a starry-eyed thanks at the door and then bounded off in search of Adele.

Henry tried not to be envious of that happy light in his eyes. If things had only transpired differently this morning....

He picked up the letter from Mr. Maurice and read it one more time. He still needed to make sure his brother was laid to rest properly, but other than that, he was a free man. He could return to London and forget what had happened at Harrowhaven over the last sennight. He could forget Miss Eliza Malcolm.

There was one thing he could not forget, however. He stood up from the desk. Before he left for London, there was one last thing he must do.

⁂

PEVENSEY PAID OUT THREE SHILLINGS at the shop that also served as a post office. Barring any new developments, he intended to return to London himself on Monday. The clues had run dry here and the chase was cold. Walter Turold had made his way to the ocean by now. The authorities at each of the likely ports had been notified, but if Turold had disguised his identity, there was little chance he would be stopped before securing passage to France or America.

"Where can I get an early luncheon?" he asked the clerk behind the counter.

The boy's Adam's apple bounced up and down as he prepared to answer such an important stranger. "Well, there's the Blue Boar, sir, if you's wanting something hot. But if you just want a bun, you can go to White's Confectionary next door."

"Thank you," said Pevensey, tipping his hat to the boy. He had already sampled the Blue Boar's cuisine, and the confectionary seemed convenient. He walked next door, and immediately, his nostrils were besieged with the smell of freshly baked grains and caramelized sugars.

"How can I help you?" said a genial man at the counter, wiping his floury hands on his apron in anticipation.

"Are you Mr. White?" said Pevensey, guessing from this fellow's eagerness that he must be the owner. His gray sideburns peeked out of a white baker's hat.

The man laughed. "There is no Mr. White, but I find the

name adds a certain charm to the establishment. We may not be Londoners, but even folks in Sussex want their bread white, an' that's the truth."

"Indeed," said Pevensey, bracing himself for the discovery of a good deal of chalk in his bread. He could see now that the man was not as old as he had first assumed and that the gray sideburns, sans flour, would normally appear brown. "I shall take a bun, if you please."

As he said it, he remembered a certain domestic's wish for free buns from his new relative. "Are you related to Frederick, the footman up at the big house?"

The man laughed again. "I suppose I must claim him. He's my wife's brother, the great, hungry lout."

"And you are but newly married?" said Pevensey, remembering the rest of the story. "Felicitations!"

"Just this Wednesday," said the man proudly. "We married up at my Lucy's village, Dealsby Cross."

"A warm day for a wedding," said Pevensey, accepting his glazed bun. He recalled how hot it had been that afternoon when Sir Richard gave him orders to report immediately at Harrowhaven.

"Aye, and an overlong wedding service," said the baker. He pounded a fresh batch of dough behind the counter. "Curate Gray is much too flowery for my taste, even when I'm not waiting to take my new wife home—if you catch my meaning."

Pevensey paused in the middle of masticating his first bite of the bun. His eyes opened wide as he swallowed. "Then Reverend Ansel did not officiate the service?"

The baker landed another punch on the dough. "He was supposed to, but he were taken ill. A bad summer cold, Mr. Gray said. Couldn't say the vows without sneezing all over us."

"Did he attend the wedding?"

"Nah, Mr. Gray showed up alone. The Reverend had tried

to come but had a sneezing fit and had to turn back. Which left Mr. Gray the whole ride to think of ways to prolong the service."

"My condolences," said Pevensey, his mind spinning. "Though surely the event was a happy one in spite of Curate Gray."

The baker gave a jolly grin and continued beating his dough into submission. Pevensey stepped outside, his fragmented thoughts crystallizing into an unbroken sequence of events. Curate Gray had gone to Dealsby Cross. Reverend Ansel had not.

He had an uncurtained look now into the window of Walter Turold's motivations. But with Turold's confession signed and witnessed, was there anything Pevensey could actually prove in a court of law?

He looked around the street. Where was Cecil? He needed to share his news as quickly as possible.

THE EARLY DEPARTURE PLANNED BY Lady Malcolm did not have its desired effect. While the Malcolms had hoped to reach London before midday, they had but barely reached the village before one of the carriage wheels lost several spokes, and they were forced to stop at The Blue Boar to make repairs.

"You should have made sure the coachman inspected the carriage before we left." Lady Malcolm sniffed out the accusation at her husband.

"How was I to know this blasted coach was so poorly built?" rejoined Sir Arthur. He shoved the door open with far too much force. Eliza could see that the failure of their mission was rankling him heavily, and even her mother was on edge. Perhaps they had done the right thing, but the penury waiting for them in London would never take their morals into account.

Sir Arthur was gone five minutes. "How long will it be?" demanded his wife when he returned.

"Dashed if I know! A half hour. An hour."

Lady Malcolm sniffed her disapproval at her husband's language. "Must we disembark?"

"Of course you must," Sir Arthur snapped. "How can they put the carriage up on blocks with you inside?"

Lady Malcolm did not dignify that question with a response. She moved towards the door, holding out her hand and forcing her husband to help her down the stairs while Eliza was left to fend for herself. The two moved off to the porch of the inn to perpetuate their pique more discreetly.

"Ollerton!" said Lady Malcolm. "Please find us some bread or a biscuit to eat. We may be here indefinitely."

The lady's maid, who had climbed down from the box, duly trotted off to the nearby bakery. Sir Arthur's valet had gone off with the coachman to effect the repair. Eliza looked around. She certainly could not stand there alone in the carriage yard. She went into the inn, hoping that her lack of chaperonage in a strange establishment would not be too noticeable.

"Ah, Miss Malcolm!" said a familiar face. The innkeeper, Ned Hornsby, was just wiping down a used table with a rag. "Carriage trouble, eh?"

"Unfortunately, yes," said Eliza softly. She wanted nothing more than to banish Henry Rowland from her mind, but here was a friend of his to make those thoughts resurface. A strange sort of friend, too. She had never interacted with an innkeeper before—but then, gentlemen of all ranks in society were more prone to mingling than ladies were.

"May I offer you a drink, miss?" He pulled out a chair for her, at a table near the counter, and Eliza, not knowing what else to do, sat down.

"That's very kind of you," said Eliza, heat rising to her cheeks, "but I am not thirsty." She recalled that she had no pin money in her reticule, and the idea of asking her father for some at the present moment was daunting.

Ignoring her protest, Mr. Hornsby fetched her a glass of lemonade anyway. She stared. It was only after he had gone whistling about his work for a few minutes, that she plucked up the courage to take a drink. It was exactly like something Henry Rowland would have done—assess her needs even better than she could do herself and provide for her without embarrassment. She set the cup down with a clunk. Oh, why must she keep thinking of that profligate!

Her green eyes watched Mr. Hornsby from behind veiled eyelashes. There was no one else in the inn except an old man, taking a nap in the chair in the corner. The solitude should have made her anxious, but instead, it emboldened her.

"Mr. Hornsby," she said, making up her mind. "I recall that Lord Henry told you on Wednesday that you might tell me some stories about him. Would you oblige?"

The bearded man stopped whistling and his eyebrows shot up into the air. "What do you want to know, miss?" He leaned his elbows on the counter and looked her full in the face.

Eliza's heart skipped a beat. She had created the opening, and now she must simply have the courage to enter it. "I know this is not a polite question for young ladies to ask, but is Lord Henry friendly with ladies of ill repute?"

The innkeeper laughed loudly. The man in the corner stirred before falling asleep again, and Eliza felt overpowered by an urge to turn and run. "Certainly not, miss," said the innkeeper. "I'd swear on the holy book itself that Henry Rowland is on the straight and narrow."

Eliza stared at her hands. "I met a Mrs. Flambard at the house...."

The innkeeper folded his arms and clucked disapprovingly. But the disapproval was not directed at Eliza. "Claimed to be his mistress, did she? I wouldna put it past that one. She's cagey, she is. The truth of the matter is—well, who am I to speak ill of the dead?"

The only dead Eliza could think of was Rufus, and his reputation certainly held no hallowed spot in her heart. "Please, sir! What do you mean?"

"Mrs. Flambard, as she styles herself, was mistress to the older brother Master Rufus for several years. Set herself up in style at the Dower House on the estate. The whole county knew of it, and Master Henry—he were steward at the time—told Master Rufus it was unbecoming for a duke and a Christian, especially with his mother and sister so close by."

"Oh!" This description of immoral activities at the Dower House comported with the dinner conversation that had puzzled Eliza several nights ago. "And did Rufus listen?"

"Certainly not! He turned Master Henry out, not La Flambard. She continued in residence for several years and then left the county a few months ago to try her fortunes in London. She came back for a short spell this week, but I saw her on her way again yesterday afternoon."

Eliza sighed inwardly. So, that tawdry blond creature had nothing to do with Henry. But what about the others? What about the maid she had seen with her own eyes? What about Catherine Ansel?

"I see now," she said to Mr. Hornsby, aware that her words might be relayed back to Henry Rowland himself, "that I was under a misapprehension regarding Mrs. Flambard. I am thankful to be corrected. There were other incidents that occurred at Harrowhaven during my stay, however, that reinforced this misapprehension. Lord Henry himself, confessed that he had behaved most vilely toward the clergyman's daughter, Miss Ansel, in past years."

Ned Hornsby leaned farther forward, his brown eyes wide with concern. "What exactly do you mean, Miss Malcolm?"

Eliza regretted at that moment, that she had said anything of the kind. Her mother, if she were here, would take her violently to task for perpetuating gossip and staining a young lady's good name. "I'm not sure exactly—apparently, a vital clue in the...murder...was Rufus Rowland's attempted seduction of Miss Ansel. Lord Henry mentioned as much to me, but then confessed that he had done far worse than his brother. But please, Mr. Hornsby,"—her voice took on a tinge of panic—"say nothing on the topic. I should not have been so free with my speech."

"Miss Malcolm," said Ned Hornsby, kneading the wet rag convulsively between his fingers, "on that subject I once swore a solemn oath of silence to a much younger Master Henry. And yet"—he cocked his head, sending his brown beard flying sideways—"he also gave me permission to tell you any stories leading to a better view of his character." He walked around the counter and pulled out a chair at the table where she sat. "May I sit down?"

Eliza nodded, her heart palpitating with fear and excitement about the revelation to come—and anxiety that her mother or father would choose this moment to walk into the inn.

Mr. Hornsby's voice quieted till it was barely above a whisper. "When Master Henry, Walt, and I were boys—Walter Turold, you understand—we were a band of lads that nothing could separate. They were both above me in station, but they treated me as if I wasna different from them in the least. The woods were our playground, and we spent many an hour hiding from their tutors among the trees.

"One day, in the middle of a wind storm, we found a downed tree in the forest, sticking out over the brook like a spaniel's leg. We climbed up on it—e'en though it was not steadily anchored in the soil—and rode it like a pony that had never been broken. The storm worsened. We'd just climbed down to go home before we were missed when little Catie Ansel appeared. She were no more than seven or eight—a pretty little girl with braids and a pinafore. She'd seen us come down from the felled tree and asked if she might go up herself. Then Walter and I shook our heads no, but Henry—he were a rascal as boys can be—taunted her some an' told her she'd be too scared by far to climb out on the log."

The mounting tension of the story constricted Eliza's throat. *Oh Henry, what is it you have done?*

"She gritted her teeth at that, and did just as he knew she would. She climbed out on the trunk and put one little foot in front of the other until she came out to the end. Then of a sudden, a great gust came up, and the tree lost the last of its bearings and rolled down into the river gulch. Down went little Catie and, I am not ashamed to say, we all shrieked like boys in shortcoats at the sight."

"What did you do?" asked Eliza, clutching a hand to her heart.

"Walt went down straightway into the water, and lifting a branch, pulled her free. But she had struck her head upon a rock or on a stump, and her blond hair was all bloodied on the side."

"What did Henry do?" demanded Eliza, not sure if she wanted to know.

"Walt demanded that we carry her home, but Henry was a-feared. He knew the matter was his fault, and he did not want to face her father or his own. He begged me and Walt to never speak of what had transpired. 'Why?' said Walt, 'She'll rat you out soon enough when she comes to.' And I couldna help but agree with him. But Henry were desperate, and so we both swore then, on our friendship, to never say what part he'd played.

"Then something had to be done, but neither Henry nor I were willing. Walt told us to go off and cry like a pair of babies, and he carried the girl home himself, half a mile in the storm up to the parsonage."

"And Miss Ansel?" said Eliza, her white fingers gripping the edge of the table.

"As far as I know, she never remembered what happened that day. She never remembered much of anything. I don't know how much Walt told the Reverend—I suspect he kept his word to Henry—but from that day on he loathed the sight of him.

"He knew the rivalry between the Rowland brothers, and so he 'came friends with Rufus from this time forward. And when his father died, Walt grew as great a wastrel as Rufus, squandering his fortune on gambling and wenches."

Ned Hornsby stared at Eliza until she looked him full in the eyes. "And if you think what Henry Rowland did is worse than what Rufus Rowland meant to do to her—to seduce a poor young halfwit for his own pleasures—then I am sorry I've broken my word to tell you all this tale. But if you think that Henry acted only in folly as boys will often do, why then, you think the same as me. He did not mean her harm, and it is not in one moment that a man's character must be measured."

"Yes, indeed, of course," said Eliza, her words coming out in a tumble. "Thank you, Mr. Hornsby!" She grabbed his hand and pressed it.

It was at that moment that Lady Malcolm and Sir Arthur entered the inn, and Eliza soon had cause to regret her impulsive response.

"Elizabeth Malcolm!" said her mother, with all the pent up frustration of a late summer thunderstorm.

"We can speak of this later," said Sir Arthur, intervening before the full force of his wife's displeasure should break upon them. "The carriage has been righted." They went outdoors to continue their journey, Eliza feeling in her bones that something else had been righted as well—albeit, now too late.

28

Red dust filled the air as Henry's boots hit the ground in the churchyard. He tied his horse's reins to an iron ring and strode quickly to the door of the parsonage. Then, he forced himself to rap on the door before his will deserted him.

He was expecting the housekeeper, but the door was answered by Reverend Ansel himself. "Henry!" His nose was still a little swollen from his summer cold, but his diction was clearer than when Henry had seen him last. "What can I do for you, my boy? Or should I say 'your grace' now?"

Henry took off his beaver and fingered the brim. "I think 'boy' is quite appropriate in this case, Reverend, since what I'm here to talk about is something that happened a long time ago."

The big man's eyebrows beetled in confusion, but he threw the door open wide and asked Henry into the parlor. In a moment's time they were seated on a pair of facing chairs for the conversation that Henry had been dreading nearly half his life.

"Now, what is it?" said the Reverend, folding his legs, leaning back, and clasping his hands over his stomach.

Henry stiffened in anticipation. "You will recall, sir, that ten years ago or so, your daughter suffered an injury during a storm."

The Reverend lost his relaxed air. "Of course I recall that—I could hardly forget such a thing."

"Did you...did you ever discover the cause of her injury?"

"Why, yes. She fell from a log and tumbled down the river bank. Walter Turold was there—he saw it happen."

"He was not the only one there, sir." Henry felt the small weight on his lungs turn into a massive boulder.

"Oh?" Reverend Ansel leaned forward.

"I was there as well," said Henry, "and what you may not know is that I...contributed to the accident, though that was not my intention."

The Reverend breathed in sharply, which led to a fit of coughing. "What do you mean?" he asked, after he had recovered himself.

Henry swallowed, fighting hard against all those years of avoiding the subject to bring it out into the open. "I taunted her. I told her she would never be brave enough to climb on that log. And she—she responded as I knew she would. She did what I dared her to, and she fell."

The Reverend opened his mouth and stared dumbfounded for a moment. "Henry, I never—"

"I made Walter swear not to tell. And, as far as I know, he kept the promise."

"That he did," said Reverend Ansel, placing his large hands on his knees. His breath became labored. "He bears many things in silence that belong to others."

"It was wrong of me!" said Henry. "Wrong of me to do it, wrong of me to hide it, and wrong of me to ask him to hide it too. I should have come to you that day. I should have come to you any day these ten years since. But now, so late, I am here at last. Can you forgive me, sir, for the harm I did your daughter?"

The Reverend sighed. "I already have, my boy. You did wrong, but nothing nearly as wrong as what...what others have done."

"Then you are not angry with me?"

"No more than I am angry with God. He created the

circumstances—the temptation, the storm, our own frailty. What else could we have done but what we did?"

Henry shifted uncomfortably. He felt—he knew—that he could have done very much differently. He stood up, hat in hand. "I thank you, sir, for your kindness. I will trespass no further on your time."

Reverend Ansel looked up absently. "Good-bye then, my boy. And remember, with what measure you mete it, so it will be meted to you."

"Yes, thank you," said Henry, and he saw himself out of the room. As he untied his horse from the iron ring, he breathed a silent prayer of thanks. There was nothing keeping him here at Harrowhaven any longer, and once he made sure his mother felt secure, he could return to London where Mr. Maurice's offer was gleaming like a lamp post in the fog.

AFTER A CURSORY SEARCH THROUGH the village, Pevensey decided that Cecil must not have been feeling strong enough to ride out after all. He mounted his horse and proceeded at a brisk trot to the young magistrate's manor house. Miss Cecil met him at the door. "My brother was overly optimistic—his head is much worse today." She arched an eyebrow at him. "But I see you have news, Mr. Pevensey, so I will provide no further descriptions of his invalid state."

"You are very perceptive, Miss Cecil," said Pevensey, barely able to keep from bouncing up and down on the balls of his feet. "Upstairs?" He reached for the banister.

"No, I let him remove to the parlor." She led the way through a set of doors to the small room where he had first seen her last night. "But I should warn you—he has covered the floor with crumbs."

Pevensey immediately spotted Cecil lying back on the couch, his curly black head encompassed by a fresh bandage and propped up with embroidered pillows. "Pevensey," he groaned, laying a half-eaten biscuit on a nearby tray. "I thought I would be back in the saddle today, but when I tried to come downstairs...."

"You almost fell and smashed your head again," said his sister succinctly. "And you are under doctor's orders not to try to get up. How fortunate that Mr. Pevensey is willing to visit to give you the news."

"What news?" demanded Cecil. "Turold?"

"Still *in absentia*. However, this morning I was presented with an interesting answer to Miss Cecil's question from last night."

"Her question?" Cecil blinked.

"Yes—why would Turold fire the second shot? And the answer, of course, is: because he didn't fire the first one. He needed to discharge his pistol before anyone came upon him."

"Then the first shot was fired by whom?"

Pevensey cast a sideways glance at Miss Cecil and decided that nothing needed to be kept from her. "Reverend Ansel."

"What?" Cecil lifted his head too quickly and, giving a yelp of pain, lay back again against the pillow. His sister sent a glare in his direction, easily interpreted as a command to mind his injury. "But he was in Dealsby Cross during the hunt."

"So we thought. But it turns out that Curate Gray conducted the wedding there. The Reverend was supposed to perform the office, but he turned back on the road—too ill to continue."

"And when he reached the parsonage—"

"—what a sight awaited him. His housekeeper locked in the broom closet while his simple-minded daughter was being led out the door by the reprobate duke."

"He would have tried to stop them." Cecil began to position biscuits on the tray to show the locations of the players in this drama.

"Yes, there must have been a struggle."

"The Reverend would have been unarmed."

"But Rufus was not." Pevensey moved the Reverend's biscuit closer to the duke's. "And Ansel seized his pistol."

"And when the duke refused to let go of his daughter—"

"He shot him in the back!" said Miss Cecil, the pitch of her voice heightened with the excitement.

Pevensey and Cecil stopped the staging of the biscuits to look at her. "Exactly so, Miss Cecil," said Pevensey, "and I daresay Turold rode up just as Rufus was falling face first into the dusty churchyard."

"Turold would have apprehended the situation immediately," said Cecil. "Dismounted, seen that his friend was dead, and known exactly why."

"The Reverend would have taken the girl inside, then panicked a little. He had just killed a man. He put the duke's pistol somewhere in the house. The girl saw it."

"Yes!" said Cecil. "She tried to tell us about it, remember? And he pretended that he had found it in the woods. And of course he had cleaned it by then to disguise that it had been fired."

"Whose idea was it," asked Miss Cecil, "to pawn it off as an accident?"

"Turold's, I wager," said Cecil. "He hoisted the duke's body back onto the duke's horse and led it away from the parsonage toward the clearing. Then, when he was far enough away, he dumped it in the clearing and discharged his own pistol."

"And shortly afterwards, you arrived," said Pevensey, "to hear his cock and bull story about firing into the bushes at a stag."

"And Turold was happy to continue calling it an accident—until we started to ask too many questions. He surmised that the truth was soon to come out, so he preempted the discovery by making his own false confession—and battering me with that fire iron to make his escape. Pevensey!" said Cecil triumphantly. "You're a wizard!"

Pevensey's freckled face split into a grin. He was not one to seek congratulations, but he would not object to them being offered, especially in front of the admiring Miss Cecil.

Cecil wrinkled his nose. "And now that we know all this—what do we do?"

Pevensey sighed. "Aye, there's the rub. Do we have any proof strong enough to counter Turold's confession?"

The three stared at each other for a long minute.

"No," said Cecil, gnawing his lip. "Unless the housekeeper gives evidence, I'm afraid that we do not."

"And I rather doubt that she saw the thing happen," said Pevensey. "For all she knows, Turold *did* shoot the duke."

Miss Cecil straightened in her chair. "I cannot believe Reverend Ansel would let someone else take the blame for his actions! He would hardly hang for defending his daughter's virtue."

"No, the worst that could happen would be transportation to Australia," said Pevensey. "And even that is hardly likely. If he pleads clergy and the judge is favorable, he'll be excused with only a branding on his thumb."

"But if he *is* transported," said Miss Cecil, "what would happen to Catie?"

"I suppose that they have no other family in England?"

Miss Cecil shook her head.

"Then she would most likely be placed in an asylum."

"A horrid thought!" said Miss Cecil, with such feeling that Pevensey suspected she must have toured an asylum at some point and known firsthand the atrocities that lay within.

"Turold must have concurred," said Cecil, "which is why he laid himself on the altar as the sacrificial lamb." He put a hand to his bandage and patted it gingerly. "Lud, if he hadn't decided to baste my head with that fire iron, I should feel a great deal of admiration for that fellow."

"What will you do?" asked Pevensey.

Cecil cleared his throat. "Do? Yes, I suppose I *am* the magistrate in charge of the case. You've provided your expertise, and now the judgment is left with me. I...I need to think on it a while. I am not sure what good a public accusation against Reverend Ansel would do—the whole county has already accepted that Walter Turold is the murderer. But at the same time, it feels a little out of place to hear divine services read by a man who killed your neighbor."

"Indeed," said Pevensey. It was not the first time he had followed a case to its conclusion only to find that conclusion too difficult to prove in a court of law. "I shall leave the matter in your hands."

They were capable hands, that he knew. Cecil, although inexperienced in the world of investigation, had proven himself eager and apt to learn. He would sort the case, as much as it could be sorted. Pevensey had no doubt of that.

"Is this good-bye then?" said Cecil, propping himself up on the sofa. His dark eyes opened wide with regret.

Pevensey smiled. "I think it must be. Now that the case is solved, Sir Richard will be needing me back at Bow Street. Murder might be the exception here in Sussex, but in London it's as common as coal."

"Well then," said Cecil, swinging his legs over the side of the sofa and attempting to rise, "I must shake your hand." A twinge of pain soon aborted his efforts.

"Lie down, you silly gudgeon," said his sister, pushing him back into a prone position. "I'm certain you can shake Mr. Pevensey's hand just as well from the sofa."

Pevensey came forward and offered his hand. "It has been a pleasure, Cecil."

"We do not always go to town for the season," said Cecil, pumping his hand with enthusiasm, "but we were thinking to go this Christmas. I shall look you up at Bow Street."

"Yes, of course," said Pevensey smoothly. He had no expectation of such an event occurring. It was not easy to sustain a friendship—or even an acquaintance—with one who moved in such a different sphere of society. "Good day," he said, and moved toward the door before any further awkwardness or sentiment could intervene.

Miss Cecil followed him into the hallway. "It has been a pleasure making your acquaintance, Mr. Pevensey." She offered her hand.

Pevensey felt a powerful twinge of surprise. "Thank you, Miss Cecil," he said, taking her hand stiffly. He dropped it an instant later, too disconcerted by her frank blue eyes to retain his usual polish. It was fortunate the case had not required him to interview this young lady. He was entirely unable to read her motives—or to read his own at the present moment.

A shadow in front of the door darkened the light coming in through the leaded glass windows. "I believe you have visitors, Miss Cecil," said Pevensey. It was not a difficult thing to deduce.

"The Bertrams, I daresay." She lowered her voice. "It's too early for a morning call, but they must think their errand as important as catching a murderer."

Pevensey looked at the overblown flower arrangement still gracing the entryway. "Or perhaps they are attempting to catch someone else."

"Indeed," said Miss Cecil dryly. She opened the door. "Oh, Mrs. Bertram!" she said enthusiastically. "And Miss Bertram!" They took hands as women do and cooed their delight at seeing one another.

Pevensey slipped out the door past the broad-bosomed matriarch who was just beginning to express her concern for "poor, poor Mr. Cecil" and their inability to wait any longer to call on the invalid.

Miss Cecil's eyes must have followed him out the door, for before it closed he heard Mrs. Bertram chortling, "What's this, Edwina? A new beau?" And the more proper Miss Bertram gasping, "Mother! What are you saying? That's the Bow Street Runner, down from London!"

Pevensey jammed his beaver onto his head with force. Exactly. He was the Bow Street Runner down from London—and London was where he was going, the place where a man like him belonged.

PART THREE

29

Eliza turned over the letter in her hands. She had not expected Adele to write at all, but here it was, two months since their stay at Harrowhaven and she had already received two letters from her. This last one was Adele's official notice that she would be coming to town soon to purchase her trousseau. The Duchess of Brockenhurst had relented and agreed to curtail the official period of mourning for Rufus so that Adele and Stephen could celebrate a Christmas wedding.

There were other tidbits of news as well. The Reverend and his family had moved away from Sussex—to America, Adele had heard. Poor Miss Ansel, thought Eliza, feeling a pity for the girl she had never met. No doubt rumors had spread about her and the duke, and her father, unable to protect her by any other means, had given up his living to his curate to re-settle elsewhere.

The Ansels were not the only ones being forced to re-settle. Eliza laid the letter down on the window sill—the only flat surface left in her room besides the bed. These were the Malcolms' last few days in their town house, their last few days in London. The house had already been put up for sale and most of their belongings sent to an auction house. A distant cousin had offered them the use of a cottage in Northumbria, and so they were preparing to go north before the cold weather set in, traveling by post and with only a few trunks containing their dearest possessions.

Adele was coming to London, but by the time she arrived Eliza might very well be gone, with little chance of ever returning to town or, indeed, to society. The disappointment of missing Adele was further enhanced by the whispering thought that where Adele was, Henry might be close. Eliza had no doubts that he was in London right now—probably had been for some time—but they orbited different suns now, and with Eliza's father descending into bankruptcy and genteel poverty, there was little likelihood that, without contrivance, their paths would ever cross again.

Contrivance—Eliza meditated on that word for a moment, as she had for the eight long weeks since they had returned from Harrowhaven. How many times she had wished that she'd never begged for Ned Hornsby's opinion on Henry's character! Better to think him a scoundrel now that he was lost to her forever than to know what a misfortune it was for her to lose him.

She placed Adele's letter in her reticule and pulled out a well-worn calling card from the handbag. Her thumb ran over the black lettering that spelled out Henry's title: Duke of Brockenhurst.

Contrivance—it was something Henry Rowland was quite skilled at. She remembered him introducing her to his family: "Miss Malcolm is a great friend of mine from London." And then later, his taradiddles about how they had promenaded together in Hyde Park. She had made that promenade with Ollerton every day for the past month—but there had been no sign of Henry Rowland on foot or on horse.

No, if she was going to contrive a meeting between them in the next few days before her departure, she must show even more imagination. She breathed in deeply. Could she—was it possible—would she dare try to discover where he lived? She breathed out. Yes, she would dare, and perhaps if she sent a letter round he would visit before it was too late.

But how could she discover his address?

"Ollerton!" said Eliza, pinning on one of the two bonnets she had kept for herself. "I am going out to take the air. Will you come?"

"Now, miss?" asked Ollerton, in the middle of cleaning out a wardrobe of linens. It was unlikely that they would be able to keep her on after the move to Northumbria, and the anxiety of separation was weighing heavily on both her and Lady Malcolm.

"If you please," said Eliza, heading for the door.

Grumbling, Ollerton fetched a shawl and followed Eliza out the door. "But miss," she said, as Eliza turned east down the street. "The park's the other way!"

"So it is," said Eliza, continuing her direction. "I would like to see the city a little today—it might be my last time."

Ollerton grumbled some more about the impropriety of the expedition, but hastened to catch up with Eliza's long legs. It was no meandering jaunt. After thirty minutes of brisk walking—and ignoring Ollerton's persistent demands to turn back—Eliza found herself staring up at a stone front of the most impressive building on Bow Street.

"Miss Eliza!" hissed Ollerton, watching a pair of blue-suited men in cavalry boots entering the building. "This is where the Bow Street Patrol meets. It's not a proper place for a lady. Come away!"

"Ollerton," said Eliza, turning to face the maid without a hint of embarrassment. "I'm going inside. You can come with me or wait on the pavement."

The elderly maid fumed, uttering half a dozen threats with Lady Malcolm's name attached to them, but in the end, she chose to escort her charge inside the building. Eliza felt a few tremors of anxiety as they went up the steps, but she stilled them courageously. "Please, sir," she said, asking the first person she saw in the foyer, "is Mr. Jacob Pevensey here? I need to speak to him."

***

"Sir Richard wants to see you in his office," said a snub-nosed errand boy, the moment Pevensey stepped into the building.

Pevensey knew better than to delay. Sir Richard doubtless wanted an update on the Southwark highwayman, the latest lawbreaker that Pevensey had been attempting to identify and apprehend. When he entered Sir Richard's office, however, he discovered that the magistrate was not alone. He was in the middle of serving tea to an elegant young lady and her older companion. Richard Ford was decidedly well-versed in the petticoat line, but it was unusual for him to entertain his Cythereans here at Bow Street. And besides, this auburn-haired female looked respectable, and—by Jove! Now that she had turned her head, Pevensey recognized her immediately as Miss Eliza Malcolm.

Pevensey bowed crisply. "Sir Richard. Miss Malcolm. How can I be of service?"

Sir Richard set down the teapot. "This young lady here needs some assistance which, I understand, only you can provide." He pursed his lips thoughtfully. "Miss Ollerton," he said, approaching the maid and offering his arm. "It's not every day that we have ladies at Bow Street. It would be an honor to provide you with a tour of the courtroom while Miss Malcolm transacts her business with Mr. Pevensey."

"Oh, I don't think…" began Miss Ollerton. But Sir Richard was not a man easily denied. The flustered lady's maid soon placed her arm in his to commence a tour of the building. They left the oak door of the office open, and Pevensey found himself alone with Miss Malcolm.

"Mr. Pevensey," said Miss Malcolm, and her color rose a

little, "I have an unusual question to put to you, about which I hope you will exercise your discretion. I am looking for the address of Henry Rowland, the Duke of Brockenhurst."

"And you are unable to locate his address through the normal channels," said Pevensey, raising a red eyebrow, "for fear of…discovery?"

"No…well, yes…but it is nothing improper."

Pevensey highly doubted that that was the case. And yet, something about the girl's hopeful eagerness made him wish to oblige. He had investigated Henry Rowland's details the day he embarked on the trip to Harrowhaven, and there had been further news about the man in the London papers just five or six weeks ago. He looked at the girl's long white fingers gripping the handles of her chair in trepidation. What harm could there be in telling her?

"You will find Henry Rowland at Maurice's Hotel."

The lady's face broke into a smile of breathless excitement. "Thank you, Mr. Pevensey! Thank you!"

Pevensey stood up and showed her back to the entrance hall where Sir Richard was manfully and charmingly combating the lady's maid's attempts to return to her mistress' side. They bid the two ladies farewell, the younger with an expression of fervent expectation, the older with thunderclouds forming on her brow.

"Very clever of you, sir, to realize Miss Malcolm wanted to speak to me alone," said Pevensey, giving his superior a wry grin.

"Yes, I do have a knack for deciphering young ladies," replied Sir Richard. It was no idle boast. "Did you locate the Southwark highwayman?"

"No, but I did help two young people establish a secret tryst."

"Hmm…very good then," said Sir Richard with a grin. "All in a day's work, Pevensey, eh?"

"Indeed, sir," said Pevensey. "Indeed."

HENRY STOOD IN THE ALCOVE, watching the waiters rearrange the tables in the dining room for the third time. It would be full every night once the season began. He knew it was possible to fit a couple more tables inside without the feeling of overcrowding—if only the correct arrangement could be found.

He overheard voices at the front desk—another client trying to book a room. There were precious few rooms left to let—an excellent problem to have. It was not so long ago that Maurice's was begging for customers, and now…now it was the most luxurious and exclusive hotel in all of London.

The maître d' floated into the dining room. "My lord, there is a young lady at the desk asking to speak with you."

"Her name?" He had been forced to grow wary ever since Rufus' demise. He was no longer the impoverished younger brother, and the London misses and their mamas were forever on the prowl.

"Miss Elizabeth Malcolm."

Henry felt his jaw twitch and the muscles in his shoulders tense. "I will be there momentarily, Gervase."

He motioned for the waiters to adjust a table by a hand's breadth, and then taking a calming breath, exited the dining room.

There she was—her auburn hair pulled up into a column of curls at the back of her head, her white hand resting lightly on the edge of the marble desktop. "Miss Malcolm," said Henry, forcing a smile onto his face and finding that one had already appeared of its own accord. "It is a pleasure to see you again." As soon as he said it, he knew that it was true. It was a glorious and ecstatic, albeit painful pleasure to see the woman who had refused him and whom he had tried, for these last two months, to utterly expunge from his mind.

He took her hand and pressed it—he wanted to press it to

his lips, but no. He would not take such a liberty. Not yet. "To what do I owe the honor of your visit?"

She blushed at that and pulled her hand away. "It seems we are to leave London, and I needed—I wanted—to say good-bye before we depart."

"How kind of you," said Henry. He felt that perhaps it was more than kind. "I must call on your family before you leave." She had forbidden him to call. But this, surely this, was a change of mind.

"We leave very soon. Perhaps tomorrow. Or the day after."

There was a tinge of desperation in her voice. Henry glanced behind her and saw the angry eyes of an old woman sitting on a bench. It was her lady's maid—he remembered the face—and she was not happy to be witnessing this conversation. There had been no change of mind, then, on Lady Malcolm's part.

"Then if I cannot call on you tomorrow," said Henry brightly, "we must have our tea now." He put Eliza's hand in the crook of his arm, nodded his head slightly at the maître d', and moved towards the dining room. Within seconds the busy waiters had vacated the room, leaving it empty except for Henry and Eliza—and the sullen lady's maid glowering at them from a nearby table.

Gervase placed a pot of the most excellent Souchong tea on the table along with some sugar dusted biscuits. "Will you pour?" asked Henry. He could see that her hands were shaking, but she filled both teacups without mishap.

"Where are you traveling to?" he asked, casually sipping his tea.

"Northumbria," she said. The word came out as dull and gray as river rock.

"Do you have family in those parts?"

"Distant relations." She put her teacup down and glanced up at the ceiling of the dining room. The carved wood around the edges had been freshly gilded, in preparation for the season. Henry kept his eyes on her, admiring the rapt look of her own admiration. "This hotel is beautiful," she said. "I have never been here before."

"It does have its charms," said Henry modestly.

"I did not expect you would be staying here still—after inheriting your brother's town house."

Henry flexed his shoulders. So, she did not know. She thought he was a guest here, too busy or too lazy to set up his own establishment.

"A wise man once told me that hotels manage themselves better when the owner is in residence."

She looked around the room. "Owner? You?"

He laughed. "Why yes, my dear, this is my hotel. The name of the place is Maurice's, but two months ago, he decided he'd had enough of catering to his guests' whims, and he allowed me to buy him out."

She picked up her teacup and stared at him. "Buy him out? How did you get involved in the hotel business in the first place?"

"It's a bit of a story," said Henry, "but three years ago I came to London poor as a church mouse. Maurice took me on as his hotel manager—my salary to be a percentage of the profits. At the time, there were no profits. The hotel was bleeding money like a stab wound. I helped Maurice right the budget and improve the quality of service. Within six months, we were starting to fill our rooms. We made the establishment more elegant. We charged more money. We filled even more rooms. There's hardly a room to be let now during the autumn, and none once the season starts."

He watched the curve of her perfect pink lips caress the edge of her teacup as she drank.

"Last season my percentage of the profits went from a trickle to a typhoon—Maurice's too. He's old now. He wants to retire. So he asked if I wanted to purchase the hotel from him, and of course, the answer was yes."

"But…how on earth did you know how to run a hotel?"

"It's not so different from being a steward," said Henry. "And in any case, I had Mrs. Forsythe's expertise whenever I ran into a matter I couldn't handle. A hotel is really just a larger version of Harrowhaven."

"Mrs. Forsythe *knows* you run a hotel?"

"Indeed. She knew it long before my own mother did. I thought she might cut me off when I poached her head housemaid—promised her higher wages to work at Maurice's—but she forgave me eventually."

"Jenny?"

"Yes, how did you know?" It was Henry's turn to be surprised.

"Never mind," said Eliza quietly. She looked around the room again, taking in all the candlesticks, the furnishings, the elegance.

The maid at the nearby table cleared her throat ominously. Her patience, Henry could see, was wearing perilously thin. Eliza laid down her napkin, and Henry rose to pull out her chair. "Thank you for the tea," she said, giving him a faint smile. Henry could see that tears were starting to form in the corners of her eyes.

"Thank you for the visit," he said gallantly. "I certainly hope that this is not good-bye. Your stay in Northumbria shall not be too long I trust."

"I am afraid it must be," said Eliza, but she did not elaborate further. "Goodbye, my lord."

"Good-bye, my dear," said Henry, leading her out to the door with the angry shadow following behind them.

As the door shut, Henry walked over to the marble counter. "Gervase, do we have any rooms available for tomorrow night?"

The maître d' walked over to the desk and examined the

ledger. "With the arrival of your mother and sister, it appears we will be full."

"Is the remodel of the blue suite finished?"

"Why, yes, my lord, we were just beginning to transfer your belongings—"

Henry held up a hand. "Hold off on that momentarily." He signaled a footman for his hat, and headed out into the streets.

30

"I THINK YOU KNOW WHAT I AM ABOUT TO SAY," SAID Ollerton, her lips compressed into a tight line. Footsore and weary, the two women had reached Grosvenor Square at last and were only a few houses away from their own residence.

"Yes, I think I do know," said Eliza.

"Going to the magistrates' office, then meeting with a gentleman on the sly? Lord have mercy! Haven't your mother and I taught you better?"

"Yes," said Eliza dully. "But what does it matter? We will be buried in Northumbria in less than three days. And I shall never see another gentleman again. Especially not *this* particular gentleman." She stopped and faced the lady's maid. "What will you tell my mother?"

Ollerton hesitated. "Why, I—"

"I know you tell her everything. You dress us both and curl our hair, but you are her maid far more than you are mine."

"Why, child," said Ollerton, "I have been your mother's lady's maid these thirty years and more. And now...." Her old hands fumbled anxiously on the handle of her reticule.

"Oh, Ollerton," said Eliza, a wave of pity suddenly overwhelming her. She had been selfish to think only of her own pain in the midst of this exile. "Northumbria is as horrid a word to you as it is to me. We must go and you must stay. And how we shall miss you!" She threw her arms around the maid and pulled her tight.

"And I shall miss you," said Ollerton, sniffing in a way that would have made her mistress proud. "And the thought of finding another position.... Well, the fact is, that your mother—perhaps I should not say it, but your mother is my best friend in all the world."

"As you are hers," said Eliza. "So tell her what you must. I am aware that my actions today must incur censure."

They reached the steps of the house that was soon to be sold and went inside. Lady Malcolm inquired where they had been. Eliza gave a vague answer about sightseeing in town and, to her surprise, Ollerton did not contradict her. She waited for the rest of the afternoon for the secret to come out, but her mother exhibited nothing more than her usual anxieties and annoyances.

Sir Arthur arrived home just in time for a late dinner. The food had been all bought in since the cook had been let go the day prior, and Lady Malcolm had no compliments for the shop that had prepared it. Eliza's father sat in his chair like a man in a daze. Eliza reflected that the tragedy of Northumbria in her own young life must pale when compared to the tragedy it symbolized for her father. He had been born into wealth and lost it through his own folly or indolence. He would leave London with little more than the clothes on his back, able to provide shelter for his family only through the kindness of others.

Lady Malcolm had nearly finished dissecting the merits of each dish when Sir Arthur laid down his fork and knife. "Margaret!" he said suddenly.

"What is it?" She sniffed petulantly. Although she was opposed in principle to worldly pomp and luxury, Northumbria was a heavy cross for her to bear too.

"I was at White's this afternoon and I ran into Brockenhurst." He looked up. "The new duke, you understand. Henry Rowland."

"What of it?"

"He's in the hotel business, it seems. Owns Maurice's."

"I repeat," said Lady Malcolm, "what *of* it?"

"I am getting to that!" said Sir Arthur, a flare of temper reddening his face. "With the season not begun, he has empty rooms. Doesn't look good, you see, for a hotel to be empty, so he's trying to fill them—make the place look alive so more people will want to stay there. I mentioned we were selling up and leaving London. He offered to let us stay at the hotel, free of charge until after Christmas. It's a favor to him, he says."

Eliza's mouth fell open in shock. After Henry's description of the hotel's popularity, she doubted he had any rooms to spare. What could this mean? She glanced back and forth between her father and her mother.

"I know you don't like the man," said Sir Arthur, "but if we take him up on the offer, we could delay going to Northumbria for another month or two. Margaret, what do you think?"

Lady Malcolm glanced around wild-eyed, from the bought pudding to the empty sideboard to her husband's earnest face. "I think it's a wonderful idea," she said before bursting into tears.

THE NEXT MORNING IT DID not take more than one hackney to transport the Malcolms' belongings to the hotel—they had pruned their wardrobes down to the most minimal selection of clothing in preparation for the trip to Northumbria. After entering the golden splendor of Maurice's, they followed the maître d' up to their rooms, a well-appointed suite of two bedrooms, a sitting room, and even their own small dining room, all decorated with a tasteful assortment of blue and white pillows, drapes, vases, and candles.

The hotel owner himself came upstairs to ensure that they

were comfortable, and Lady Malcolm, although not effusive, proclaimed herself exceedingly grateful for the accommodations. "My pleasure to host you," said Henry politely. "My mother arrives today, with Adele, so you shall have some company to keep you entertained. Please feel free to use any of the mounts in the hotel stables or arrange with Gervase to borrow the carriage."

"I say, very generous of you! Very generous!" said Sir Arthur, who had already discovered a cupboard liberally stocked with spirits. Sir Arthur poured himself a glass while Lady Malcolm examined the capacious wardrobes, and Henry seized on the opportunity to step out into the hallway with Eliza for a brief moment.

Eliza looked at Henry, so in his element as lord and master of this domain, his iron hand inside the velvet glove of courtesy. "Thank you," she whispered.

"But of course," he whispered back.

"Extra rooms? I hardly think so. I do not know how we shall ever repay you."

"I do. Come riding with me this afternoon."

"Dear me," she said, all her old fears of equestrian pursuits returning to her. "I might have misplaced my riding habit."

"Then I shall have another one made for you," said Henry, his voice still intimately soft.

"No, no...I have it," she said. "Very well, I will come."

"Good," he said, and taking her hand he pressed it to his lips. "I shall see you at three o'clock."

⁂

ELIZA STRAIGHTENED HER BACK AS she sat on the bench in the entrance hall, adjusted the skirt of her emerald green riding habit to drape more becomingly, and tried not to think about the terror awaiting her. She had been able to ride Marigold without mishap, but what were the chances that the stables at Maurice's held another horse so absolutely docile?

After what seemed like hours, Henry entered in full riding dress, crop in hand. "The groom is out front," he said and gave her his arm. The groom's horse was a piebald nag, but the two horses waiting for them were perfectly matched blacks—long-legged, well-bred, and no doubt high-mettled. Eliza closed her eyes as Henry put his hands around her waist and lifted her onto the side saddle.

"Eliza, listen to me," he said. "Guide the horse—he will do whatever you wish. Speak to him—he will listen to you."

"I...don't think he will," said Eliza tremulously, frightened that the duke would let go of the reins before she was ready.

"He will," Henry insisted. "You are stronger than you think. And you have found your voice."

He placed the reins in her hands and climbed onto his own horse next to her. "Hyde Park?" he asked with a smile.

"Of course," she said, forcing herself to smile as well. "Did we not used to promenade there together?"

"Ha! How could I have forgotten?" He urged his horse forward into a walk, and almost instinctively she felt her foot urging her horse forward as well. The groom trailed along behind them, and within ten minutes they had reached the entrance to that great island of green in the middle of the stone city. They took the path, still walking at an easy pace.

"I cannot believe I have not fallen off yet," said Eliza, gritting her teeth.

"You underestimate yourself."

They passed a few other riders out to take the air. Henry tipped his hat, and Eliza—although she recognized none of them—managed a nod. She was eminently thankful that the season had not begun. Then there would be dozens of riders hoping to see and be seen, and her anxiety would only have increased.

They reached a fork in the road and Henry took the narrower, less used path. Trees grew on either side as they entered a more forested area of the park. "Shall we go faster?" asked Henry.

"Oh...I think my horse would not like that at all," said Eliza.

"Your horse?" said Henry with a grin.

"Yes. I think there is something wrong with his shoe—a loose nail perhaps. It would bother him excessively if we did anything faster than a slow walk."

"Hmm...is that so?" Henry slowed his horse to a stop and dismounted. "Come here then, and let me look at the poor fellow." He lifted Eliza down from her horse and then proceeded to lift the horse's legs one by one examining the hooves. When he reached the right foreleg, his brow furrowed. "My dear Eliza, I do believe you are right. This horse's shoe is far too loose for you to ride him without mishap."

Eliza's face registered surprise. "The accuracy of my own prognosis astounds me. What shall we do now?"

"Why, promenade, of course," said Henry. He snapped his fingers for the groom and handed him the reins of the horses. As if by prior instruction, the groom began to lead the horses back down the narrow path towards the entrance of the park. Within a few minutes he was out of sight. Henry took Eliza's arm and wrapped it around his to begin the return journey. "How is this?" he asked. "More comfortable than the horse?"

Eliza blushed. "Yes, I suppose it is." She began to feel a slight unease about the disappearance of their chaperone, but that disquiet left as quickly as it had come. Whatever was about to happen needed no witnesses but themselves. "And better for conversation," she said, stopping in the path, looking him in the eye, and willing him to speak.

"How fortunate, for I have some conversation to make with you." Henry cleared his throat. "At our last meeting at

Harrowhaven, I picked a particularly unpropitious time to declare my feelings for you."

"It was not so much the time," said Eliza shyly, "as that I had formed some inaccurate conceptions of your character."

"Indeed? And what were those?"

Eliza blushed and looked away.

"I am hesitant to assume," said Henry, "but I think you may be referring to that blond maid who borrowed my handkerchief in the hall."

"The maid, and Mrs. Flambard, and Catie Ansel, and—"

"Dear me! You must have thought me quite the scoundrel. I am altogether innocent of your suspicions, I assure you."

"I know that now," said Eliza, "thanks to your friend Ned Hornsby, but at the time I was overwrought and not at all sure what to think...."

"Ned is a good fellow! I am delighted to hear that you have revised your opinion of me." Henry's eyes twinkled. "And, as I was saying, the timing, I know, was unpropitious. I realize that it was not enough for your boundless ambition to see me as Duke of Brockenhurst and master of Harrowhaven. But now that you have seen Maurice's also, the plum of the pudding, as it were, perhaps the timing is improved. Are all these things enough, my dear Eliza, for you to consider me as a suitor for your hand?"

"How can you talk so?" demanded Eliza, her face hot with indignation. "If it had not been for those foolish misunderstandings, I would have married you two months ago when you were a second son without any prospects or a penny to your name."

"Truly?"

"Yes! I would have married you when you met me at the bottom of the stairs, when you found me crying in the garden, when you saved me from eating breakfast alone with the investigator, or even when you served me that awful platter of fish!"

Henry wrapped his arms around Eliza's waist and brought her closer.

"You see, my dear? I told you that you had found your voice."

Eliza lifted her arms and placed them around his neck.

"Eliza Malcolm will you marry me?"

"Yes," she said. "I will."

And then Eliza was truly grateful that the groom had disappeared, for Henry's lips found hers and did not leave them until she was fully satisfied that she was the only woman in the world for him, yesterday, now, and in the future.

⸙

Eliza's eyes were still shining like green stars when Henry escorted her up the front steps of Maurice's. "Shall I kiss you again?" he whispered in her ear.

"Not here!" she said, her sense of propriety struggling against the pull of temptation. "I must tell my family."

"And I mine," said Henry, "for there is the Harrowhaven carriage, arrived in our absence."

He squeezed her hand encouragingly, and they parted ways in the entrance hall.

Eliza went first to their rooms, but no one was there. She came back downstairs and caught sight of her parents seated in the hotel dining room, enjoying a late tea together. She saw her father laugh and lean over to pat his wife's hand. She saw her mother's green eyes sparkle. Their aging faces showed the lines of struggle born from years of contradictory temperaments, goals, and dreams, but today, at least, they were savoring each other's company.

"Papa," Eliza said, crossing the room to join them at their table. "I have something to tell you."

Their conversation halted, and they stared at her, anxiously, as if they already knew what she was going to say.

"The Duke of Brockenhurst has proposed marriage to me this afternoon, and I have accepted his offer."

Sir Arthur let out a cry of delight. "'Pon rep, Eliza! I had not dared to let myself hope you would act reasonably. The fellow came to me earlier today and asked permission to put the question to you."

"You did not warn me, Papa!" said Eliza. She was not altogether certain that she would have preferred to know what was coming in advance.

"I know, I know," said her father, clearing his throat, "but I thought that with the last proposal, I may have applied...too great a pressure on you, Eliza. I am overjoyed that you made the decision on your own."

Eliza turned to her other parent. "Mama," she said anxiously, "I know that you had doubts about Henry Rowland's character—"

Lady Malcolm held up a hand. "Ollerton has informed me that she was mistaken about that maid Jenny. Apparently, her removal from Harrowhaven was to seek a better position, not to hide an indiscretion."

"Then you are not opposed?"

Lady Malcolm sipped her tea and looked around the room at the exquisite painting and paneling that had so impressed Eliza yesterday. "No, my dear. If you are happy, then I must be too." She sniffed. "And we will simply trust the Almighty to make up the deficiencies in all of us."

"Eliza!" said a gleefully loud voice, disrupting the Malcolm family conference, and indeed, every one of the hotel guests who had sat down to read their newspaper in quiet in the dining room.

Adele hurried over to the table, clad in a frothy yellow confection of lace. "Henry tells me we are to be sisters...again!"

Eliza rose from her seat to embrace Adele. There was no use blushing at her forwardness or her *faux pas*. They were family now, and Eliza refused to be embarrassed by her.

"I told you he had a *tendre* for you," said Adele, taking Eliza's hands in hers. "And, what delightful timing, for now we shall buy our trousseaus together. Henry cannot complain about any amount I spend at the modiste's if you are getting gowns too!"

"How fortunate!" said Eliza, trying to keep the irony out of her voice.

"I shall help you choose your wedding gown," said Adele, eager to launch into the specifics of this new venture. "Brussels lace, and silver lamé—"

"I think Eliza is quite capable of choosing her own gown," said a firm voice. The owner of the hotel strode over to the table to make sure all of his guests were comfortable. "She has excellent taste, I find, when other people allow her to make up her own mind."

"Yes," said Eliza, looking at Henry's broad shoulders in his perfectly-tailored black jacket. "I rather think that I do."

FINIS

Author's Note

What does "a single man in possession of a good fortune" have in common with the "triumph of barbarism and religion," as Edward Gibbon so affectionately termed the Middle Ages?

In my studies of history, the manners of the Regency era and the characters of the medieval period are the two things which have most captured my imagination. While reading Georgette Heyer and Elizabeth Chadwick, an interesting thought occurred to me: what if I took the characters and events of the Middle Ages and transposed them into the high society of the British Regency?

In my first Regency, *To Wed an Heiress*, I imagined the characters of the Norman Conquest set during the Regency era. Harold, the Earl of Anglesford, tries at all costs to save the family fortune, coming into conflict with the rapacious William Hastings and his alluring daughter Arabella. Murder most foul occurs, bringing the insightful Jacob Pevensey, an investigator from Bow Street, on the scene to sort out the tangled web of love and lies.

This novel, *The Duke's Last Hunt*, was inspired by the events surrounding the death of William Rufus, the second king of England after the Norman Conquest. Rufus was killed by an arrow while hunting in the New Forest. Before the hunt, Rufus had bestowed arrows on his friend Walter Tyrel (or Thurold), saying, "To the best hunter, the best arrows." The commonly accepted story was that his friend shot him accidentally while firing at a stag. Walter Tyrel then fled to France where he was sheltered by Abbot Suger.

Over the centuries, many theories have sprung up regarding Rufus' death and laying the blame on others besides Walter Tyrel. Rufus' brother Henry was the one who benefitted directly from the event. He was also hunting in the forest that day, and it is said that as soon as he heard the news, he rushed to consolidate power and take the crown. Some think that Henry orchestrated the death, perhaps commissioning Walter Tyrel or others to carry out the deed.

Abbot Suger himself seems to doubt Tyrel's guilt. He wrote: "It was laid to the charge of a certain noble, Walter Thurold, that he had shot the king with an arrow; but I have often heard him, when he had nothing to fear nor to hope, solemnly swear that on the day in question he was not in the part of the forest where the king was hunting, nor ever saw him in the forest at all."

Whether the death was murder or manslaughter, it is certain that William Rufus was not a beloved monarch. The historian William of Malmesbury gave this ungentle assessment: "He was a man much to be pitied by the clergy, for throwing away the soul they labored to save...not to be lamented by the people, because he suffered their substance to be plundered."

Rufus was renowned for his opposition to the church. During his reign he attempted to keep the see of Canterbury empty in order to increase his power and revenue. He finally agreed to appoint Anselm as Archbishop, a scholarly fellow who would become famous for the *Proslogion*, which proved the existence of God, and *Cur Deus Homo*, which explained why Jesus became Man to atone for our sins. But besides being a writer, Anselm was also a fighter. He refused to let Rufus trample on the rights of the church, and during Rufus' reign, he was forced to go into exile.

Most of the secondary characters in this book are my own creation, but a couple found inspiration from the historical record. William Rufus had a sister, Adele, who married Stephen of Blois. Stephen became one of the adventurers on the First Crusade, which retook Jerusalem from the Muslims. Somehow, however, his mild-mannered exploits never quite measured up to the doughty deeds of Adele's father, William the Conqueror. Her letters to Stephen still survive, showing Stephen to be the quintessential henpecked husband of the medieval era.

Also from Madison Street Publishing

TO WED AN HEIRESS
By Rosanne E. Lortz

HARO EMISON, THRUST INTO HIS new role as Earl of Anglesford, discovers that his late father has left the family teetering on the edge of financial ruin. Intent on rescuing the estate, Haro abandons his long-held interest in his cousin Eda and searches instead for a wealthy heiress. But when pride and jealousy cause his plan to spiral out of control, he begins to wonder if he has made a dreadful mistake....

Eda Swanycke is enjoying her first season in London when her debut comes to a crashing halt. Jilted by her cousin, she suffers the indignity of watching Haro's new intended lay claim to his person and position. But when a brutal murder upends the household with Haro as chief suspect, Eda must put her wounded pride aside, match wits with the investigator from London, and try, at all costs, to save Haro Emison's neck from the gallows....

Printed in Poland
by Amazon Fulfillment
Poland Sp. z o.o., Wrocław